$\mathcal{L}$YDIA'S
CHARM

WANDA & BRUNSTETTER

*L*YDIA'S
CHARM

**Doubleday Large Print
Home Library Edition**

BARBOUR
PUBLISHING

Cover design: Müllerhaus Publishing Arts, Inc.
www.mullerhaus.net

Published by Barbour Publishing, Inc., P.O. Box 719,
Uhrichsville, OH 44683

**Our mission is to publish and distribute
inspirational products offering exceptional value
and biblical encouragement to the masses.**

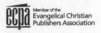
Member of the
Evangelical Christian
Publishers Association

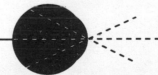

**This Large Print Book carries the
Seal of Approval of N.A.V.H.**

DEDICATION/ACKNOWLEDGMENT

To all my Amish friends who live in Ohio. To Mae Miller: thanks for having us for supper and for sharing with me your wonderful recipe for Frogmore Stew. A special thanks to Bill Westfall, who encouraged me to write this story set in Charm.

Who can find a virtuous woman? for her price is far above rubies.
PROVERBS 31:10 KJV

PROLOGUE

A sob rose in Lydia King's throat as she stared at the calendar on her kitchen wall. A year ago today, she'd buried her husband after having been married only five short years. Oh, how she wished she could bring Jeremiah back.

She glanced at her four-year-old son, Josh, who sat at the table, coloring a picture of a yellow cat. The sweet-tempered boy had Lydia's tawny blond hair and his daddy's big brown eyes. He was endlessly curious and enjoyed all kinds of animals—two more of his father's traits.

Lydia blinked to keep her tears from

spilling over. Josh needed his father as much as she needed her husband. It wasn't fair that Jeremiah had been killed in a logging accident, leaving her alone to earn a living and raise their son.

The muscles in the back of her neck tightened. It wasn't fair that two weeks ago she'd lost her job at the restaurant in Arthur, Illinois, because business was so slow that the restaurant may have to close. She'd looked everywhere for another job, but there were none to be had.

The rent on their small home was coming due in a few days, and with her funds running low, Lydia didn't know what she should do. She needed to provide for Josh, and without a job, she'd soon be out of money and unable to pay any of her bills. Unlike her English friends who'd also been laid off, Lydia would not rely on unemployment checks because her Amish community believed they should rely on each other and God rather than on insurance.

Lydia had no family living nearby to offer her support. When she and Jeremiah had first moved to Illinois from their home in Wisconsin, they'd made quite a few friends in the local Amish community. Those friends had been quick to help Lydia financially after Jeremiah's death, but she couldn't expect them to provide for her and Josh forever. They had families of their own to support, and Lydia wanted to make it on her own.

Oh Lord, please tell me what to do, she prayed. *I need some direction.*

Her gaze came to rest on the stack of mail lying on the table, unopened. She thumbed through the envelopes, noting several bills that only fueled her frustration.

When she spotted an envelope from her mother, who'd moved to Charm, Ohio, a year ago, she quickly tore it open.

Dear Lydia,

I received your letter the other day and was sorry to hear that you'd lost your job. It's not good for you to be there with no family, and I think you and Josh should come here to live with your grandfather and me. Since Holmes County has the largest population of Amish in America, a lot of tourists visit here every year. I'm sure it would be easy for you to find a

job in the area. I could watch Josh
while you're working, and you'd have a
place to stay where you wouldn't have
to worry about paying rent. Please
think about this and let me know your
decision.

As Always,
Mom

Tears welled in Lydia's eyes. Things had
been strained between her and Mom for a
long time. It touched Lydia that Mom cared
enough to suggest that she and Josh move
to Charm.

Mom had found it hard to leave her
home in Wisconsin to take care of Grandpa,
who'd suffered a stroke a year after Lydia's
father died. Since Mom was Grandpa's only
daughter, and her two older brothers lived
in Missouri, she'd felt obligated to care for
him. Lydia had figured her mom would be
happy living in Ohio, where she'd been
born and raised, but after reading several
of her letters, she'd realized that Mom was
miserable. Maybe taking care of Grandpa
was too much for her. She probably needed
some help.

"I'm *hungerich*. What's for *mattsait*,

Mama?" Josh asked, breaking into Lydia's thoughts.

Lydia had no appetite for food, but she couldn't let her boy go without his supper. She forced a smile and gave his shoulder a gentle pat. "We have some leftover chicken noodle soup in the refrigerator. Does that sound good to you?"

He nodded enthusiastically and grinned.

Lydia glanced at Mom's letter one more time. Lifting her shoulders and letting them droop with a sigh, she made a decision. She didn't want to leave their home in Arthur, but she had no other choice. It would be a new beginning for Josh and her, and she was sure that Mom would appreciate some help with Grandpa. Maybe her loss of a job was God's way of letting her know that it was time for a change.

CHAPTER 1

The teakettle whistled. Lydia started to rise from her chair, but Mom beat her to it.

"I'm glad you decided to move here," Mom said, removing the teakettle from the stove. "Your *grossdaadi* doesn't talk much these days, and I get terribly lonely sometimes." Lydia noticed the dark circles under Mom's pale blue eyes as she poured hot water into their cups. Mom's flaxen hair was streaked with gray, and the wrinkles in her forehead were more defined. She was only fifty, but she'd aged quite a bit since the last time Lydia had seen her.

"Unless someone comes to stay with Dad, I don't get out much these days," Mom explained as she dropped a tea bag into her cup. "Even then, I worry about how he's doing, so I don't stay away any longer than necessary."

Lydia plopped a tea bag into her cup, bounced it up and down a few times, and placed it on her saucer. "Maybe now that I'm here, you can get out a little more."

"Don't you want your tea to steep awhile longer? It looks awfully pale in your cup," Mom said.

"My tea's fine. I like it weak." Lydia held her voice in check, determined not to give in to her frustrations. Some things never changed. Mom telling her what to do was one of them.

Maybe I'm being oversensitive, Lydia told herself. *I've been used to being on my own for the past year and doing things pretty much the way I choose. Hopefully, things will get better after Josh and I have been here awhile. I just need to keep a positive attitude and ignore the things I find irritating.*

She glanced around the small kitchen

and noticed a pot of primroses sitting on the windowsill. That was something positive—a sign of spring.

Mom reached for the jar of honey sitting on the table and put a spoonful in her cup of tea. She pushed the jar toward Lydia, but Lydia shook her head. She'd always preferred her tea unsweetened and figured Mom should know that. But then, Mom had more important things on her mind these days, so maybe it had slipped her mind.

"If you don't need me for anything this afternoon, I'd like to take Josh into town to look for a new pair of boots," Lydia said. "His feet have grown, and his old boots are pinching his toes."

"Do you have enough money?"

Lydia nodded. Truth was she barely had enough, and she hoped she could find something within her price range.

"That's fine. I'll hitch my horse to the buggy for you whenever you're ready to go."

Lydia frowned. "I know how to hitch a horse, Mom."

"Yes, but Buttercup's kind of temperamental. She might not cooperate with you the way she does for me."

Lydia couldn't imagine any horse with a name like Buttercup being temperamental. "I'm sure I can manage, but if I have any trouble, I'll come in and get you."

The awkward angle of the gas lamp hanging overhead etched Mom's face in sharp shadows as she pursed her lips and nodded slowly. "You might try Charm Harness and Boot for Josh. If you can't find the right boots there, you should go to the Wal-Mart in Millersburg."

"It'll take too long to go to Millersburg," Lydia said. "Hopefully we'll find what we need at the local store. I might stop by Miller's Dry Goods, too. If there's anything you need, I'd be happy to pick it up."

"I can't think of anything right now," Mom said. "Since I spend most of my days taking care of your grossdaadi, I'm too busy to do any quilting, so I don't buy much from the dry goods store these days."

"I'm sorry to hear that. I know how much you like to quilt." Lydia took a sip of tea and let it roll around on her tongue. She loved the zesty taste of peppermint.

"With the exception of the new store Kiem Lumber built a few years ago, I think you'll find that things haven't changed much in Charm," Mom added.

"It's nice to know that some things haven't changed. So many things in our world have."

Mom nodded. "We do have a couple of new store owners in town."

"Which ones?"

"The woodshop on the outskirts of town is now owned by a man named Menno Troyer. He and his wife, Sadie, moved here from Pennsylvania about a year ago, but she died six months ago from cancer. That left Menno with four boys to raise on his own."

"That's too bad." As a widow, it was hard enough for Lydia to raise one child on her own; she couldn't imagine trying to bring up four boys without the help of her husband.

"Oh, and then there's the general store," Mom continued. "It's run by a family of—"

The back door slammed shut, and Mom jumped, nearly spilling her cup of tea.

"Ich hab ken halt draa grict!" Josh hollered as he raced into the kitchen.

"What couldn't you catch hold of?" Lydia asked.

"Derr katz!" Josh jumped up and down, his dark eyes big as saucers.

Mom put her finger to her lips and frowned. "Be quiet, Josh. You might wake your *urgrossvadder.*"

A gray cat with four white paws zipped into the kitchen and hid under the table, curling its bushy tail around its fluffy body.

Josh dove under the table and grabbed the end of its tail. *Meow!* The cat let out a screech and raced across the room. Josh tore after it, but his feet tangled in the throw rug in front of the sink, and he dropped to the floor with a grunt. He sat a few seconds, then scrambled to his feet. Dashing across the room, he grabbed for the cat, but it sought refuge under the table again.

"Ich hab ken halt draa grict!" Josh hollered.

"I told you to be quiet!" Mom raised her voice as she pointed to the cat and then to the back door. *"Duh die katz naus!"*

Josh's lower lip trembled, and his eyes filled with tears as he gathered up the cat and took it outside, as Mom had asked.

Irritation welled in Lydia's soul. Josh wasn't used to his new home or having to be quiet when his great-grandfather was sleeping. What harm could there be in letting him play with the cat in the house?

Mom was being too harsh and critical of his behavior. Didn't she realize the boy was only four years old? Besides, if Josh was supposed to be quiet, then why was it all right for Mom to raise her voice?

Lydia grimaced as she thought about how many times Mom had been critical of her when she was a child. She had never been able to do anything right, and whatever she'd done, Mom had usually ended up redoing.

I need to remember that this isn't my house and that Mom and Grandpa are doing us a favor by letting us live here, Lydia reminded herself. *As long as we're staying in this house, we'll need to do things Mom's way, or there won't be any peace.*

When Josh returned to the kitchen with his head down and shoulders slumped, Lydia gave him a hug and quietly said, "Why don't you go back outside and play with the katz?"

Josh nodded and scurried out the door.

Mom took a sip of tea and released a lingering sigh. *"Der grossdaadi hot net genunk scholof grickt lescht nacht."*

"I'm sorry Grandpa didn't get enough sleep last night. I'll make sure that Josh doesn't disturb him when we get home from shopping this afternoon."

"I appreciate that. Dad's not doing well, and he isn't used to having little ones in the house running around, making noise."

Lydia stared into her half-empty cup and blinked back tears. So much for her resolve to remain positive and ignore the things she found irritating. If Josh had to keep quiet all the time, she wasn't sure how long they could stay here. What Lydia needed most was to find a job so that she and Josh could eventually have a place of their own.

⁓

Menno Troyer stepped into the kitchen and groaned. Not only were the cabinets old and in need of repair, but the rest of the kitchen looked messy, as well. A stack of dirty pots and pans from last night's supper had been piled up in the sink, and the dishes they'd used for breakfast this morning still sat on the table.

He flung open the cupboard door under the sink and grimaced. The garbage can was heaped with even more trash than it had held last night. Since it was late spring and there'd be no school for the next few months, his boys would be home by them-selves most of the time while he was at work in his woodshop behind their house.

This morning before Menno had headed to the shop, he'd given the boys a list of chores to do. Here it was almost noon, and they hadn't completed anything.

Menno moved into the living room. It needed a fresh coat of paint, and the cracked windows had yet to be replaced. He frowned when he saw his two dark-haired boys, five-year-old Kevin and seven-year-old Carl, sleeping on the floor. Nine-year-old Dennis, who had reddish-blond hair like his mother's, sat in Menno's recliner with his scruffy-looking mutt, Goldie, draped across his lap. Ike, who'd turned twelve a few weeks ago, was sprawled on the sofa, reading a book. This was ridicu-lous!

Menno clapped his hands, causing Den-nis and Ike to jump, but the two younger boys slept on. "Get yourselves up and be quick about it! I'll be heading to Kiem Lum-ber soon, and if you want to go along, then you'd better get with it."

"You don't hafta shout, Papa." Ike sat up and yawned. "We ain't *daab*, ya know."

"I know you're not deaf, but you sure do act like it sometimes." Menno pointed to the kitchen door. "Doesn't look as if you heard a word I said this morning about doing your chores."

"I fed and watered the horses," Ike said.

"And I fed Goldie." Dennis stroked the golden retriever's ears and offered Menno a freckle-faced grin.

"That's fine, well, and good, but no one cleared the breakfast table or did last night's dishes."

Ike motioned to his sleeping brothers. "That was *their* job."

Menno's patience was beginning to wane. "Who said?"

"Ike said so," Dennis spoke up before his older brother had a chance to reply. "He thinks he's the boss when you ain't home."

"Ike's supposed to be in charge when I'm working in the shop." Menno turned to Ike and snapped his fingers. "Being in charge means you need to see that everyone gets his chores done before I come home from work every day. It doesn't mean that you get to lie around while your brothers do all the work."

"But you're home early today," Ike said. "So you didn't give us a chance to get everything done."

"I'm home early because I'm goin' to Kiem's. I told you this morning that if you wanted to go along, you'd need to have your chores done by noon."

Ike frowned. "Sorry, Papa, but my lazy brothers won't listen to anything I say."

Menno felt overcome by a sense of guilt. Ever since Sadie had died, he'd put a lot of responsibility on the boys—especially Ike. It was either that, or he'd have to hire someone to come in and do the household chores, and he really couldn't afford that right now. He'd just gotten Sadie's hospital bills paid off and had been trying to put some money away for future needs they might have. With the tourist season starting up again, Menno figured he might sell more furniture and that would help their finances. But he had two employees he needed to pay, not to mention four growing boys who had to be fed and clothed. At the rate things were going, he'd never get this old house fixed up like he'd promised Sadie when they'd first moved to Charm.

Menno glanced at the rocking chair he'd made for Sadie soon after they were married. A wave of sadness washed over him. She'd used that chair to rock each of their sons.

As much as Menno hated to think about it, he really needed a wife—a mother for his boys. But the only widowed women in the area were much older than him. A few younger women weren't yet married, but they seemed so immature. What Menno needed was someone who'd had experience raising children. The question was, who?

CHAPTER 2

Do you like your new *schtiwwel*?" Lydia asked Josh as they left Charm Shoe and Boot.

He grinned and pointed to the pair of shiny black boots on his feet. *"Sei nett."*

"Jah, they're very nice." As Lydia helped Josh into the buggy, his stomach growled noisily. "Are you getting hungry?" she asked.

He patted his belly and gave a nod.

"All right then, we'll stop over at Grandma's Restaurant and get some lunch."

Josh's eyes widened. *"Grossmammi* has a restaurant?"

Lydia chuckled. "No. That's the name of the restaurant where we'll be eating. It has nothing to do with your grandma."

As they traveled the short distance to town, Lydia noticed that the picturesque landscape looked the same as she remembered it: Same curving, hilly roads with many Amish farms scattered along the way. Some had been built close to the road, while others were set farther back. Some had their place of business connected to their homes, and some were in separate buildings.

As they continued along County Road 70 with Buttercup behaving herself quite nicely, Lydia noticed that the roots of several old-looking trees were exposed along the edge of the road. They'd probably been there for a good many years, just like the little town of Charm, which had been founded in 1840. It was originally named Stevenson, but when the first post office was opened in 1885, the town's name was changed to Charm. Lydia remembered her father saying that some folks had given the town the nickname of *Putschtown*, which meant "a small clump."

A bird fluttered from one of the trees

and swooped in front of the buggy. Josh let out a whoop and ducked his head.

"It's all right, son," Lydia said. "The *voggel* can't get in our buggy. I think he's just trying to make it to one of the trees on the other side of the road."

Josh flashed Lydia a grin that nearly melted her heart. Oh, how she loved spending time with her precious little boy.

As they came down the hill into Charm, she spotted the building for Kiem Lumber, which had been built a few years ago and was more modern than the last one had been. She was anxious to see what it looked like inside.

Across Highway 557, she spotted Grandma's Restaurant. When she pulled Buttercup into the restaurant's parking lot, she was surprised to see so many cars. Since it was a weekday and an hour past noon, she hadn't expected so many people would still be having lunch. She hoped they could get a table right away, because she had a couple more stops to make before they headed back to Grandpa's place, and she wanted to get there in plenty of time to help Mom with supper.

When they entered the restaurant, Lydia

was disappointed to see several people standing in the entryway, waiting for a table. She thought about leaving, but Josh was really hungry. As she recalled from her last visit several years ago, this was the only restaurant in the center of town. Of course, there was the Chalet in the Valley, but that was farther out. Also, she'd never eaten at the Chalet and wasn't sure if they'd have anything on the menu that Josh would like.

Lydia stepped up to the counter and told the hostess that they needed a table for two; then she took Josh's hand and stood off to one side. While they waited, Josh alternated between playing with the lever on the gumball machine and watching out the window, while Lydia read the names and comments in the guest book. One comment in particular caught her attention: *I'm glad we came to visit this charming little town. There are so many quaint and unusual shops here; no wonder they call it Charm.*

Lydia had never really thought about the quaintness of Charm or heard anyone who lived here refer to it is as charming. She supposed that most people who lived in a certain area for any length of time took everything about it for granted. People from outside the area, especially tourists, no doubt viewed traditional Amish towns like Charm in a much different way.

They waited about twenty minutes and were finally shown to a table. Several more minutes passed before a young English woman came to take their order.

"Sorry about the wait, but we're short-handed right now and didn't expect such a big lunch crowd this afternoon." The dark circles under the waitress's eyes and the perspiration glistening on her forehead gave indication of her obvious fatigue.

Lydia smiled, hoping to encourage the young woman. "It's okay. We didn't mind waiting."

The waitress offered a faint smile as she looked at Josh, sitting on a booster seat with an expectant look on his face. "What can I get you to drink, little fellow?"

"A glass of milk." Lydia spoke for Josh, since he wasn't proficient in English yet. That would come after he started school in a few years. "And I'd like a glass of iced tea, please," she quickly added.

The waitress left the table, and when

she returned with their beverages, she took their order: a hot dog for Josh and a turkey sandwich for Lydia.

While they waited for their food, Lydia looked at her shopping list. They still needed to stop by the general store to pick up a few things Mom had mentioned she needed at the last minute, and then they'd go to Kiem Lumber to buy some paint. Shortly before Lydia and Josh had left for town, Lydia had told Mom that she'd help her paint the kitchen tomorrow morning. Lydia was more than willing to help because Mom wouldn't have time to do the painting on her own.

"How come that little Amish girl looks like a lady in her face?" Josh asked in their Pennsylvania-Dutch language.

Lydia took a sip of her tea and nearly choked when Josh pointed at a woman who had just entered the restaurant. She was dressed in Amish clothes and couldn't have been more than four feet tall.

Lydia noticed that the little woman's chestnut brown hair was sprinkled lightly with gray, and soft wrinkles framed her lips and eyes. She was definitely not a girl. More than likely, she was in her early fifties.

"How come that little Amish girl looks like a lady in her face?" Josh repeated as he continued to point.

Lydia shook her head sternly. "Put your hand down, Josh. It's not nice to point."

"But how come she looks—"

"Not now, Josh. I'll explain things to you later."

When the little woman followed the hostess past Lydia and Josh's table, Lydia held her breath, hoping Josh wouldn't say anything more. To her relief, he kept quiet, but he continued to stare at the little woman.

Lydia was glad when the woman was seated near the back of the restaurant, out of Josh's sight. She didn't want to deal with any more of his embarrassing questions, at least not until they were in the buggy where no one else could hear.

Lydia managed to keep Josh occupied by talking about other things until their food was brought to the table. Then, after a silent prayer, she told Josh to enjoy his hot dog.

When they finished their meal, Lydia took the bill to the counter to pay. They were almost to the front door when she spotted a

sign in the window that read: WAITRESS
WANTED. Could this be the job she'd been
hoping to find? A job this close to Grandpa's house would be perfect, because she
could walk or ride her bike to work.

Lydia was so excited about the prospect
of working here that, if Josh hadn't been
squirming and tugging on her hand, she
might have inquired about the job right
then. Under the circumstances, she figured it would be best to leave Josh with
Mom and come by in the morning to put in
her application. Hopefully, the job would
still be available. If it wasn't, she would
have to accept it as God's will and trust
that He'd provide something better for her.

When Lydia and Josh entered the general
store, a nice-looking Amish man with
reddish-brown hair and dark brown eyes
greeted them with a cheery smile. He was
of average height with muscular arms, and
his cleanly shaven face let Lydia know that
he wasn't married.

"Can I help you with something?" he
asked as Lydia turned toward one of the
aisles.

"I just need some toothpaste and a few

other things, but I think I can find them," she replied.

"I'll be at the front counter when you're ready to pay for your purchases." He disappeared around the corner, and Lydia moved up the aisle with Josh.

She'd only been looking a few minutes when Josh tugged on her hand. *"Schpielsach."*

Lydia looked down at Josh and shook her head. "I don't have enough money to buy you a toy."

"Zuckerscheifli?"

"No, Josh. You just had lunch. You don't need any sugar candy."

The corners of his mouth turned down, and his eyes filled with tears.

Lydia sighed. She wished she could have left Josh at home with Mom. It would have saved her the embarrassment of him pointing at the little person at the restaurant, and she'd have been able to shop without him begging for things. But if she'd left him at home, they couldn't have shopped for new boots.

Guess I should be grateful for the time I get to spend with my boy, she chided herself. *Once I get a job, I won't be with Josh nearly as much as I'd like.*

Lydia lifted the corner of Josh's straw hat and ruffled his hair. "Why don't you look at the toys while I finish shopping? If I have enough money left after I pay for my purchases, I'll buy you some gum or a piece of candy."

Josh grinned and scampered away.

When Lydia finished shopping and stepped up to the counter, she was surprised to see the Amish man kneeling on the floor next to Josh.

Wearing a contented smile, Josh held a red lollipop in his hand. "Zuckerscheifli."

Lydia was about to reprimand him for taking the candy without asking, when the man spoke up.

"I hope you don't mind that I gave him a lollipop. He was eyeballing the candy, and I couldn't resist."

"I don't mind. That was kind of you." Lydia tore her gaze away from the man's handsome face. "Did you say thank you?" she asked Josh.

"Danki." Josh swiped his tongue over the lollipop and grinned at the man.

"You're welcome. Are you finished shopping now?" he asked Lydia.

She nodded and placed her purchases on the counter.

"Are you new to the area? Don't believe I've seen you in our store before."

Lydia introduced herself, as well as Josh, and then explained how she'd come to live with her mother, Mae Weaver. "Mom used to live in Wisconsin, but she moved to Charm a year ago to care for my gross-daadi, Wilbur Hershberger," she added.

"Oh yes, I've met your *mamm* a couple of times, but not Wilbur yet." The man extended his hand, which was nearly twice the size of Lydia's. "It's nice to meet you. My name's Levi Stutzman. My family moved here a few months ago from Geauga County, in the northeastern part of the state, and we bought this place." He motioned to the other end of the store. "My *daed* and two sisters are in the back room, unpacking some pots and pans we just got in. My younger brothers, who help out in the store on occasion, are at home, and my mamm's out running some errands right now."

"Maybe I'll get to meet some of your

family the next time I come in." Lydia paid for her purchases and picked up the paper sack. "We have one more stop to make, so I guess we'd better be on our way."

Lydia and Josh were almost to the door when it swung open. The same little Amish woman they'd seen at the restaurant entered the store.

Josh tugged on Lydia's dress, and she held her breath. She hoped he wouldn't say anything that might embarrass her. She really should have taken the time to explain about little people after they'd left the restaurant.

The little woman looked up at Lydia and smiled; then she moved on past. Lydia thought about introducing herself, but with Josh standing there wide-eyed and mouth hanging open, she decided it was best to make a hasty exit.

"How come that little Amish girl looks like a lady in her face?" Josh asked as Lydia was putting the paper sack in the buggy.

"I'll tell you in a minute." Lydia hoisted Josh into the passenger's seat, untied the horse from the hitching rail, and took her seat on the driver's side. She'd better give Josh an explanation right away, because if the little woman lived nearby, there was a good chance they'd see her again.

"Listen to me, Josh," Lydia said, carefully choosing her words. "You know how some *bopplin* are born with a lot of hair and others have none?"

He gave a slow nod.

"Some bopplin have blue eyes, and some have brown."

"Jah."

"Well, most bopplin grow up to be tall, but some are short."

"Ich katzbehnich."

Lydia bit back a chuckle. "You're short-legged now, but someday when you grow up, I'm sure you'll be tall just like your daed."

Josh blinked and stared at Lydia as though he had no idea what she was trying to tell him. Truth was, she wasn't exactly sure how to explain dwarfism to Josh. If she told him that some babies were born with a genetic defect causing short stature, he'd never understand. She needed to keep her explanation simple.

She reached across the seat and touched Josh's arm. "Some people, even when they grow up, never get tall. They stay small, like that little woman in the store." She paused to gauge his reaction, but he still wore a look of confusion.

"But why'd the little girl look *alt*?"

Lydia sighed. "She looks old because she's a woman, Josh."

He shook his head vigorously. "She's a *bissel maedel*."

"She's not a little girl." Lydia turned Josh to face her. "You're not understanding what I'm trying to say. The little woman was born different than you and me. You'll grow up to be tall someday, but she'll never grow any taller than she is right now."

"How come?"

"Because God made her different than us, and she'll always be short."

"Even when she's alt like Urgrossvadder?"

"Jah, even when she's old like your great-grandfather."

Josh swiped his tongue across the lollipop a couple of times and tipped his head, as though trying to process all that she'd said. "Does the little woman sleep in a little bed, and eat at a little table?"

"I don't know. Maybe." Lydia had never been inside a little person's house, so she really couldn't say.

Josh made another quick pass at his lollipop. "Can we go to her house sometime and see?"

"I don't think so, Josh. I don't even know the woman's name, much less where she lives. Right now, we need to go to Kiem Lumber and get some paint for Grandma's kitchen." Lydia backed the horse away from the hitching rail. She was glad to have this discussion over and hoped she'd put Josh's curiosity about the little woman to rest.

CHAPTER 3

How's business?" Nona asked as she walked up to the front counter where Levi stood. "Have you been keeping busy?"

Levi gave a slow nod. "But not so busy that I haven't been able to handle things on my own. How'd things go with your errands?" he asked. "Your horse didn't give you any trouble, I hope."

"Of course not. Tinker's gentle as a kitten." Nona peered up at Levi. "Any idea who that young woman was with the little boy? I didn't recognize them."

"Her name's Lydia King. She's Wilbur Hershberger's granddaughter."

"I see. Do you know where she's from?"

"She mentioned that she's a widow and that she and her son Josh moved here from Illinois."

"Guess we'll probably be seeing a lot of them then."

"Maybe so."

"Did you notice her pretty face and shiny blond hair?"

Levi gave a brief shrug.

"Her boy's sure cute."

"Jah. He was eyeballing the candy, so I gave him a lollipop."

"That was nice." Nona smiled. "Maybe Lydia and her son will come into the store often and you'll have a chance to get better acquainted."

Levi's eyebrows drew together. "Don't get any ideas, Mom. You ought to know by now that I'm not lookin' for a *fraa*."

"Never said you were looking for a wife."

"I'm perfectly happy helping you and Pop here in the store."

"Never said you weren't." Nona moved around the counter and climbed onto the stool where Levi had previously been sitting. "You can't blame a mamm for trying," she said with a chuckle.

"There's a twinkle in your eye that has me worried." Levi leaned over, so he was looking Nona in the face. "I hope you're not getting any ideas about trying to play matchmaker."

She swatted him playfully on the arm. "Wouldn't think of it, son."

❧

"I'm hungerich," Josh complained as Lydia tied her horse to the hitching rail in front of Kiem Lumber.

"I don't see how you can be hungry," Lydia said. "Not long ago we had lunch, and you just finished eating a lollipop."

"I'm still hungerich."

Lydia gave his belly a gentle poke. "I guess that's because you're a growing boy."

Josh giggled and bobbed his head. "Jah. *Waxich bu.*"

"You'll have to wait until we get back to Grandma's for a snack, because I don't think there's anything to eat inside the lumber store." Lydia took Josh's hand, and they headed across the parking lot. When they entered the store, she paused, searching for the aisle where the paint was located. Kiem Lumber had expanded since she'd been here last, and there was so much more to see. Besides the variety of lumber available, displays of fancy electric light fixtures, plumbing supplies, all kinds of flooring, lots of garden items, and many other things filled the aisles.

Lydia finally located the paint section, but Josh tugged on her dress.

"What is it, Josh?"

He pointed across the room. "Ice cream."

Her gaze went to a young English girl coming down the open staircase with an ice-cream cone in her hand. Apparently food was sold someplace on the second floor.

"Ice cream," Josh said again.

Lydia groaned. She figured it would be easier to get her shopping done if she let Josh have a treat, so she took his hand and started up the stairs.

Menno took a seat inside Carpenter's Café as he waited for his boys to come out of the bathroom so they could place their order. Since they hadn't taken the time to eat lunch before they'd left home, he'd decided to stop at the café for a late lunch. The little troublemakers had been arguing ever since they'd left home, and he hoped some cheeseburgers and milk shakes might put them in better moods. If nothing else, maybe the boys would be too busy eating to fuss at each other.

Menno's stomach rumbled as he stared at the menu in front of him. Except for the meals that had been brought in by some of the women in their community, he and the boys ate simply—soup and sandwiches, mostly. It was nice to eat out once in a while, where there was a variety of food. The lunch menu here was varied: cheeseburgers, hot dogs, smoked sausage, fish and chicken sandwiches, tacos, and several kinds of salad.

Menno drummed his fingers along the edge of the table. What could be taking the boys so long? He needed to get back to his woodshop soon. He wished he'd asked the boys what they wanted before they'd headed to the bathroom.

I sure hope they're not fooling around in there.

He drew in a deep breath and leaned back in his chair. Since Sadie had died, he never seemed to have a free moment; something always demanded his immediate attention.

The sound of running feet and high-pitched voices pulled Menno's thoughts back to his surroundings. His boys were racing down the hallway like a herd of runaway horses. Suddenly, Kevin darted in front of a young, blond-haired Amish woman, who walked beside a little boy whose hair was also blond. They managed to sidestep Kevin just in time, and Menno breathed a sigh of relief.

"You'd better watch where you're going," Menno said as Kevin slid into the chair beside him. "You know you're not supposed to run in here."

"Sorry, Papa," Kevin mumbled. "I was in a hurry to get back to the table."

"Jah, well, I guess no real harm was done. Now tell me what you want to eat so I can put in our order." Menno motioned to the menu. "Does anyone want a hot dog, or would you rather have a cheeseburger?"

Ike flopped into the chair next to Menno. "I'll have a cheeseburger."

"Same here," Carl said with a nod.

"What about you two?" Menno asked, looking at Dennis and Kevin.

"Hot dog!" they both hollered.

Menno frowned. "Lower your voices. I'm

not hard of hearing, and remember, you're in a public place."

The woman with the little boy glanced over at Menno and offered him a faint smile; then she quickly looked away.

I wonder who she is. Don't think I've seen her around here before.

Dennis tugged on Menno's shirtsleeve. "Papa, I'm hungerich. Are you gonna get us somethin' to eat?"

Menno jerked his head. "'Course I am. Stop badgering me." He left the table and got in line behind the young Amish woman. Just then, she turned and came face-to-face with him, almost spilling her glass of iced tea and dish of ice cream.

Her dimpled cheeks turned pink. "Excuse me. I—I didn't realize anyone was standing behind me."

"No harm done." Menno stepped aside, watching as she and the little boy took seats at the table across from his boys.

Menno placed everyone's order, and when he returned to his table, he was surprised to see that Kevin was talking to the little blond-haired boy, who was eagerly eating his dish of ice cream.

Menno was on the verge of calling Kevin

back to their table but figured it could wait until their food was ready. One less brother at the table meant less opportunity for an argument to begin.

When their order was called, Menno picked up their food and told Kevin to return to their table and take a seat.

"In a minute, Papa. I wanna finish tellin' Josh about our pet *frosch*."

"Forget about the frog. You need to eat your hot dog before it gets cold."

Kevin said something else to the boy; then he scampered over to Menno's table and sat down. A moment later, the young woman and the little boy left the café.

Menno watched them head down the stairs to the main part of the store. "Looks like you made a new friend," he said, handing Kevin his hot dog.

Kevin grinned. "His name's Josh King. His mamm's name is Lydia. His daed's dead, and they moved here from Illinois to live with his grossmammi, who lives with his urgrossvadder."

"Is that so?"

Kevin nodded. "Sure hope I get to see Josh again, 'cause he said he'd like to see my frosch."

Menno smiled. "If Josh and his mamm will be living in Charm, then I'm sure we'll see them again. But right now, let's pray so we can eat."

As Menno closed his eyes, a vision of the blond woman popped into his head. *She's young, but not too young—maybe in her late twenties. She's a widow with a son, so she's had experience raising children. Hmm . . . I wonder. . . .*

CHAPTER 4

The stairs creaked as Lydia made her way down to the kitchen. She'd slept longer than she'd planned and hoped Mom hadn't already started breakfast. When she'd looked in Josh's room a few minutes ago she'd discovered that he wasn't there. She figured he was probably in the kitchen waiting to be fed.

Much to Lydia's surprise, when she stepped into the kitchen there was no sign of Mom or Josh, and nothing was cooking on the stove. Deciding that Josh might have gone outside to check on the kittens he'd discovered in the barn last night, and knowing Mom must be with Grandpa, Lydia removed a carton of eggs from the propane-operated refrigerator. She'd just started cracking them into a bowl when she heard Grandpa's gravely voice coming from his bedroom at the end of the hall.

"Don't want no juice! Ya can't make me drink it! Get outa my room!" Grandpa's words, though slurred from his being partially paralyzed, clearly made his point.

"But you've got to drink something, Dad," Mom argued. "You'll become dehydrated if you don't."

"Don't matter. *Mei hoig aawle-daag sin verbein.*"

"I realize your hay-pitching days are over," Mom said, "but you can't give up on life."

"Probably gonna die anyway. Why don'tcha let me die in peace?"

Lydia cringed. She hated to hear Grandpa talk like that. Life was precious, and each day should be lived to the fullest. But then, she reasoned, Grandpa's life wasn't so full anymore. From what Mom had said, since his stroke, Grandpa hadn't been able to do much more than sit in his wheelchair and stare out the window. Even so, that was no reason to give up on life. Where there was life, there was hope. That's what Lydia's father used to say before he'd died of an unexpected heart attack.

Feeling the need for a cup of coffee, Lydia set the eggs aside, filled the coffeepot with water and coffee grounds, then set it on the stove. While she waited for it to perk, she began setting the table.

In an attempt to drown out the loud voices that continued from Grandpa's room, Lydia hummed the melody of her favorite hymn, "Faithful Love." It was no use; Grandpa's angry tone sliced through the air like a knife as he continued to holler and argue with Mom.

When Lydia could stand it no longer, she turned off the stove and headed down the hall. She was almost to Grandpa's room when the door flew open, and Mom rushed out. Her face was flushed, and her eyes rimmed with tears. She looked at Lydia and slowly shook her head. "Nothing I do is ever good enough for him."

Lydia hesitated a minute, then opened the door to Grandpa's room and stepped in. She found him in bed, a well-worn quilt pulled up so that only his face and full gray beard stuck out. As she approached, he blinked his pale blue eyes a couple of times but said nothing.

Lydia picked up the glass beside Grandpa's bed and tipped the straw toward him. "Would you like a drink?"

"Not thirsty," he mumbled.

"But you have to drink something. If you don't, you'll . . ."

"Go away! Leave me alone. Wanna die in peace."

Lydia was tempted to tell Grandpa that he would die sooner if he didn't keep fluids in his body, but after hearing the way he'd hollered at Mom, she didn't want to say anything that might rile him further.

"After breakfast, I'll be going to town to apply for a job at Grandma's Restaurant," Lydia said. "Is there something I can pick up for you at one of the stores in Charm?"

"No."

Taking a seat beside his bed, she reached over and touched his arm. "Is it all right if I sit with you awhile?"

"Rather be alone."

Tears pricked the back of Lydia's eyes.

No wonder Mom had looked so upset. Maybe Grandpa needed one of the ministers from the church district to pay him a visit. Maybe someone outside the family would have better luck getting through to him than she or Mom.

Lydia gave Grandpa's shoulder a gentle squeeze, rose from her chair, and quietly left the room. She was almost to the kitchen when the back door flew open, and her rosy-cheeked little boy darted into the house with a fluffy gray kitten in his arms. Before Lydia could say anything, Josh made a beeline for the kitchen. "Look, Grossmammi," he said excitedly, "*en bussli.*"

"Jah, I see the kitten. Now take it outside!" Mom's voice was tinged with irritation. "You know I don't allow animals in the house!"

Lydia flinched, and Josh started to howl. This was not a good way to start the day. "Maybe it would be best if I didn't go to the restaurant to apply for that job this morning," she said, stepping up to Mom. "Maybe I should stay home and give you a break from caring for Grandpa. Besides, I said I'd help you paint the kitchen today."

Mom shook her head. "The kitchen can wait. If you don't apply for the job now, it might be gone."

"You're right, so maybe I should take Josh with me. That way you won't have to worry about keeping an eye on him."

"I'll manage. Besides, it wouldn't be good for you to take Josh along when you're applying for a job."

"I guess you're right." Lydia sighed. "I just don't feel good about—"

"We'll be fine." Mom glanced around the kitchen and frowned. "Where is Josh? I hope he didn't take that critter into the living room." As she started that way, the sound of laughter floated down the hallway.

"That sounds like my daed." Mom's eyebrows lifted as she looked at Lydia. "I haven't heard him laugh like that since I came here to care for him. I'd better go see what's going on."

Mom rushed down the hallway, and Lydia followed. When they entered Grandpa's room, Lydia was stunned. Josh sat on the edge of Grandpa's bed, and the kitten he'd brought into the house lay curled in a ball on Grandpa's chest.

Grandpa's crooked lips formed a smile. "En bussli," he said.

"That dirty kitten does not belong on the bed." Mom looked at Josh. "You are not supposed to be in here when your urgross-vadder is trying to rest."

"Let him be," Grandpa mumbled.

Mom stood, frozen in place. Then with a disgruntled look, she rushed from the room.

❧

As Levi headed home from Berlin, where he'd gone to get Mom a few things from the health food store, his buggy passed Wilbur Hershberger's place. He'd never met the man personally but had heard from others in the community that Wilbur had suffered a stroke some time ago. His daughter, Mae, had come into their store a couple of times, but she'd never seemed too friendly, especially toward Mom. Levi figured Mae might be shy or have a lot on her mind. Taking care of her ailing father had to be difficult.

His thoughts went to Mae's daughter, Lydia, and how she'd come into the store with her son the other day. She'd seemed a lot friendlier than Mae, but maybe she was more outgoing than her mother.

Levi reflected on Mom's comment about Lydia being pretty and hoped she didn't have any ideas about trying to get him and Lydia together. Mom had tried to play matchmaker a few times before, and Levi had called a halt to it real quick. He'd made up his mind a long time ago that he would never get married. Aside from Mom and Pop needing his help in the store, any children he might have could be born with dwarfism. Not that he'd be opposed to having a child who would never grow tall. Having grown up in a home full of little people, he was perfectly comfortable around them. What concerned him was how a woman of normal size might feel about having a child with dwarfism. He was also worried about how the child might be treated by other children of normal size. Over the years, Levi had seen many rude people stare at or make fun of his parents and siblings because of their short stature, although Mom and Pop had always dealt with it well.

A car honked as it passed Levi, and his

horse whinnied and pulled to the right. "Whoa, boy. Steady now," he said, gripping the reins. "Sure wish our horse and buggies didn't have to share the road with cars," he mumbled. "But then I guess the Englishers probably wish they didn't have to share the road with our horse and buggies."

As Levi approached Grandma's Restaurant, his stomach rumbled noisily, so he decided to stop for a quick lunch before he returned to the store. He guided his horse to the hitching rail, made sure it was secure, and went inside.

Menno had just entered Grandma's Restaurant when he spotted the young, blond-haired woman he'd seen yesterday at Carpenter's Café. She was speaking with Edith, the owner of the restaurant.

Menno was about to take a seat when he noticed Levi Stutzman sitting at a table near the window. "Is this seat taken?" he asked, motioning to the empty chair across from Levi.

Levi shook his head. "I'm here by myself."

"Mind if I join you? I'm not in the mood to eat alone."

Levi smiled. "Have a seat. I'd be glad for the company."

"How are things going at your folks' store?" Menno asked as he sat down. "Are you keeping busy?"

"We sure are, and with the tourist season about to begin, I'm sure we'll be busier than ever."

"Guess stayin' busy is a good thing. Jobs are hard to come by in many places in the country, so I suppose those of us who have plenty of work should be grateful."

Levi nodded. "I just worry that running the store will become too much for Mom and Pop. They're not getting any younger, and because they're both so short, it's harder for them to do some things."

"I'm sure they appreciate having you there to help out."

"My family means the world to me. There isn't anything I wouldn't do for them."

"I understand. I feel the same way about my boys." Menno reached for his glass of water and took a drink. *I'll even give them another mamm if I can find the right one.*

"How are things going for you?" Levi asked.

"About the same. I'm workin' hard in my shop and trying to hold things together at home. Raising four active boys can be a challenge sometimes."

"I imagine. Where are the boys today?"

"Left the two younger ones with a neighbor. The two older boys are at the shop, sweeping sawdust from the floors, under the supervision of my employees, John and Mark." Menno slowly shook his head. "Things were a bit easier when the boys were in school. At least then I didn't have to worry about 'em during the day. Never know what's going to happen next. What one boy doesn't come up with, the others likely will." He grimaced. "The other day they were foolin' around with a frog they found at the pond, and that night while I was fixin' supper, I found the critter in the kitchen sink. Dennis finally admitted that he was the one who put the frog there."

"How'd you handle that?" Levi asked.

"Ich hab ihm die leffidle lese misse."

Levi reared his head back and laughed.

Menno frowned. "Just what's so funny about me givin' Dennis a lecture?"

"It's not the lecture that made me laugh. It was picturing the look you must have had on your face when you discovered a frog sitting in your sink."

Menno chuckled. "Guess it is kind of funny, but it sure wasn't at the time."

"I don't think being a parent is ever easy," Levi said. "I'm sure me and my brothers and sisters have put our folks through a lot over the years. For that matter, the younger ones are still pretty rambunctious at times."

"You're right about parenting not being easy. Fact is, nothing's been easy for me since Sadie died." Menno's face contorted. "It's been six months since her death, and I wonder if the pain of losing her will ever subside."

"Since I'm not married I don't know how it would feel to lose a mate, but I do know that when my grossmammi died, my gross-daadi found joy again by spending time with his *kinnskinner.*"

Menno nodded. "It'll be a long time before I have any grandchildren, but your point's well taken. I should enjoy whatever time I have to spend with my boys." He gave his left earlobe a tug. "Just wish they'd learn to behave themselves."

Levi glanced over his shoulder. "Changing the subject, I wonder if we're ever going to get waited on. Someone should have been here by now to take our order, don't you think?"

"I think they may be shorthanded."

"Guess I ought to be more patient," Levi said, "but Mom and my sisters are the only ones working in the store right now, and I don't want to leave 'em alone too long."

"Where's your daed and *brieder* today?"

"Pop and my brother Peter went fishing. Mom said Pop's been working too hard lately, and she insisted that he take the day off. And if Andy's up and dressed by now, he's probably at the store or home doing his chores."

"How come you didn't join 'em at the fishing hole?"

"I had some errands to run in Berlin this morning and figured Mom would need me in the store this afternoon." Levi fingered his silverware as he stared out the window. "Can't remember the last time I went fishing. Sure would be nice to spend a few hours at the pond."

Just then, a waitress finally came and took their order.

When their soup and sandwiches arrived, they ate while they talked about the warm spring weather, and discussed some safety issues folks had been having with their horse and buggies lately.

"It scares me the way some Englishers drive their cars around here," Menno said. "With all the dips and turns on the back roads, it's hard to see when one of our buggies is up ahead. If a car's going too fast there's just no way they can stop in time once they realize a buggy's at the bottom of one of those dips."

He lifted his glass of water, and someone bumped his arm. The cold liquid sloshed out of his glass and trickled down the front of his shirt.

"I–I'm so sorry. I didn't mean to bump you."

Menno looked up and recognized Lydia King. "It's okay. No harm's been done," he said, blotting his shirt with a napkin.

"Would you like me to see if I can find you a towel?"

"I'm fine. It's just a little *wasser.*"

"Do you work here, Lydia?" Levi spoke up.

She nodded then shook her head. "Not yet. I'll be starting here tomorrow, though."

"Then I'll probably see you again, because I come in for lunch quite often," Menno said.

She smiled. "I'll try not to make a habit of spilling water on you."

"Might feel kind of good if it's a real hot day." Levi chuckled, then looked over at Menno and said, "Have you met Lydia King? She and her son just moved here from Illinois. Lydia is Wilbur Hershberger's granddaughter."

"Jah, I know." Menno smiled at Lydia. "You and your son were talkin' to one of my boys at Carpenter's Café yesterday. He told me who you were." Menno extended his hand. "I'm Menno Troyer. I own the woodshop here in town."

"It's nice to meet you." Her cheeks flushed as she shook Menno's hand. "I'd better go so you two can finish your lunch. It was good seeing you both again."

"So how'd you meet her?" Menno asked Levi after Lydia walked away.

"Met her briefly when she and her little boy came into our store yesterday," Levi replied. "Didn't say a whole lot to her, though."

Menno gulped down what was left of

his water. "When Kevin came back to our table after talking to her son at Carpenter's Café, he said the boy's daed had died."

Levi nodded. "When Lydia and Josh were in our store, she mentioned that she was a widow and had lost her job in Illinois."

"Ah, I see."

"Sure hope she's not as clumsy as she was today," Levi said, "or she won't keep the job very long."

Menno nodded and pushed away from the table. "Whelp, guess it's time for me to pay my bill. I need to get back to work."

Levi stood. "Same here."

❧

"Mom, look out!"

As Nona turned to see what Levi was yelling about, the ladder she stood on wobbled, and she hung on tight. "Don't scare me like that! You nearly made me fall."

Levi's eyebrows furrowed. "You shouldn't be up there at all. You should've called me if you needed something that was too high for you to reach."

"You can't always do everything for me." Nona climbed down the ladder, holding a small box of cleaning rags in one hand.

"But Mom . . ."

"Just stop it, Levi. What's it going to take for you to realize that your daed and I are just as capable as you? We can pretty much do what everyone else does, just in a different way."

"But there's no reason for you to be climbing ladders when I'm right here." Levi exhaled with a grunt. "You and Pop work too hard and do many things that I could easily do for you."

"If we didn't work, we'd get fat and lazy." She winked at him. "Laziness is the habit of resting before you get tired, you know."

He snickered, despite his obvious attempt at maintaining a straight face.

"Just remember one thing. Your daed and I may be small, but we're not lazy, and we're not incapable." Nona brushed past him and moved toward the front of the store. "I think you should have gone fishing with your daed and Peter this morning," she called over her shoulder.

"I had errands to run," he said, catching up to her. "Besides, I wasn't about to leave you alone in the store this afternoon."

She stopped walking and turned to face

him. "I'm not alone. Betty and Andy are in the back room, unpacking that new shipment of dishes we got in yesterday." She motioned to the front counter. "And Selma's right there, ready to wait on customers."

"But since Betty and Andy are . . ."

"Short and incapable? Is that what you were going to say?"

Levi shook his head. "I was going to say that since Betty and Andy are busy in the back room, you might need my help out here."

She motioned to the broom leaning against the wall. "If you want to make yourself useful, why don't you sweep the floor?"

"What are you going to do?"

"I'd planned on dusting the shelves and cleaning fingerprints off the front counter. Is that okay with you, or is it your intent to hover over me the rest of the day?"

"Didn't plan to hover, but I will sweep the floor."

"Danki."

As Nona picked up her dust rag, Levi grabbed the broom. She appreciated all that he did around here, but sometimes he

got on her nerves with his overprotective-
ness. If it weren't for the fact that Levi
was her only normal-size child, Nona
might have thought he was overprotective
because he was her oldest child and believed it was his duty to look out for his
parents, but Levi's concerns went deeper
than that. He saw their short stature as a
handicap, and thought because he could
do some things easier than they could, he
had to hover around and do everything for
them. Nona wished there was some way
she could get through to Levi, but he
seemed determined not to make a life of
his own.

Just then, eight-year-old Andy skittered
in from the back room. "I'm bored, Mom.
Sure wish I could've gone fishin' with Pop
and Peter."

"You could have if you hadn't slept so
late. By the time you got up, your daed
and *bruder* were long gone."

The skin around Andy's pale blue eyes
crinkled as he wrinkled his freckled nose.
"Somebody's shoulda woke me."

"I called you twice." Gently, she pinched
his cheek. "*Somebody* should have lis-
tened when they were told that they'd

need to get up early if they wanted to go fishing."

Andy turned and tipped his head up to look at Levi. "Will ya take me to the pond so I can do some fishin'?"

"Not today."

"How come?"

"There's too much work here to be done."

"How 'bout tomorrow?"

Levi bent down so he was eye level with Andy. The boy's hair and eyes were the same color as his, but that's where the similarity ended. Andy would never be tall like his oldest brother. "I don't think tomorrow will work, either," Levi said.

"How come?"

"I'll be busy then, too."

"Your daed and Peter will be helping in the store tomorrow," Nona interjected. "So you're free to take Andy fishing in the morning."

"Oh, good! I can hardly wait." Andy bounced up and down on his toes. "Think I'll dig me some worms as soon as we go home tonight. That way I'll be sure to have plenty of bait." He grinned up at Levi, then turned and trotted into the back room.

Levi looked at Nona and his eyebrows furrowed. "I don't have time to go fishing."

"Jah, you do." She gave his shirtsleeve a quick shake. "You'll go, and you'll have a good time."

CHAPTER 5

As Lydia walked along the shoulder of the road toward Grandma's Restaurant the following day, she drew in a breath of damp, earthy air. It had rained during the night, but now the sun was out, and a vivid rainbow glistened in the sky. A bird twittered from a nearby tree, adding to the joy of the moment. She was glad Grandpa's house was within walking distance of the restaurant so she could enjoy the beauty of God's creation in a more personal way.

Today would be Lydia's first day on the job, and she'd been given the late morning/ early afternoon shift. She hoped everything would go well. The last thing she needed was to bump someone's arm like she'd done yesterday when she'd spilled water on Menno Troyer. He must have thought she was a clumsy fool. Lydia's only excuse for not watching where she was going was that she'd been anxious to get home and tell Mom and Josh that she'd gotten a job. She'd make sure to stay focused today and watch what she was doing.

Lydia was surprised when she stepped into the parking lot and saw all the cars, not to mention several horse and buggies tied to the hitching rail. She figured the lunch crowd must be here already.

She hurried into the restaurant and had just put on her apron when she spotted an Amish man with light brown hair sitting at a table on the side of the room that she'd been assigned to work. It was Menno Troyer.

Drawing in a deep breath to help steady her nerves, she stepped up to him and smiled. "I didn't think I'd see you again so soon."

"I come here often because the food is real good." He returned her smile, although it never quite reached his hazel eyes. From the slump of his shoulders, he appeared tired. "So how are things going with your new job?"

"You're my first customer, but so far, so good." She motioned to the menu in front of him. "Have you decided what you'd like to order?"

He tapped his fingers on the table. "Guess I'll have my favorite—a Rueben sandwich and a glass of iced tea."

"I promise I'll be careful not to bump you this time." She shifted her ordering pad to the other hand. "I'm usually not as clumsy as I was yesterday. Guess I was so excited about getting the job that I wasn't watching where I was going."

His mouth moved in a slight slant when he smiled. "Not to worry. With four rowdy boys, I've had a lot worse things than water dumped on me."

She chuckled. "I know what you mean. My son can be accident prone at times, too."

"Is Josh your only child?"

She nodded, surprised that he remembered Josh's name.

"My youngest boy, Kevin, mentioned that Josh had told him you're a widow and that you moved here from Illinois."

"That's right."

"What part of Illinois?"

"We lived near Arthur, but the restaurant where I worked there wasn't doing well, so I lost my job."

"Do you miss Illinois?"

"I miss my friends there. I was born in Ohio, but my folks moved to Wisconsin when I was a year old, so that's actually where I grew up. Soon after I married, my husband and I moved to Illinois."

"So what brought you back here?"

"My mamm, Mae Weaver, moved here a year ago to care for my grossdaadi, and when she heard I was out of a job, she suggested Josh and I move to Charm to live with her and Grandpa."

He handed her the menu. "I'm a transplant, too. I moved my family here from Pennsylvania about a year ago to open a woodshop." His eyes darkened, and he dropped his gaze to the table. "But my wife died six months ago, so my boys and I have been on our own ever since."

"I'm sorry to hear that. I'm sure it's not easy raising four boys alone."

"No, it's—"

"How's everything going here?" Lydia's boss asked as she stepped up to the table.

Lydia's faced heated. She was taking much longer to turn in Menno's order than she should have. Talking too much was a fault of hers, and she hoped Edith wouldn't think she was slow.

"Everything's fine," Menno spoke up. "I've just finished placing my order, and your new waitress was about to turn it in."

A sense of relief swept over Lydia. He was covering for her so she wouldn't get in trouble with her boss. What a nice man.

Edith pushed an unruly strand of curly dark hair back under her Mennonite head covering and motioned to the table behind them. "Those people have been sitting there awhile. As soon as you're done here, could you please wait on them?"

"Yes, of course." Lydia glanced at Menno. "Will there be anything else?"

He shook his head. "Just the Rueben sandwich and a glass of iced tea."

Lydia hurried toward the kitchen to turn in his order. After Edith's reminder to wait on the couple sitting behind Menno, she'd have to stick to business.

As Mae lifted a loaf of warm bread from the oven, tears spilled onto her hot cheeks. She'd been so busy all morning caring for Dad's needs and trying to keep Josh out of trouble that she still hadn't had time to paint the kitchen, much less take a few minutes out for herself. She felt drained most of the time from caring for Dad, and now that she had Josh to watch, she had even more responsibility on her shoulders.

She loved to quilt and wished she could spend her days doing that, but it wasn't likely to happen. Not when she was stuck taking care of other people's needs instead of her own. It wasn't fair that Abe and Dan, her two older brothers, had moved to Missouri several years ago and weren't available to help Dad.

She placed the bread on a cooling rack and flopped into a chair at the table, as a wave of guilt washed over her. She had no right to be thinking this way. Abe and Dan were both struggling financially, and each of them had several children still living at home. It was her responsibility to care for

Dad, and she was doing Lydia a favor by allowing her and Josh to live here.

When Mae first heard that Lydia had lost her job at the restaurant in Arthur, she'd known it was only a matter of time until she was forced to move out of the house she rented. At least now Lydia and Josh had a roof over their heads, which was one less worry for Mae.

Since Lydia was working at Grandma's Restaurant, she could help with some of the household expenses. With all of Dad's doctor bills and the medicine he had to take, bills added up. Mae wasn't sure how long the money in Dad's bank account would last. She could ask for help from their church district if necessary, but she preferred to make it on her own.

Mae reached for the teapot on the table and poured herself a cup of chamomile tea, hoping it might help her relax. She was about to take a drink when Josh raced into the room, red-faced and sweaty.

With all the enthusiasm of a four-year-old, he hollered, *"Kichli,* Grossmammi? *Sei so gut!"*

Mae frowned and put her finger to her lips. "I know that a cookie is good, but you need to keep your voice down, because your urgrossvadder is sleeping."

"Kichli! Kichli!" Josh darted across the room and pointed at the cookie jar on the counter.

Mae jumped up, grabbed his arm roughly, and pulled him to her side. "You need to be quiet."

Tears welled in Josh's eyes, and his chin quivered like a leaf blowing in the wind.

Mae let go of his arm. He probably thought she was mean, but he needed to understand that he couldn't yell in the house. "Take a seat and I'll get you some cookies and milk."

Josh, a bit calmer now, climbed into a chair, folded his hands, and watched as she took three chocolate chip cookies from the cookie jar and placed them on a napkin in front of him. Then she poured a glass of milk and set that on the table, too.

"Danki." Josh smiled up at her, his blue eyes bright and cheerful again.

She patted his head and returned to her seat on the other side of the table.

Josh ate the first cookie then washed it down with a gulp of milk. He dunked the second cookie in the milk until it broke in

two and fell to the bottom of the glass.
Before Mae had a chance to offer him a
spoon, he stuck his fingers inside the glass.

"*Nee*, not like that," she scolded. "If
you're not careful, you'll . . ."

Thunk! The glass toppled over, and the
milk spilled onto the tablecloth and trickled
on the floor.

Mae jumped up and grabbed the sponge
from the sink. "You've been nothing but
trouble for me all day!" She shook her
finger at Josh and drew in a shaky breath,
trying to compose herself.

"*Keep your temper; nobody wants it.*"
Mae remembered Dad saying that to her
plenty of times when she was a girl. Well,
it had been easier to keep her temper before she'd had a noisy child in the house.

Josh sat several seconds, blinking his
eyes. Then he opened his mouth and let
out a piercing wail.

"What's goin' on?" Dad shouted from
his room. "Don'tcha know I was tryin' to
sleep? Just stop hollerin' at the boy!"

"Now look what you've done!" Mae's
hand shook as she set his glass upright.

Josh grabbed the other cookie, hopped
off the chair, and raced out of the room.

"Come back here!" Mae ran down the hall after him, but Josh was too fast for her. He slipped into Dad's room and quickly shut the door.

Mae gritted her teeth. *That boy deserves a good spanking.*

She jerked open the door, and when she stepped into the room, she barely noticed the smile on Dad's face as he nibbled on the cookie Josh had given him. It angered her that Josh would disobey like he did.

"You come with me right now!" Despite Dad's protests, Mae grabbed Josh by his arm, pulled him out of the room, and led him back to the kitchen. Then she took a seat in a chair, put Josh over her knee, and was about to give his rear-end a slap, when the back door opened and Lydia stepped in.

When Lydia realized that Mom about to spank Josh, she was stunned. "What's going on here?"

Mom's face was a mask of anger as she set Josh on the floor. "Your son has caused so much trouble today!"

"What's he done?"

"He's been noisy when I've asked him to be quiet; he's interrupted me several times when I've been busy; he spilled milk on the table and floor; and then he ran into my daed's room with a cookie."

Lydia could see how frustrated Mom was, but her heart went out to Josh, whose chin trembled as tears dripped onto his flushed cheeks. She pulled him into her arms and gave him a hug. "Why don't you go outside and see if you can find the kittens? I need to talk to Grandma right now."

Josh nodded as he sniffed and swiped at his tears.

Lydia gave his shoulders a gentle squeeze. "I'll come out to see the kittens when I'm done talking to Grandma."

"Okay." Josh shuffled across the room and went out the back door.

Lydia turned to Mom and frowned. "Josh is only four years old. He doesn't understand why he needs to be quiet all the time or can't make any mistakes. I'd like for him to get to know you better, but if you keep getting upset about everything he does, or spank him for something as simple as taking Grandpa a cookie, he'll be afraid to come near you." She held her shaking hands firmly at her sides. "Maybe it would be best if I find somewhere else for Josh and me to live."

"How are you going to do that? You just started working, so there's no way you can afford to pay rent on a house right now." Tears pooled in Mom's eyes and dribbled onto her cheeks. "I—I want you to stay here with me. I'm going through a lot taking care of my daed, and I need your support." She sniffed several times. "I'm sure Josh doesn't misbehave on purpose, and I'll try to be more patient with him."

Lydia stepped forward and wrapped her arms around Mom. "We've both been through a lot in the last several years, and we really do need each other." She gently patted Mom's back. "I'll have a talk with Josh and see if I can make him understand how important it is to be quiet in the house when Grandpa's resting and remind him that he needs to listen and do what you say."

CHAPTER 6

Friday morning had dawned warm and clear, and the grassy area where Levi sat with his youngest brother at the pond near their home felt cool and inviting.

Zeep! Zeep! A bird called to its mate from a nearby tree. It was the perfect day for fishing, and even though Levi hadn't wanted to leave the store, he was glad he was here.

He thought about how Pop had strained his back last night while carrying a box full of used books Mom had decided to donate to the Care and Share secondhand store near Berlin. The poor man would probably be hobbling around for days before Mom convinced him to see the chiropractor.

Because Pop had injured his back, he wouldn't be working in the store today, which meant Mom would only have Peter, Selma, and Betty's help. Levi had tried to convince Mom that he should forget about fishing and work in the store, but she'd insisted on him going and reminded him that he'd promised to take Andy.

"Right," Levi mumbled under his breath. "Mom's the one who told Andy I'd take him fishing, not me."

Andy, who sat several feet away with his fishing line cast into the water, looked over at Levi with raised eyebrows. "Were ya talkin' to me?"

Levi shook his head and swatted at a pesky fly that kept buzzing him.

"Who were ya talkin' to then?"

"No one."

"Had to be talkin' to someone or ya wouldn't have said anything."

"I was talking to myself, so don't worry about it." Levi cast his fishing line into the water and leaned back on his elbows. *Guess I may as well enjoy this sunny day and quit worrying about how things are going at the store,* he decided. *When I get back this afternoon, if Mom says things were real busy this morning, I'll give her a break and insist that she go home and rest.*

Levi and Andy had only been fishing an hour or so when Andy's friend Raymond showed up. "When I stopped by the general store, your mamm said I'd find ya over here," he said, flopping onto the grass beside Andy. "Can ya come over to my place and see my new *haase*?"

Andy dropped his fishing pole and thumped Levi's arm. "Can I go see Raymond's haase?"

Levi frowned. "You made such a big deal about wanting to fish, and now you want to take off and see a rabbit?"

Andy shrugged. "I did wanna fish, but I haven't caught a thing all mornin'. Think I'd rather go over to Raymond's instead."

"If that's what you want to do, it's fine with me," Levi said. "I'll either go back to the store or hang around here awhile longer. I'll come by Raymond's place in a few hours to pick you up. How's that sound?"

Andy grinned. "Sounds good to me." He

grabbed his fishing pole and handed it to Levi. "You can fish with both poles if you want."

Levi chuckled and placed Andy's pole on the ground. "Think I'd better concentrate on just one pole for now." He squeezed Andy's shoulder. "Now go on with Raymond and have fun. I'll see you in a few hours."

The boys scampered off, and Levi continued to fish. As the warm sun beat down on his head, he decided it felt kind of good to take part of the day off. It felt so good he propped his fishing pole against a rock, leaned back in the grass, and closed his eyes.

~

Lydia looked down at Josh as he trudged through the tall grass beside her, wearing a contented smile. She was glad she didn't have to work today and had decided to take Josh to a nearby pond for a picnic lunch. They needed some time alone together, and Mom needed a few hours without having to deal with Josh.

Right after breakfast, Lydia and Mom had painted the kitchen. Then, when Josh became restless and noisy, Lydia came up with the idea of taking him to the pond. After seeing how close Mom had come to spanking Josh yesterday, Lydia didn't want to risk upsetting Mom again. Even though Mom had apologized to Josh for losing her temper, he'd been wary of her ever since. The tension Lydia felt between her and Mom was a little better since they'd had their talk yesterday, but Lydia still found herself wishing she hadn't felt forced to move here.

Yet it was too late for regrets. She was here, had a new job, and would make the best of her situation. Hopefully, things would go better between her and Mom, as well as Mom and Josh, and then she wouldn't feel the need to find a place of her own.

The sun disappeared between the cottony blanket of clouds, and Lydia feared it might rain. But then as quickly as the sun vanished, it reappeared.

Josh tipped his head back and squinted his eyes. "I like it when God turns on His light."

Lydia smiled. What a way with words her little boy had. He was just like his father in that respect. Jeremiah had often said things to Lydia that took her by surprise.

"I'm hungerich," Josh said, tugging on her hand.

"We'll eat as soon as we get to the pond."

Josh looked up at her and grinned, and Lydia's heart almost melted. Josh was so exuberant and loved being outdoors. He liked to eat, too—another trait of his father's. She remembered how, whenever she'd made cookies, Jeremiah had always managed to snitch a handful or two. Then a short time later, he'd be back in the kitchen, asking for more.

When the pond came into view a few minutes later, Josh took off on a run.

Dropping her picnic basket to the ground, Lydia ran after him. "*Absatz*—stop! Don't go near the water!"

She'd no sooner said the words, when—*Splash!*—Josh stepped off the bank and fell into the pond.

CHAPTER 7

Levi's eyes snapped open. He'd heard a splash, and then someone had screamed. When he looked to the left he was surprised to see Josh, the young boy he'd met the other day, thrashing about in the water. Josh's mother shrieked as she raced toward the pond. Levi had to do something quick or the boy might drown.

He jerked off his boots and leaped into the pond. With a few quick strokes, he reached out to Josh, grabbed his suspenders, and lifted him from the water. When he stepped onto shore a few minutes later, he was relieved to see that the child was breathing and hadn't taken in too much water. Except for being thoroughly drenched, Josh appeared to be unharmed.

Lydia dropped to her knees beside Josh and pulled him into her arms. "Thank the Lord you're all right," she said breathlessly as she stroked his damp head with her shaky hand.

Levi motioned to the lightweight blanket that had fallen from Lydia's picnic basket when she'd dropped it. "I think you'd better wrap him up in that so he doesn't get chilled."

"Of course." Lydia scooped up the blanket and bundled it around Josh's trembling body. "I'm not a strong swimmer. If I'd jumped into the water and tried to save my boy, we might have both drowned, but if you hadn't jumped in when you did, I certainly would have." Tears welled in her eyes as she looked at Levi. "How can I ever thank you for saving my son's life?"

"No thanks needed."

Josh's teeth chattered as he pointed to the picnic basket. "I'm hungerich."

Lydia smiled, despite the anxiety still

rippling through her body. Apparently the dip in the pond hadn't frightened Josh nearly as much as it had her. "We'd better go home and get you out of those wet clothes. We can eat lunch when we get there."

Josh leaned close to Lydia's ear and whispered, *"Kummt er aa?"*

"What'd he say?" Levi asked.

"He wondered if you will come, too." Lydia quickly added, "If you have no other plans, we'd like you to join us for lunch. It'll be my way of saying thank you for rescuing Josh."

Levi pulled out his pocket watch and realized that he'd been sleeping awhile. It was almost time to get Andy. "I appreciate the offer," he said, "but I have to pick up my little brother soon, and I'll need to help in my folks' store this afternoon."

"How about supper? Could you join us for that?" Lydia asked.

Josh nodded enthusiastically. *"Kumme. Mattsait."*

Levi rubbed his chin a few times as he smiled at Josh and said, "I'd be happy to come to your place for supper this evening."

❧

"Where's Levi?" Nona asked when Andy entered the store that afternoon.

"Went home to change 'cause his clothes were wet."

"How'd he end up with wet clothes?"

"Said he jumped into the pond to save some *bu* who was gonna drown."

"Seriously?"

"Uh-huh."

Concern welled in Nona's soul. "Who was it? Is the boy all right?"

"Levi didn't say who it was, but I guess he's okay." Andy shrugged. "Think Levi would've said so if he wasn't."

Nona's forehead wrinkled. "Weren't you there? Didn't you see it happen?"

"Huh-uh. Raymond came by the pond and invited me over to his place to see his *haase*. Levi said I could go, and that he'd pick me up when he was done fishin', but when he got there, his clothes were all wet." Andy shuffled over to the candy counter and stood on his tiptoes, peering into the glass. "Can I have some licorice, Mama? I'm *hungerich*."

"Didn't you have lunch?"

Andy shook his head. "Levi didn't bring

nothin' for us to eat while we was at the pond, and I got busy playin' with Raymond's haase and never thought about bein' hungerich until now."

"The rest of the family has already eaten, but you can find some apples and cheese in our cooler. I'd rather you eat those than candy." Nona motioned to the other end of the store. "You can sit in the back room and eat your snack, or take it outside if you like."

"Okay." Andy whistled as he scampered away.

"Can I take a break from doing this?" Selma asked when Nona walked past the shelf she'd been stocking with scrapbooking supplies. "My back hurts from standin' so long."

Nona rolled her eyes. "You're only twelve . . . Too young to be having back problems like your daed."

Selma squinted her gray-blue eyes as she reached around and rubbed a spot on her lower back. "I may be too young, but my back still hurts."

Nona realized from her daughter's serious expression that she wasn't faking a sore back. "All right then, you can sit on the stool behind the counter and wait on customers. I'll take over for you here."

"Danki, Mom."

"If your back still hurts by Monday, I'll see about getting you in to see our chiropractor."

"Okay." Moving slowly, as she continued to rub her back, Selma made her way to the front of the store.

Nona began stocking the shelves and was nearly finished when Levi showed up.

"Did Andy tell you what happened at the pond?" he asked.

She nodded. "Only he didn't say who the boy was who fell in the water, and he didn't know if the boy was okay or not."

"The boy's name is Josh King. Remember, when he and his mamm came into the store the other day and I told you about them moving here from Illinois?"

"I remember. Is Josh okay?"

"He's fine. I got out him out before he'd taken in too much water." Levi smiled. "His mamm was very appreciative of me saving her son's life. Fact is, she invited me to eat supper at their house this evening."

"Is that so?"

Levi gave a quick nod. "I said no at first, but the boy seemed sad, so I changed my mind."

"I'm glad you did. You hang around with your family way too much, when you ought to be out having fun."

Levi's eyebrows drew together so they almost met at the bridge of his nose. "What's wrong with a fellow hanging around his family?"

"Nothing, but in my opinion, a twenty-eight-year-old man should be married and raising a family of his own by now."

Levi opened his mouth as if to reply, but she cut him off. "And don't give me that old story about you having to be here to see to our needs. Your daed and I are perfectly capable of taking care of things at home, as well as raising our *kinner*. Even if you weren't working at the store, we'd make out here, too." Nona plunked down on the stool she'd used when she'd been stocking the lower shelves. "Now tell me about Josh's mother."

Levi turned his hands palm up. "What's to tell?"

"Do you think she's pretty?"

Levi's face flamed, and he quickly averted her gaze. "I . . . uh . . . really hadn't noticed."

"Then how come you look so flustered right now?"

He shuffled his feet a few times, the way he used to do when he was a boy and had been caught telling a fib. "I'm not flustered. Just don't like being quizzed is all."

Nona snickered. "Whatever you say."

Levi lifted his gaze and narrowed his eyes. "I hope you're not getting any ideas about me and Josh's mother, because I barely know her and . . ."

"I know. I know. You're not interested in getting married."

"That's right." Levi turned and called over his shoulder, "I'll be outside cleaning the front porch. Thanks to me, there are muddy footprints all over it now."

Nona smiled. The eager look she'd seen on Levi's face when he'd told her that he'd been invited to supper gave her some hope that despite what he'd said, he might be interested in Josh's mother. For the last few years, Nona had been praying that her oldest son would find a good woman and settle down to marriage. A few of the young women in the area had their eye on Levi, including their bishop's daughter Mary Rose. But so far, Levi hadn't shown an interest in anyone. Did Nona dare hope that Lydia might be the woman who would finally capture her son's heart?

CHAPTER 8

As Lydia scurried around the kitchen, preparing for their guest, her stomach did a little flip-flop. She hoped she hadn't been too bold inviting Levi to come here for supper, but she'd wanted to do something to say thank you to Levi for saving Josh's life. Besides, Josh was so excited about Levi coming that he was sitting on the porch waiting for him to arrive.

"I wish you would have checked with me first before you decided to invite someone here for supper," Mom said, opening the oven door and lifting the lid on the

roasting pan. "It's just a good thing I had
this ham in the refrigerator."

"Sorry, but I didn't think you'd mind."
Why was it that every time Lydia did something, Mom seemed to scold her for it?
She treated her like a child instead of a
twenty-six-year-old woman.

Mom shut the oven door and turned to
face Lydia. "It's too late to worry about it
now, but the next time you want to invite a
guest over, I'd appreciate it if you asked
me first."

"I doubt that I'll be inviting a guest over
anytime soon, since I don't know many
people in the area yet. But if and when I
do want to invite someone, I'll make sure
that I check with you first." Lydia hated it
when Mom made her feel guilty. She'd
done that so many times in the past. If
Lydia had a place of her own, inviting
guests over wouldn't even be an issue.
Of course, if she and Josh lived alone,
she wouldn't have invited Levi, a man she
barely knew, into their home unless she'd
invited someone else to join them, as
well.

"Do you think you can you manage in

here without me for a few minutes?" Mom asked. "I need to check on Dad."

"Sure. I'll start mashing the potatoes."

As Mom hurried from the room, Lydia gritted her teeth. *Doesn't Mom think I'm capable of getting supper ready without her help? Does she have to treat me like I'm a still a little girl?*

The whinny of a horse drew Lydia's attention to the window. When she peeked out, she saw a horse and buggy rumbling up the driveway and figured it must be Levi.

As Levi guided his horse and buggy up to the hitching rail his palms grew sweaty. He hoped he was doing the right thing by coming here for supper. If Mom thought he was interested in Lydia, maybe Lydia did, too. "Don't be ridiculous," he mumbled. "I barely know the woman. I'm sure the only reason she invited me to supper was to say thank you for saving her son."

Levi had just finished putting his horse in the corral when Josh rushed up to him. "Do ya wanna see some *busslin*?"

"Sure," Levi said with a nod.

Josh grabbed Levi's hand and led him

to the barn, where a gray mother cat and five furry kittens were curled up together on a bale of straw. As they approached, the mother cat cracked her golden eyes open and stretched slowly.

Josh scooped up one of the kittens and held it out to Levi. *"Es feischtielich."*

Levi stroked the kitten's head. "Jah, it's very soft."

Josh took a seat on another bale of straw, and Levi did the same. The kitten purred contentedly as Josh cuddled it against his chest. "Have ya got any busslin?" he asked.

"No, but my bruder Andy has a pet goat."

Josh's eyes widened. "Can I see it sometime?"

"Maybe so." Levi glanced at the barn door. "I think we should go to the house now. Your mamm probably has supper waiting for us."

"Okay." Josh placed the kitten back with its mother, and the two of them left the barn.

When they entered the kitchen Levi was treated to a tantalizing aroma. "Something smells mighty good in here," he said, smiling at Lydia, who stood at the counter, mashing potatoes.

She glanced his way, wearing a slip of a grin. "I think it's the baked ham that smells so good."

Levi smacked his lips. "I like baked ham."

"Me, too!" Josh grinned up at his mother. "Me and Levi was in the barn. We petted one of the busslin."

"That's nice." Lydia motioned to the hallway outside the kitchen door. "We'll be ready to eat soon, so go into the bathroom and wash. If you've been holding a kitten, your hands are dirty."

Josh looked up at Levi with a serious expression. "You pet the busslin, so you'd better wash, too."

"Good thinking." Levi chuckled and winked at Lydia. "We'll be right back."

❧

While Josh and Levi were in the bathroom, Lydia finished mashing the potatoes. She didn't know why, but seeing the way Josh had looked at Levi just now made her feel weepy all of a sudden. *A boy needs his father,* she told herself. It wasn't fair that Jeremiah had been taken from them before Josh got to know him well. A few years from now, Josh probably wouldn't even remember his father.

Knowing this was no time for self-pity, Lydia added butter to the potatoes and set them on the table.

She'd just begun making the gravy when Levi returned to the kitchen.

"Where's Josh?" she asked.

"He went upstairs. Said he had something in his room he wanted to show me."

"Oh, great. Now his hands will probably be dirty again."

Levi glanced around the room. "Where's your mamm? Won't she be joining us for supper?"

"She's in my grossdaadi's room right now, feeding him his supper. As soon as she's done, we'll eat." Lydia motioned to the chair at the head of the table. "If you'd like to take a seat, we can visit while I finish dishing things up."

"Is there anything I can do to help?" he asked. "I'm used to helping in the kitchen at home, and it'll be better than sitting and watching."

Lydia pointed to the pitcher of water on the counter. "You can fill our glasses if you like."

"No problem."

Levi had just finished filling the glasses with water when Josh returned to the kitchen, carrying a book, which he handed to Levi. "Read me a *schtori*?"

"Sure, I'll read any story you'd like." Levi took a seat at the table and lifted Josh into his lap. As he read about a cat named Blue, a lump formed in Lydia's throat. She remembered all the times when Jeremiah used to hold Josh and tell him stories about when he was a boy. She remembered the look of love she'd seen on her husband's face as he held Josh in his lap.

Mom stepped into the kitchen and cleared her throat real loud. "I'm done feeding my daed. Is supper ready yet?"

Lydia nodded.

Levi set the book aside and smiled at Mom. "It's nice to see you again, Mae," he said, lifting Josh into the chair beside him.

Mom's only reply was a quick nod.

Lydia took a seat on the other side of Josh, and Mom sat across from Lydia. As they bowed their heads for silent prayer, Lydia prayed the Lord's Prayer, and then asked God to help Mom relax and be more hospitable toward Levi.

When the prayer ended, Levi looked over at Mom and said, "How have you been? We haven't seen you at the store for some time."

"I don't get out much these days," she replied stiffly. "Taking care of my daed is a full-time job."

Lydia forked a piece of ham onto Josh's plate and then handed the platter to Levi. "When Josh and I moved here, I'd planned to help Mom more with Grandpa, but now that I'm working at the restaurant, my time is limited." She smiled at Mom. "However, I'm more than willing to run any errands you need after I get off work and on my days off."

"Today was your day off, and you went to the pond." The bitterness in Mom's tone was obvious, and it caused Lydia to cringe. Didn't Mom care that they had company? Did she have to let the discord between them show in front of Levi—or Josh, for that matter?

"I thought you'd get more done today if you didn't have Josh underfoot," Lydia said, passing the plate of mashed potatoes to Mom. "And I did ask if you minded."

Mom merely shrugged in reply.

Lydia picked up her glass and drank some water. *This isn't going well. I need to think of something to lighten the mood and ease the tension between me and Mom. Levi probably thinks we have a terrible relationship.*

"Can we go over to Levi's house?" Josh asked, bumping Lydia's arm. "His bruder has a gees, and I wanna see it."

Levi looked over at Lydia. "Maybe you can bring Josh by our house some day when you're not working. We live directly behind the store, so it's easy to find."

Lydia smiled. "Maybe we will sometime."

The rest of the meal was eaten in silence, except for when Josh asked Levi or Lydia a question. Mom didn't eat much and kept fidgeting in her chair. Lydia couldn't figure out what was wrong.

When supper was over, Levi and Josh went to the living room so Levi could finish reading Josh his story, while Lydia and Mom did the dishes. Mom didn't say much while they worked, either. Every once in a while, she'd purse her lips and glance at the living room door. Lydia didn't know why, but Mom was clearly uncomfortable having Levi here.

Levi entered the kitchen just as Lydia finished washing the last dish. "Josh fell asleep in my arms. I laid him on the sofa."

"Danki." Lydia motioned to the stove, where the teakettle whistled and steam poured from the spout. "Would you like a cup of tea or some hot chocolate?"

"I appreciate the offer, but I really should head for home. There are chores waiting to be done."

Mom said a quick good-bye to Levi, slipped past them, and headed down the hall toward Grandpa's room.

Levi opened the back door, then turned to face Lydia. "I appreciate the meal. Everything was very good."

"You're welcome."

"Tell Josh I'll be looking forward to showing him Andy's goat."

"I'll tell him."

Levi's fingers brushed hers as they reached for the doorknob at the same time. Lydia felt a strange tingling travel up her arm and quickly stepped aside so he could open the door.

"*Gut nacht,*" she murmured.

"Good night." The door clicked shut behind Levi.

Lydia stood there a moment, trying to make sense out of the strange sensation she'd felt when their fingers touched. Had there been some static electricity in the air?

With a shake of her head, she started toward the living room to get Josh. She was almost there when Mom came up the hallway, wearing a serious expression. "I need to speak with you. Let's go into the kitchen."

Alarm rose in Lydia's chest as she followed Mom to the kitchen. "You look upset. Is it Grandpa? Is he worse?"

"He's sleeping."

"Then what's wrong?"

Mom poured them both a cup of tea, and they took seats at the table. "I don't think it's a good idea for you to take Josh to see Levi's brother's goat."

"Why not?"

"Josh might not understand about Levi's family. He might be frightened."

"Why would Josh be frightened of Levi's family?"

Mom leaned closer to Lydia and lowered her voice. "Levi's mother, father, as well as his brothers and sisters are little people. Levi's the only one in his family of normal size."

Lydia inhaled sharply. "The little woman I saw the other day at the restaurant, and then again at the general store must be Levi's mother. I wonder why he never said anything."

"I don't know, but I don't want you to get involved with him."

"I–I'm not involved with Levi, but why would it be wrong if I were?"

"Think about it." Mom stared hard at Lydia. "If you married Levi, you might have *zwarich* bopplin."

"You're worried about me having dwarf babies?"

Mom gave a decisive nod.

Laughter bubbled in Lydia's throat. "I barely know Levi, and you already have us getting married and having babies? That's *lecherich*, Mom."

Mom slapped her hand on the table, causing their teacups to vibrate and Lydia to jump. "It's not ridiculous! You saw how much attention Levi showed Josh." She grimaced. "And Josh ate it up. He looked at Levi with such affection and even spoke to him like he was his daed, for goodness' sake."

Lydia gripped the edge of the table until her knuckles turned white. "It did my heart good to see how happy my boy was tonight. He hasn't had a man in his life since Jeremiah died." She paused and drew in a quick breath. "Besides, it's not me Levi's taken an interest in, it's Josh."

"Well, if you're not careful, you'll be next."

Lydia's chair scraped noisily as she pushed away from the table and stood. "I'm tired. If you don't need me for anything I'm going up to bed." She paused and waited for Mom's response.

"I don't need your help with anything, and it's good that you're going to bed now, because you and Josh will need to get up early for church tomorrow." Mom rose from her chair. "I'm going to check on my daed, and then I'm going to bed myself."

Lydia hurried from the kitchen. She was about to climb the stairs, when she remembered that Josh was still asleep on the sofa. She went straight to the living room, gathered Josh into her arms, and trudged up the stairs.

I just can't believe Mom's worried about

me marrying Levi and having zwarich bop-plin. She paused outside of Josh's room as a sickening thought popped into her head. *Could Mom be prejudiced against Levi's family because they're different?*

CHAPTER 9

Are you sure you don't want me to stay home with Grandpa so you can go to church today?" Lydia asked Mom as they set the table for breakfast the following morning.

Mom shook her head. "Your grossdaadi's not doing well this morning, and I need to be here with him. Besides, I think it'll be good for you and Josh to go so you can get to know the people in our church district."

Lydia didn't argue. Once Mom made up her mind, there was no changing it. Besides, maybe Mom was right about getting

to know people. If Levi and his family belonged to the same district, she'd get the
opportunity to meet them today. At least
that was something to look forward to.

Just then, Josh zipped into the room—
red-faced, sweaty, and chasing the gray
mother cat.

"Oh no," Lydia groaned. "Not again."

Mom whirled around and clapped her
hands so hard that the cat leaped straight
into the air. When it landed on the floor, it
quickly darted under the table.

"Get that *katz* and put it outside!" Mom's
voice rose to a high-pitched squeal.

With eyes wide and chin trembling, Josh
dropped to his knees and crawled in after
the cat. "Kumme. Kumme."

The cat's hair stood on end as it me-
owed and hissed at Josh.

Josh crawled in farther. He was almost
touching the cat, when it swiped the end
of his nose with its sharp claws.

"Yeow!" Josh jumped up, bumping his
head on the underside of the table. *"Mop-
skopp,"* he mumbled, rubbing the top of
his head as he backed out slowly.

"No, you're the stupid fellow," Mom said,
shaking her finger at Josh. "You shouldn't

have let the cat in the house. How many times must you be told?" She reached under the table, grabbed the cat by the scruff of its neck, and put it outside.

When Josh looked up at Lydia with tears rolling down his cheeks, she struggled to keep her own tears at bay. How could Mom talk to her only grandchild like that? Didn't she feel any love for Josh?

When Menno pulled his horse and buggy into Rueben Miller's yard, he noticed Lydia and her boy walking across the grass toward the house. She had a graceful way about her . . . and a pleasant smile, too. He'd seen that at the restaurant the other day. But there was also a kind of shyness about her, like she was unsure of herself. Of course, having lost her husband a year ago, she was probably still grieving, same as him. It wasn't easy to get over the loss of a mate.

He glanced at Ike, sitting on the seat beside him, and wondered if he missed his mother. If he did, he never said so. Fact was, none of the boys said much about their mother. Maybe they'd had enough time to heal. Or maybe it was easier to deal with the pain if they didn't talk about it. *That's sure true with me,* Menno thought as he climbed down from the buggy and unhitched his horse. *Every time I think about Sadie, it feels like someone's punched me in the stomach.*

"Want me to take Midnight to the barn?" Ike asked when he and his brothers clambered out of the buggy.

"I'd appreciate that." Menno moved toward the group of men who'd gathered outside the buggy shop where church would be held, while his three youngest boys ran off to join several other children playing in the yard.

"How are things with you and the *buwe*?" Rueben Miller asked, stepping up to Menno.

Menno shrugged. "We're gettin' along as well as can be expected, but the boys can sure be a handful at times."

Rueben thumped Menno's arm. "Maybe what they need is a *mudder* to keep them in line."

Menno gave a nod. "I've been thinkin' that myself. Just need to find the right woman, is all."

"Better take your time lookin'. You wouldn't want to pick the wrong wife, that's for sure."

For the next several minutes, Menno visited with Rueben, until he saw the ministers file into the buggy shed. Then Menno, along with the other men, followed.

After the men and boys were seated, the women and girls entered and took their seats on the opposite side, facing the men. Menno's two oldest boys sat on the bench in front of him, and the two younger ones sat on either side of him. He figured as restless as they usually were, it was a good idea for him to keep them close so he could supervise their behavior.

The service opened with a song from their hymnal, *The Ausbund*. As the congregation sang, the ministers filed out of the buggy shop so they could meet in a room at the house where they'd decide who would deliver the two sermons today.

Menno grimaced. He was glad the lot had never fallen on him to fulfill a ministerial role. Between running his business and trying to raise the boys, he had enough responsibility on his shoulders. Of course, if he were ever chosen for one of the ministerial positions, he'd do his best to be a good leader.

Menno glanced across the room, and his gaze came to rest on Lydia. He wondered if she felt overwhelmed with the burden of raising her son, the way he often did with his exuberant boys. *But then,* he reasoned, *she does have the support of her mother right now. I'm sure Mae's a big help in taking care of Josh while Lydia works at the restaurant.*

Lydia glanced his way, then quickly looked away, her cheeks turning pink. He hoped she didn't think he was staring at her—and that no one else had noticed his gaze, either. It wouldn't be good if any rumors got started about the two of them.

Turning his attention to the book in his hand, Menno concentrated on the song they were still singing.

The congregation continued to sing until the ministers returned. Soon after that, the first sermon was given by Alvin Schrock. He spoke from Luke 18, verse 1, and emphasized the need for people to spend more time in prayer. Menno had been remiss in that area lately. He'd been so busy keeping his business going and trying to stay on top of things at home that he spent very little time in prayer.

The brief prayers he offered before and after meals weren't enough to keep him walking close to God. But prayer didn't come easy for Menno these days. God had seemed far away ever since Sadie died. Menno wasn't sure God really cared about him anymore. He'd prayed that Sadie's life would be spared, but God had said no to that request.

Tears clouded Menno's vision as he stared at his hands, clasped firmly in his lap. Life wasn't fair. There were too many injustices in the world, and as far as he was concerned, the death of a loved one was the worst injustice of them all.

The nicker of a horse drew his attention toward the windows. Several horses were moving about in the corral, and he wished he could be outside, where it wasn't so hot and stuffy.

The murmur of youthful voices pulled Menno's thoughts in another direction. He blinked a couple of times when he saw Ike and Dennis on the bench in front of him, poking each other.

Menno leaned forward and was about

to tap Dennis on the shoulder, when Kevin, who'd been leaning heavily against his arm, fell off the bench and landed on the floor with a *thud*.

Kevin let out a yelp and rubbed at the lump that had quickly formed on his forehead. "Wh—what happened, Papa? Did somebody push me off the bench?"

Menno, sensing that all eyes were on Kevin, put his fingers to his lips. "Shh . . ."

Kevin started to whimper, so Menno lifted the boy to his feet and led him out the door.

Once everyone had been served at the noon meal following church, Lydia spent the next hour getting acquainted with some of the women, while Josh played with a group of children his age. She was pleased that she'd been welcomed so warmly, and Bishop Yoder's wife, Sarah, a pleasant woman with thinning gray hair, had been the friendliest of all.

After questioning Sarah about the Stutzman family, Lydia was disappointed to learn that they were in a different church district.

"However, they have come to a few of

our services on the Sundays when their own district isn't having church," Sarah said as the two women seated themselves in wicker chairs that had been set up on the lawn. "I'm guessing they probably had other plans for today."

"That's too bad. I've met Levi, but I was looking forward to meeting the rest of his family."

"If you go to the general store very often, I'm sure it won't be long before you've met the whole family." Sarah smiled. "Now tell me, how's your mamm doing these days? I've been really busy lately and haven't been by to see her for a few weeks."

"Mom has her hands full taking care of my grossdaadi," Lydia replied. "She doesn't get out much."

Deep wrinkles formed across Sarah's forehead. "Several of the women in our community have offered to stay with Wilbur so Mae could attend some of our social functions, but she's always declined. The only time we've been able to get her to accept our help is when she needs to go shopping or has an appointment." She patted Lydia's arm in a motherly fashion. "Of course, now that you're here, I'm sure it's taking some of the burden off Mae's shoulders."

Lydia gave no reply. There was no point in telling Sarah that, other than when they'd painted the kitchen, Mom hadn't accepted much help from her. It was as if she took pleasure in doing everything herself. It made Lydia wonder if Mom liked to martyr herself so she'd have something to complain about.

I shouldn't be thinking such thoughts, Lydia reprimanded herself. *I'm sure Mom feels responsible for Grandpa and is only trying to do the right thing by taking care of him. Even so, that's no reason for her not to accept my help or to be so harsh with Josh.*

Pushing her thoughts aside, Lydia smiled at Sarah and said, "Do you think your husband or one of the other ministers would have a talk with my grossdaadi? He doesn't cooperate with Mom very well, and I think he's probably depressed because he can't do much except sit in his wheelchair or lie in bed."

"My husband, as well as our other ministers, has tried talking to Wilbur several times, but the poor man seems determined to feel sorry for himself." Sarah sighed. "Of course, we're all praying for him, too."

"We appreciate that." Lydia rose to her feet. "I think I'd better find Josh and head for home. It's been nice visiting with you, Sarah."

"Same here. Please tell your mamm I said hello and that I'll try to get by to see her soon."

"I'm sure she'd appreciate the company." Lydia said good-bye to some of the other women; then she headed across the yard in search of Josh. She caught sight of him playing with two of Menno's boys on the other side of the barn.

She'd just started in that direction, when a tall, middle-aged man with dark hair streaked with silver-gray stepped up to her.

"I understand you're Mae Weaver's daughter."

Lydia nodded. "That's right."

He extended his hand, and the skin around his deeply set blue eyes crinkled. "I'm Rueben Miller."

Lydia assumed from the full beard Rueben wore that he was married. "It's nice to meet you." She glanced at the group of women gathered on the lawn. "Which of the women here today is your wife?"

"My wife died three years ago." A shadow crossed Rueben's face. "Our five boys and their families moved to Oklahoma several years ago, so except for my friends, I'm pretty much alone here in Charm."

"Have you considered moving to Oklahoma to be near your family?"

"I have considered it, and they've suggested it, but I'm hoping . . ." Rueben's voice trailed off; then he spoke again. "How's your mamm doing? I haven't seen her in a while."

"Mom's been busy taking care of Grandpa. She doesn't go many places these days."

"Now that you're living here, I thought maybe Mae would have more time to herself and might be able to get out more."

"I've offered to help with Grandpa, but Mom always says no."

"I see. Well, tell her I said hello and that I've missed seeing her at church."

"I will." Lydia glanced across the yard where Josh was playing. "I think I'd better get my son and head for home. It was nice meeting you, Rueben."

"Same here."

The wistful look on Rueben's face made Lydia wonder if he might be interested in Mom. If so, did Mom know about it?

CHAPTER 10

I don't wanna go home," Josh said as Lydia led him toward their buggy. "I wanna play with Kevin."

"You can play with him some other time. It's getting late, and we need to get home." She gently squeezed his fingers. "When we get there, you can play in the barn with the busslin."

"Okay."

Lydia lifted Josh into the buggy; then she went to the barn to get her horse. As she was leading him out, she nearly bumped into Menno, who was coming into the barn.

"It's nice to see you," he said. "Are you getting ready to head for home?"

"Jah."

"Me, too."

Lydia's horse whinnied and flipped its head from side to side.

Menno patted the horse's flanks. "Seems like she's kind of anxious to go. Either that, or she's got a fly up her nose."

Lydia snickered. "If there's a fly up Buttercup's nose, then it must have been there awhile, because she was tossing her head like that on the way here this morning."

"Something must be bothering her." Menno made his way around the horse, checking for sores under the bridle, and then looking at each hoof. "Found the problem," he announced.

"What is it?"

"She's missin' a shoe."

Lydia groaned. "No wonder Buttercup kept pulling to the left and flipping her head. She'll probably do it all the way home, too."

"More than likely. Think I'd better follow your rig home. That way if the horse acts up, I'll be there to help you," Menno said.

"You don't have to do that. I'm sure we'll be fine."

"I'd feel better if I knew you'd made it home okay."

Lydia finally nodded her consent. It would be comforting to know he was behind her and could offer help if she needed it.

"Would you like me to hitch your horse to your buggy?" he asked.

She smiled. "I appreciate the offer, but I'm sure I can manage."

"All right then, I'll get my rig and my boys and meet you out by the driveway."

A short time later, Lydia and Josh were heading for home, with Menno and his boys following in their buggy. Buttercup flipped her head a few times, but Lydia managed to keep her under control. When they neared the driveway leading to Grandpa's house, Lydia leaned out of the buggy and waved at Menno. She thought about inviting him and his boys to join them for a light supper, as a way of saying thanks for following her home, but decided against it. After she'd promised Mom that she wouldn't invite anyone to the house for supper without asking, she knew better than to invite Menno and his boys in.

Mae had just taken a seat on the porch swing when she spotted a horse and buggy coming up the driveway. "So much for peace and quiet," she mumbled. She'd checked on Dad a few minutes ago, and seeing that he was asleep, had come out here for some time alone. Now that Lydia and Josh were back, she'd have no time to herself, and there'd be no peace and quiet, either.

I shouldn't be so selfish, she told herself. *I invited Lydia and Josh to move here, so I should enjoy the time I get to spend with them.*

Thump. Thump. Thump. Josh bounded onto the porch and flung the back door open.

Mae jumped up from her chair and grabbed the door before he could go inside. "I'd like you to stay out here awhile," she said. "Your urgrossvadder's taking a nap, and I don't want you to wake him."

Josh looked up at her and tipped his head. "Gotta change my clothes. Gonna play with the busslin."

"That's fine, but be very quiet when you go up the stairs."

"Okay." Josh disappeared into the house, and Mae returned to the porch swing.

A few minutes later, Lydia stepped onto the porch. "I got Buttercup put away, but we'll need to call someone to shoe her tomorrow. She's missing a shoe on her back left hoof and acted kind of spooky because of it."

"Were you able to keep her under control?"

"Jah. Menno Troyer followed us home after church to be sure we made it okay."

"That was nice. Did you invite him in?"

Lydia shook her head. "After what you said the other day, I was sure you wouldn't appreciate the unexpected company."

"Well, I did just get Dad settled down for a nap, so we would have had to sit out here to visit."

The screen door opened and banged shut. "I'm goin' to the barn!" Josh hollered, as he bounded down the stairs and into the yard.

Mae frowned. "I wish he wouldn't slam the door like that. If he woke Dad, I'll really be upset." She jumped up, opened the door, and stuck her head inside. Not a sound. Thankfully, Dad must still be asleep.

"I'm sure Josh didn't slam the door on purpose," Lydia said when Mae returned to her seat. "He's full of energy and isn't used to being quiet all the time."

Mae yawned. "I know, and I wish I had half his energy. Seems like I'm always so tired."

"That's because you're always busy. It might help if you got out more and did something fun."

"I can't. Dad's very fussy, and he can be difficult at times."

"You've said that before, but I'm sure I could manage to care for him."

Mae lowered her gaze. "You probably think I worry too much."

"I think if you got out more and enjoyed yourself, you wouldn't worry quite so much. I'm not the only one who thinks you need to get out more, either."

"Oh?"

"I met Rueben Miller today, and he said the same thing. He also said he's missed seeing you."

"Is that so?"

Lydia touched Mae's arm. "The way he said it made me wonder if he has a special interest in you."

Mae cheeks grew hot, and she fanned

her face with her hand. "There's nothing going on between me and Rueben."

"I didn't say there was, but would you like there to be?"

"I—I don't have time to think about such things."

"But if you did?"

"Well, I don't, so there's no point in us talking about it." Mae stood. "Think I'll go inside and make some sandwiches. Are you hungry?"

Lydia nodded. "Josh probably is, too. I'll go out to the barn and see what kind of sandwich he wants; then I'll come inside and help you."

"That's fine." As Mae stepped into the kitchen she thought about Rueben and what he'd said to Lydia. When she'd first moved home to take care of Dad, Rueben had come around a lot, but after she'd discouraged him, his visits became less frequent.

Mae wasn't about to tell Lydia, but the truth was, she'd been attracted to Rueben when they were teenagers. But nothing had ever come of it, for she and Rueben had both found someone else. In fact, she'd forgotten about her attraction to him until she'd returned to Charm.

Mae figured there was no point in encouraging him when she wasn't free to pursue a relationship while she was taking care of Dad. If the time ever came that she was free, she was sure Rueben would have found someone else by then. With the exception of Dad, most of the Amish widowers she'd known had remarried within the first year. Truth was, she was surprised Rueben hadn't found himself another wife by now.

&

Levi and his family had just returned home after visiting friends at another church district. Since it was such a warm evening, Levi decided to sit on the porch awhile and enjoy the fresh air. It was relaxing to watch the stars come out and listen to the crickets sing their nightly chorus.

"Mind if I join you?" Mom asked a few minutes later.

"'Course not."

She took a seat in the wicker chair beside him. "We haven't had a chance to really talk since you had supper last night at Wilbur's place. How'd things go with that?"

"It went okay. Lydia's boy got real excited when he showed me a batch of kittens."

"What'd you have to eat?"

"Potatoes, ham, peas, bread, and a tossed green salad."

"Did Lydia cook the meal?"

He shrugged. "I think she made some of it."

"Is she a good cook?"

He nodded. "Probably ate more than I should have, too."

Mom chuckled. "Speaking of food, are you hungry now?"

"Not yet. Maybe later I'll fix myself something to eat."

"You don't have to do that. I'd be happy to fix it for you."

He shook his head. "I'm perfectly capable of making myself a sandwich."

"Okay." She leaned back in her chair and clasped her hands in her lap. "You know what I've been thinking?"

"What's that?"

"I think it would be nice if you invited Lydia and her boy over here for supper sometime."

"I don't think that's such a good idea."

"Why not? Are you ashamed for her to meet us?"

"'Course not. I just don't want her getting any ideas that I might have a personal interest in her."

"Do you?" Mom asked with a hopeful expression.

Levi shook his head forcefully.

"You don't like her?"

"It's not that. I don't plan on getting serious about anyone, so there's no point in my doing anything that might make her think I'm interested."

Mom sighed. "Levi, Levi, it's always the same old thing with you, isn't it? You think that just because you were born to a family of little people you have to take responsibility for us."

"It's not just that."

"What else is holding you back?"

Before Levi could respond, the back door swung open, and Betty rushed out. A wisp of dark hair had fallen into her face, and her brown eyes were full of fear. "Levi! Mom! Come quickly! Pop fell down the stairs, and I think he's hurt bad!"

CHAPTER 11

Nona paced between the cluster of chairs in the hospital waiting room and the window overlooking the parking lot. A multitude of shimmering stars dotted the night sky, but she barely took notice. It had been over an hour since Harold had been taken to the examining room, and they'd still had no word on his condition.

Please, Lord, don't let it be anything serious, she prayed. When Harold had fallen down the stairs, he'd hit his head and passed out for a few minutes. When he came to, he'd acted disoriented. She feared he might have a concussion. She was also pretty sure from the swelling in his left arm that it was broken. She could only hope and pray that he had no serious injuries.

"I wish you'd sit down," Levi said when she glanced in his direction. "You're gonna wear a hole in the floor if you don't stop pacing."

Nona ambled across the room and hoisted herself into a chair that was too high for her short stature. She glanced at the area that had been set up for children and noticed a couple of smaller chairs, but they were too narrow for her wide frame. "Sure wish we'd hear something on your daed's condition. I'm usually a patient person, but not knowing how he's doing is making me *naerfich*."

"I'm nervous, too," Levi said, "but we have to be patient."

Nona sighed. "The longer we wait, the more worried I become. What if he's seriously hurt? What if . . ."

Just then, a middle-aged man entered the room and stepped up to Nona. "Mrs. Stutzman?"

She nodded.

"I'm Dr. Jorgenson." He took a seat in the chair beside her. "Your husband's suf-

fered a pretty serious concussion, so we'll
need to keep him here a day or so for ob-
servation. His left arm and a couple of ribs
are also broken, and he has several nasty
bruises on the left side of his body."

Nona's shoulders sagged as she
reached for Levi's hand. While she felt terrible knowing that her husband must be in
pain, she was relieved because his injuries could have been much worse.

"His broken bones and bruises will heal,"
the doctor said. "Unless there are complications from the head injury, he should be
fine."

"Can we see him now?" Nona asked.

"Yes, of course." The doctor rose from
his chair. "Follow me."

When Levi woke up the following morning,
he felt as if he carried the weight of the
world on his shoulders. It would be several
weeks before Pop could help in the store
again, which meant Levi would have to
work there full-time. There would be no
time for any of his woodworking projects,
and there sure wouldn't be time to do anymore fishing. Mom had stayed at the hospital last night, insisting that she couldn't

leave Pop. Knowing that someone needed to oversee things at home, as well as at the store, Levi had come home alone.

He followed the welcoming smell of coffee and bacon coming from the kitchen, where he found Betty and Selma cooking breakfast. Both stood on wooden stepstools Levi had made for them. Betty glanced over her shoulder and smiled at Levi. "Breakfast is almost ready, so if you'll call the boys, we can eat as soon as everyone's at the table."

Levi looked at the chairs where his folks normally sat. It didn't seem right that they wouldn't be sitting there this morning. He wondered how long Pop would have to stay in the hospital. He figured Mom would stay there until Pop came home.

"Levi, what's wrong?" Selma asked. "You look upset."

"I was just thinking about Pop."

"Do you think he'll get to come home today?"

Levi shrugged. "Guess it all depends on how well he's doing and what the doctor says."

"Pop won't be able to work in the store for a while, will he?" Betty asked.

"Afraid not, but I'll be there, so we'll get along okay."

Selma's nose crinkled. "You won't try to boss us around, I hope."

Levi stepped up to her and tweaked her nose. "Someone needs to keep you in line."

"Well, I'm in charge of the kitchen this morning," Betty said. "So would you please get Peter and Andy so we can eat?"

"Enjoy being in charge while you can." Levi snickered and sauntered out of the room.

≈

Mae had just finished mopping the kitchen floor when she heard the rumble of buggy wheels. She peered out the window and was surprised to see Rueben Miller in his work wagon pulling up near the barn. She'd gone to the phone shed early this morning and left a message on his voice mail letting him know that her horse needed to be shoed, but she hadn't expected him to be here so soon.

Mae felt relief when he headed to the barn, although when he was finished shoeing the horse, he'd probably knock on the door to give her his bill.

I hope he doesn't pressure me to go out to supper with him, the way he did the last time he was here.

She emptied the bucket of dirty water into the sink and focused on the windows that needed cleaning. She'd deal with Rueben when the time came and not worry about what he might say to her.

For the next hour, Mae kept busy cleaning house, until a knock sounded on the back door. She set her cleaning rag down and went to answer it. When she opened the door and saw Rueben standing on the porch, a rush of pleasure flooded her being, and her heart began to pound. With the exception of Lydia's father, she thought Rueben was the nicest-looking man she'd ever met. His thick dark hair, streaked with silver gray, and his piercing blue eyes made him look quite distinguished. His hands were strong and capable; his fingers long and narrow. Even in his faded work clothes, with his face glistening with perspiration, she thought he looked good.

"Hello, Rueben. Have you finished shoeing my horse?"

His eyes twinkled as he gave her a nod. "Did you have any trouble with her?"

"Nope, none at all." Rueben scrutinized Mae in such a way that her cheeks turned warm.

She leaned against the doorjamb for needed support. "Do you have my bill?"

Rueben reached into his pocket and handed her a slip of paper. "I did all four shoes. Also cleaned and trimmed the hooves real good."

"I'll get the money I owe you." Mae stepped quickly into the kitchen, leaving Rueben on the porch. She was tempted to invite him inside for a cup of coffee but decided against it. It was best to keep their relationship strictly business, because as long as she had Dad to care for, she and Rueben had no future together.

When Mae returned to the porch, she found Rueben leaning against the railing with his arms folded. "I missed you at church yesterday. I always look for you there."

"Dad needed me, and I thought it was better for Lydia to go so she could get acquainted with some of the women in our district."

"I guess that makes sense." Rueben motioned to the barn. "I met your grandson in there. He showed me a nice batch of kittens."

She nodded. "They were born a few weeks ago but didn't show themselves until recently. I guess the mother cat had them hidden pretty well."

"I asked the boy if he'd like to walk with me up to the house, but he said he'd rather stay in the barn with the kittens."

"Josh spends a lot of time out there, which is good, because he's too noisy in the house, and my daed likes things nice and quiet." Mae handed Rueben the money, and in so doing, her fingers brushed his. Just the simple contact made her chest flutter. "I—I appreciate that you came here so quickly."

"No problem. Didn't want you to be without your horse for transportation." He took a step closer to her—so close that she could see the dark flecks in his blue eyes.

"I have no plans to go anywhere this week, and Lydia rode her bike to work this morning, so there was really no hurry in getting Buttercup's shoes put on."

"You never know what might come up. Since I had this morning free, I figured I'd get it done for you now." Rueben started for the stairs but hesitated and turned back around. "How's your daed doing these days?"

"He's about the same. Sleeps a lot and doesn't want to leave his room much, even though I have a wheelchair for him."

"That's too bad. Think he'd feel up to company? I'd like to say hello."

Mae shook her head. "He's sleeping right now, and I'd rather he not be disturbed."

"Maybe some other time then. It's been nice seeing you, Mae. Take care of yourself." Rueben gave her a nod and hurried down the stairs.

Mae's heart ached as she watched him step into his wagon and ride away. Oh, how she wished things could be different.

A few minutes before Lydia's shift ended that afternoon, she overheard a man who'd come into the restaurant say that Harold Stutzman had fallen down the stairs the night before and was in the hospital in Millersburg. Not wishing to appear as if she were eavesdropping, Lydia didn't ask the man for details. Instead, she decided that she would stop by the Stutzman's store and find out for herself how Harold was doing. It was on her way home and would give her an opportunity to pick up a few other things they needed.

When Lydia left the restaurant and stepped into the parking lot, the glare of the sun nearly blinded her vision. If this warm spring weather they'd been having was any indication of what was to come, they were probably in for a hot summer. That was fine with her. Hot sunny days were better than cold rainy ones like they'd had last spring in Illinois. She just wished she didn't have to work in order to provide for her and Josh. It would be nice if she could stay home with her boy all the time, but she hadn't been able to do that since Jeremiah died.

With a weary sigh, Lydia climbed onto her bike. Unless she got married again, she'd always have to work outside the home, and unless she fell in love again, another marriage wasn't likely.

When Lydia arrived at the general store, she parked her bike near the front door and went inside.

"How's your daed?" she asked, stepping

up to the counter where Levi sat. "I heard that he fell down a flight of stairs."

Levi grimaced. "Pop hit his head and ended up with a concussion, some broken ribs, lot of bruises, and a broken left arm."

"I'm sorry to hear that. Will he be okay?"

"We think so, but since he has a concussion, the doctor wanted to keep him at the hospital for a day or so. Mom stayed with Pop last night, so I'm in charge of the store." Levi motioned to a stack of papers on the counter. "Things have been kind of hectic around here today. I've been trying for the last couple of hours to get some orders placed and some bills paid. Guess I'll probably have to work on 'em at home this evening."

Lydia thought about inviting Levi and his siblings to their house for supper, but she was sure Mom wouldn't appreciate that. "Is there anything I can do to help—maybe bring a meal over for your supper tonight?"

"I appreciate the offer, but we'll be fine. My sisters, Betty and Selma, can both cook fairly well, so I'm sure they'll fix supper."

Just then, a small girl with dark brown hair, who Lydia assumed was one of Levi's sisters, stepped out of the back room and motioned to Levi. "Could you help me a minute? There's something on one of the shelves I'm not able to reach, and I can't find the ladder."

"I'll take care of it. You shouldn't be up on a ladder anyway." Levi hurried off.

His sister seated herself on the stool behind the counter and smiled at Lydia. "My name's Betty. Can I help you with something?"

"I just need some mouthwash and a box of tissues, but I'm sure I can find them." Lydia turned down the first aisle, where she found exactly what she needed. When she returned to the counter, Betty was still there, but no Levi. She'd hoped for the chance to say good-bye to him but guessed it wasn't to be.

When she stepped out the door a few minutes later, she met two small boys, both with dark brown hair, coming up the stairs, and figured they must be Levi's brothers. They were jabbering to each other in Pennsylvania Dutch, and didn't seem to notice Lydia as they entered the store.

Lydia wondered when she'd get the opportunity to visit with Levi's family. She hoped to bring Josh by their house to see the goat Levi had told him about, but now wasn't a good time. Maybe in a week or two, after Levi's dad was home from the hospital.

CHAPTER 12

Levi stretched his arms over his head, hoping to ease the kinks out of his back. For the last hour, he'd been hauling boxes full of kitchen items into the store. Normally, Pop would be helping with this, but he'd only been out of the hospital two weeks and wasn't up to doing much of anything yet. Besides, with only one good arm, he wouldn't be able to carry any heavy boxes. Levi had thought about asking his two younger brothers to help, but they were both at home, mucking out the barn.

Levi was about to enter the store with another box, when he was met by Mom coming out the door. "Are you about done with that?" she asked, looking up at him.

"Almost. Just a few more boxes to unload."

"Will you be able to help Betty and Selma in the store for a while then? I need to run a few errands."

"Jah, sure. I'd planned to do that anyway."

She smiled. "You're such a helpful son. Don't know what we'd do without you right now."

"You'll never have to find out, because I'm not going anywhere. As long as you and Pop own this store, I'll be here to help."

Her forehead wrinkled. "We don't expect you to sacrifice your own needs for us. We want you to have a life of your own."

Levi shifted the heavy box. "I have a life . . . with my *familye*."

"But wouldn't you like to have a family of your own . . . a fraa and a houseful of kinner?"

"We've been through all this before, Mom, and it's getting old. I really wish you wouldn't keep bringing it up."

"But if you found someone you truly loved, I'm sure you'd change your mind about getting married."

"You know, this box is sure getting heavy. I need to get it inside before my arms give out."

"Okay. I shouldn't be gone too long. When I get back, you can take your lunch break." Mom looked up at him, and a slow grin spread across her face. "Say, I have an idea. Why don't you eat lunch over at Grandma's Restaurant today? Now that strawberries are in season, I'm sure they'll have strawberry pie on the dessert menu, and I know how much you like that."

"I brought my lunch today, remember? Fixed it myself while you were making breakfast."

"Oh, that's right. Well, it's in the cooler, so maybe you could save it for tomorrow's lunch."

"I don't think so. See you later, Mom." Levi stepped through the open door. He had a pretty good idea that Mom was trying to get him to eat at Grandma's Restaurant because Lydia worked there. Even though he was more than mildly attracted to Lydia, which he wasn't about to admit to anyone, he couldn't begin a relationship that had nowhere to go, because he was definitely not getting married!

It had been a busy morning at the restaurant, and Lydia, having just returned from a short break, had the lunch crowd to deal with. From what she'd been told, things would get even busier throughout the summer months, when many tourists came to visit the shops here in Charm.

I wonder if this town will ever really feel like my home, Lydia thought as she glanced out the window at a horse and buggy moving slowly down the street. Here in Doughty Valley, which was part of Holmes County, lived the largest population of Amish in America, and business seemed to be booming. It gave her hope that her job was secure.

As Lydia headed for the kitchen to turn in the order she'd just taken, someone touched her arm. It was the little woman, whom she realized now was Levi's mother. She sat on a stack of newspapers in a booth, no doubt to bring her closer to the table.

"Can I bring you something to drink while you look over the menu?" Lydia asked.

The woman shook her head. "I can't stay long enough for lunch. Just came in for a cup of coffee and to speak to you."

"What'd you need to speak to me about?"

"I'm Nona Stutzman." She flashed Lydia a friendly smile. "Levi's my son, and I understand that he had supper at your house a few weeks ago."

Lydia nodded and reached for the coffeepot on the shelf behind her. "I heard that your husband had fallen down the stairs. Is he doing okay?" she asked as she poured some coffee into Nona's cup.

"He's been home from the hospital for two weeks now and is getting along pretty well with the use of only one arm." Nona smiled as she added some cream and sugar to her coffee. "We were glad his injuries weren't any worse."

Lydia nodded.

"The reason I wanted to talk to you is I was wondering if you and your son would be free to have supper at our place this Friday evening. Levi mentioned that he'd promised your boy he could see Andy's goat. If you come a little early, the boys can play with the goat before we eat."

Lydia smiled. It would be nice for Josh to have someone to play with and for her to spend an evening in the company of someone who didn't find fault with everything she did. Since she didn't have to work on Friday, she could spend the day helping Mom do whatever chores needed to be done, and then she'd be free to go to the Stutzmans' for supper. "We'd love to come," she said. "What time?"

"We'll eat around six, so why don't you come over at five?"

"That sounds fine. Is there anything I can bring?"

"Nothing at all. Just make sure you come hungry. Oh, and our house is directly behind the store, so it's not hard to find."

"Sounds good. Josh and I will be there by five."

Lydia turned from Nona's table and spotted Menno Troyer sitting in a booth by himself. She stepped up to him and smiled. "Have you decided what you'd like to order?"

He pointed to the daily special on the menu—ham and cheese sandwich, with home-style fries. "Oh, and I'd like a glass of milk."

"Would you like the milk now or with your meal?"

"Now's fine." He picked up the salt-shaker and passed it from one hand to the other. "How's your horse? Were you able to get shoes put on her right away?"

"Rueben Miller came out the very next day."

"That's good."

"I'll turn your order in now, and then I'll be back with your milk."

Lydia returned shortly with Menno's milk. "I'm sure it won't take long until your sandwich is ready." She started to leave, but he called her name.

"Is there something else you'd like to order?"

"No, I—" He cleared his throat, took a swallow of milk, and cleared his throat again. "Uh . . . this Friday's my son Kevin's birthday, and I'm planning to take him and his brothers out for supper. I wondered if you and your boy would like to join us."

"It's nice of you to include us, and I'm sure Josh would enjoy helping Kevin celebrate his birthday, but we already have plans for Friday evening."

"Oh, I see." His shoulders dropped as he stared at the table.

Lydia felt bad seeing the look of disappointment on Menno's face. "How about Saturday night?" she asked. "Do you think

Kevin would mind if we went out to supper with you the day after his birthday?"

Menno smiled. "Don't think he'd mind a bit. We'll come by your place to pick you up around five. How's that sound?"

"That should be fine." As Lydia moved away from the table, a warm feeling settled over. She had a lot to look forward to this weekend.

"Guess who I saw this afternoon?" Mom asked Levi when she returned to the store later that day.

He shrugged. "Beats me."

"Lydia King."

"Where'd you see her?"

"I stopped by Grandma's Restaurant for a cup of coffee." Mom flashed Levi a sly-looking smile. "It's the first chance I've had to really meet her. She seems very nice."

"Uh-huh." Levi grabbed a roll of paper towels and a bottle of glass cleaner and began scrubbing the fingerprint smudges someone had left on the candy counter.

"I invited Lydia and her son to come over to our place for supper this Friday evening," Mom said as she placed her packages behind the counter.

"How come?"

"They're new to the area. I figured it'd be a good chance for us to get to know them. Besides, you said you had promised to show Andy's goat to Lydia's boy."

Levi's forehead wrinkled. "I did promise, but I never thought you'd invite them to supper, especially with Pop's injuries and all."

She squinted at him. "I'm the one who'll be doing the cooking, not your daed."

"I know, but you've been running yourself ragged ever since Pop came home from the hospital. You don't need one more thing to do."

"I'll have Betty and Selma's help in the kitchen; and if you're concerned about it, you can help, too." Mom shook her finger at him. "Now take that worried look off your face. Everything will go fine, and we'll all have a good time."

CHAPTER 13

Mae had just taken a bowl of leftover vegetable soup from the refrigerator when Lydia stepped into the room. "Josh and I will be leaving for the Stutzmans' soon, but if there's anything you need me to do before we go, I can take a few minutes to do that now," she said.

"I don't need anything done, but I wish you wouldn't go."

Lydia's forehead wrinkled. "How come?"

"I just don't, that's all."

"Josh has really been looking forward to seeing Andy's goat, and he'd be disappointed if we didn't go."

"You'll be going out with Menno and his boys tomorrow night. That ought to be good enough."

"I'm sure our supper with Menno and the boys will be nice, and Josh is looking forward to that, but it doesn't mean we shouldn't go to the Stutzmans' tonight."

"How about you, Lydia? Are you looking forward to Saturday night?"

Lydia's only reply was a brief nod.

"At least Menno's an appropriate suitor for you."

Lydia's eyes widened. "Menno is not my suitor, and neither is Levi. He didn't even invite Josh and me to supper tonight; his mother did. Nona said they wanted an opportunity to get to know Josh and me. And as far as Menno's concerned, I'm sure the only reason he invited us to join them for supper was so that Kevin could spend some time with Josh."

As if on cue, Josh bounded into the room. "I drew Urgrossvadder a picture and took it to his room. I know he liked it, 'cause he smiled at me and said, 'Danki.'"

Mae frowned. Josh had gone into Dad's room several times in the last few weeks, and each time she found him there, Dad had been smiling. It was good to see Dad smile, but did it have to be Josh who'd put that smile on his face? Mae would have given anything if Dad would smile at her that way.

Lydia placed her hand on Josh's shoulder. "I'm glad he liked your picture." She lifted her dark bonnet from the kitchen wall peg and placed it on her head. "Are you ready to go?"

He nodded and grinned up at her.

"Good-bye, Mom. We'll see you later tonight." Lydia took Josh's hand, and they hurried out the door.

Mae's stomach clenched as she watched out the window as Lydia and Josh got into the buggy. She hoped Lydia wouldn't be swayed by Levi's wit and handsome face and would have a better time with Menno and his boys tomorrow evening than she did with Levi and his family tonight. Lydia needed someone stable and serious-minded like Menno.

When Lydia pulled her horse and buggy into the Stutzmans' yard, she spotted Levi kneeling on the ground beside a scruffy-looking, black-and-white terrier. Next to him stood a small boy with reddish-brown hair and a face full of freckles. He wasn't much bigger than Josh.

When Levi caught sight of them, he left the dog and hurried over to their buggy. "I'll put your horse away, and then Andy and I will take Josh to the barn to see the goat."

"I'd like to see it, too," Lydia said. "That is, if you don't mind me tagging along."

Levi hesitated a minute, then shook his head. "We won't be eating for a while, so you're welcome to join us."

As soon as Levi put the horse in the corral, he led Lydia, Josh, and Andy to the barn.

"Here's my gees." Andy pointed to the small white goat, munching on a clump of hay in one of the stalls.

"Can we pet him?" Josh asked.

"Sure." Levi opened the gate, and the boys stepped inside.

When Josh dropped to his knees and stroked the goat's head, the goat stopped eating and nuzzled his hand. "The gees likes me," he said, looking up at Lydia with a wide grin. "He's feischtielich."

She smiled. "I'm sure he's very soft."

While Josh and Andy petted and fussed over the goat, Lydia and Levi sat on a bale of straw and visited.

"How do you like it here in Charm?" Levi asked. "Is it much different from your home in Illinois?"

Lydia shifted on the prickly straw. "The area's definitely different, but what I miss most are my friends."

"I know what you mean. When my family moved here from Geauga County, we left lots of good friends." He yanked a piece of straw from the bale he sat on and stuck it between his teeth. "Fortunately, Geauga County isn't that far from here, so we can hire a driver and be there in less than two hours. Only trouble is, we're so busy in the store most of the time that we have a hard time getting away."

"Do your friends from Geauga County ever come here to visit?"

"Not yet, but I'm sure some of them will, eventually."

"Do you have family living there, too?"

Levi nodded. "My aunt and uncle on my daed's side, and I also have a few cousins there."

Lydia was tempted to ask if Levi's relatives were little people, but she thought that might appear rude.

"How about you? Do you have relatives living in Illinois?"

She shook her head. "My husband's family lives in Wisconsin. After he died, they invited me to move there, but I had a job and didn't want to leave my home in Illinois."

They lapsed into a comfortable silence, broken only by the sound of an occasional *ba–a–a*, and the boys' laughter as they played with the goat. Every once in a while, Levi looked at Lydia and smiled, but instead of making further conversation, he leaned his head against the wall and continued to chew on his piece of straw.

Lydia wondered if Levi felt uncomfortable around her. But if that were so, then why'd he invite her to bring Josh over to see Andy's goat? Maybe the conversation had lagged because he'd run out of things to say or was tired.

Ding! Ding! Ding!

"That's the dinner bell," Levi said, jumping up. "Mom must have everything ready to eat. Guess we'd better get the boys and head for the house."

Lydia rose from her seat and followed Levi to the goat's stall. "It's time for supper," she said to Josh. "We need to go into the house now."

He scrunched up his nose. "Do we hafta go? Me and Andy was havin' fun pettin' the gees."

"My mamm rang the dinner bell, and that means she's ready for us to eat." Levi gave Josh a light tap on the head. "You can come over and play again some other time."

Andy scrambled to his feet and held his hand out to Josh. "Let's go. I'm hungerich."

The goat let out a loud *ba–a–a* when they walked away, but Josh kept going, with only a quick glance over his shoulder.

As they made their way through the cool grass, a warm wind rustled the trees overhead and caressed Lydia's face. Despite being a bit nervous over meeting the rest of Levi's family, she was glad she and Josh had come here tonight and hoped by the time they left that she'd feel fully relaxed.

❧

When Lydia entered Nona's kitchen, a savory aroma greeted her. She was surprised to see a clean plastic runner covering the table, but at each place setting there was only a napkin and a glass of water—no silverware or plates.

Nona stood on her tiptoes and greeted Lydia with a hug; then she introduced her and Josh to the rest of the family. "This is Peter, who's ten; Betty, who's sixteen; Selma, age twelve, and Andy, whom you've already met, is eight." She glanced over at the small man with thinning light brown hair who stood near the table. "And this is my husband, Harold, who'd probably prefer that I don't tell his age."

Harold looked up at Lydia and grinned. "I don't mind admitting that I turned fifty not long ago." He held out his hand. "And it's real nice to meet you."

"It's nice to meet you, too," Lydia said. "I was sorry to hear about your accident."

He gave a nod. "Jah, it was clumsy of me to trip and fall down the stairs, but my injuries could have been much worse." He pushed his metal-framed glasses back in place and lifted the arm that bore a cast. "All I can say is, I'm glad to be doin' as well as I am."

"I hope you're hungry," Nona said, "because I made plenty of Frogmore Stew."

Josh's eyes widened as he shook his head. "I don't want no frosch for supper."

Levi's brothers and sisters exchanged glances; then they all began to laugh.

"There are no frogs in the stew," Nona said, "but I think you're in for a pleasant surprise." She motioned to the table. "Now if everyone will wait a few minutes to have a seat, Betty, Selma, and I will dish up the 'good stuff.'"

Lydia watched with interest as Nona held a large pot, and Betty ladled a blob of food on the table where each person would sit. The "good stuff" consisted of pieces of cutup chicken, smoked sausage, shrimp, potatoes, carrots, mushrooms, onions, and green peppers. Next to each blob of food Selma placed small containers of barbecue sauce, cocktail sauce, melted butter, and sour cream.

"This is a fun meal that was passed down to me from my grandparents," Nona explained after she'd directed everyone to take a seat. "It's cooked in a broth we call the 'icky stuff,' and then we eat the 'good stuff' with our fingers. Now, if you should run out of anything, just call out what you need. If someone has extra pieces of that food, they'll toss it to you."

Despite the unusual way they'd be eating this meal, Lydia thought it sounded like fun. Josh must have thought so, too, for the smile he wore stretched from ear to ear. Lydia figured he'd probably enjoy eating with his hands without being corrected for not using proper table manners.

Lydia noted with interest that Nona's children sat on stools that were higher than the chairs, so they could easily reach the table. Josh was also given a stool to sit on. Lydia and Levi sat on regular chairs, of course, and Levi's folks were seated on a couple of thick catalogs that had been placed on their chairs.

They bowed for silent prayer then dug right in. Everything tasted so good. Lydia especially enjoyed the shrimp dipped in cocktail sauce.

The conversation around the table was pleasant, as Harold shared several humorous stories about his childhood days. Despite his arm being in a cast, he did quite well eating with only one hand. It didn't take Lydia long to realize that everyone in Levi's family had a sense of humor.

She was pleased to see how well Josh fit in and was relieved that he didn't ask any questions about why everyone in Levi's family, with the exception of Levi, was so small. It was a lot different sharing a meal with these fun-loving people than sitting down to supper with Mom, who did nothing but complain and pick apart everything Josh or Lydia did. Being here this evening reminded Lydia of how it had been when Jeremiah was alive and the three of them had shared happy times together.

Sometime later, Lydia looked down at her place at the table and was surprised to see that she'd eaten everything that had been set before her. She'd been having such a good time that she'd finished her meal without even realizing it.

"The food was delicious, and so much fun to eat." Lydia smiled at Nona. "I've never had anything like it before."

"No, I wouldn't imagine so." Harold chuckled and stroked his full, dark beard, streaked with a bit of gray. "Until I married Nona, I'd never had anything like it, either."

"I'd be happy to give you the recipe," Nona said.

Lydia smiled. "That'd be nice."

"What's for dessert?" Andy asked when everyone finished eating and their final prayer had been said.

Harold stepped down from his seat. "After all that food you put away, you can't possibly be hungry."

Andy bobbed his head a few times. "If Mama made strawberry pie, then I'm hungerich."

"I think we'll let our food settle awhile before we eat dessert," Nona said. "Maybe after the pots and pans are done, we'll be ready for pie."

While the women cleared the glasses off the table and washed them, along with the pots and pans, Levi and his father kept the boys entertained in the living room.

I really have enjoyed being here tonight, Lydia thought as she carried several glasses to the sink. *I can't remember the last time I've had so much fun. I hope Mom will allow me to invite the Stutzmans to our house for supper sometime.*

CHAPTER 14

Hold still and quit your *rutschich*," Menno said as he attempted to comb Carl's hair.

"He's squirmin' 'cause he's got an *ie-mense* in his pants." Dennis snickered and poked his brother's arm.

Carl wrinkled his nose and returned the poke. "Do not have an ant in my pants."

"Bet ya do." Another poke.

"Do not!"

"Do so!"

"Sit down on the sofa and stop bothering your brother!" Menno had been rushing around for the last half hour trying to get the boys ready to go out to supper, and he was nearly out of patience with their silly antics. If they weren't ready soon, they'd be late picking up Lydia and Josh.

Dennis shuffled across the room and sank onto the sofa next to Ike. "How come Papa ain't combin' your hair?"

"I combed my own, and get away from me 'cause you're sittin' too close." Ike elbowed Dennis in the ribs.

"Stop it!" Dennis slid to the other end of the sofa.

"I want you all to be on your best behavior tonight," Menno said. "And be nice to Lydia and Josh."

"Okay, Papa," the boys said in unison.

When Menno finished with Carl's hair, he worked on Kevin's. "I think we'd better go out to the kitchen and wet this comb," he said in frustration. "Your hair's sticking straight up, and I can't get it to lay flat."

Kevin followed Menno out to the kitchen, while Carl joined his brothers on the sofa.

When Menno returned to the living room he discovered that Carl and Dennis were gone.

"Where's your brieder?" he asked Ike.

The boy shrugged. "Don't know. Think they went outside."

"What makes you think that?"

"They left the room as soon as you and Kevin went to the kitchen, and I heard the front door open."

"That's just great." Menno grunted. "At this rate we *will* be late picking up Lydia and Josh."

He stepped onto the porch and cupped his hands around his mouth. "Dennis! Carl! I need you in here, right now!"

No response. No sign of the boys in the yard, either.

He gritted his teeth and started across the lawn. Most likely, they had gone to the barn and were fooling around. With his luck they'd probably gotten dirty, too.

The barn door squeaked as he opened it, reminding him that it needed a good oiling. He grimaced. It seemed like there were more jobs to do around here than he would ever get done. If he didn't have to cook, clean, and take care of the boys, he'd have more time to keep up with all the outside and inside repairs that needed to be done. When Sadie was alive, he'd never really appreciated everything she'd done to keep up the house and look after the boys.

Of course, he reminded himself, *if we*

hadn't moved here from Pennsylvania, I'd have the help of my family right now and wouldn't be trying to do everything on my own.

Seeing no sign of Carl or Dennis in the barn, he called their names, thinking they might be hiding in the loft.

No reply.

Menno groaned. *Those boys had better not be hiding from me.* He stepped out of the barn and went around back to look out in the field. As he approached the silo, he stopped and cupped his hands around his mouth. "Carl! Dennis!"

"We're in here, Papa," came a muffled voice. "We're trapped in the silo."

Menno started grabbing silage and pulling it away from the opening leading to the chute. "What in the world are you two doing in there?"

"We got bored waitin' for you to comb Kevin's hair, so we went outside, and then . . ." Dennis's voice trailed off as he sneezed. "We came in here to play, and when we tried to get out, we couldn't, 'cause the entrance was blocked."

"We cried for help, but no one came."

Carl sounded like he was on the verge of tears.

"Well, that was a dumb thing to do," he scolded. "You could have suffocated in here."

By the time Menno managed to get enough silage moved away so the boys could slip out, his clothes were dirty, and of course, theirs were, too.

"Now, because of your little stunt, all three of us will have to wash up and change our clothes." Menno motioned to the house. "Thanks to you two, we'll be late picking up Lydia and Josh."

The boys hung their heads as they shuffled toward the house.

Menno lifted his face toward the cloudless sky. *Oh Lord, what am I gonna do with these boys of mine?*

Lydia glanced at the battery-operated clock on the kitchen wall. It was almost five thirty, and Menno had said he'd pick them up at five. She hoped he hadn't forgotten or changed his mind about taking her and Josh to supper, because Josh was really looking forward to going. For the last thirty minutes, he'd been sitting on the porch swing, staring at the driveway.

"Wasn't Menno supposed to pick you up at five?" Mom asked, stepping into the kitchen.

Lydia nodded and glanced at the clock again.

Mom touched her arm. "Don't look so worried. I'm sure something must have come up to detain him. He'll probably be here any minute."

"I hope so, because Josh will be very disappointed if we don't get to go."

Mom headed over to the stove and removed the teakettle. "Would you like a cup of tea while you're waiting?"

"No thanks."

"I think I'll have one." Mom poured hot water into a cup and added a bag of chamomile tea. "I've been trying all day to get your grossdaadi to eat something, but he's refused everything, saying he's not hungry."

"I know how stressed that must make you."

"Jah." With a heavy sigh, Mom dropped into a seat at the table. "To make matters worse, I didn't get much sleep last night."

"Would you rather I not go out to supper?

I can send Josh with Menno and the boys and stay home to keep an eye on Grandpa. That way you can go to bed early."

Mom shook her head. "I'm sure Menno's looking forward to your company. He's bound to be lonely now that his wife is gone." She took a sip of tea. "Besides, Dad is sleeping right now, so I after I fix myself something to eat, I'll probably stretch out on the sofa and take a nap."

"Okay, but I'd really like to stay home and take care of him tomorrow so you can go to church. I know from what some of the others said a few weeks ago that it's been some time since you were able to attend."

"I've gone a few times, when one of the other women in our community came to stay with Dad, but he seems to be getting weaker every day, and I don't want to leave him alone."

Lydia glanced out the window and spotted a horse and buggy coming up the driveway. "Looks like Menno's here," she said, moving toward the door. "I'd better get Josh so we can go."

"Have a nice evening," Mom said as Lydia slipped out the back door.

"Sorry for being late," Menno apologized

as he helped Lydia and Josh into his buggy. "I had a little trouble getting the boys ready to go. First Dennis and Carl got trapped in the silo, and then Kevin couldn't find his jacket." He chuckled and shook his head. "Silly boy had it on the whole time."

Lydia smiled. "That's okay. I understand."

"Sure is a nice evening," Menno said as they pulled onto the main road.

"Jah. Summer's not far away."

They engaged in idle chitchat as they traveled the back road to Berlin. While Lydia and Menno visited, Josh chattered away in the back of the buggy with Carl and Kevin. The older boys were quiet, and Lydia wondered if they'd fallen asleep. But when they arrived at the restaurant, she knew they weren't sleeping because they were the first ones to clamber out of the backseat.

Soon after they entered Boyd and Wurthmann's Restaurant, they were shown to a table near the window. As they waited for their waitress to come, Dennis and Ike sat with their heads together, whispering, while Kevin, Carl, and Josh giggled and chattered like a bunch of magpies.

"Would you like to give Kevin the present we bought him now?" Lydia asked Josh as she removed the gift from the plastic sack she'd brought along.

Josh nodded and happily handed the gift to Kevin. "Here ya go. *Hallich gebottsdaag.*"

"Jah. Happy birthday," Lydia added.

Kevin tore the wrapping off the package and pulled out the engine of a toy train. "Danki," he said with a wide grin.

"Let me see it!" Dennis reached across Lydia, who sat between him and Josh.

"Boss uff!" Menno warned, but it was too late. The boy's hand bumped Lydia's glass, and it toppled over, spilling water on the skirt of her dress.

Menno frowned. "Now look what you've done! I told you to watch out."

"Sorry," Dennis mumbled. He cast a quick glance in Ike's direction, then handed Lydia a wad of napkins. "Here ya go."

"It's all right." Lydia blotted her skirt. "It's only water, and it'll soon dry." She smiled at Menno, hoping to put his mind at ease. "I doused you with water once, so I guess tonight it was my turn to get a little wet."

A look of relief crossed Menno's face,

and he grinned. "I'm glad you're such a good sport about it."

Their waitress came then and took their orders. As they waited for their food, Menno kept scolding his boys for whispering and poking each other, while Lydia tried to keep Josh entertained.

Finally their meal came, and after their silent prayer, all five boys dug into the hamburgers they'd ordered. Lydia and Menno both had pork chops, which included mashed potatoes, cooked carrots, and a garden salad. For dessert, the boys had ice cream, and Menno ate a piece of strawberry-rhubarb pie. Lydia passed on dessert, saying she was too full.

On the way home, Lydia reflected on how the evening had gone. During supper, Menno hadn't said a whole lot to her. He'd seemed too busy watching out for his boys. He hadn't told her any amusing stories or humorous jokes and had seemed rather reserved. He was nothing like Levi, who, along with his parents, had told a host of funny stories and jokes during the Frogmore Stew supper.

Levi's two young brothers had been better behaved than Menno's boys, too. While this evening was pleasant enough, last night had really been fun.

I don't know why I'm making such comparisons, Lydia told herself as they headed for home. *I'm not giving Menno a fair chance. I'm sure he's a lot more relaxed at home, and his boys probably behave better there, too.*

"We're here," Menno announced as he directed his horse and buggy up Grandpa's driveway.

As they drew closer to the house Lydia leaned forward in her seat and gasped. An ambulance was parked in the yard, the reflection of its red lights blinking against the side of the house.

CHAPTER 15

Lydia leaped from the buggy and dashed into the house. There was no sign of Mom in the kitchen or living room, so Lydia ran down the hall to Grandpa's room. Grandpa was lying on his bed, with two paramedics bent over him. Mom stood nearby, slowly shaking her head.

"Wh–what happened?" Lydia asked, touching Mom's shoulder.

"They think he's had another stroke." Mom's hand shook as she swiped at the tears running down her cheeks. "This time, I'm afraid he might not make it."

"I'm so sorry, Mom."

"They're getting him ready to go to the hospital, and I'll need to go along."

"I'd like to go with you, but I don't know what to do about Josh."

"He can go home with me and the boys," Menno said, stepping into the room. "He can spend the night with us, and you can pick him up tomorrow. I'm sure Kevin and Carl would enjoy having Josh sleep in their room."

"That's so nice of you," Mom said before Lydia could respond. "I really would like to have my daughter with me."

"But tomorrow's a church day," Lydia said to Menno. "Won't that make things hectic for you with five boys to get ready?"

He shrugged. "I've been gettin' four boys ready for church and school over the past six months, so I don't think one boy more will make much difference."

Lydia contemplated the offer a few seconds and finally nodded. She just hoped that Josh would be good and wouldn't give Menno any problems.

"You boys go on up to the house while I put my horse in the barn," Menno said when he pulled his horse and buggy into his yard sometime later.

"Can we have somethin' to eat?" Dennis asked.

Menno frowned. "You just finished eating supper not long ago, and now you're hungry again?"

Dennis patted his stomach. "I've got room for some *kichlin* and *millich*."

"Me, too," Carl said.

The other three boys nodded in agreement and raced into the house.

"Cookies and milk, huh?" Menno shook his head. "Sure hope they settle down before it's time for bed," he mumbled as he trudged through the tall grass toward the house.

When Menno entered the kitchen, he was nearly run over by Josh and Kevin, who had removed their shoes and were racing across the kitchen floor. "Whoa! Slow down, you two."

"We're gonna get us some kichlin before my brieder eats 'em all." Kevin whirled around so fast his elbow connected with Josh's nose. Blood squirted out, and Josh let out an ear-piercing howl.

Menno dashed into the kitchen and

grabbed a towel. Then he wet it with water and held it against Josh's nose.

Josh cried so loud that Menno thought his head would explode. In the meantime, Kevin pulled a chair over to the counter and stuck his hand into the cookie jar.

"Give me that yo-yo!" Ike hollard from the other room.

"You said I could play with it!" Dennis shouted.

"Did not!"

"Did so."

Menno grimaced. Josh's nose was still bleeding, so he couldn't leave the boy alone while he dealt with the argument going on in the next room.

Crash!

Menno's head snapped to the right. Kevin now stood in a puddle of milk, with broken glass scattered around his bare feet.

"Don't move, Kevin! Stay right where you are so you don't get cut!" Menno placed Josh's hands over the towel. "Hold onto this and don't let go!"

As Menno bent to pick up the broken glass, he wondered if he'd made a mistake agreeing to keep Josh overnight. Well, he was doing it as a favor to Lydia, so he'd just have to make the best of things and pray for the strength to get through the night.

Guess I'd better pray for Wilbur Hershberger, too.

Mae's stomach clenched as she stared at her father's pale face. He'd definitely had another stroke, and a few minutes ago, the doctor had told her that Dad probably wouldn't survive. Mae had asked Lydia to stay in the waiting room so she could be alone with Dad to say good-bye, but she feared she might not get the chance. He could die without ever knowing the way she felt, or without them being able to make peace with each other.

Tears trickled down her cheeks. She and Dad had never had a good relationship. Ever since she could remember, he'd been harsh and demanding. Never with Mae's two older brothers, though. Despite Dad's belittling words and frequent negative comparison of Mae to the mother she'd never met, she had done her best to please him. Nothing ever seemed to be good enough, though. Mae had cooked, cleaned, and helped her brothers with the chores, but Dad never even once said thanks.

Mae's mother had died giving birth to her, and she'd often wondered if Dad blamed her for her mother's death, but she'd always been afraid to ask. When Mae married David and they'd moved to Wisconsin a year after Lydia was born, she'd been relieved that she didn't have to see Dad too often anymore.

Then, a year after David's unexpected death, Dad had suffered his first stroke. So Mae had felt obligated to return to Ohio to take care of him. She'd hoped that her arrival might make Dad love her and appreciate the sacrifice she'd made by taking care of him. But that hadn't happened. Instead, he'd been indifferent and uncooperative, often refusing to eat or do anything that might help him regain the use of the left side of his body.

Only Josh had been able to get through to Dad, but Mae had been jealous when she'd seen them laughing together. She'd felt that way many times when she was a girl and Dad had joked around with her brothers. Even so, she still loved him and wanted his approval. She desperately needed it.

Dad's eyes fluttered, and he moaned. "Iva?"

Mae swallowed around the lump in her throat. Iva was her mother's name. "It's me, Dad. It's your daughter, Mae." She took a seat in the chair beside his bed and reached for his icy-cold hand.

"Mae," he murmured in a garbled voice. "Jah."

"I—I love you, Mae."

More tears fell, as she gently squeezed his fingers. "I love you, too, Dad."

And then he was gone . . . slipped away into eternity. Had he made his peace with God? Would Mae see him in heaven someday? She didn't know. Right now, she wasn't sure about her own salvation, much less where Dad stood with the Lord.

One thing she did know was that she needed to get on her knees and thank God for allowing her and Dad to say their good-byes. Despite the sadness over his passing and the way he'd treated her all these years, it uplifted her soul to know that he'd said he loved her.

CHAPTER 16

Lydia clung to Josh's hand as they stood on the uneven ground at the cemetery next to Mom and her two brothers, Abe and Dan. It was hard watching Grandpa's casket being set into place. It had nearly broken her heart when at the close of the funeral service this morning, Josh had asked, "Why's Grandpa in that box, Mama? Why won't he smile when I talk to him?" She'd explained that Grandpa had gone to heaven and someday Josh would get to see him again.

Being at the cemetery brought back memories of the day Lydia had buried

Jeremiah. She'd felt such pain and despair when her husband died but had forced herself to remain strong for Josh's sake. Now she'd need to be strong for Mom's sake.

As the graveside service began, Lydia thought about Grandpa and how she'd never really gotten to know him well. Lydia and her folks had made a few trips to Ohio when she was a girl, but she couldn't remember Grandpa ever coming to see them at their home in Wisconsin, and he'd never visited her and Jeremiah in Illinois. She'd always figured it was because he didn't like to travel, but after the last few months of living in his house, and seeing how he often snapped at Mom, Lydia decided that he probably hadn't visited them because he was upset with Mom for marrying Dad and moving away. While growing up in Wisconsin, Lydia had been close to her father's parents, but they'd both passed away a few years ago. After Lydia married Jeremiah and they'd moved from Wisconsin to Illinois, she hadn't come back to Ohio to visit. No wonder she'd never felt close to Grandpa.

Maybe I should have made an effort to

get to know him better during the time I've been here, Lydia thought with regret. She glanced at her uncles, Abe and Dan, and realized that she didn't know either of them very well, either. She'd only seen them a couple of times during her childhood. She supposed that was because they both lived in Missouri and didn't travel much because of their business, making and repairing buggies. Both brothers had blue eyes like Mom, but their hair was brown instead of blond. As Lydia recalled, Grandpa's hair had been brown when he was younger, too.

We should not take our families for granted, Lydia thought. *We should spend more time together and get to know them well.*

She look over at Mom. Her face was pale, and her eyes glistened with tears. Ever since Grandpa had died, Mom had been weepy, yet she seemed unwilling to talk about her feelings.

In spite of the tension between her and Mom, they had to work things out, because Mom was going to need her in the days ahead.

"I think we should speak with Lydia and her mamm and offer our condolences," Levi's mother said when they'd finished eating the meal that had been served at Wilbur's home, following his graveside service.

"I think you're right," Pop said. "But then we need to go home, because my arm's starting to throb, and I forgot to bring my pain medicine along."

"That's my fault," Mom said. "I should have thought to put the bottle in my purse." She looked over at Levi. "Are you coming with us to talk to Lydia and her mamm?"

"Sure." Levi knew he needed to offer his condolences, but after the cool reception he'd gotten from Mae the evening he'd eaten supper at her house, he felt uneasy about how she might respond to Mom and Pop. Well, it was too late to worry about that. Mom and Pop were already moving across the yard in the direction of the house. Mae stood on the porch beside Lydia, talking to some others who'd come back to the house after the graveside service.

When Mom and Pop stepped onto the porch, Mom touched Mae's arm and said, "I'm sorry for your loss."

Mae shrank back, as though repulsed by Mom's touch.

Levi grimaced. He remembered the few times that Mae had come into their store and how she'd avoided talking to Mom, hurrying out the door as soon as she'd paid for her purchases. He had wondered if Mae was prejudiced against people who were different than her. It wasn't the Christian way, and here, among those who were supposed to be Christians, Levi had hoped his family would find love and acceptance by everyone.

Mom didn't seem to be put off by Mae's coolness, for she just smiled and said, "If there's anything we can do for you, please let us know."

Mae only nodded, but Lydia smiled and clasped Mom's hand. "We appreciate that very much."

"I can't do a whole lot for you right now," Pop said, lifting his arm, "but as soon as my cast comes off, and I'm able to use my arm again . . ."

"Don't trouble yourself. I'm sure we'll be fine," Mae said, cutting him off.

A blotch of red erupted on Lydia's

cheeks. "We'll let you know if we need anything, Harold."

Josh tugged on Levi's hand. "Where's Andy?"

"He's at the store today, helping my sisters."

"Can I come see the gees again?" Josh asked with an eager expression.

"Of course you can," Mom said. "Maybe we can have your mamm and you over for supper again." She smiled at Mae. "You're invited, too, of course."

"We'll have to see how it goes." Mae glanced across the yard. "Oh, there's Menno Troyer and his boys." She nudged Lydia's arm. "Don't you think we should thank him for keeping Josh the other night?"

"I did thank him when I picked Josh up."

"Well, I want him to meet my brothers, and it looks like he's getting ready to leave. So if we're going to catch him it had better be now." Mae hurried away, apparently oblivious to what Lydia had just said.

The color in Lydia's cheeks deepened. She was obviously embarrassed by her mother's rudeness. "I appreciate your coming today," she said to Mom.

Mom patted Lydia's arm. "Don't forget now. Let us know if you need anything."

"Lydia, are you coming?" Mae called from across the yard.

"I–I'd better go." Lydia glanced at Levi; then she hurried away.

❧

After Menno had visited awhile with Lydia, Mae, and Mae's two older brothers, he looked across the yard where his boys were playing with Josh and some of the other children. So far, they'd been on their best behavior today, and for that he was grateful.

"I want to thank you again for keeping Josh the other night," Lydia said. "It was important that I be with my mamm at the hospital."

"No problem. I was glad to do it."

"When I picked Josh up, I was so upset about Grandpa dying that I didn't even think to ask how everything went. Was he a good boy?"

Despite the craziness that had gone on that evening, Menno assured Lydia that everything had been fine, and that Josh had gotten along well with his boys.

"I'm impressed with how well-behaved

your boys seem to be. I just don't know how you do it." Mae looked at Lydia. "Don't you think they're well-behaved?"

Lydia nodded in response.

They're not always this well-behaved, Menno thought ruefully. *What they need is a mother.* He studied Lydia, until he saw her blush; then he quickly averted his gaze. *Could you be that mother?*

CHAPTER 17

Over the next several weeks, Mom was sullen and often snapped at both Lydia and Josh. Given the loss Mom had just suffered, Lydia tried to be supportive and ignore her negative attitude, but it was getting increasingly difficult.

Josh had spent the night at Menno's house a few times, and that gave Josh something fun to do while easing the tension at home. Lydia didn't know why, but she suspected that Mom resented her only grandson.

One morning, as Lydia and Mom were getting breakfast ready, Mom turned to her and said, "There's something I need to tell you."

"What's that?"

"I was under a lot of tension while I was taking care of my daed."

Lydia nodded.

"Things were never good between me and Dad, and I always figured it was because he blamed me for my mamm's death."

"How could that be your fault, Mom?"

"She died giving birth to me." Tears welled in Mom's eyes. "I—I think Dad was so angry and hurt when she died that he needed someone to blame. Since my mamm had complications and bled to death, he thought he was justified in blaming me."

Lydia's heart went out to Mom, for she could see the anguish on her face. She touched Mom's arm. "If that's the case, then Grandpa was wrong for putting the blame on you."

"Dad must have loved my mamm a lot, because he never remarried." Mom sniffed deeply. "All the years I lived at home I tried to please him, but nothing I did ever seemed to be good enough. He treated my brothers like they were special, and that made me bitter and envious. When your daed and I moved to Wisconsin, I was glad for the opportunity to get away from Dad. Then when Dad had his first stroke, I thought if I came back here to care for him, he might appreciate it and finally show me some love." She dabbed at the tears that had splashed onto her cheeks. "But he didn't appreciate anything I did, and the thanks I got were angry words and his unwillingness to do anything I suggested that might help him to get better."

Lydia slipped her arm around Mom's shoulder. "I'm so sorry, Mom. I knew things were strained between you and Grandpa, but I had no idea what all you'd been through."

Mom turned down the stove and blew her nose on a napkin. "At the hospital, just before Dad died, he said that he loved me. You have no idea how much that meant to me."

Lydia nodded slowly. She did have an idea, because it would mean a lot to her if Mom would say she loved her and was sorry for the tension there'd been between the two of them. Lydia was beginning to think that the reason Mom had been so sharp with her and Josh was because of how things had been between Mom and Grandpa. She wished Mom had talked to her about this sooner. It might have helped ease some of the tension between them.

"It's good that Josh could get through to my daed when I couldn't," Mom continued, "but I must admit, I felt envious when I saw how Josh made Dad smile. It brought back the pain of the past and reminded me once again that Dad showed my brothers more attention than me. I always felt left out."

"I'm glad Grandpa told you that he loved you before he died," Lydia said.

Mom dropped into a chair at the table and motioned for Lydia to do the same. "There's something else I want to discuss with you."

"What's that?"

"Much to my surprise, my daed left this house to me. Probably because I came here and took care of him. So for now at least, the three of us have a roof over our heads." Mom paused and blew her nose again. "While you were at work yesterday, I went to the bank. I discovered that there was hardly anything left in Dad's account, and I had to use most of it in order to pay his doctor bills. There's still the hospital bill, and I don't have enough money for that."

"Maybe I can ask for more hours at the restaurant," Lydia said.

Mom blinked, as though trying to hold back her tears. "That might help a little, but I don't think it'll be enough."

"We'll make out; I'm sure God will provide."

"I hope so."

Lydia thought about suggesting that Mom look for a job, but if Mom worked outside the home, who would take care of Josh?

🐍

"Breakfast is ready!" Menno called up the stairs. "Come and get it now before it gets cold."

A few seconds later, Dennis and Ike tromped down the stairs. "It's summer break, and we ain't got no school, so I don't see why we hafta get up early every morning," Dennis complained.

"You get up early because there are chores to do." Menno looked up the stairs. "Where's Carl and Kevin?"

Ike shrugged and released a noisy yawn. "Probably still in bed."

"You're in charge around here when I'm at work," Menno said. "You know that, don't you?"

"Jah."

"Well, it's also your job to see that your brothers get out of bed and come down to breakfast on time."

Ike grunted. "Never had to do it before. Not until after Mama died, anyhow."

"Things are different now, and I really do need your help."

Ike turned and tromped back up the stairs. "Carl! Kevin! You'd better get outa bed right now!"

It's not fair that Ike has to be responsible for the care of his brothers. He's still just a boy himself, Menno thought as he followed Dennis into the kitchen. *It's not right for me to be hollering at the boys all the time, when I ought to enjoy being with them. My boys need a mother.*

Nona had just taken a seat at a table inside Grandma's Restaurant, when she spotted Lydia talking with her boss, Edith. Since they stood a few feet from her, she couldn't help but overhear what they were saying.

"My mother and I are having some financial struggles right now, so it would help if I could get more hours in every week. . . ." Lydia's voice trailed off as she and Edith moved toward the back of the restaurant.

Several minutes later, Lydia returned and stepped up to Nona's table. "Are you ready to order?" she asked.

"I'll just have the soup of the day and a garden salad."

"What would you like to drink?"

"Water will be fine."

"I'll turn your order in right away."

Nona reached out and touched her arm. "Is everything all right? You look upset."

Lydia shifted her ordering pad from one hand to the other. "I'm concerned about our finances right now, but I've asked Edith for more hours so the extra money will help."

"Is there anything we can do?"

"It's nice of you to offer, but I'm sure we'll be fine."

As Lydia walked away from the table, Nona glanced to her right, where Rueben

Miller sat in a booth. Deep wrinkles etched his forehead as he glanced in her direction. Had he also heard Lydia's conversation with her boss? Was he concerned about Lydia and her mother, too?

CHAPTER 18

One morning a week later, Mae discovered an envelope in her mailbox with a typewritten note that said: *To help with your expenses.*

She tore open the envelope and gasped. One thousand dollars was inside! "Now who could this be from?" she murmured.

Mae hurried back to the house, hoping to catch Lydia before she left for work. "Look what someone left us," she said breathlessly, holding the envelope out to Lydia.

"What is it?"

"Someone gave us one thousand dollars to help with our expenses."

When Lydia took the envelope and looked inside, her mouth opened wide. "Who could it be from?"

Mae shrugged. "I'm wondering if it might be Menno."

"What makes you think the money came from him?"

"I'm almost certain he's interested in you."

"I'm not so sure about that." Lydia tapped the envelope as she stared at the money. "I wonder if Rueben Miller could be the one responsible."

"What made you think of him?"

"I'm almost certain he's interested in you."

"I seriously doubt he put the money in our mailbox."

"Maybe we should quit trying to guess who did it and just be thankful for the money," Lydia said.

Mae gave a slow nod. She was thankful, but she wished she didn't have to rely on others during a time such as this. She wished they could make it on their own.

When Nona entered the restaurant and was ushered to a seat, she was pleased to see Lydia waiting on tables.

"Wie geht's?" Nona asked when Lydia stepped up to her table.

"I'm doing all right. How are things with you?"

"Just fine."

"How's Harold? Is he recuperating from his fall?"

"Yes, and he's looking forward to getting his cast off soon."

"I'm sure he must be." Lydia handed Nona a menu. "Can I bring you something to drink while you decide what you want to eat?"

"Iced tea sounds good to me."

"I'll be right back." Lydia hurried from the table.

Nona figured Lydia was putting up a brave front. With the financial situation she and her mother faced, she had to be feeling more than a little stressed.

A few minutes later, Lydia returned with Nona's iced tea. "Have you decided on what you'd like to order?"

"Think I'll have a toasted cheese sandwich."

"Anything else?"

"That should be enough." Nona patted her stomach. "The older I get, the easier it seems to gain weight."

Lydia smiled. "I'll put in your order."

"Before you go, I wanted to ask you a question."

"What's that?"

"I was wondering if you, Josh, and your mamm would like to come to our place for supper on Friday night."

Lydia tapped her chin with the end of her pencil. "Josh and I would love to come, but I can't speak for Mom."

"Please mention it to her, and tell her we'd like the chance to get to know her better."

"I'll do that," Lydia said with a nod.

"I'm going to the back room to get the boxes of towels that just came in," Levi said to Selma, who'd been sitting behind the counter on a stool. "When I come back, you can unpack the boxes and put the towels on the shelf over there." He pointed to one of the shelves he'd just cleared off.

Selma frowned. "Can't Betty unload the towels? I'd rather sit here and wait on customers."

"You've been waiting on customers all morning. It's Betty's turn to do that."

Selma groaned. "My back hurts, Levi. If I have to unload boxes it'll hurt even worse."

"Haven't you been doing those back exercises Dr. Langley gave you?"

Her thick eyebrows drew together. "It makes my back hurt more when I do those exercises."

"Maybe that's because you're not doing them regularly."

She folded her arms and stared at him. "Just because you're bigger than me doesn't mean you can tell me what to do. You're not my daed, you know."

"Never said I was, but I am older than you, and I think I know what's good for you."

"Humph! You'd better get married and have a few kinner of your own before you start tellin' me what to do!"

Levi was stunned by Selma's outburst. She'd never talked to him like that before. "You're right," he said. "I'm not your daed, but today I'm in charge of things here at the store, so you'd best do what I say."

Selma folded her arms and glared at him. "I'll be glad when school starts up again and I don't have to work at the store."

"Well, you'll probably be working here

full-time after you graduate from the eighth grade, so you may as well get used to being told what to do."

She shrugged her shoulders. "I may not be workin' here at all. May get a job at the bed-and-breakfast where Betty works part-time."

"Whatever." Levi started to walk away, but just then Mom entered the store.

"How are things going?" she asked, looking at Selma. "Did you get many customers while I was gone?"

"Not so many." Selma climbed off the stool and reached around to rub a spot on her lower back. "My back hurts, Mama, and Levi's tryin' to make me unload some boxes."

Mom's gaze went to Levi.

"Never said she had to lift anything heavy; just wanted her to put some towels on a shelf."

"Even so, bending over the box might aggravate her back." Mom touched Selma's shoulder. "You can stay behind the counter and wait on customers. I'll put the towels on the shelf."

Selma smiled. "Danki, Mom."

Levi groaned as he lifted his gaze to-

ward the ceiling. He couldn't believe the
way Mom was babying Selma.

He headed for the back room, and when
he returned with the first box, he found
Mom waiting in front of the shelf where the
towels were supposed to go. "Did you get
all your errands run?" he asked.

"Sure did, and then I stopped by Grandma's Restaurant and had lunch." A smile
lifted the corners of Mom's lips. "I saw
Lydia while I was there, and I invited her
and Josh to come to our place for supper
this Friday night." Mom's smile widened.
"She said they could come, and I included
Lydia's mamm in the invitation."

Levi grunted. "I'd be real surprised if
Mae shows up."

"What makes you say that?"

"Have you forgotten how she acts whenever she's around you and Pop?" He
frowned deeply. "It was all she could do to
say hello to you the day of her daed's funeral."

"Maybe she's shy. Probably just needs
a chance to get to know us."

"And you think that inviting her to our
place for supper's the answer to that?"

"It could be." She patted Levi's arm.

"Even if Mae doesn't come, it'll be nice to spend time with Lydia and Josh, don't you think?"

Levi gave a noncommittal shrug. No way would he admit to Mom that he enjoyed being with Lydia and Josh. He didn't even want to admit that to himself.

CHAPTER 19

I saw Nona Stutzman at the restaurant today," Lydia said to Mom as they did the
supper dishes that evening.

Mom reached for another plate to dry.

"She invited Josh and me to go over to
their house for supper this Friday evening."

"What'd you tell her?"

"I said we'd love to come." Lydia smiled.
"She invited you to come, too."

Mom shook her head forcefully. "You
two can go if you like, but I won't be going."

"Why not? Have you made other plans
for Friday evening?"

"No, but I'd rather not go."

"Do you have something against Levi's family?"

"Of course not. It's just that . . ." Mom's voice trailed off as she stared out the window. "There's a horse and buggy coming up the driveway. I'd better see who it is." She dropped the dish towel on the counter and hurried out the door.

Lydia watched out the window as the horse pulled up to the hitching rail. She was surprised to see Menno and his four boys get out of the buggy. After Menno tied up the horse, he and the boys followed Mom into the house.

Lydia wrung out the dishcloth and greeted them when they entered the kitchen.

"We were driving by and thought we'd drop in and see how you're doing," Menno said, smiling at Lydia.

Josh, who'd been playing in the living room, raced into the kitchen and rushed over to Kevin. "Wanna go out to the barn and play with the busslin?"

Kevin looked up at Menno, as though seeking his approval.

"Jah, sure," Menno said. "Why don't all of you boys go out to the barn while I sit and visit with Lydia and Mae?"

When the boys rushed out the door, Mom turned to Lydia and said, "It's kind of stuffy in the house. Why don't you and Menno go out on the porch and visit? I'll be there in a minute with some refreshments for us."

"I'll help you," Lydia was quick to say. She didn't want Menno to think she was the kind of daughter who'd let her mother do all the work while she sat and visited.

Mom shook her head. "Go on out to the porch. I can manage fine on my own."

Lydia was tempted to argue, but that would be pointless. She'd never won an argument with Mom. Besides, it would be embarrassing to make an issue of it in front of Menno. So she followed him silently out the door and took a seat on the porch swing.

"You look tired," Menno said, lowering himself onto the swing beside her.

"I've been working longer hours at the restaurant lately."

"How come? Are they shorthanded?"

Lydia twirled the ties on her head covering around her fingers while shaking her head. "With Grandpa's hospital bills, we need the extra money." She chose not to mention that there was very little money left in Grandpa's bank account.

Before Menno could respond, Kevin bounded out of the barn and leaped onto the porch. "Come see the busslin, Papa!"

"In a minute, son. I'm talkin' to Lydia right now."

Kevin tugged on Menno's shirtsleeve. "Kumme, before they run away."

Menno grunted as he rose from the swing. "Guess I'd better have a look at those kittens," he said to Lydia.

She gave a nod. "You go ahead. We can talk later."

A few minutes went by, and Mom stepped out the door with a tray of chocolate chip cookies, a jug of milk, and some paper cups. "Where's Menno?" she asked as she placed the tray on a table near the door.

"He went to the barn to look at the kittens," Lydia replied.

"How come you didn't go with him?"

"I've seen the kittens plenty of times and thought it would be nice just to sit here and relax."

Mom motioned to the tray she'd brought out. "Help yourself to some cookies."

"No thanks, I'm not hungry."

"How about some milk?"

"I'm fine, Mom."

Mom seated herself in one of the chairs on the porch. "It was nice of Menno to stop by, don't you think?"

"Uh-huh." Lydia leaned against the porch swing and closed her eyes.

"Don't fall asleep. I'm sure Menno will be back any minute, and you don't want to be rude."

Lydia's eyes snapped open. "I wasn't planning to sleep. I'm just trying to relax."

"Oh."

Lydia was relieved when Mom didn't say anything more. She turned her attention to a robin tugging on a fat worm it had pulled from the grass.

Several minutes later, with a whoop and a holler, Menno's boys and Josh raced from the barn. Menno lagged behind. When they stepped onto the porch, Mom motioned to the tray. "Please, help yourselves."

The boys grabbed a handful of cookies and ran back into the yard, hollering and chasing each other around the maple trees.

Menno took two cookies and a cup of

milk, then sat beside Lydia on the swing. "The cookies are good," he said, after he'd taken a bite. "Did you make 'em, Lydia?"

"No, Mom did. Since I'm working full-time I don't have time to do much baking."

"I'm just thankful you have a job, be-cause one of us needs to be working right now," Mom said.

Just then, Josh and Kevin bounded onto the porch, each holding a kitten. "Can I take this busslin home?" Kevin asked, holding the kitten out to his father.

Menno shook his head. "We've got enough to deal with at our place right now without havin' to worry about a kitten un-derfoot."

Kevin thrust out his lower lip. "Dennis and Ike have a *hund*. Why can't I have a bussli?"

"Ike and Dennis are old enough to take care of their dog," Menno said. "You and Carl can't even keep your toys picked up."

"You can come here and see the kittens anytime you like," Mom said, smiling at Kevin. "Why don't you bring the boys here for supper on Saturday evening?" she added, looking at Menno.

He smiled. "That'd be real nice."

Mom looked down at Josh. "See now, you can play with the boys when they come over on Saturday."

Josh nodded eagerly and gave Kevin a big grin. *"Ich schpiele gem."*

"I like to play, too," Kevin said.

The boys grabbed two more cookies, tromped down the steps, and joined the others chasing each other around the trees.

"It's sure hot out today," Ike shouted as he thumped Dennis on the back. "Wish we woulda brought some balloons along, 'cause we coulda put water in 'em and then pitched the balloons at each other to cool off."

"I'm glad they didn't bring any balloons," Menno mumbled. "The last time they played with water balloons, Kevin started bawling because the others ganged up on him." He grabbed another cookie and dunked it in his milk. "Then Ike threw a balloon that landed on the porch, and I slipped in the water, fell, and skinned my knees."

"I don't know how you manage to keep up with four active boys," Mom said. "Makes me almost glad Lydia was an only child."

Lydia was tempted to comment on that but chose to remain silent. Truth was, she'd always wished she'd had a few siblings. Unfortunately, Mom's uterus had been damaged when Lydia was born, so she wasn't able to have more children.

Menno grimaced. "Almost every day, I wonder how much longer I can keep up with my boys. But I love 'em, and we try to make the best of our situation."

The boys continued to romp around the yard, playing with the kittens and chasing each other in a game of tag. Every once in a while, Menno hollered something at one of them; then he turned to Lydia and said, "Gotta stay on those boys all the time."

I think Menno's boys need a mother more than Josh needs a father, Lydia mused. *I wonder if Menno will ever get married again.*

CHAPTER 20

Are you sure you won't change your mind and go with us?" Lydia asked Mom as she and Josh prepared to leave for the Stutzmans'.

Mom shook her head. "I've got a *kop-pweh*, and I wouldn't be good company this evening."

"I'm sorry to hear you have a headache. Is there anything I can do for you before Josh and I leave?"

Mom flapped her hand. "I'll be fine. Besides, it'll be kind of nice to spend some quiet time alone."

Josh tugged on Lydia's hand. "Can I

take my bussli to show Levi and his brieder?"

Lydia shook her head. "If Levi and his brothers want to see the kittens, they'll have to come over here."

Josh's eyes brightened. *"Mariye?"*

She patted the top of his head. "Probably not tomorrow, but they'll come over sometime, I'm sure."

As Nona rushed around the kitchen getting supper ready, her heart swelled with hope. Lydia and Josh would be here soon, and from the way Levi had been whistling for the last hour, she had a hunch he was looking forward to their visit even more than she was. Could it be because he'd taken an interest in Josh, or did Levi have his eye on the boy's mother?

Nona couldn't help but hope for the latter. Despite Levi's insistence that he would never marry, she had a hunch that he really wanted to fall in love and start a family of his own. From the short time Nona had known her, she'd concluded that Lydia would make a good wife. She seemed to be hardworking, even-tempered, and a good mother to Josh. She liked to laugh and have a good time. She also seemed to accept Levi's family for who they were and didn't appear to be the least bit put off by their small stature. Lydia was nothing like her mother, who seemed to want to keep her distance.

I wonder if Mae will come with Lydia and Josh this evening, Nona thought as she opened the oven to check on the roast. *If Mae got to know us, maybe she wouldn't be so standoffish.*

"Do you want us to start setting the table yet?" Betty asked when she and Selma entered the kitchen.

Nona smiled. Such thoughtful girls she had. "That's a good idea. Then we'll be ready when our company gets here."

"How come we're having Lydia and Josh over again?" Selma wanted to know. "They've never had all of us to their house for supper, just Levi."

Nona shook her finger. "We don't have others for supper in the hopes of getting an invitation to eat at their house."

"That's right," Betty put in. "Besides, Lydia and her mamm are having a hard time financially right now. They probably can't afford to feed a bunch of people."

Nona's eyes narrowed. "Where'd you hear that?"

"Heard you telling Levi and Pop about it the other day at the store."

"Were you eavesdropping?"

"No, Mom. I was coming out of the back room and heard you say that Lydia had asked her boss for extra hours because she needed more money."

Nona guessed she couldn't reprimand Betty for overhearing the conversation she'd had with Levi and Harold. After all, she herself, had overheard the conversation Lydia and her boss had been having, and she hadn't intentionally been listening. "Well girls, just be sure you don't mention what you heard to anyone," Nona said. "We don't want rumors getting started in our community, and we don't want Lydia to think I invited them for supper because I feel sorry about their situation."

"We won't mention it to anyone," Betty said.

Selma nodded. "Will Lydia's mamm be comin' with them this evening?"

Nona shrugged. "I don't know, but I hope so."

"Guess we'll know soon enough," Betty

said, looking out the window. "A horse and buggy's coming up the lane right now."

As soon as Lydia pulled her horse and buggy to a stop, Josh scrambled out of the buggy and raced across the yard to the swing set, where Levi's brother Andy was playing.

A few seconds later, Levi stepped out of the barn. "I'll take care of your horse," he said to Lydia.

"Danki, I appreciate that." Levi seemed like such a thoughtful man. In many ways he reminded her of Jeremiah—kind, easygoing, and full of good humor. She wondered why Levi wasn't married. Surely some woman should have set her *kapp* for him by now.

Levi led Buttercup into the barn, and Lydia followed. "I see your mamm didn't come with you," he said.

"Mom came down with a koppweh, so she stayed home to rest."

He put the horse in one of the empty stalls. "Sorry to hear she has a headache. Mom will be disappointed that she couldn't come."

"Maybe some other time." Truth was,

Lydia doubted that Mom would ever come here for supper.

"Shall we get the boys and head up to the house?" Levi asked after he'd brushed the horse down and given her some water to drink. "Everyone else is inside, and I'm sure Mom has supper ready by now."

Lydia followed Levi out of the barn and across the yard. When they approached the swings, Levi told the boys it was time to go inside.

"Aw, do we have to?" Andy wrinkled his nose. "Josh and me were gonna play with my gees awhile."

"Maybe you can play with the goat after supper." Levi thumped Andy's shoulder. "Mom's fixing roast beef and mashed potatoes tonight. You wouldn't want to miss out on that, now would you?"

"No way!" Andy grabbed Josh's hand, and they ran toward the house as fast as their short legs would take them.

"Roast beef sounds good," Lydia said as she and Levi stepped onto the porch.

He jiggled his eyebrows playfully and grinned at her. "Mom didn't want you to think the only thing she could cook was Frogmore Stew."

Lydia laughed. "I'd never heard of Frog-more Stew before that night, but it was sure good—and fun to eat."

"We're all about having fun around here," Levi said as he opened the back door for Lydia.

When they stepped into the kitchen, Lydia was greeted with the tantalizing aroma of freshly cooked beef. She glanced at the table, which was set with plates and silverware.

Nona's face broke into a wide smile. "It's good to see you again, Lydia. We're glad you could come."

"Josh and I are glad to be here," Lydia said. "We appreciate your inviting us to join you for supper again."

"I'm sorry your mamm's not with you. Did she have other plans for this evening?" Nona asked.

Lydia explained about Mom having a headache, and then she asked if there was anything she could do to help with the meal.

"Nope, not a thing." Nona motioned to the table. "Everything's on, and we'll be ready to eat as soon as Harold and the others get washed up."

Lydia looked down at Josh. "I think you'd better wash your hands, don't you?"

"I'll take him to the bathroom," Andy offered.

"Andy, you be sure and wash, too, and don't forget to use soap," Nona called as the boys bounded out of the room.

When they gathered around the table a short time later, Lydia asked Harold how he was doing.

He lifted his arm and grinned. "Real well. I'll be getting the cast off in another week or so."

"That's good to hear."

Everyone bowed for prayer. When it was over, Nona passed the platter of roast beef.

As they ate the meal, plenty of conversation and a few jokes were shared around the table—mostly from Harold and Nona, although Levi contributed a joke he'd heard recently, as well.

"Why don't eggs tell each other jokes?" he asked Josh.

Josh shrugged. "I don't know."

"Because they'd crack each other up."

Everyone but Josh laughed. Lydia wasn't sure he'd understood Levi's joke.

Harold looked over at Lydia. "Have there

been a lot of tourists at the restaurant since you've been working there?"

"I'm really not sure. I haven't figured out how to tell the difference between a tourist and someone who lives in the area," she replied.

"Many times a tourist will have a camera with 'em, and some of the things they say can be a dead giveaway."

"Like what?"

"Well, the other day a man and his wife came into the store, and I knew right away that they were tourists when the woman said she'd noticed that she'd seen lights on our Amish buggies and wanted to know if the buggies had batteries in them. I told her they did, and then her husband bobbed his head a few times and said, 'I told ya so, Helen. I knew those horses couldn't pull such big buggies all by themselves." Harold leaned his head back and roared. "Can you believe anyone would actually think such a thing?"

Lydia, wondering if the story was true, looked over at Nona for confirmation.

Nona nodded and grinned. "It's true all right; I was there when those English tourists came in."

Lydia snickered. She guessed she'd have to listen better to what some of her restaurant customers said. Maybe after she'd worked there awhile, she'd have some humorous stories to share with the Stutzmans.

"Can Andy come over to see my bussli tomorrow?" Josh asked around a mouthful of mashed potatoes.

Andy looked at Levi with a hopeful expression. "Can ya take me over there tomorrow?"

Levi nodded. "Not until evening, though. I'll be working at the store all day."

Lydia was about to say that tomorrow would be fine, but then she remembered that Mom had invited Menno and his boys for supper. "Actually, we have other plans for tomorrow evening," she told Levi. "Could you come by to see the kittens on Sunday afternoon?"

"Sure, that'll be fine."

"All this talk about Andy seeing Josh's kittens makes me think about a story I heard the other day," Harold said.

"What story's that?" his ten-year-old son Peter asked.

"Well, it seems that a little boy lost his

kitten." Harold paused to push his glasses back in place. "Anyway, the boy's daed decided to call the sheriff to see if he could help find the kitten. He was told that looking for a kitten wasn't a job for the sheriff, and he was too busy for that." Harold leaned closer to Josh with a serious expression. "You know what the man said?"

Josh shook his head.

"He said, 'You don't understand, Sheriff. This is a very smart kitten. He's so smart he can almost talk.' Then the sheriff said, 'Well, mister, you'd better hang up the phone, 'cause that clever little kitten might be tryin' to call you right now.'"

Everyone laughed, especially Harold. If there was one thing Lydia had come to realize about Levi's family, it was that they liked to laugh at their own jokes.

The rest of the evening went much the same—filled with lively banter and lots of good food.

When Lydia saw the clock and realized how late it was getting she said it was time for her and Josh to go home.

Josh's chin jutted out. "But me and Andy didn't get to play with the gees."

"You can do that the next time you come

over," Nona said. She hurriedly put some of the leftovers, including three pieces of chocolate cake, into a box and insisted that Lydia take it home with her.

"Danki for the delicious meal," Lydia said. "We had a really good time."

Nona smiled and stood on her tiptoes to give Lydia a hug. "You're more than welcome. We'll have to do it again sometime."

All heads nodded in agreement.

"Don't forget to come see my bussli," Josh said to Andy as they headed out the door.

"*Sunndaag.*" Andy grinned widely. "I'll see ya on Sunndaag afternoon."

"I'll get your horse and buggy." Levi hurried past Lydia and headed to the barn.

By the time Lydia and Josh got there, Levi had taken Buttercup out and was hitching her to the buggy.

Once again, Lydia appreciated Levi's kindness. But then, was it any wonder he was so kind and helpful? His folks had obviously set a good example for Levi and his siblings, who'd been most gracious this evening.

When Levi bent down and scooped Josh up, Josh wrapped his arms around

Levi's neck. "Wish I could stay here," he said, nuzzling Levi's cheek with his nose. "Wish you were my daed."

Levi's cheeks flamed. Lydia could only imagine how embarrassed he must be.

"Say good-bye to Levi," she said, reaching for Josh. "We need to get home now."

"Bye, Levi," Josh said, before she placed him in the buggy.

"See you on Sunday." Levi lifted his hand in a wave. "Drive safely."

Lydia climbed into the driver's side and took up the reins. She'd need to have a talk with Josh on the way home about his comment to Levi. It wouldn't be good for Josh to get any ideas about Levi becoming his father, because from what she could tell, Levi saw her as nothing more than a friend.

"Is *Daadi* in heaven?" Josh asked suddenly.

"Jah, I believe he is."

"Wish I could go to heaven and visit Daadi and Urgrossvadder."

Before Lydia could think of a response, the buggy began to wobble. When it tipped toward one side, she wondered if the right front wheel had come loose.

"Oh, great," she mumbled as she pulled to the shoulder of the road so she could look things over. If the wheel wasn't too loose, they might be able to make it home. If not, she'd leave the buggy here, unhitch the horse, and lead it home. Tomorrow morning, she'd call the buggy maker to fix the wheel.

"Stay in your seat while I have a look at the wheel," Lydia said to Josh. She stepped down from the buggy and had just knelt on the ground beside the wheel, when Josh hopped out and darted into the road.

Before Lydia could get to her feet, a car crested the hill and slammed into Josh.

Lydia gasped and dashed into the road. Her precious boy's head and shirt was covered with blood as he lay there, unmoving. A scream tore from Lydia's throat. "No! No! No!"

CHAPTER 21

Soon after Lydia and Josh left, Levi decided to sit on the porch awhile and enjoy the cool breeze that had come up.

When he leaned against the back of his chair and closed his eyes, a vision of Josh playing with Andy popped into his head. Even with four years between the boys, they got along remarkably well. He wondered if it was because they were almost the same size, or because they liked so many of the same things.

Levi's thoughts went to Lydia, and he smiled, remembering how hard she'd laughed at his family's silly jokes. It was obvious by the way Mom made over Lydia that she liked her a lot.

I like her, too, Levi thought. *I just can't allow myself to give in to those feelings.*

The wail of a siren brought his thoughts to a halt, and his eyes snapped open. He glanced toward the road and saw a rescue vehicle with flashing red lights whiz by.

Curious as to where the vehicle was going, Levi stepped off the porch and grabbed his bike. As he started down the road, he saw the red lights up ahead, where the vehicle seemed to be stopped. There'd been an accident.

With heart pounding and hands sweating, Levi peddled faster. He dreaded what he might find. Accidents involving Amish buggies happened too often here in Holmes County.

As Levi drew closer to the rescue vehicle he heard a woman sobbing. Shock and concern stabbed his heart when he saw Lydia bent over a small body covered in blood. *Oh dear Lord, not Josh!*

Levi leaped off his bike, letting it fall to the ground, and rushed over to Lydia. "What happened? Were you involved in an accident?"

Lydia's eyes were wide as she lifted her tear-stained face to him and slowly shook her head. "My buggy was wobbling, so I . . . I stopped to see if the wheel had come loose, and then—" Her voice faltered as she choked on a sob. "Josh jumped out of the buggy and—and he ran into the road. Then a car came over the hill, and . . ."

Levi slipped his arm around Lydia's trembling shoulders; she was clearly in shock. "The ambulance is here. They'll take Josh to the hospital, and everything will be all right." As the words slipped off Levi's tongue, he knew they weren't true. Josh was barely breathing. From the looks of all the blood on the boy's head and shirt, he'd no doubt sustained serious injuries.

When the paramedics lifted Josh onto a stretcher and placed it in the back of the ambulance, Lydia followed.

"I'll take your horse and buggy to your house and let your mamm know what's happened," Levi told Lydia as she climbed into the ambulance. "I'll see that she gets a ride to the hospital."

Lydia gave a brief nod, but Levi wasn't sure she'd even heard what he'd said.

Heavenly Father, Levi prayed, as he lifted his bike into the back of her buggy, *please be with Josh, and give Lydia the strength to deal with what lies ahead.*

&

As Lydia sat in the hospital waiting room, anxious for some news on Josh, she pled with God to spare her son's life. She nearly choked on the bile rising in her throat as she thought about how still Josh had been on the way to the hospital, and how he'd never even opened his eyes. Josh couldn't die. She needed him, and he needed her. What had happened to the happy time they'd had this evening? All the joy Lydia had felt when they'd left the Stutzmans' had been snatched away in one split second.

Lydia wondered about the young English woman who'd been driving the car. She'd apologized to Lydia several times and said she hadn't been speeding, that she couldn't stop in time because Josh darted in front of her so quickly. The woman had used her cell phone to call for help and then stayed right beside Lydia while they waited. Lydia was sure the woman hadn't hit Josh on purpose, but she couldn't help feeling angry, nonetheless. *She should have been watching closer. One never knows what they'll find when they come over the crest of a hill.*

Someone touched Lydia's arm, and she jerked her head. Mom stood beside Lydia's chair with a pained expression. "Levi told me what happened. He arranged for me to get a ride to the hospital." She took a seat in the empty chair beside Lydia and reached for her hand. "Has there been any word on Josh's condition?"

"Not yet." Tears welled in Lydia's eyes and dribbled onto her cheeks. "I'm trying to be patient. I'm trying to be brave. I—I'm praying for the faith to believe that Josh is going to be okay." The words stuck in her throat.

"Levi said when he was getting ready to take your horse and buggy home that he'd noticed a cat on the other side of the road. I wonder if Josh saw the cat, too, and decided to chase after it."

"M—maybe." Lydia swallowed hard. "If only he'd stayed in the buggy like I told him to. I wish . . ." She stopped talking and leaned back in her chair. Wishing wouldn't change a thing.

They sat in silence for the next hour until a doctor came into the room and called Lydia by name.

"I'm Dr. Cummings. I need to speak to you about your son."

Lydia leaped out of her chair and moved quickly toward the doctor. "Is . . . is Josh going to be all right? Is he seriously hurt?"

"I'm sorry to tell you this, but your boy has suffered severe head and internal injuries, and he's in a coma." The doctor's dark eyes were filled with compassion. "I'm not God, so I don't know what the future holds, but if Josh is going to pull through, he'll need a miracle."

Lydia squeezed her eyes shut. *Send us a miracle, Lord. Oh, please, heal my son.*

CHAPTER 22

For the next four days, Lydia never left the hospital. She sat in the chair beside Josh's bed, holding his hand and praying for a miracle. She even slept in the chair and left Josh's room only long enough to use the restroom or get something to drink. She had no appetite for food and hadn't eaten much of anything, despite constant pleadings from Mom. The concern she felt for Josh had robbed her of any appetite.

As Lydia sat beside Josh's bed, staring at his still form, her heart felt heavy with grief. The doctors and nurses had done all they could, but there'd been no change in his condition, and she was beginning to doubt he'd ever come out of his coma.

She reached out to stroke Josh's pale cheek. It was bruised and swollen, and the bandage on his head nearly covered his eyes. He didn't even look like her boy anymore.

She drew in a deep breath and tried to relax. Worrying wouldn't change anything; she needed to hold strong to her faith and keep praying until Josh got well. She needed to believe that God would heal her boy, but her faith was weakening with each passing hour.

Lydia leaned her head against the back of the chair and closed her eyes, reflecting on how many people had come to the hospital to offer their support: Nona and Levi, Menno, Rueben, the bishop and his wife, and several women from their Amish community.

Lydia's boss had also come by. She'd told Lydia that she didn't have to worry about returning to work until she felt ready and that her job would be there for her. That was a relief. Lydia didn't know what they'd do without her job. But her meager income wouldn't be enough to pay all of Josh's hospital bills that were quickly mounting up. She'd be paying those for a long time and would probably have to rely on others for assistance. But whatever money she had to spend wouldn't matter at all if Josh got well. His precious life was worth any amount of money.

The door to Josh's room swished open, and Lydia opened her eyes just as Mom entered the room.

"How's he doing?" Mom asked, stepping up to Josh's bed. "Has there been any change?"

Lydia shook her head as she fought for control. "I talk to him all the time, but he never moves or gives any response to my voice."

"You look awful." Mom touched Lydia's shoulder. "When was the last time you had something to eat?"

Lydia shrugged. "I can't remember."

"You're going to make yourself sick if you don't eat. What good will you be to Josh then?"

"Do you think he'll ever wake up, Mom? Do you think God will answer our prayers?"

"If it's God will for Josh to recover, then

he surely will." Mom took Lydia's hand and pulled her gently to her feet. "I want you to come with me to the cafeteria so we can get something to eat."

With a heavy sigh, Lydia followed Mom out the door.

Menno had just finished lining out the work that needed to be done in his shop this morning, when, *floop!*—a fat little frog landed in the cup of lukewarm coffee sitting on his desk. It stayed a few seconds, then leaped to the desk and sat there like it had found a new home.

"What in the world?" Menno glanced around the room and spotted Kevin and Carl giggling and running back and forth between a stack of lumber. "All right now, which of you boys brought a frog in here?"

Kevin pointed at Carl, and Carl pointed at Kevin.

Menno grimaced. "When I brought you in here to help today, I said there'd be no fooling around."

"Sorry," Carl mumbled as he lifted the frog from Menno's desk. "We'll take it outside and put it in the creek."

"When you get that done, I want you back in here to help Ike and Dennis sweep the sawdust that's piled up on the floor."

"Okay, Papa," the boys said before they scooted out the door.

Menno went to the sink across the room, dumped out what was left of his coffee, and poured himself another cup. As he sat at his desk, looking over some paperwork, he thought about Josh and wondered how he was doing. Due to Josh's accident, he and the boys hadn't been able to go to Lydia and Mae's for supper last Saturday as planned. Even if Josh survived, it would be some time before he was up to company.

Menno glanced at Ike and Dennis as they swept the floor. *Don't know what I'd do if something happened to one of my boys. Can't imagine what Lydia must be going through right now.*

Menno had gone to the hospital a couple of times since Josh's accident, but so far, there'd been no change in his condition. Kevin had wanted to go along, but Menno had said no. It wouldn't be good for Kevin to see his friend in such a horrible state.

※

"I'm really not hungry." Lydia pushed her food tray toward the edge of the table. "I don't want to be away from Josh's room too long. If he wakes up and doesn't find me there, he'll be scared."

"Lydia, please . . . you've got to eat a little bit," Mom coaxed.

"I can't. I'm going back to Josh's room." Lydia jumped up and raced from the cafeteria. She knew Mom had followed her, for she heard her footsteps echoing in the corridor behind her.

When they stepped into the hallway outside Josh's room, Dr. Cummings rushed up to Lydia. "I've been looking for you."

Hope welled in her chest. "Is it Josh? Is he awake?"

The doctor slowly shook his head. "I'm sorry to have to tell you this, but Josh is gone."

Gone? The words barely registered in Lydia's brain.

"He died a few minutes ago."

A chill rippled through Lydia's body, and she swayed unsteadily as her blood ran cold and her head began to spin. "I need to see him. I need to see my boy."

"Of course."

Dr. Cummings opened the door to Josh's room, but before Lydia could go inside, Mom touched her arm. "I'll go with you."

A sob rose in Lydia's throat and came out in a scream. "No! I need to be alone with him!"

Mom moved aside, and Lydia stepped into the room. As she approached Josh's bed, her knees threatened to buckle. He was no longer hooked up to any machines. There was no sign of life in his little body, and she knew for a certainty that he wouldn't be coming back to her. Josh had gotten his wish; he was in heaven now with his daadi and urgrossvadder.

CHAPTER 23

Tears trickled onto Lydia's cheeks as the pallbearers took Josh's small casket from the wagon and carried it to the gravesite that had been prepared for him. As she watched the casket being placed on three wooden boards that had been set over the gaping hole, the shrill cry of a crow pierced the quietness that lay over the cemetery.

It seemed so unreal, as if it was happening to someone else. Josh couldn't be dead. That couldn't be the body of her sweet little boy inside the cold wooden box. The anguish Lydia felt was like nothing she'd ever experienced. Losing Jeremiah, as painful as it had been, hadn't compared to the emptiness and grief that consumed her whole being right now.

Her legs trembled as she stood on the uneven ground next to Mom and the other mourners who'd come to share in her grief. Lydia wished more than anything that she'd never moved to Charm. If she and Josh had stayed in Illinois, this wouldn't have happened. Josh would still be alive, happily playing in their yard or coloring a picture at Lydia's kitchen table. Should she go back? But what was there to go back to? Jeremiah was gone, and so was Josh. Nothing would ever be the same.

I wish I'd been nicer to Josh when he was alive, Mae thought as she stared at the small handmade coffin that held her grandson's lifeless body. As the pallbearers set Josh's coffin in place, Mae glanced over at Lydia. Her shoulders shook. Tears streamed down her face. First she'd lost her husband, and now her only son. It didn't seem right that someone as young as Josh should die. The death of a loved one was never easy to accept, but for a mother to lose her child—that just wasn't natural. Parents were supposed to die before their children, not the other way around.

Mae glanced at the group of mourners standing nearby and noticed the look of compassion on Rueben's face. She hadn't been free to begin a relationship with him because of Dad, and now she wasn't free because Lydia would need her.

Maybe someday, she thought, *if he hasn't found someone else by then. But I can't worry about that right now.*

Mae slipped her arm around Lydia's waist. Her first priority was to help her daughter through this horrible time of grief.

As the graveside service came to a close, it tore at Levi's heart to see the look of agony on Lydia's face. It wasn't that long ago that they'd buried her grandfather, and now here they were saying good-bye to her only son. Levi hadn't known Josh very long, but he'd quickly established a fondness for the boy. He couldn't imagine how Lydia would deal with the loss of her son in the days ahead. It would probably be a long time before she'd come to grips with it. If there was only something he could say or do to comfort Lydia during this time of grief.

Levi's brother Andy had taken Josh's death hard, too. He'd been looking forward to visiting Josh last Sunday and seeing the kittens he'd found in the barn. Andy had been so upset that he hadn't wanted to come to the funeral today. Mom had agreed to let Selma stay home with him, while Betty and Peter took care of things at the store.

When Levi heard a familiar series of honking, he looked up and saw a flock of geese flying overhead in a perfect V formation. He didn't know why, but it made him think of Josh, whom he felt certain, was flying free in heaven with no more pain.

During the funeral dinner that followed the graveside service, Lydia received condolences from many people, including Levi and his family. It was hard to know what to say in reply to their sympathetic comments, and with each hug or look of concern, her heart felt like it was being torn in two. Even with the support of these caring people, she couldn't accept the fact that

God had taken her son, and she wasn't sure that she could go on without him. Besides missing Josh for the joy that he'd brought to her, Lydia's precious boy was the last link she had to Jeremiah. She missed them both so much. Why hadn't God answered her prayers and made Josh well? She felt as though He'd turned His back on her.

"Let us know if there's anything we can do to help," Nona said, giving Lydia a hug.

Lydia, feeling as though she were in a fog, could only manage a nod.

Levi stepped forward then, speaking in a tone of comfort and hope, but his words barely registered in her brain. She just wanted the day to be over so she could go to her room and be alone.

When Levi's family moved aside, Menno and his youngest boy, Kevin stepped up to Lydia. "I'm sorry for your loss," Menno said. "I know how hard it can be to lose someone you love."

"Jah." Lydia's throat felt so swollen she could barely speak, and her fuzzy head had begun to pound.

Kevin looked up at her with tears in his

eyes. "Papa says Josh went to heaven. He said my mamm's there, too."

All Lydia could do was nod. *Please leave me alone. I wish everyone would just stop talking to me and go home.*

As though he could read her mind, Menno nudged Kevin's arm. "Go find Ike now, and tell him I said to get our horse and buggy ready. It's time for us to head home." He touched Lydia's arm lightly before he moved away.

"Why don't you go up to your room and rest awhile?" Mom said when she joined Lydia a few minutes later. "You look so *mied*."

"I . . . I am tired, and I've developed a koppweh."

"Go rest then. You really need it."

Lydia shuffled toward the stairs. She wished she could crawl into bed, close her eyes, and never wake up. She wished God had taken her instead of Josh.

CHAPTER 24

Lydia blinked against the first rays of morning sunlight streaming through her bedroom window. She didn't want it to be morning. She didn't want to get up. She wanted to stay in bed but knew she couldn't. There were bills to pay, and she was the only one in this house with a job.

It had been one week since Josh's death, and despite the agonizing depression Lydia felt, she'd forced herself to go to the phone shed yesterday and call Edith, letting her know that she planned to return to work today.

A dog howled from a neighboring farm, and June bugs thumped against Lydia's bedroom window as though calling her to get up.

Drawing in a deep breath and mustering all the strength she could, Lydia pulled herself out of bed and plodded over to the window. Pushing the curtains aside, her gaze came to rest on two furry gray kittens scampering across the lawn as they chased after a butterfly. Across the road, in the neighbor's pasture, she saw a spindly colt nursing from its mother.

Tears flooded Lydia's eyes and dribbled onto her cheeks. Josh had loved to play with the kittens and always enjoyed watching the horses. He'd enjoyed anything that involved being outdoors. Were there animals in heaven for Josh to play with? She surely hoped so.

Lydia caught sight of the sign out by the road, a few feet from the entrance of their driveway. It read: WELCOME TO CHARM.

"Welcome, indeed," she mumbled. "Moving to Charm has brought me nothing but misery." She bit down on her bottom lip in an effort to hold back the sob rising in her throat, but it was no use—more tears flowed, and she hiccupped on the cry that erupted.

She gripped the edge of the windowsill and tried to compose herself. She had to get control of her emotions if she was going to return to work. If she didn't start making some money soon, they wouldn't be able to pay any of their bills, and she couldn't expect Edith to keep her job open indefinitely.

I can't keep thinking about the way things might have been if we hadn't moved to Charm, Lydia told herself as she moved determinedly toward her closet. *I must learn to live with things the way they are.*

Soon after Lydia left for work, Mae filled a glass with iced tea and went outside to sit on the porch. It was a warm summer day, and the sun felt good on her tired body. But it did nothing to relieve the ache in her soul. She missed Josh's cheerful smile and felt horrible about all the unkind things she'd said to him when he was alive, even though things had been somewhat better between them before he'd died. She missed Dad, too, and still felt that she'd failed him. Lydia was all she had now, but their relationship continued to be strained, even though Mae had been trying to be supportive.

"It's probably my fault she doesn't respond to me now," she murmured. "I've been nothing but critical and demanding ever since Lydia was a little girl. If only I knew what to do to make things better between us. If I could just give her the comfort she needs."

The *clip-clop* of horse's hooves, and the rumble of buggy wheels, drew Mae's attention to the road. A few seconds later, a horse and buggy turned up the driveway and stopped in front of the hitching rail near the barn. She was surprised when Rueben climbed down, secured the horse, and started for the house.

"Wie geht's?" he asked, stepping onto the porch.

"I . . . I'm okay," she said as she rose to greet him.

He eyed her curiously. "You sure about that?"

Mae shrugged and sighed.

"I just finished shoeing a horse at the next farm over and wondered if there was anything I could do for you here."

She shook her head.

As he leaned against the porch railing with his arms folded, his piercing blue eyes seemed to bore right through her. "There must be something you need to have done."

"I can't think of a thing." Mae didn't want Rueben hanging around, because he might start asking her out again. She wasn't ready for that and didn't know if she ever would be.

He stepped forward and cradled her shoulders in his strong hands. "I'm your friend, Mae. I really do want to help."

"I . . . I don't need any help."

"I think you do. I think if nothing else, you need a friend who'll listen to how you're feeling right now." Rueben sounded so sincere, and Mae wondered if he might have an even softer heart than she'd imagined.

"I feel like a failure in so many ways." She lowered her gaze, unable to look at him because she didn't want him to see the tears in her eyes.

"No one is a failure who has friends," he said, lifting her chin with his thumb, so she was forced to look at his face. "A friend is someone who knows the song in your heart and sings it back to you when you've forgotten the words."

She held her arms stiff at her sides, unsure of how to respond.

"I've seen the way you cared for your daed—always putting his needs ahead of your own. Sometimes we get so busy trying to please someone else that we forget about our own needs." Rueben pulled her slowly against his chest.

Mae hesitated at first, but finally relaxed and leaned into his embrace, realizing that it felt wonderful and safe. They stood like that for several minutes, until she finally pulled away.

Rueben's soft, gentle smile filled an empty place in her heart, yet she couldn't give in to her feelings. "I have some things I must do in the house," she said abruptly.

"Okay, but I'll be back to check on you soon. If you need anything between now and then, please leave a message on my answering machine." Rueben slid one finger down the side of Mae's cheek; then he turned and sprinted for his buggy.

Mae, feeling quite shaky and very confused, lowered herself into a chair and drew in a deep breath. She sat like that for several minutes, until another horse and buggy rumbled into the yard. It was Sarah Yoder.

"I brought you a loaf of freshly made raisin bread and a casserole," Sarah said when she stepped onto the porch with a box in her arms. "Shall I put it in the kitchen?"

"That'd be fine. If you're thirsty, help yourself to something cold to drink. There's a jug of sweet meadow tea in the refrigerator."

"All right, I will." Sarah disappeared into the house and returned a few minutes later with a glass of iced tea.

"It was nice of you to bring the food. We can have the casserole for supper this evening, because I know I won't feel like cooking, and I'm sure when Lydia gets home from work she won't be up to it, either."

Sarah quirked an eyebrow. "Lydia went back to work so soon?"

"Uh-huh. I tried to talk her out of going, but she was determined and insisted that we needed the money."

"Maybe you should try to find a job."

"I don't have the energy to go looking, and even if I did, I'm not sure what kind of work I could do." Mae released a lingering sigh. "I've never had to work outside my home, and I have no real skills other than quilting."

"I'm concerned about you." Sarah took Mae's hand. "You look so *verleed*."

"You're right; I am depressed."

"That's understandable. It's only been a week since Josh's funeral, and not long before that you lost your daed."

"I'll admit, losing them has been very upsetting, but I'm also depressed about the way I treated Josh when he was alive."

"How'd you treat him?"

Mae drew in a deep breath and released it with a moan. "I was often impatient and never took the time to enjoy him like I should." She slowly shook her head. "I'm not a good mother to Lydia, either."

"Why do you say that?"

"Things haven't been good between me and Lydia for some time, although they're a little better now, I think. Even so, I blame myself because I've been harsh and demanding with her ever since she was a girl."

Tears welled in Mae's eyes. "My husband's gone, my father's gone, and now my grandson's gone. I can't seem to help Lydia deal with her grief, and I feel as though she's pulling further and further from me." She blinked and swiped at the tears that had fallen onto her cheeks. "I . . . I feel as though I have nothing left."

Sarah reached into her purse and handed Mae a tissue. "You have God. And when you feel as if you have nothing left, then you'll realize that God is enough. You also have your friends."

Mae blotted the dampness on her cheeks with the tissue and blew her nose. "I . . . I know I do, and I appreciate that, but I feel so guilty, and I wish I could change the past."

"No one can change the past, but we can seek forgiveness and go on from there, trying to be a better person."

Mae nodded. "That's what I want . . . to be a better mother to Lydia and try to build a stronger, more loving relationship be-tween us, but it may take some time."

Sarah wrapped her arms around Mae, and Mae found comfort, just as she had in the hug Rueben had given her.

"I need to go now," Sarah said, rising from her chair. "But I want to leave you with a verse of scripture that I think might help. Psalm 32, verse 8, says: 'I will instruct thee and teach thee in the way which thou shalt go: I will guide thee with mine eye.'"

As Mae watched Sarah walk to her buggy, a sense of peace flooded her soul. If she allowed God to teach her in the way she should go, maybe she'd know how to help Lydia deal with her pain.

❦

"I hope we get served right away," Selma said to Nona as the two of them crossed the parking lot of Grandma's Restaurant. "I'm really *ausghungert.*"

Nona chuckled. "You don't look starved to me."

"I am, though. That appointment with the chiropractor took longer than I thought, and it's way past lunchtime."

"Well, we're here now, so let's see if they have a table for us." Nona opened the door to the restaurant and stepped in.

They waited a few minutes and were shown to a table in the back of the room near the kitchen. Several minutes went by, and then Lydia showed up at their table.

"I'm surprised to see you here today,"

Nona said. "I didn't think you'd be back at work so soon."

Lydia gave no reply.

"How are you and your mamm doing? Is there anything you need?"

"We're fine." Lydia stared out the window with a strange expression. Nona noticed that her eyes were red-rimmed, and there were dark circles beneath them.

"Isn't she gonna ask what we want to drink?" Selma whispered to Nona.

Nona pursed her lips. Lydia was sure acting strange. It was probably way too soon for her to have come back to work. She touched Lydia's arm. "Selma and I would like something to drink."

Lydia blinked a couple of times. "Wh–what would you like?"

"I'll have a glass of iced tea," Nona said.

"I'd like some lemonade." Selma smiled up at Lydia, but Lydia just turned toward the kitchen without a word.

Ten minutes later, Nona and Selma were still waiting for their beverages, and Lydia hadn't returned to see what they wanted to eat.

"I'm really hungerich, Mama," Selma complained.

"I'm getting pretty hungry myself." Nona glanced around. She hadn't seen Lydia since she'd left their table and couldn't figure out what could be taking her so long to bring their beverages.

A short time later, Lydia walked by, carrying a pot of coffee.

"Excuse me," Nona said, motioning to Lydia, "but we're still waiting for our beverages."

"Oh, I forgot." Lydia hurried off. When she returned, she set a cup of coffee in front of Nona and a glass of milk at Selma's place.

"That's not what we ordered," Selma spoke up.

Nona leaned close to Selma and whispered, "It's okay. Just drink the milk."

Lydia started to move away, but Nona touched her arm and said, "Can you please take our orders now?"

"Oh, okay."

Nona asked for a chef salad, and Selma said she'd like a hamburger.

Lydia walked away without even writing down their orders.

Twenty minutes went by, with no sign of Lydia. Nona was on the verge of asking

Lydia's boss if she knew why their orders hadn't come yet, when she caught sight of Lydia running into the small room at the back of the restaurant. A few seconds later Lydia appeared, carrying her purse. Without a word or glance in Nona's direction, Lydia rushed to the front of the restaurant and hurried outside.

"Now that was sure *fremm*," Selma said.

"You're right, it was strange," Nona agreed. "Lydia hasn't been acting like herself at all today, and I'm very concerned."

CHAPTER 25

As Menno Troyer went to open the restaurant door, Lydia came rushing outside and bumped his shoulder. "Are you all right?" he asked.

Without even looking back, she tore across the parking lot as if she was running from a fire. Could something have happened at home that caused her to leave the restaurant in such a hurry? Should he go after her and ask?

His stomach growled. *Maybe I should mind my own business and get something to eat. She might have just gotten off work and been anxious to get home.*

"I can't believe Lydia would walk off the job and not tell anyone she was leaving," Carolyn, one of the waitresses said to Lydia's boss, Edith.

Menno's ears perked up, and he moved closer to where the women stood near the front counter.

"Several of the customers complained that she'd taken their orders some time ago but never brought their food." Edith slowly shook her head. "It's not like Lydia to do such a thing. I'm wondering if she came back to work too soon. Maybe the pressure of waiting tables during the busy lunch hour was too much for her to handle."

"If I'd just lost my little boy a week ago, I don't think I could have returned to work so soon," Carolyn said.

"Lydia said she needed the money, and since we're shorthanded right now, I couldn't say no when she phoned and said she'd like to return to work today." Edith sighed. "Guess I'll have to go over to her house this evening and see what's up. If she can't work, I may need to find someone to take her place, because now that summer's here, we're busier than ever." She glanced over at Menno, and her cheeks turned pink. "Are—are you waiting for a table, Mr. Troyer?"

He nodded. "I was, but if you're too busy here, I can get some lunch over at Carpenter's Café."

Edith slowly nodded. "We're shorthanded right now, so if you're in a hurry, maybe eating somewhere else would be the best idea."

"Okay, thanks." Menno turned and went out the door.

As he crossed the street to Kiem Lumber, he glanced down the road. There was no sign of Lydia, so he figured she must have made it home already. She'd taken Josh's death pretty hard and probably shouldn't have returned to work yet.

Think I'll head over to her place after I close my shop for the day. I really do need to see how she's doing.

"I can't believe I did such a thing." Lydia blinked at the tears stinging her eyes as she sat at the kitchen table telling Mom how she'd walked off the job. "I . . . I don't know what came over me," she wailed. "We were real busy, and it seemed like everyone wanted something at the same time." She sniffed and dabbed at the tears that had dribbled onto her cheeks.

"The strain of working was probably too much for you. I think you went back to the restaurant too soon." Gently, Mom patted Lydia's back. "You really need to take more time off to rest and deal with your grief."

"I can't. We need the money—not just for food, but to pay all the bills that have been mounting up."

"Maybe I can sell some of the quilts I have tucked away," Mom said. "That would help with some of our expenses."

"But it won't be enough, and you only have a few quilts set aside."

"I can make more." Mom sipped her tea. "Of course, that will take some time."

"With Josh gone, I feel so empty inside." The words caught in Lydia's throat, and she nearly choked on a sob she couldn't control. "I feel like I have nothing left."

"That's not true. You have me, and we both have God."

Lydia sniffed and blew her nose on a napkin. "Right now it doesn't seem like I have God at all. Since Josh died, I haven't felt God's presence."

"Sarah Yoder came by this morning, and she gave me some good advice."

"What was it?"

"She said that when you feel as if you have nothing left, then you'll become aware that God is enough."

Lydia felt a dull throb in the back of her neck as she let Mom's words roll around in her mind. "I know God should be enough, but I miss Josh so much."

"I know you do. I thank God that I've never lost a child, but when I lost your daed, I had an ache in my heart that I wasn't sure would ever leave. Every day, I've had to remind myself that life goes on and that I must make the best of my situation." Mom slipped her arm around Lydia's shoulders. "I know I haven't been the best mother, and I'm sorry for being so critical and harsh with you over the years. Will you forgive me for that?"

Lydia leaned her head on Mom's arm and sniffed deeply. "I forgive you."

Mom and Selma showed up just as Levi had set the ladder in place so he could wash the inside of the store windows.

"It went well at the chiropractor's today."

Mom motioned to Selma. "Dr. Langley said that if Selma continues to do the exercises he gave her and goes in for regular adjustments, she won't have so much pain in her back."

Levi nodded.

"You're awfully quiet today," Mom said, touching Levi's arm.

"It's hard to talk when you've got a sore throat," he mumbled.

She squinted as she looked up at him. "I didn't realize you had a sore throat. How long's this been going on?"

He shrugged. "A couple of days, I guess."

Deep wrinkles etched her forehead. "And you've never mentioned it?"

Levi rubbed his throat as he spoke in a near whisper. "Thought it would go away on its own."

"Let's go in the back room where there's a flashlight, and I'll have a look at your throat."

Levi groaned. "I don't think there's any need for that."

She pursed her lips as she shook her head. "Don't argue with me now. I need to see if your throat looks infected."

Levi followed Mom into the back room.

If he didn't let her look at his throat, she'd pester him about it the rest of the day.

"Have a seat, and I'll get the flashlight," Mom instructed.

Levi pulled out a chair at the small table and sat down. Mom stepped up to him a few seconds later with the flashlight. "Open your mouth and stick out your tongue."

Levi did as she'd said. *"Ahhh . . ."*

Mom frowned deeply. "Oh, oh. It doesn't look good, Levi. Your throat's awful red, and your tonsils look swollen." She placed her hand on Levi's forehead. "Feels to me like you're running a fever. You need to see the doctor right away because you've obviously got some kind of infection going on."

"That's just great," Levi mumbled. "This is not what I need; I don't have time to be sick."

"No one ever has the time to be sick, but the sooner you see the doctor, the sooner you'll get well. I'll phone Dr. Shaffer's office and see if you can be seen today." She was almost to the door when she halted and turned around.

"Is there something else?" he asked.

"I hate to bring this up when you're not feeling well, but I'm concerned about Lydia.

After Selma's appointment, we went to Grandma's Restaurant for lunch, and I was surprised to see Lydia there, waiting tables."

"It's only been a week since Josh's funeral. She shouldn't have gone back to work so soon."

"I know." Deep wrinkles creased Mom's forehead. "She wasn't acting like herself at all and ended up rushing out of the restaurant without even bringing us our food."

"You're kidding?"

"Huh-uh. Lydia just went into the back room, grabbed her purse, and ran out the front door." Mom compressed her lips like she often did when she was deep in thought. "I'm thinking about going over to her place to check on her."

"You mean, right now?"

"No, after we close the store for the day."

"I don't think that's a good idea, Mom."

"Why not?"

"The last time you were there, Mae gave you the cold shoulder. Besides, Lydia might not appreciate you butting into her business."

"I don't plan to butt in. I just want to check and see if she's all right."

Levi shook his head. "The best thing

you can do is pray for Lydia and give her more time to grieve for Josh."

"Maybe you're right," Mom finally said. "I don't want to seem pushy, and I don't want Lydia to think I'm upset with her for running out on us today. For the time being, I'll just pray for Lydia." She turned toward the door again. "I'm going to call the doctor now."

Levi let his head fall forward into the palms of his hands. It wasn't bad enough that his throat felt so sore he could barely swallow; now he was worried about Lydia.

CHAPTER 26

That evening after supper, Lydia had just begun to help Mom clear the table when a knock sounded on the front door.

"I wonder who that could be," Mom said. "Most folks we know use the back door, not the front."

"Want me to go see?"

"No, that's all right. I'll go." Mom put the plates she held into the sink and hurried from the room. A few minutes later, she was back with Lydia's boss.

"This afternoon, when you rushed out of the restaurant without a word to anyone, I became concerned and decided I'd better check on you," Edith said.

"I'm sorry for my strange behavior," Lydia apologized. "I just couldn't keep up with things today, and I ran out the door without even thinking. I'll understand if you fire me."

Edith shook her head. "You're not fired, but I think you need to rest a few more weeks before you try to come back to work."

"I agree with that," Mom said. "I knew Lydia was going back way too soon."

"But I can't afford to miss too many days of work," Lydia argued. "With all the expenses we have, we need the money even more than before."

"I'll talk to some people in our community about bringing you some food and helping with your expenses," Edith said. "But while you're taking the time you need to rest, I will have to hire someone to take your place."

"I understand."

"When you're ready to return to work, just let me know."

Relief flooded Lydia's soul. At least she still had a job. For that, she was grateful.

Soon after Edith left, Menno showed up without his boys.

"Came to see how you're doing," he said to Lydia when he entered the kitchen. "You looked upset when you rushed out of the restaurant today."

"I was. I don't even remember seeing you there." Lydia released a lingering sigh. "I realize now that I went back to work too soon."

"I wondered about that."

"Edith was here a short time ago," Mom interjected. "She's going to hire someone to fill in for Lydia until she's up to working again."

"That's good to hear," Menno said.

"Where are your boys this evening?" Mom asked.

"Left 'em at home to clean their messy rooms." He grimaced. "Our house looks like a disaster these days. I have to holler at those boys all the time in order to get 'em to do anything. It's been that way ever since their mamm passed away."

"Have you thought about hiring someone to come in and clean the house?" Mom asked.

He shook his head. "Don't want to spend

the extra money. I'd figured Ike was old enough to keep the boys in line when I'm not at home, but they don't listen to him."

"Would you like a cup of coffee or something cold to drink?" Mom asked.

"Some iced tea would be nice, if you have it." Menno pulled out a chair at the table and sat down.

Lydia, not wishing to appear rude, also took a seat, while Mom poured each of them a glass of iced tea.

"Would anyone care for a slice of homemade raisin bread?" Mom asked. "Sarah Yoder brought some over this morning."

"That sounds real good," Menno said. "I'm not much of a cook. Fact is, the boys and I only had soup and crackers for supper tonight."

"We still owe you a supper, so we'll have to make it soon," Mom said, handing Menno a plate full of the raisin bread she'd sliced.

"That'd sure be nice." Menno smiled. "I've never been one to turn down a good, home-cooked meal."

Lydia couldn't believe Mom was worried about having Menno and his boys over for supper. Had she forgotten that their finances were limited? Besides, neither of them felt up to doing much cooking right now—or entertaining guests, for that matter.

She yawned and covered her mouth as a feeling of exhaustion settled over her like a heavy quilt.

Menno gulped down the rest of his iced tea and pushed away from the table. "I'd better go."

"Do you have to leave so soon?" Mom asked.

"Lydia looks tired, and I should get home and check on my boys. Let me know if you need anything," Menno said as headed out the door.

A few minutes after he left, Lydia said good night to Mom and went up to her room. Too exhausted to even get undressed, she flopped onto her bed and quickly fell asleep.

Levi moaned and rolled over in bed. He'd been to see the doctor and had been told that he had tonsillitis. In addition to the antibiotic he was given, he'd been told to stay home and rest for the next several days.

"How are you going to get along if I have to stay here in bed?" he asked Mom as she handed him a glass of water to take his pill.

"Don't you worry about it. We'll do okay."

"But I'm needed at the store, and there are chores to do here at home."

"We all know how to do the chores, Levi. Everyone will chip in and do the work that needs to get done at the store, as well as here at the house."

"But, Mom, what if . . ."

She held up her hand. "We'll manage just fine; you'll see. You need to rest like the doctor said. If you don't start taking better care of yourself and your tonsils keep flaring up like this, they'll eventually have to be removed."

Surgery was the last thing Levi wanted to have, so he took a drink of water and swallowed the pill. His throat hurt something awful, and his head ached, too. He felt too lousy to keep arguing with Mom. Besides, he'd never won an argument with her. She was a wonderful mother, and sweet as bread pudding, but she could also be quite stubborn.

She patted his arm and fluffed up his

pillow. "Close your eyes now and rest. After a bit, I'll bring you some chamomile tea and some of those cherry-flavored Echinacea lozenges to suck on."

Levi nodded and closed his eyes. He hoped this whole mess with his tonsils cleared up soon because he couldn't afford to spend too much time here in bed. It would be hard not to worry about how his family was getting along without him.

When Lydia awoke the following morning, she felt drained, even though she'd slept almost nine hours. She couldn't remember when she'd felt so exhausted.

Will I ever get my strength back? she wondered as she plodded across the room to her closet. *Will I ever feel like life's worth living again?*

Her gaze came to rest on a cardboard box filled with Josh's clothes. *Maybe I should give them to the Care and Share Store, or maybe Menno's youngest boy could wear them. At least they'd be going to good use.*

Tears dribbled down Lydia's cheeks. Oh, how she missed her precious little boy. If

Josh was here, she could hug him tightly and stroke his soft cheek.

On second thought, she decided, *I think I'll hang on to his clothes for now. I don't think I could stand seeing anyone else wear them.*

She shuffled back across the room and knelt beside her bed. *Dear God, please give me the strength to endure this and remind me daily that I still have You.*

⁂

When Lydia entered the kitchen, she found Mom sitting at the table, staring at a basket full of fresh produce.

"Where'd that come from?" Lydia asked.

Mom shrugged. "Found it on the back porch when I went out to shake the flour from the dish towel I'd been using to roll out biscuit dough."

"Did you hear anyone come into the yard?"

"Huh-uh. There was no note with it, either." Mom stroked her chin as she continued to study the basket. "I wonder if one of the women in our community left it. Edith said yesterday that she was going to see about getting us some food."

"It seems strange that they'd leave it there and wouldn't bother to knock."

"Maybe they were in a hurry or didn't want to disturb us."

"I suppose that could be." Lydia poured herself a cup of coffee and moved over to the kitchen window. "Looks like another warm day. Maybe we should eat breakfast on the porch."

"That's a nice idea," Mom agreed. "You go ahead, and I'll bring breakfast out on a tray when it's done."

"I should help you with it."

"I can manage." Mom motioned to the door. "Go on now. Listen to the birds and enjoy the warm summer sun."

"Okay."

Lydia had only been sitting on the porch a few minutes when she saw the mailman's car pull up. She waited until he pulled away from their box, then set her coffee on the porch and headed down the driveway.

The flutter of wings drew her attention upward. The leaves in the trees overhead quivered in the breeze, offering shade for the beautiful cardinal sitting on a limb. Despite the sadness in her heart, Lydia realized how many things she had to be thankful for if she just looked around.

When she brought the mail up to the house and started sorting through the bills, she was surprised to see a blank envelope with no name or address. She tore open the envelope and gasped. Five thousand dollars lay inside! A typewritten note included with it read: *To help with Josh's hospital bills.*

Lydia hurried into the house and showed the money to Mom. "Do you think the same person who left the basket of produce on the porch left this, too?"

"I don't know." Mom squinted as she stared at the money. "I wonder if Menno left it. He seemed concerned about you when he was here last night."

Lydia shook her head. "Menno has four growing boys. He probably doesn't have that kind of money to spare."

"That's true. He did say he didn't have the money to hire anyone to clean the house." Mom drummed her fingers along the edge of the table. "I wonder if Rueben left us the money."

"What makes you think that?"

"He dropped by here yesterday morning and asked if he could help with anything."

"What'd you tell him?"

"I said we were getting along okay."

"But we're not, Mom. We have a lot of bills to pay, and now that I'm not working . . ."

"I realize that, but it's hard for me to accept help from others. If I'd told Rueben we needed his help, he'd be hanging around here all the time."

"Would that be so terrible? Don't you like Rueben?"

A red blotch erupted on Mom's neck and quickly spread to her cheeks. "I do like him. I just don't want him thinking there's a chance for us to . . ." She stopped talking and drew in a quick breath. "Never mind all that. I guess I just need to be thankful that someone cared enough to help us and not worry about who left the money or the produce."

Lydia nodded. She was pleased that God had provided for them through a secret giver but wished she knew who it was so she could say thanks.

CHAPTER 27

Lydia spent the next two weeks resting, praying, and reading her Bible. Not a day went by that she didn't think about Josh. Even a simple thing like watching the cats lapping milk from a dish or hearing them purr made her think about her boy. But through the process of spending more time in the Word, she'd come to realize that she needed to yield her will to God and accept her loss rather than fighting against it. As much as it hurt, she knew God could use the accidents that had claimed Jeremiah and Josh to draw her closer to Him. For the first time in many weeks, Lydia felt God's presence and knew He had a purpose for her life; she just didn't know what it was.

God was providing for her and Mom's needs, too. Several women in their community had been bringing in food, and a few of the men had come to do some of the more strenuous outside chores. They were managing financially, thanks to the large amount of money that had been left in their mailbox to help pay Josh's hospital bills.

By the end of the third week, Lydia felt stronger and ready to return to work. She'd called her boss and asked if she could come to work on Saturday. Since it was one of their busiest days at the restaurant, Edith suggested that Lydia wait until Monday, when things were usually a little slower. Lydia agreed and planned to spend Saturday working in the garden, thinking the physical exercise would do her some good.

She'd just taken out the hoe to do some weeding between the rows of beans when Mom came outside, carrying a cardboard box.

"I'm going to Miller's Dry Goods to see if

they'd be interested in taking two of my quilts on consignment. If there's any interest, I'll get busy and start quilting again."

"You could check with the quilt shop in Berlin, too," Lydia suggested.

Mom nodded. "Would you like to go with me?"

Lydia motioned to the garden. "I'd planned to do some weeding today."

"The weeds will still be here when we get back, and if you go with me now, I'll help you in the garden later this afternoon."

Lydia contemplated Mom's offer, then nodded. "I'll just need a minute to get my outer bonnet. Then I'll be ready to go."

🕊

"While you take your quilts in I think I'll go over to the Stutzmans' store and speak with Nona," Lydia told Mom as they approached Miller's Dry Goods Store.

"What do you need to speak with Nona about?" Mom asked.

"I want to apologize for the way I behaved at the restaurant a few weeks ago."

"Oh, I see."

"I shouldn't be gone long, so you can wait for me in the dry goods store, if you like."

"Okay."

Mom went into the store, and Lydia hurried down the street. When she entered the general store, she spotted Levi sitting on a stool behind the counter with a ledger in front of him.

"Guder mariye," he said as she approached the counter.

"Good morning. Is your mamm here today? I'd like to speak with her."

Levi shook his head. "She took Selma to see the chiropractor. Is there something I can do for you?"

"I just wanted to tell your mamm how sorry I am for my strange behavior at the restaurant a few weeks ago." Lydia fiddled with the ties on her head covering, embarrassed to be talking to Levi about this. What if Nona hadn't told him about the way she'd acted? Should she offer an explanation?

"I wasn't myself that day," she murmured, avoiding his gaze. "I kept forgetting what I was supposed to do, and I didn't want your mamm to think I'd intentionally been rude to her and Selma when I didn't bring their meal."

"Mom told me about it, and she didn't

think you were being rude. She figured you'd probably come back to work too soon and were overwhelmed."

"I was, but I'm doing better now. I've been off work since then, but I'm planning to return Monday morning." She sighed. "I'm relieved that Edith didn't fire me, because I really do need my job."

"I understand, and I'll give Mom your message as soon as she gets here."

"How have you and your family been?" Lydia asked.

"Pop's arm has healed well, and Selma's doing a little better with the pain in her back." Levi rubbed the side of his neck. "A few weeks ago I was down in bed for a while with infected tonsils, so that wasn't much fun."

"I'm sorry to hear that. Have you considered having your tonsils removed?"

"The doctor did mention that. Said if it keeps happening I might have to get it done." He grimaced. "Sure hope that doesn't happen. It was bad enough for me to be laid up for several days with tonsillitis. I wouldn't want to be away from the store again for any length of time."

"Did your family manage all right without your help?" she asked.

He nodded and gave her a little-boy grin. "At least Mom said they did."

Just then, Levi's brother Andy ambled into the room. He halted when he saw Lydia, then dropped his gaze to the floor. "Sorry about Josh," he mumbled. "Sure do miss him."

Lydia blinked against the tears gathering in her eyes. "I miss him, too, but I'm sure he's in heaven."

"That's what my mamm said." Several seconds ticked by. Then Andy looked up at Levi and said, "Pop's in the back room tryin' to stack some things on a shelf, but he can't reach that high, so he was wonderin' if you know where the ladder is."

"I took it outside yesterday when I was patching the roof. Guess I must have forgotten to bring it in." Levi frowned. "I don't want Pop climbing the ladder, though. It hasn't been that long since his arm healed, and we don't need him falling and breaking it again." Levi turned to Lydia. "Would you mind keeping an eye on things while I do the job my daed was planning to do? Normally, Betty would be here to help, but she's working at the B&B near Sugarcreek today."

"What is it you'd like me to do?" Lydia asked.

"Just wait on any customers who might come into the store."

"I guess I can manage that."

"Danki, I appreciate it."

When Levi and Andy walked away, Lydia stepped behind the counter. She was impressed with Levi's concern for his father. From what she could tell, he seemed to put the needs of his family ahead of his own.

A few minutes later, an English woman came into the store, looking for something to buy as a souvenir. She picked out a wooden yo-yo and had just brought it to the counter when Levi returned.

"This is really nice. Is it the only one you have in the store?"

Lydia looked to Levi to answer the woman's question.

"I made the yo-yo a few months ago," he said, "but I've been too busy with chores at home and helping here in the store to make any more."

"That's too bad," the woman said. "I have

six grandchildren, so I would have bought more if you'd had them."

"I do have some other wooden toys that I've made. They're in the back room." Levi motioned with his head. "Would you like me to get them so you can take a look?"

The woman smiled. "I'd appreciate that."

Levi hurried off, and when he returned with a cardboard box, he placed it on the counter and pulled out several wooden horses, and a wooden game with marbles and a chute.

"Those are perfect," the woman said. "Now I'll have something to give each of my grandchildren."

Lydia rang up the woman's purchases on the battery-operated cash register, while Levi wrapped the toys in bubble wrap and placed them back in the cardboard box.

After the woman left the store, Lydia turned to Levi and said, "I had no idea you were so talented. Those wooden toys you made are sure nice."

Levi shrugged. "It's something I like to do in my spare time. I don't have much time for woodworking during our busier months, but when things slow down here in the winter, I drag out my woodworking tools and get busy."

"Do you make other things besides toys?" Lydia asked.

"I made the table and chairs that are in our kitchen at home, as well as a few other pieces of furniture for our house."

"I'm surprised you're not working at one of the woodshops in the area."

"I've thought about it, but I'm needed right here."

Just then the door opened, and several more customers entered the store.

"I'd better go so you can take care of business," Lydia said. "Don't forget to give your mamm my message."

"Will do."

Lydia hurried out the door and turned in the direction of the dry goods store.

She'd only gone a short ways when she spotted Menno and his boys heading her way.

"We're going over to Kiem Lumber to have lunch at Carpenter's Café," Menno said when they caught up to her. "Would you like to join us?"

"That sounds nice, but I'm on my way to Miller's Dry Goods Store. Mom went there to see about selling some of her quilts."

"Why don't you see if your mamm would like to have lunch with us?"

Lydia hesitated, wondering whether she should tell Menno that she didn't have enough money with her to buy lunch.

"It'll be my treat," Menno said, as though he already knew. "And I won't take no for an answer."

Seeing the sincerity on his face, Lydia finally agreed.

"Are we goin' or what?" Carl tugged on his father's hand. "I'm hungerich, and I might pass out if I don't eat somethin' soon."

"I'm hungerich, too," Dennis put in.

"You boys are always hungry." Menno ruffled Carl's hair. "I think the whole lot of you must have holes in your legs." He looked at Lydia and grinned. "Guess I'd better head over to Kiem's and put in an order for my half-starved boys. I'll wait to order my food until you and your mamm show up."

"We shouldn't be too long." Lydia turned and hurried down the street.

When she entered the dry goods store, she found Mom talking with Sylvia, one of the Amish women who worked there. When they finished their conversation, Mom turned to Lydia and said, "They've agreed to let me leave both of my quilts. The only trouble is, they have a lot of quilts right now, so there's no guarantee that mine will sell."

"You can always make more and try to sell them to some of the other quilt shops in the area," Lydia reminded her.

"That's true." Mom opened the door and stepped onto the sidewalk. "I don't know about you, but I'm getting hungry. I think we ought to head for home now, don't you?"

"Actually, I spoke with Menno a few minutes ago, and he invited us to join him and the boys for lunch over at Carpenter's Café."

"Lydia, you know our finances are tight, and we shouldn't be spending what little money we do have to eat out."

"Menno said our lunch would be his treat."

"Why, that's sure nice of him. I haven't eaten lunch out in a very long time, so this will be a real treat."

Menno had just gotten the boys seated with their hot dogs and fries, when Lydia and Mae showed up.

"Take a minute to look over the menu," he told them. "When you've decided what you want, I'll put in your orders."

The women took a menu and found seats at the table across from the boys.

"I think I'd like a ham and cheese sandwich and a glass of lemonade," Lydia said a few minutes later.

"Same here." Mae handed the menu to Menno. "It was nice of you to invite us to join you for lunch."

"Glad to do it," he said. "I'll turn in our orders, and then we can visit while we wait for our food."

When Menno returned to the table, he took a seat beside Lydia. They talked about the warm weather they'd been having, and then Menno answered a few questions Lydia had about his woodshop. When their food came, they bowed for silent prayer.

"Any idea when you'll return to work?" Menno asked Lydia as they ate their meal.

"I'm going back on Monday," she replied.

"Sure you're ready for that?"

"I believe so. I'm feeling more rested now, and I'm think I'll be able to cope with things better."

Zing! Flop! A napkin wadded into a ball sailed past Lydia's head and landed in her glass of water.

Menno snapped his fingers and glared at the boys. "Which one of you did that?"

Carl pointed at Dennis.

"We were makin' pretend snowballs," Dennis said.

"This isn't the place to be doin' that. You can wait for winter to make real snowballs. Right now, you need to finish your lunch and quit fooling around."

"I'm done with my hot dog," Ike said. "Can I have an ice-cream cone?"

"I want one, too!" Kevin shouted.

"Same here," Dennis and Carl echoed.

"All right, but only if you promise to behave yourselves while you eat."

All four heads bobbed, so Menno handed Ike some money. "Go ahead and get a cone for you and your brothers." He turned to face Lydia. "Sorry about that."

"No harm done," she said, squeezing water from the fake snowball and plucking it from her glass.

Soon after the boys returned to the table with their ice-cream cones, Ike let out a loud burp.

"What do you say?" Menno asked, giving Ike a stern look.

"It's better to burp and be in shame, than not to burp and—"

Menno held up his hand. "That's enough. Just eat your cone and be quiet."

Lydia had just picked up her sandwich, and was about to take a bite, when— *floop!*—a little green frog landed in the middle of her plate. It sat there a few seconds, and hopped to the floor.

"*Ach*, my!" she squealed. "Now where did that come from?"

Menno leaned over and snatched up the frog; then he looked at his sons and said, "Who does this belong to?"

Three heads turned in Carl's direction.

Menno's eyes narrowed. "Did you bring that frog in here?"

The boy's face quickly turned pink as he nodded. "Had the frosch in my pocket but never expected he'd hop out."

Menno thrust the frog into Carl's hands. "Tell Lydia you're sorry, and then take the critter outside."

"Sorry," Carl mumbled. He gave Lydia a sidelong glance, then dashed out of the café.

Menno groaned. "Don't know what's gotten into my boys lately. They never acted like this when their mamm was alive—especially not in public." He glanced at Lydia, wondering what she must think of his rowdy sons. It seemed like they were always doing something to embarrass him whenever she was around.

"I think it's time for us to go home," Lydia said, rising from her chair. "Danki for the lunch, Menno."

"We appreciate it very much," Mae added.

"You're welcome."

Soon after the women left, Carl showed up without the frog.

"I want to talk to you boys," Menno said, taking a seat at the table between Kevin and Dennis.

"What about?" Ike asked.

"It's about your rude behavior." Menno grimaced. "I've never seen any Amish children misbehave in public the way you did here today, and I never want to see you act like that again. Are we clear?"

All heads nodded.

"When we get home, you'll have extra chores to do, and from now on, whenever we're with Lydia, you'd better be on your best behavior."

CHAPTER 28

On Monday morning Lydia returned to work. Even though they were quite busy, she managed to keep up and stay focused on what she was doing. By the end of her shift, however, she was exhausted and anxious to call it a day.

Lydia had ridden her bike to work, but there was one stop she wanted to make before going home. She felt a strong need to go to the cemetery to visit Josh's grave, even though it would hurt.

When Lydia arrived at the cemetery, she saw Menno kneeling in front of one of the graves. Not wishing to intrude, she held back, staying near the wooden fence that surrounded the graveyard.

"I miss you, Sadie," Menno murmured. "I'm sure our boys do, too." His shoulders shook as he gulped in a couple of deep breaths.

Lydia's heart went out to him, for she understood fully the grief he felt. Even though Jeremiah had been gone over a year, she still missed him. And the ache in her heart from losing Josh was still so fresh she could barely deal with seeing his grave, just on the other side of the fence.

Lydia waited until Menno stood and moved away from his wife's grave. Then she opened the gate and stepped inside.

When the gate clicked shut, Menno whirled around. "I didn't know anyone was here. Thought I was alone."

"I haven't been here long. I was on my way home from work and decided to stop and visit Josh's grave."

He lifted the brim of his straw hat and ran his fingers through the ends of his hair. "When I was a boy and lost my grandparents, I was sad, but it was nothing like the pain I felt when my wife died."

Lydia's throat burned, and she could

barely swallow. "I know. Losing my husband and then our son was the worst kind of pain I've ever had to endure."

He nodded with a look of empathy. "I still have my boys, and for that, I'm grateful, but they're so hard to deal with at times. It makes me miss Sadie all the more, because she was so good with 'em."

Lydia knew her situation was different from his, but she felt the need to offer some advice. "During the last few weeks, I've spent a lot of time praying and reading my Bible. While I'm still hurting from the loss of my husband and son, I've come to realize that God is with me and He can use my situation to make me a stronger person and to help someone else who might also be hurting."

"I know you're right, and I really haven't spent as much time praying or reading the Bible as I should. When I get up in the mornings, I'm usually in a hurry to get the boys going so I can head to work. When I come home in the evenings, I'm so tired it's all I can do to throw something together for us to eat and see that the boys do their chores and get ready for bed." He squinted and rubbed the bridge of his nose.

"Guess I should start reading my Bible and spending some time in prayer before I go to bed at night."

"That's when I usually spend time with God, but I often pray throughout the day."

"I need to start doin' that, too." Menno pushed his hat back in place. "I'd better get back to work. I left the boys at my shop, and my workers are overseeing 'em while I'm gone. Don't want to take advantage of John and Mark's good natures."

He turned and was about to open the gate, when she called out to him. "Would you and the boys be free to have supper at our house tonight?"

He pivoted toward her, a slow smile spreading across his face. "That'd be real nice. What time would you like us?"

"How about six o'clock?"

"That should work out just fine. See you then, Lydia."

❧

"I hate goin' to the dentist," Levi's brother Peter complained as they left the dentist's office in Berlin.

"But your tooth doesn't hurt anymore, does it?" Levi asked.

"How should I know? I'm all numbed up."

Peter rubbed the side of his face. "Can't feel a thing, 'cept for a prickly sensation."

"It'll wear off in a few hours, and then you'll be good as new." Levi gave the top of his brother's head a couple of light raps. "Let's go over to Heini's Cheese Store. Mom asked me to pick up a few things for her."

Peter's brow puckered. "It ain't fair."

"What's not fair?"

"Goin' to Heini's when my mouth's too numb to eat. Won't be able to try any of those tasty cheese samples they always have settin' out."

"I'll be buying some cheese to take home," Levi said as they climbed into his buggy. "You can have a hunk of it after the numbness wears off."

"Won't be the same as goin' up and down the aisle, samplin' all kinds of cheese." Peter frowned and folded his arms. "They've usually got several kinds of fudge there, too."

"I think you'll live without it this time," Levi said as he backed the horse away from the hitching rail.

When they arrived at Heini's, Levi went in, while Peter wandered around some of the other stores that were located in the same building. Levi promised that when he was done shopping he'd buy Peter an ice-cream cone, figuring it would be easy enough for the boy to eat.

Levi took his time picking out the kinds of cheese Mom had on her list, and he sampled several as he walked up and down the aisles between the refrigerated cases.

When he found everything he needed, he placed it all on the counter. Mary Rose Yoder, who stood near the cash register, rang up his purchases. "Hi, Levi. It's good to see you." Her blue eyes twinkled as she pushed a wisp of dark hair that had escaped her head covering back into place.

He gave a quick nod.

"How's your family?"

"Doin' okay."

She smiled sweetly. "I've missed seeing you. Since I started my new job here, I don't get into your folks' store very often anymore. Mama does most of our shopping now."

"Guess that's understandable."

"I heard there's going to be a volleyball game at the Masts' place on Saturday evening. Think you might go?"

"I don't think so. Saturdays are usually busy at the store, and by the time I get home and do all my chores, I'm usually too tired to go anywhere."

"That's too bad. I was hoping you might be there."

Levi was relieved when another customer stepped up behind him. That meant Mary Rose wouldn't have time to keep talking to him. Not that she was unpleasant or anything. She was a nice-looking young woman and had a pleasing personality. Levi just wasn't interested in a relationship with her, and he was pretty sure that's what she was hoping for.

Once Mary Rose had rung up his purchases, Levi grabbed the sack, said a quick good-bye, and scooted out the door. He found Peter sitting on a bench in the entryway, head down and shoulders slumped.

"What's wrong?" Levi asked. "Did you think I'd forgotten about you and gone home?"

"Naw. Some big English kids came by and made fun of me for bein' so small." Peter's nose wrinkled as he squinted his eyes. "They kept pointin' at me and sayin'

I was funny lookin' and would never grow into a man."

Levi's face heated as he glanced around. "Where are the boys now?"

Peter pointed to the door. "They took off runnin' when their mamm called 'em."

Levi frowned. It upset him when people made fun of his family. He shouldn't have let Peter wander around by himself. People could be so insensitive and cruel.

⁂

"I hope you don't mind that I invited Menno and his boys to join us for supper this evening," Lydia said to Mom as they set the table. "I know you asked me not to invite anyone without checking with you first, but when I saw the dejected look on Menno's face at the cemetery, I wanted to do something to help cheer him up."

"I don't mind a bit," Mom said with a shake of her head. "Remember I'd mentioned before that we needed to have Menno and his boys here for supper?" She smiled. "I still think that nice man's interested in you."

Lydia shook her head. "I think he's more interested in eating a home-cooked meal than he is in me."

"I don't think so. I can tell that he's lonely, and I think he might be looking for another wife."

"Well, he hasn't given me any indication that he's interested in me as a wife." Lydia shrugged. "Even if he did, I'm not sure I'm ready to get married again."

"But you will be someday, don't you think?"

"Maybe . . . if I ever fall in love and find the right man." Lydia touched Mom's arm. "What about you? Have you thought about getting married again?"

"No, I don't think so." Mom's face flamed, and she lifted her apron and fanned her face with the edge of it. "After all, who'd be interested in marrying me?"

"Rueben Miller. I've seen the way he looks at you, Mom. I think if you'd give him half a chance . . ."

A horse whinnied outside, and Lydia thought Mom looked relieved.

"Our guests are here," Mom said, peeking out the kitchen window. "Why don't you greet them while I check on the chicken?"

Lydia opened the back door and stepped onto the porch just as Menno pulled his horse and buggy up to the hitching rail.

❧

"Now remember what I said," Menno told his boys as they clambered out of the buggy. "Watch your manners at the table, and be nice to Lydia and her mamm."

"We will, Papa," they said in unison.

By the time Menno had his horse put in the barn and had made his way up to the house, the boys were already on the porch, talking with Lydia. He hoped they hadn't said or done anything rude. If they had, he hoped she would say something so he could deal with it.

"I was just telling the boys that we're having chicken for supper," Lydia said when Menno joined them on the porch.

He smiled. "Sounds good. We all like chicken."

"Not me," Dennis said with a shake of his head. "I've never liked chicken."

Menno nudged the boy's shoulder. "Since when?"

"Dennis don't like nothin'," Carl said. "Remember the time you made him eat spinach, and he threw up all over the kitchen floor?" He groaned as he held his stomach. "Nobody wanted to eat after that."

"That'll be enough. We don't need that

kind of talk," Menno said sternly. He looked over at Lydia and smiled. "It was nice of you to invite us to supper. I've been looking forward to it all afternoon."

She pulled the screen door open. "Let's go inside. I'm sure Mom has everything just about ready."

As they stepped into the kitchen, the tantalizing aroma of baked chicken greeted Menno, and his stomach rumbled. He hoped Lydia hadn't heard it.

"It's good you could come," Mae said with a smile. "If everyone would like to have a seat, Lydia and I will set the food on the table."

Menno pulled out a chair at the head of the table, and his boys took a seat on the wooden bench to his left. After Lydia and Mae put the food on the table, they seated themselves in the chairs on Menno's right, with Lydia sitting closest to him. All heads bowed for prayer.

When Carl started rustling his napkin, Menno nudged the boy's leg under the table. *That boy can't sit still for more than a few minutes,* he thought.

When the prayer was over, the serving dishes were passed. Besides the chicken,

Mae and Lydia had prepared mashed potatoes, steamed carrots, pickles, homemade rolls, and a lemon-flavored gelatin salad.

The adults visited while they ate, but the boys said very little as they gorged on the food—even Dennis, his pickiest eater. Menno was sure they were enjoying the tasty meal as much as he was. It was a far cry from the bland meals he tried to cook, and the female company was kind of nice, too.

Toward the end of the meal, Kevin looked over at Lydia and said, "So, what's for dessert?"

Menno would have nudged Kevin with the toe of his boot, but the boy sat too far away for his foot to reach.

"How does applesauce and maple-nut cookies sound?" Lydia asked. "I made them because I knew you were coming."

Kevin smacked his lips. "Sounds real *gut* to me."

The other three boys bobbed their heads in agreement.

Mae served up the applesauce while Lydia set out the cookies.

"It's a nice evening," Mae said as she

poured Menno a cup of coffee. "Why don't we go outside and play a game of croquet?"

Ike scrunched up his nose. "I don't like that game. I'd rather play volleyball."

"We don't have a volleyball or a net," Mae said. She looked over at Lydia. "Why don't you and Menno go out to the barn and get the croquet set while I do up the dishes?"

"Don't you want my help?" Lydia asked.

Mae shook her head. "By the time you get the game set up, I'll be done with the dishes."

Lydia hesitated but finally went out the back door. Menno and his boys followed.

"The croquet set's in the barn," Lydia said to Menno. "If you'd like to have a seat at the picnic table, it shouldn't take me long to get the game."

"Why don't I come with you?" Menno hurried along beside her.

As they passed the flower bed along the side of the house, the sweet fragrance of roses wafted up to Menno's nose. He missed not having any flowers growing in their yard. Since Sadie had died, the flower beds had gone untouched.

As they neared the barn, he glanced at

the vegetable garden and noticed several clumps of weeds were coming up between the rows of tomatoes. Menno didn't even plant a garden this spring much less have the time to maintain it.

When they entered the barn, Lydia pointed to the area where the horse's grooming supplies were kept. "I think the croquet set is over there."

"I'll get it." Menno strode quickly across the barn and glanced over his shoulder at Lydia as she leaned against a wooden beam. She appeared to be watching a fluffy gray cat skitter across the floor, no doubt in search of a mouse.

"Here we go," Menno announced when he joined her again. "Found all I could of the croquet set." He hesitated a minute, hoping to draw her into a conversation, but she turned and hurried out the door.

The boys, who'd been sitting at the picnic table under the shade of an enormous maple tree, joined them on the grass. Once they had all the wickets put in place, Dennis and Carl started an argument about who would go first and who would get to use the red ball. Since there were only four balls, it was decided that the boys could play the first game, and whoever lost would sit out while one of the adults played the second game.

"Don't wanna play this stupid game," Ike said with a grunt. "Someone else can have my mallet." He handed it to Lydia and bent down to pick up one of the cats that had run out of the barn.

Menno took a seat beside him on the grass, and a few minutes later, Mae showed up with a couple of folding chairs. "If you'd like to play, I can have one of the boys sit out," he told her.

"That's okay; I'm content to sit and watch." Mae lowered herself into one of the chairs. She motioned to the other chair. "Wouldn't you rather sit there? It'll be a lot more comfortable than sitting on the hard ground."

"Guess you're right about that." Menno brushed away some pieces of grass that had stuck to his pants and seated himself beside Mae.

"I hope the boys don't get upset if Lydia wins," Mae said. "She's always been good at croquet."

"Don't think they much care who wins or loses; they just like to smack the ball around." Menno watched as Kevin lined up his ball and gave it a good whack. He groaned when the ball missed the wicket.

Kevin lined up the ball, swung, and missed once more.

"Try it one more time," Lydia urged.

With a determined expression, Kevin swung the mallet, but missed yet again.

"Let me do it!" Ike jumped up, grabbed the mallet from Kevin, and smacked the ball hard. It sailed across the yard with such force that Menno heard it *zing*.

Whack!—it hit Lydia in the knee, and she crumpled to the ground.

Menno leaped out of his chair and dashed across the yard. "Are you hurt? Can you put weight on your leg?"

"I think it's just a bruise," Lydia said, rising slowly to her feet. "I'd better go into the house and put some ice on it."

Menno grimaced. If his boys kept doing things like this, he'd never gain Lydia's favor.

CHAPTER 29

Mae felt anxious as she left the quilt shop in Berlin. The store owner had said she'd be interested in selling some of her quilts, but Mae didn't have anything ready except for a table runner and a few potholders. If she was going to help out financially, she'd have to get busy and start working on another quilt right away.

Before heading home, Mae decided to stop by the health food store down the street to get some Arnica lotion. Lydia had used all they had on her sore knee, and even though the bruise was better, Mae didn't want to run out of the wonderful, healing cream.

When she stepped inside the health food store, she noticed Levi in the homeopathic section, where the Arnica was located.

"Guder mariye," Levi said with a smile.

"Good morning." Mae moved closer to the shelf and picked up a bottle of Arnica.

"That's pretty good stuff," Levi said. "Someone at our house always seems to be falling or bumping into things, so we keep Arnica on hand because it helps bruises heal."

Mae gave a nod and started to move away.

"How's Lydia doing? Is she working full-time at the restaurant again?"

"Jah." Mae moved quickly to the cash register, made her purchase, and left the store. She was sure Levi was concerned about Lydia, and he really did seem like a nice man. Too bad he'd been born into a family of little people, or she might have hoped that he and Lydia would get together. Mae still felt that Menno would make a better husband for Lydia. He needed a wife, and Lydia needed the opportunity to be a mother again.

When Mae reached Spector's Hardware, where she'd tied her horse, she was surprised to see Rueben standing beside her buggy.

"I was pretty sure this was your rig," he said when she joined him. "Figured you might be in the Christian bookstore or over at Spector's."

"I went to the health food store," Mae said.

Rueben's eyes looked even bluer than usual. As he gazed at Mae, her heart began to pound. Why did he have to look at her that way? Why'd he have to be so nice looking?

Rueben took a step closer. "Have you had lunch yet?"

She shook her head. "I thought I'd get something to eat after I got home."

"How'd you like to join me for a sandwich at Java Joe's? It'll be my treat."

Mae nibbled on her lip as she considered his offer. The thought of a sandwich and something cold to drink seemed appealing.

"I won't take no for an answer, so you may as well say yes," Rueben said with a chuckle.

"Oh, all right." Mae had turned the poor man down so many times in the past, maybe it wouldn't hurt to join him for a meal this once.

A look of relief swept over his face. "Whatever I decide to order will taste a lot better with you sitting across the table from me."

She suppressed a giggle, feeling much like a young woman on her first courting date. What a way with words this determined man had.

⁊

Anxious to see how Lydia was doing, Menno slipped into a booth for a cup of coffee and a piece of pie.

"How's your knee?" he asked when Lydia came to wait on him.

"The bruise is almost gone, and it's feeling much better." She smiled. "You really don't have to come in here every day to check on me."

"I know, but since it was one of my boys who smacked the ball that hit your knee, I feel responsible."

She shook her head. "It was an accident, and I'm really doing okay."

"Glad to hear it."

"So what would you like to order?"

"Just pie and coffee."

"What kind of pie?"

Menno leaned forward, resting his elbows on the table. "Let's see now. Have you got any lemon meringue?"

She nodded. "Last time I looked there were two pieces left."

"Great. I'll take 'em both."

Her eyebrows shot up. "Are you really that hungry?"

He chuckled and shook his head. "Thought I'd take one to go. It'll be a nice snack for me to have after the boys are in bed this evening." Menno drummed his fingers along the edge of the table. "Speaking of the boys, I promised to take 'em fishing this Saturday, and I was wondering if you'd like to go along. Thought maybe we could pack a picnic lunch to take to the pond."

"That sounds nice, but I'm scheduled to work this Saturday."

"What time do you get off?"

"Not until four."

"Guess we could do some evening fishing and have a picnic supper instead of lunch."

"That's a nice idea. I could buy some sandwiches and chips from the restaurant and put a picnic supper together before I leave work on Saturday."

"Sounds good. Should we pick you up here at the restaurant?"

"That'll be fine. I'll get your pie and coffee now."

As Lydia walked away, Menno smiled. If things kept going this well, before the end of the year, his boys might have a new mother.

⁊◌

By the time Lydia's shift ended, she was more than ready to go home. She had ridden her bike so she could get to and from work faster than walking.

As she peddled her bike up the hill just a ways past Kiem Lumber, her knee began to throb. *Maybe I'd better get off and walk the rest of the way home,* she decided.

Lydia winced as she grabbed the handlebars and began to push. Apparently, her knee hadn't healed quite as well as she'd thought. Being on her feet all day, and then peddling a bike had probably put too much strain on it.

The sun bore down mercilessly, and she

stopped to draw in a deep breath, wishing she had some ice to put on her knee.

Clip-clop. Clip-clop.

Lydia heard a horse and buggy coming down the road. She turned, and when it crested the hill, the driver pulled the rig along the shoulder behind her. She shielded her eyes from the glare of the sun to see who was driving the buggy, and soon realized that it was Levi.

"What's going on?" he asked, sticking his head out the driver's side of his rig. "Is there a problem with your bike?"

"It's not the bike, it's my knee."

Levi hopped down from the buggy and rushed up to Lydia. "What happened to your knee?"

She quickly explained about the accident during the croquet game.

"That must have been why your mamm was buying Arnica at the health food store in Berlin when I saw her the other day."

"Mom mentioned buying Arnica, but I didn't know she'd seen you."

"Guess she didn't think it was worth mentioning."

Lydia wasn't sure how to respond. Mom didn't care much for Levi—or at least not

his family. Did Levi sense Mom's disap-
proval, too?

"If you'll hang on to my horse so he
doesn't take off, I'll put your bike in the back
of my buggy and give you a ride home."

"I'd appreciate that," she said, stepping
up to his horse.

Levi lifted Lydia's bike into the back of
his rig; then he helped her into the passenger's side and climbed in himself.

"How's business at your store?" Lydia
asked as they headed down the road.
"Have you been keeping busy this summer?"

"Sure have."

"I guess things will stay busy even into
the fall. Mom said a lot of tourists come to
the area during September and October."

"That's how it usually goes all right."

"It looks like someone's found the time
to do some fishing," Lydia commented as
they passed a pond where two young
Amish boys sat on a log with their fishing
poles.

"Probably stopped to do some fishing
on their way home from school." Levi directed his horse and buggy up Lydia's
driveway. "Do you like to fish?"

She nodded. "In fact, I'll be going fishing with Menno and his boys this Saturday evening."

"Oh, I see. Well, I'm sure you'll have a good time."

Was that a look of disappointment she saw on Levi's face, or was she imagining things? Could Levi be interested in her? *No,* she decided, *it's probably wishful thinking on my part.*

Levi halted the horse near the barn, jumped down, and took Lydia's bike out of the buggy. By the time he came around to help her, she'd already climbed down. "Danki for the ride. I appreciate it," she said.

"Sure, no problem. See you, Lydia." Levi stepped into his buggy and drove away.

I wish it were Levi who'd asked me to go fishing, Lydia thought as she pushed her bike toward the barn. *I wish he would look at me tho way Jeremiah used to.*

CHAPTER 30

Saturday morning dawned bright and clear. As soon as Lydia left for work, Mae planned to wash the material for quilts and a few other things that she'd packed away several months ago. Now that she was free to do some sewing again, she wanted the material to be fresh and clean.

"How late do you have to work today?" Mae asked as she and Lydia finished washing their breakfast dishes.

"I get off at four."

"How would you like to do some quilting with me this evening after we've had supper? I'll have all my material washed and dried by then, and I might even get a little sewing done before you get home."

"Maybe some other time, Mom," Lydia said. "I'm going to the pond with Menno and his boys this evening, remember?"

"Oh, that's right." Mae smiled. "I'm glad you'll be spending time with Menno. The more I get to know him, the more I'm convinced that he's really a nice man."

Lydia nodded and reached for a clean dish towel to dry her hands. "Guess I'd better go. I don't want to be late for work." She grabbed her purse from the counter. "Menno will be picking me up at the restaurant when my shift is over at four, so I won't see you until he drops me off here later this evening."

"That's fine. I'll fix myself something simple for supper and spend the rest of the evening at my quilting frame."

As soon as Lydia went out the back door, Mae headed downstairs to the cellar, where the washing machine was kept.

Later, when she brought the clean material outside to hang on the line, she was surprised to see Rueben coming up the driveway in his open buggy.

"My horse is overheated," he called to

her. "Mind if I use your hose to cool him down?"

"No problem. Go right ahead!"

Mae hung the material on the line while Rueben hosed down his horse. When he finished, he strolled across the lawn toward her.

"Sure is hot out today." He wiped his forehead with the back of his hand. "Never would know that fall's not far away."

"Would you like something cold to drink?" she offered.

"That'd be much appreciated."

"If you'd like to have a seat on the porch, I'll go in the house and get some iced tea."

"Sounds good."

Mae hurried into the house. When she returned, she found Rueben sitting in a chair with his eyes closed and his feet propped on the porch railing. He looked so relaxed she hated to disturb him. He looked so handsome, her heart started to pound. She hadn't felt this giddy since she was a teenager.

She set the pitcher of iced tea and two glasses on the table, then took a seat in the chair beside him, watching his chest rise and fall. If only she were free to open her heart to him. If Lydia were to marry Menno, then maybe . . .

Rueben's eyes snapped open suddenly, and he blinked a couple of times. "Guess I must have dozed off for a few minutes."

"That's okay. I was trying to be quiet so I didn't wake you." Mae motioned to the iced tea. "Are you ready for something cold to drink?"

"Sure am. I shoed four horses this morning, and then I had some errands to run in Berlin. I only had one bottle of water with me, and when that was gone, I was so busy that I didn't even think about stopping for something to eat or drink."

"In this heat, you're probably dehydrated." Mae poured him a glass of iced tea and hurried into the house to get the banana bread she'd made yesterday. "You'd better have some of this," she said, handing him a slice of the bread. "If you haven't eaten anything all morning, your blood sugar's probably low."

Rueben gobbled down the bread and gulped the iced tea. "That sure hit the spot. Danki, Mae."

"You're welcome." She held out the plate

of bread again. "Help yourself to another piece."

"Don't mind if I do." Rueben plucked off a piece and ate it quickly. "This is sure moist and tasty. You're a real good cook."

Mae's face heated. She wasn't used to receiving such a compliment, especially from such a nice-looking man. "I'm glad you like it. I substituted honey for sugar, and used whole wheat flour, so it's a healthy treat."

"Are you managing okay financially since your daed died?" Rueben asked, taking their conversation in another direction.

She nodded, unwilling to admit that even with Lydia working again they were struggling to pay the bills.

Rueben's expression turned serious. "I meant what I said the other day. If you need anything—anything at all—just ask."

"I appreciate that." Mae kept her focus on the porch, unable to meet his steady gaze. She wished she wasn't so attracted to Rueben.

For the next several minutes they sat in comfortable silence, until Rueben finally set his empty glass down and stood. "I have another horse to shoe this afternoon,

so guess I'd better get going." He smiled
at her in such a way that her heart nearly
melted. "Thanks again for the snack and
for letting me borrow your hose to cool off
my horse."

"You're welcome."

Rueben hesitated, like he wanted to say
something more, but then he turned and
sprinted across the yard to his horse and
buggy.

ॐ

"Would you help your daed carry those
boxes of dishes from the storage room?"
Mom asked Levi.

"Sure will. I don't think he should carry
them alone." Levi started for the storage
room, where Pop had been working all
morning.

"Oh, and if you get some free time this
afternoon, would you look for Andy's fishing pole?" Mom called.

Levi turned around. "What does he need
it for?"

"Your daed and I decided that we should
all go to the pond this evening, and Andy
and Peter want to do some fishing while
we're there. Maybe you'd like to fish awhile,
too."

"I'll look for Andy's pole, but I don't think I'll go with you this evening," Levi said.

Mom's eyebrows lifted high on her forehead. "And miss all the good food I'm planning to take?"

He shrugged. "I can eat something at home."

"What about fishing? I know how much you like to fish."

"I'm not in the mood to fish." Levi thought about how Mary Rose Yoder had invited him to the volleyball game this evening, and he'd said he was usually too tired on Saturday evenings to go anywhere. After telling her that he wasn't going to the volleyball game, would it be wrong to go to the pond with his family? It would be a lot more relaxing than playing volleyball all evening. But if he went to the pond, he might see Lydia, and he wasn't sure he could deal with seeing her and Menno together.

"I think you'll disappoint the boys if you don't go with us," Mom added.

"You've got to go, Levi," Pop said, sticking his head around the storage room door. "We'd like the whole family to be together."

Mom nodded. "Your daed and I have

been looking forward to spending the evening with our kinner, and it won't be nearly as much fun if you're not there."

Levi didn't want to disappoint his folks, so with a sigh of resignation he said, "Okay, I'll go."

❧

"How late are we workin' today?" John Schwartz, one of Menno's employees, asked as the two of them sanded the legs of a large, dining room table.

"Thought I'd close the shop around three. Me and the boys are going to the pond this evening." Menno smiled. "Lydia King's going with us. We'll be picking her up at Grandma's Restaurant at four o'clock."

John's blue eyes twinkled as he tipped his red head and gave Menno a sly-looking grin. "Is there something going on between you and Lydia?"

"Not really. We're just friends." Menno hoped the eagerness he felt didn't show on his face.

"Would you like there to be something more than just friendship between you two?"

Menno shrugged. "Maybe so, but we'll have to wait and see how it goes."

"Do the boys like her?"

"I'm sure they do. I mean, what's not to like? She's a good cook, a hard worker, kindhearted, and on top of all that, she looks pretty good in the face."

John smiled. "Those are all good things."

"Papa, you'd better come quick!" Ike hollered, as he raced into the shop.

Menno's eyebrows furrowed. "What's wrong?"

"Kevin's missin'. We've looked every-where for him!"

CHAPTER 31

I've got to go look for my boy," Menno told
John. "See if Mark can stop what he's doing and help you with the table. If I'm not
back by three, you can close up the shop."

John gave a nod, and Menno rushed
out the door behind Ike.

When they reached the house, Menno
found Dennis and Carl sitting on the front
porch.

"When Ike came to get me, he said Kevin
went missing." Menno touched Carl's
shoulder. "Where'd you last see your little
brother?"

"Can't remember."

Menno looked at Dennis. "What about you? Do you know where Kevin might be?"

Dennis dropped his gaze and scraped the toe of his boot on the step below him. "We . . . uh . . . was all playin' in the barn, and then . . ." He looked over at Ike. "You tell him what happened."

Menno ground his teeth together. "Were you boys up to some kind of mischief?"

Ike shook his head. "I was muckin' out the horse stalls, the way you told me to do, and then I heard this commotion goin' on in the main part of the barn."

"What kind of commotion?"

Ike pointed at Carl and then at Dennis. "They had a rope tied around Kevin's waist, and said he had to be their horse. They were makin' him pull the wagon with a bunch of bricks in it."

"The bricks I asked you boys to move for me?"

Dennis and Carl both nodded.

"Figured it'd get done quicker if we used the wagon," Dennis mumbled.

"That's fine, but you shouldn't have expected Kevin to pull a wagon full of bricks. That was way too heavy for him."

"I told 'em that," Ike said, "but they kept

tryin' to make Kevin pull the wagon, and then he started bawlin' like a wounded heifer." His face contorted. "Finally got sick of watchin' it, and so I untied Kevin."

"Then what happened?" Menno asked.

"Kevin ran out of the barn," Dennis interjected. "Then after Ike got our sandwiches made and called us into the house for lunch, everyone but Kevin came."

Ike nodded. "So we all started lookin', but we couldn't find him anywhere."

"Where did you look?" Menno questioned.

"In the barn, in the house, in the buggy shed." Dennis pointed to the field of corn growing beside their place. "We even looked out there, and also up the road apiece, but Kevin's just vanished."

"Well, he has to be someplace. Are you sure you looked everywhere?" Menno's fears mounted, and he sent up a quick prayer. What if Kevin had wandered up the road and got hit by a car? What if . . . ?

"I know one place we didn't look," Ike said.

"Where's that?"

"In the cellar."

"Don't think Kevin would go down there,"

Carl said. "He gets scared when he's in the dark."

Menno knew Carl was right. Kevin had been afraid of the dark since he was a toddler. Even so, if he wanted to get away from his brothers badly enough, he may have braved the dark cellar.

"I'll get the big flashlight I keep by my bed," Menno said. "Then we'll check out the cellar."

Menno took the stairs two at a time and hurried down the hall toward his bedroom. When he opened the door, he halted. The bottom drawer of the oversized dresser he'd given Sadie for Christmas two years ago was wide open. Kevin was sleeping in it, his legs and one arm dangling over the edge. In his other hand he held a woman's handkerchief.

The drawer held some of Sadie's hankies, along with several old letters she'd written to Menno when they were courting. After Sadie died, he'd kept them for sentimental reasons.

He bent down and gently shook the boy.

Kevin's eyes popped open, and he sat up quickly and looked around. "Wh–where am I?"

"You're in my room, in the dresser drawer."

Kevin quirked an eyebrow. "What am I doin' in here?"

Menno shook his head "You tell me."

"Let me think." Kevin rubbed his forehead and puckered his lips. "Well . . . uh . . . Dennis and Carl tied me up and tried to make me pull the wagon with bricks in it."

"So I heard."

"Then Ike made 'em let me go, and I—I ran out of the barn and came up here." Kevin dropped his gaze. "Guess I must've conked out."

"Why were you sleeping in the drawer?" Menno asked, raising the boy's chin.

"Wanted to be near Mama's things." Kevin lifted the hanky in his hand and held it against his nose. "Thought maybe I could smell Mama on her things. It's real lonely without her."

Menno's throat constricted. Kevin obviously still missed his mother.

He gathered Kevin into his arms and gently patted his back. If he gave his boys a new mother, they'd never have to be home by themselves, and they wouldn't be lonely anymore.

Lydia glanced at the clock on the restaurant wall. It was four o'clock—time for her shift to end—and time for Menno to pick her up for their picnic supper at the pond. She grasped the picnic basket she'd prepared for them and went outside to wait in the parking lot.

A few minutes later, Menno guided his horse and buggy into the parking lot. He handed Ike the reins, hopped down, and helped Lydia into the buggy.

"Are we late?" Menno asked, taking his seat beside her.

"No, you're right on time."

Menno grunted. "Kevin went missing this afternoon, and I thought for a while I might have to cancel our plans for this evening."

"Where'd you find him?" Lydia asked.

"Sleeping in a dresser drawer in my room." Menno rolled his eyes as he slowly shook his head. "Never know from one minute to the next what my boys are gonna do."

"Josh was like that, too. Always rambunctious and full of curiosity." She sighed. "I still miss him so much."

"Of course you do, but hopefully the pain of losing him will ease in time."

"I . . . I hope so."

"Papa, Dennis is pokin' me," Carl hollered from the back seat.

"Stop poking your bruder," Menno called over his shoulder.

"He poked me first."

"Did not."

"Did so."

"No, you poked me first."

A muscle in Menno's cheek quivered. "It doesn't matter who started it. Just sit back and be quiet, and please keep your hands to yourself."

They rode in silence until the pond came into view. When Menno stopped the horse, the boys hopped down from the buggy.

"I'm hungerich!" Kevin shouted. "Can we eat right now?"

Menno looked over at Lydia. "What do you say? Should we feed these hungry buwe?"

"I don't see why not," she said with a nod.

Menno helped Lydia set the food and paper plates on the blanket he'd brought along, and after their silent prayer, everyone dug in.

The boys jabbered as they ate, and every once in a while one of them poked the other or let out a loud burp.

"What do you say?" Menno asked, looking at Dennis, who'd just released a disgustingly noisy burp.

"It's better to burp and be in . . ."

Menno pointed his finger at the boy. "That's not what you're supposed to say, and you know it."

"You're 'sposed to say, 'excuse me.'" Ike thumped Dennis's shoulder.

Dennis wrinkled his nose. "Get your hands off me."

Ike thumped Dennis's shoulder again. "Aw, I ain't hurtin' ya none."

"Are so."

"Am not."

"Are so."

Menno clapped his hands so hard that Lydia jumped. "That's enough!" He looked over at Lydia with a sheepish expression. "Sorry for yelling. Didn't mean to startle you, but the boys were getting on my nerves."

"Maybe we should get busy fishin'," Carl said. "That way we can't get on anyone's nerves."

"Good idea," Menno said. "Get your fishing poles from the back of the buggy."

"Can ya help me bait my hook?" Kevin asked, looking up at Menno with his big brown eyes.

"Sure."

Dennis, Carl, and Kevin raced over to the buggy and grabbed their fishing poles. Menno followed them to the pond. Lydia expected Ike to join them, but he remained seated on the blanket beside her.

"Aren't you going to fish with your brothers?" Lydia asked.

"Maybe I will. Maybe I won't. Not sure what I'm gonna do yet."

Unsure of what to say, Lydia started putting their leftovers in the picnic basket.

"You like my daed?"

Lydia almost dropped the paper cups she held. "Of course. He seems like a very nice man."

"He snores real loud when he's sleepin'. He also picks his teeth with the end of a paper clip. Oh, and sometimes, instead of usin' a napkin, he lets our hund lick his dirty fingers. "

Lydia grimaced. Why was Ike telling her these things? Surely the boy had to be exaggerating.

"Hey, Ike," Menno called. "Come on over here and do some fishing with us. You, too, Lydia."

Lydia rose to her feet, but Ike just sat there with his arms folded.

When Lydia approached the water, she bent down to see how the boys were doing, and—*Swish!*—Dennis snagged her head covering with his fishing hook, pulling it right off her head.

Lydia grabbed for it, pulled the hook carefully out, and put her covering back on her head, relieved that there wasn't a big hole in it.

Menno shook his finger at Dennis. "I think you'd better apologize to Lydia for not watching what you were doing."

"Sorry," Dennis mumbled.

"It was an accident. I'm sure you didn't do it on purpose." Lydia smiled and gave Dennis's shoulder a gentle squeeze. "I shouldn't have been standing so close to where you were fishing."

Menno handed Lydia a fishing pole.

"Since it doesn't look like Ike's going to use this, would you like to try your hand at fishing?"

"Sure, I'll give it a try." Lydia took the pole and positioned herself on the grass.

⁂

As Levi and his family shared a picnic supper at the pond, he had a hard time taking part in all the joking and silly bantering that was going on.

"Say, did ya take a bath last night?" Andy asked Peter as he poked his arm.

Peter snickered. "Why? Is there one missin'?"

Andy groaned. "Very funny. Ha! Ha!"

"Could you pass me the potato salad?" Betty asked.

Peter yawned and took his sweet time handing Betty the bowl of potato salad.

Betty frowned. "You're the laziest boy I know. Don't you do anything fast?"

"Jah, I get tired real fast."

Everyone but Levi laughed. He felt nothing but irritation, as he struggled not to watch Lydia and Menno sitting beside each other at the edge of the pond.

"Did you hear that the smartest man in

the world is becoming deaf?" Pop asked, nudging Mom's arm.

"No, tell me about it," she said.

Pop leaned closer to Mom and cupped his hand around his ear. "Eh? What was that you said?"

Everyone roared. Everyone but Levi. He just couldn't take his eyes off Lydia.

"What do you say, Levi?" Mom asked. "Should I cut the pie into six or eight pieces?"

Levi shrugged in reply.

"Better make it six," Pop said. "Don't think I can eat eight pieces all by myself."

Selma snickered. "Ha! That's a good one, Pop."

Someone hollered, and Levi glanced toward the pond. A couple of Menno's boys were running back and forth on the grass behind Menno and Lydia, tossing water balloons around. Suddenly, one of the balloons sailed through the air and smacked Selma right in the face!

"I can't see!" Selma covered her eye and rocked back and forth. "My *aage* hurts, and it's swellin' shut!"

CHAPTER 32

Let me have a look at your eye." Mom pulled Selma's hands away from her face. "Ach, it's all red, and you're right, it's beginning to swell really bad."

"I think we should go home right now and call one of our drivers to take Selma to the hospital emergency room," Levi said.

"Let's try to get the swelling down before we make a decision on that." Pop turned to Mom. "Don't you have some ice we can put on it?"

"As a matter of fact, I do." Mom reached into the cooler and withdrew a small ice pack. "Hold this against your eye for a while, and we'll see if it gets any better," she told Selma.

Levi picked up the soggy water balloon and ground his teeth. So much for their fun-filled picnic supper! "One of Menno's boys threw this, and I'm going over there and find out who it was." He leaped to his feet and dashed through the tall grass between them.

"What's wrong? You look *umgerennt*," Menno said when Levi strode up to him.

"I am upset. Two of your boys were tossing water balloons around, and one of them hit Selma in the eye."

"Is she okay?" Lydia asked before Menno could respond. She looked genuinely concerned.

"We don't know yet. Her eye's all red and starting to swell shut."

"Which one of my boys threw the balloon?" Menno questioned.

Levi shrugged. "Didn't see who threw it; just saw them tossing the balloons around. We were about to have some dessert when—*wham!*—Selma got hit in the eye. Right after that your boys darted into the woods."

"I'm sorry about your sister's eye, and I'll take care of my boys right away." Menno stalked off toward wooded area behind them.

⁑

When Menno entered the woods, he discovered Dennis and Carl crouched behind a tree. "Come out here, you two, and be quick about it!"

The boys stepped out, faces red and heads hanging down.

"Were you throwing water balloons?"

Dennis nodded.

"Where'd you get them?"

"Brought 'em from home," Carl said. "We filled the balloons with water from our hose and put 'em in a box in the back of our buggy."

"Which one of you threw the water balloon that hit Selma Stutzman in the eye?"

"It wasn't me," Carl said.

Dennis shook his head. "Wasn't me, neither."

Menno's brows furrowed, and he clenched his fingers. "Well, one of you did it, and if you don't own up to it right now, I'll break a switch from one of these trees and give you both a *bletsching*."

Dennis squirmed nervously, and Carl started to cry.

"It . . . it was me, Papa, but I . . . I didn't do it on purpose." Carl sniffed a couple of times. "Wasn't aimin' at Selma a'tall."

"That's right," Dennis put in. "We were tryin' to see who could throw the farthest, and Carl's balloon didn't make it too far."

"You shouldn't have been pitching water balloons so close to where the Stutzmans were sitting, and you should have checked with me first before you brought the water balloons from home." Menno was tempted to follow through with his threat to spank the boys, but decided he should wait until he was calmer to decide how to discipline them.

"Come with me now." He took both boys by the arm.

"Where are we goin'?" Carl's lower lip trembled.

"You need to tell Selma you're sorry, and then we'll be heading for home."

"Do we hafta go so soon?" Dennis whined. "I haven't done any fishin' yet."

"If you'd wanted to fish so bad, you

wouldn't have been fooling around with water balloons."

Menno led the boys over to where the Stutzmans were gathered around Selma. Lydia was there, too, talking with Levi's mother.

"Is she going to be all right?" Menno asked Levi's father.

Harold shrugged. "Don't know yet. Her eye's still swollen, and she says that everything looks blurry."

"I'm real sorry this happened, and now my boys have something to say." Menno nudged Carl's arm.

"Sorry," Carl said in a shaky voice. "I wasn't aimin' the water balloon at you, Selma."

Dennis gave a nod. "It was just an accident."

"We figured that," Nona said in a gentle tone of voice.

Selma said nothing; just sniffed and rocked back and forth as she held the ice pack against her eye.

"You should have been watching where you were throwing those things," Levi admonished. "You know, I read in *The Budget* not long ago about a boy in Missouri who lost his eyesight after getting hit in the face with a water balloon. You ought to be more careful from now on."

"We will," Dennis and Carl both said.

Menno looked at Lydia. "I think it's time we gathered up our things and headed for home."

"We'd better go, too," Harold said. "After what Levi told us about that boy in Missouri, we're not taking any chances. Selma needs to have her eye looked at this evening."

Lydia leaned closer to Nona and said, "I'll be praying that there will be no permanent damage to Selma's eye."

Nona smiled. "We'll appreciate the prayers."

Lydia rose to her feet and followed Menno to his buggy. *I probably have no chance with Lydia now,* he thought. *Who'd want to be a mother to my troublesome boys?*

Lydia was quiet on the ride home, thinking about Selma and worrying about her eye. She was glad the Stutzmans planned to see that Selma's eye was looked at right away. Something like this could be very serious if left untreated, and it would be tragic if Selma lost the sight in her eye.

"You're not sayin' much." Menno reached across the seat and placed his hand on Lydia's arm. "Are you upset because our evening was cut short?"

"No, I'm concerned about Selma."

He nodded. "Hopefully she'll be all right. Think I'll stop by their place tomorrow to find out for sure."

"That's a good idea."

"I feel bad about you seein' my boys act up like they did this evening. It seems like they're always getting into some kind of trouble."

Lydia glanced over her shoulder. All four boys were slouched in their seats with their eyes closed. Were they sleeping or keeping quiet so Menno didn't yell at them anymore?

"I know I've said this before, but it's been hard for me to handle them since their mamm died," Menno said quietly. "As time goes by, it doesn't seem to be getting any easier."

"I think it's always harder for a parent to raise a child alone."

"Or in my case, four rowdy kinner." Menno's lips compressed. "There's so much responsibility resting on my shoulders. Sometimes I feel like I might cave in."

"Have you thought about moving back to Pennsylvania where your family lives? I'm sure you'd have a lot of help there."

He pulled back on the reins to slow the horse, as it had begun to trot when they neared Lydia's driveway. "When Sadie first died, my sisters practically begged me to move back to Pennsylvania, but my business is here, and I need to keep it going so I can support my family."

"I understand. That's the reason I moved to Ohio—so I could find a job to support myself and Josh." She sighed and relaxed against the seat. "I haven't been living in Charm very long, but I've made many new friends, and it's finally beginning to feel like home."

"It felt like home to me until Sadie died. Now our house feels like an empty building instead of a home." Menno glanced over at Lydia and cleared his throat. "I've thought about getting married again. If my boys had a mother, I'm sure they'd settle right down."

Lydia shifted uneasily. Was Menno hinting that he might be considering her as a candidate for marriage? Oh, surely not. They didn't know each other well enough for that. He was probably just making conversation.

"Looks like your boys might have fallen asleep," she said, glancing over her shoulder again.

"Humph! They may as well enjoy their rest now, because when we get home there'll be plenty of chores for them to do—especially Carl and Dennis."

Menno guided his horse up to the hitching rail, jumped down, and helped Lydia from the buggy. "Maybe we can have another picnic sometime before the fall weather sets in," he said with a hopeful expression.

"Maybe so." She lifted her picnic basket out of the buggy. "I'll see you at church tomorrow, Menno. Tell the boys I said goodbye."

"Sure will."

Lydia hurried toward the house, anxious to tell Mom about her evening and what had happened to Selma's eye.

When she stepped into the house, she

found that none of the gas lamps had been lit in the kitchen or living room. That was strange. Mom usually made sure there was light in all the downstairs rooms as soon as the sun started going down.

"Mom, I'm home," Lydia called. "Where are you?"

No answer. Just the steady *tick-tock* from the clock on the fireplace mantel.

"Mom, are you here?"

Still no response.

Lydia lit the lamp hanging over the kitchen table and glanced around to see if Mom might have left a note. Maybe she'd gone out for a walk or had decided to pay a call on one of her friends. There was no note in sight, however.

Lydia was about to head outside to see if Mom's horse and buggy were there, when she decided to check upstairs first. Maybe Mom was in her room with the door shut and didn't hear Lydia calling.

Lydia quickly ascended the stairs, and when she got to the top, she halted. Mom lay in the hallway. Beside her was a ladder tipped on its side.

CHAPTER 33

I'm really sorry about this," Mom said as Lydia helped her get settled in bed.

Lydia shook her head. "It's not your fault you fell and broke your arm."

"I shouldn't have climbed that rickety old ladder." Mom yawned noisily. "But I couldn't reach the shelf in my closet where I store some of my material, and . . ." She yawned again. "I'm feeling so sleepy. Can barely keep my eyes open."

"You have every right to be tired. We've just spent the last several hours at the hospital, and now it's past midnight. Besides, the doctor said the pain medicine he gave you would make you sleepy."

Mom's forehead wrinkled as she frowned. "Thanks to my carelessness, I won't be able to do any sewing or quilting. Sure can't do that with only one good arm." Tears welled in her eyes and splashed onto her cheeks. "So much for me helping out with our finances. I won't be able to do most of the household chores now, either."

Lydia patted Mom's shoulder. "Don't worry about it. Once the word gets out, I'm sure some of the women in our community will come over to help."

"Just when I thought things were getting better. Just when . . ." Mom's eyelids fluttered and then closed.

Lydia knew from the rise and fall of Mom's chest that she'd fallen asleep. She turned off the battery-operated light by Mom's bed and slipped quietly from the room.

Outside in the hall, she leaned heavily against the wall. Was there no end to their troubles? Things were just starting to go better, and now this!

"How's your eye feeling?" Nona asked when Selma entered the kitchen on Sunday morning.

"It feels a little better, but it's still swollen."

"The doctor said it might take a few days for all the swelling to subside," Nona said. "Your daed and I was so relieved when we were told that there was no permanent damage done to your eye."

"I'm glad it's an off-Sunday for us today," Selma said. "I sure wouldn't want to go to church and have everyone see me lookin' like this."

Nona glanced at the door leading to the kitchen. "Where's Betty? Didn't she come downstairs with you?"

"She did, but she's in the bathroom."

"While we're waiting for her to join us, why don't you get busy and set the table? The men and boys will be in from doing their chores soon, and it would be nice to have breakfast waiting for them."

Selma went to the cupboard, climbed onto her stool, and took out some plates. She'd just placed them on the table when Levi stepped into the room. "How's that eye doing this morning?" he asked.

"A little better, but there's still some swelling, and everything's a little blurry yet."

"I still think Menno's boys shouldn't have been throwing water balloons so close to where you were sitting. I don't think Menno pays enough attention to what his kinner are doing."

Nona couldn't help but notice Levi's furrowed brows. Was he that upset about Selma's eye, or was he irritated because Lydia had been with Menno and his boys at the pond? Nona thought she'd seen a look of jealousy on Levi's face yesterday evening. She had a hunch that Menno was looking for a new wife, and she couldn't really blame him for that. Those four boys needed a mother to help raise them. She just hoped it wouldn't be Lydia he chose.

She'd been wishing Lydia and Levi might get together. She'd seen the way Levi looked at Lydia and felt sure he was fighting his attraction to her. Should she try to convince him to pursue a relationship with Lydia, or would that push him further away?

If only she could make Levi see that he was free to make a life of his own. Maybe it would have been better if he'd been born with dwarfism like the rest of her children. At least then he wouldn't think he had to do everything for them.

Church was being held in Bishop Yoder's buggy shop, less than a mile from Menno's place. Since the boys had fooled around so much while getting ready, he'd been glad that they hadn't had to travel far, or they surely would have been late.

As Menno took a seat on a bench on the men's side of the room, he quickly scanned the faces of the women sitting across from him. There was no sign of Lydia or her mother.

He glanced over at Carl and Dennis, already beginning to fidget on their bench, and hoped he wouldn't have to end up taking one of them out this morning. Never when Sadie was alive had the boys been disruptive during church. She'd always managed to maintain control. He needed a mother for his boys.

I wonder if everything's all right with Lydia. Seems strange that neither she nor her mamm are here today. Think I'll

drop the boys off at home after church and head over to Mae's place to see what's up.

⁂

Lydia had just taken the teakettle from the stove when she heard a horse and buggy pull into the yard. Not wishing to wake Mom, who was asleep in the living room, she quickly opened the door and stepped outside.

When the horse and buggy pulled up to the hitching rail, she was surprised to see Menno step down.

"I was concerned when I didn't see you at church today," he said as she approached his buggy. "Wondered if you'd gotten sick or something."

Lydia shook her head. "My mamm fell and broke her arm last night. She's not feeling up to going anywhere right now."

Menno's eyebrows shot up. "How'd that happen?"

Lydia explained what had happened, then added, "We didn't get home from the hospital until close to midnight, so we were both pretty tired this morning."

"I can imagine, and I'm sorry to hear about Mae. Is she in much pain?"

"She is, but the pain pills help with that, although they make her sleepy. We saw the Stutzmans when we were at the hospital last night," Lydia added, "but I never got a full report on how Selma's eye is doing."

"I stopped by their place before I came here," he said. "Selma's eye looked a little better, and Nona said the doctor told them there'd be no permanent damage."

"I'm glad to hear it." Lydia glanced toward the house, thinking she really should check on Mom.

"Guess I'd better let you go. Besides, I should get home. No telling what those boys of mine are up to by now." Menno stepped into his buggy. "See you soon, Lydia."

As Meno drove away, Lydia turned toward the house. Just as she reached the back porch, another horse and buggy pulled into the yard. This time it was Rueben. He secured his horse to the hitching rail and headed for the house. Lydia met him halfway across the lawn.

"I missed seeing you and your mamm at church this morning and thought I'd stop by on my way home and check up on you."

Rueben glanced toward the house. "Mae's not sick, is she?"

"No, but she fell and broke her arm yesterday." Lydia once again related the story of the evening's events.

"That's a shame." His brows furrowed. "Is she feeling up to company? I'd like to say hello and let her know I'm concerned about her."

"She's sleeping right now," Lydia said. "After her last pain pill took affect, she couldn't keep her eyes open."

"Guess I won't disturb her then. Please tell Mae that I stopped by, and do let me know if you need anything."

As Rueben's buggy pulled out of the yard, Lydia thought about the look of concern on his face when he'd heard about Mom.

I wonder if I should invite him to join us for supper some evening, Lydia thought as she stepped onto the porch. *Maybe when we have Menno and his boys over again, I'll make sure Rueben's included. Surely Mom won't mind.*

CHAPTER 34

Are you sure you're going to be all right here by yourself?" Lydia asked Mom on Monday morning.

Mom, who sat at the kitchen table drinking a cup of tea, nodded. "You helped me get dressed, made my breakfast, and even put a sandwich in the refrigerator for my lunch, so I'm sure I'll be fine." She held up her left arm. "I still have one good arm, so I'm not completely helpless."

"I know, but you need to be careful not to do too much."

"I won't; I promise."

"I need to head for work now," Lydia said,

glancing at the clock. "Is there anything you want me to do before I leave?"

Mom shook her head. "You go ahead and don't worry about me."

"I'll try not to, but I'm going to stop by Sarah Yoder's on my way to work and ask her to check up on you."

"There's no need for that."

"Sarah's your friend," Lydia said. "She'd want to know that you broke your arm, and I'm sure she wondered why we weren't at church yesterday."

"I suppose you're right."

Lydia gave Mom a hug and opened the back door. She was about to step out when she noticed a cardboard box sitting on the porch, a few feet from the door.

"What's that?" Mom asked when Lydia returned to the kitchen and set the box on the table.

Lydia opened the flaps on the box. "It's full of canned food items and some root vegetables. It looks like our secret gift-giver is at it again."

Mom peered into the box. "Hmm . . . I wonder who it could be."

"I don't know, but I have my suspicions.

I'm really thinking it must be either Menno or Rueben."

Mom pursed her lips. "Hmm . . . You did say that they both stopped by here yesterday when I was napping, so they're the only ones who know I broke my arm. Of course, one or both of them might have told someone else by now. Anyone could have left the food, I suppose."

Lydia motioned to the box. "I'll put these things away when I get home from work."

"I can do it," Mom said.

Lydia shook her head. "These things need to be put on the shelves in the basement."

Mom's jaw tightened. "My legs aren't broken, Lydia. I'm perfectly capable of going down to the basement."

"But with only one good arm, you can't carry jars and hold onto the railing."

"Guess you have a point."

"Promise not to go down to the basement?"

"I won't go down."

"I've really got to go now, or I'll be late for my shift." Lydia gave Mom another hug.

"Take it easy while I'm gone, and I'll see you later this afternoon."

⁂

After Lydia left, Mae decided to rest on the sofa. Her eyes felt so heavy she could barely keep them open. *It must be the pain medication,* she thought as she reclined on the sofa and closed her eyes. *I'll just rest here awhile . . .*

Tap-tap-tap!

Mae's eyes snapped open. When she glanced at the clock, she realized that she must have fallen asleep, because Lydia had been gone nearly an hour.

"Come in," she called.

The back door squeaked open, and Sarah Yoder stepped into the room.

"Lydia stopped by on her way to work and said you fell and broke your arm." Sarah took a seat in the chair closest to Mae. "I came over to see if you needed my help with anything."

Mae yawned and sat up. "Actually there is something you could do."

"What's that?"

"Someone left us a box of food this morning, and Lydia made me promise not to put the things away myself."

"No problem. Where do you want me to put things?"

"It's canned items and some root vege-tables, so you can put them in the base-ment."

"I'll do that right now. Is the box in the kitchen?"

Mae nodded. "But you don't have to do it this minute. If you have the time, we can sit and visit awhile."

"Let me get the things put away first, and then I'll make us a pot of tea, and we can visit."

Mae smiled. "I appreciate your coming by."

"That's what friends are for." Sarah hur-ried from the room.

A few minutes later, there was another knock on the door.

Knowing that Sarah had gone to the basement, Mae went to the door and opened it. Nona Stutzman stood on the porch.

☙

"We were at the hospital last Saturday night, waiting to hear some word on our daughter Selma's eye, and saw Lydia. She explained that you'd broken your arm,"

Nona said to Mae. "I came over to see if you needed my help with anything."

Mae shifted from one foot to the other and dropped her gaze to the porch. "I . . . uh . . . Sarah Yoder's helping me." She glanced over her shoulder. "She's in the basement right now."

"Oh, I see. Well, isn't there something else I can do to help?"

Mae shook her head. "I can't think of a thing."

"Are you sure, because I'd be glad to—"

"I'm doing fine. Thanks for stopping."

"All right then. Please let us know if you think of anything we can do for you." Nona turned and walked back to her buggy. Normally she felt accepted among the Amish, but not so with Mae, who obviously felt uncomfortable around her. The question was, why?

CHAPTER 35

It had been two weeks since Lydia's mother broke her arm. Nearly every day, one or more women from their community had come over to help out while Lydia was at work. Although it was hard to accept help from others, Lydia had a sense of peace knowing that Mom wasn't at home by herself trying to do things she shouldn't.

At least twice a week, secret gifts were left on their porch. That morning before Lydia left for work, she'd found a basket full of homemade bread. Three days ago, they'd been given a ham, as well as a stack of cut firewood, which was appreciated, since Mom liked to sit by the fire in the evenings and read.

Sure wish I knew who to thank for their generosity, Lydia thought as she donned her work apron at the beginning of her Wednesday shift.

She glanced across the room and saw Rueben being seated by the hostess. *I wonder if I should say something to him about the things that have been left on our porch. If he's the one responsible, maybe he'll admit it.*

Lydia picked up her order pad and walked over to his table. "Good morning, Rueben. Would you like to look at the menu, or did you want to order the breakfast special?"

"I have a couple of horses to shoe this morning, so I don't have much time. Think I'll just have a cup of coffee and a few glazed doughnuts."

Lydia's forehead wrinkled. "If Mom was here right now, she'd lecture you about not eating right. She's always stressed the importance of eating a nutritious breakfast."

He chuckled. "Your mamm's always been kind of a health nut. Even when we were kinner in school, she used to lecture me and the other scholars about not eating too many sweets. Said we ought to bring fruit in our lunchboxes instead of doughnuts and cookies."

"I didn't realize you knew Mom when she was a girl."

"Jah. We went to the same school here in Charm." Rueben ran his fingers down the length of his nose. "I had a crush on her for a time, but then she chose David Weaver instead of me, so I started courting Rachel Mullet."

"Hmm . . . that's interesting." Lydia wondered why Mom had never said anything about knowing Rueben when they were children. Did Mom know that Rueben had been interested in her back then?

"Speaking of your mamm," Rueben said, "I haven't checked on her in a while and wondered how she's getting along with her arm."

"Pretty well. Some of the women in our community have been helping, so that's kept her from doing too much. She has about four weeks left until the cast comes off."

"Glad to hear she's allowing others to

help. Your mamm's always tried to do too much on her own."

"I know, but she and I are both learning to accept help, as well as the gifts that have come from others." Lydia paused, hoping Rueben might ask what gifts she was referring to. Instead, he changed the subject.

"Since Mae and I are both widowed, I was hoping there might be a chance for us to get together." Rueben's forehead wrinkled as he slowly shook his head. "Every time I think she might be showing me some interest, she cools off again. Sometimes when I've stopped over to see her, she's been friendly. Other times she's been distant—like she couldn't wait for me to leave. Makes me wonder if I ought to give up on the idea of us becoming a couple."

Lydia shook her head. "I wouldn't give up on her yet. If you spend more time with Mom, I'm sure she'll see what a nice man you are. I've been planning to invite you over to our place for supper. Would you be free to come this Friday evening?"

Rueben's eyes brightened as he nodded. "Friday would be fine for me. Is there anything I can bring to help with the meal?"

"Just a hearty appetite. Someone's been leaving food on our porch for the last couple of weeks, so we'll have a good selection to choose from for supper."

Rueben grinned and thumped his stomach. "I'll make sure I don't eat too much breakfast or lunch that day so I'll have plenty of room for that good supper."

Lydia felt deflated. Rueben certainly hadn't given any hint that he had been leaving the food on their porch. Of course, if he didn't want her to know, he might have been playing dumb.

"I'd planned to invite Menno and his boys to join us for supper, too," Lydia said. "Is that all right with you?"

Rueben nodded. "That'll be fine."

"Good. We'll look forward to seeing you on Friday evening." *I just hope Mom's as happy about it as Rueben seems to be,* Lydia thought as she walked away.

As soon as Nona entered the restaurant, she spotted Lydia waiting on Rueben Miller. Hoping she'd have a few minutes to visit with Lydia, she indicated to the hostess that she'd like to be seated on the side of the room where Lydia waited on tables.

"Oh, and I'll need something to sit on," Nona reminded the hostess.

The young English woman smiled and said, "I'll bring you a stack of newspapers."

Once Nona was seated, she glanced at the menu the hostess had given her.

"How's Selma's eye?" Lydia asked, stepping up to Nona's table.

"Much better. The doctor said she's going to be just fine."

"That's good to hear." Lydia motioned to the menu. "Are you here for breakfast?"

Nona shook her head. "I'll just have a cup of hot tea and a cinnamon roll. I really came by in the hopes that I could talk to you for a few minutes. If you have the time, that is," she quickly added.

Lydia glanced around the room. "We don't have too many customers right now, so I probably have a few minutes."

"I wanted to ask about your mamm—to see how she's getting along with her broken arm."

"She's doing fairly well and has been getting some help from others in our community."

"I'm glad to hear it." Nona tapped her fingers along the edge of the table, wondering how best to say what was really on her mind.

"Is something bothering you?" Lydia asked.

"Actually, there is." Nona cleared her throat a couple of times. "When I went over to your place a couple days after your mamm broke her arm, I offered to help out, but she said she was getting along just fine. Now you say that she's getting help from others in our community. It makes me wonder why she can accept help from them but not me."

Lydia moistened her lips with the tip of her tongue. "Well, I—"

"I get the feeling that I'm not welcome at your mamm's house, and she never comes into our store anymore. Do you know if I've done something to offend her?"

"I don't think so. I . . . I mean, I can't imagine what it could be." Lydia shifted uneasily. "As far as I'm concerned, you and your family are welcome to visit us anytime."

"Are you sure about that?"

"Jah."

Nona smiled. "All right then, we'll be over for a visit sometime soon."

CHAPTER 36

I still can't believe you invited Rueben for supper this evening without asking me first," Mae said as she sat at the table, watching Lydia scurry around the kitchen.

Lydia turned from peeling potatoes and smiled. "I figured you might say no."

"What would make you think that?"

"Because sometimes when Rueben's stopped by, you've given him the cold shoulder."

"How do you know that?"

"Rueben said so."

Mae frowned. "When did he tell you that?"

"Wednesday morning when he came into the restaurant for coffee and dough-nuts."

"Humph! He should have eaten a better breakfast than coffee and doughnuts."

Lydia snickered. "He said you'd say that."

"Oh, he did, did he?" Mae thumped her cast. "What else did Mr. Miller say about me?"

Lydia's face colored, and she turned back to the sink.

"Lydia, what'd Rueben say?"

"He said he had a crush on you when you were kinner, and now that you're both widowed, he'd been hoping that the two of you might get together." Lydia glanced over her shoulder. "He said he'd thought for a while that he might have a chance with you, but now he's not so sure."

Mae straightened the silverware on the table in front of her as she tried to formulate the right words. She wasn't sure how Lydia would take it if she told her that she'd been fighting her attraction to Rueben ever since she'd returned to Charm to take care of Dad.

Lydia left the sink and took a seat beside Mae. "Do you have feelings for Rueben?"

She nodded slowly. "Truth is whenever he comes around, I can barely take my eyes off him."

Lydia's eyes widened as her mouth formed an O.

"Are you upset because I have feelings for Rueben?"

"Why would I be upset?"

Mae leaned over and blew on her tea. "I know how close you and your daed used to be. I've been concerned that if you knew how I felt about Rueben you might think I'd stopped loving your daed."

"Dad will always hold a special place in your heart, just like Jeremiah will hold a place in mine. But I think Dad would want you to go on with your life and be happy," Lydia said. "He'd be pleased if you found love again."

"I appreciate hearing you say that, but I can't get involved with Rueben right now."

"Why not?"

"Because you need me."

"Oh, Mom, don't let that be your excuse. I'm a grown woman and can make it on my own." Lydia placed her hand over Mae's. "I would never stand in the way of your happiness. If being with Rueben makes you happy, then you need to give him a chance."

A sense of relief flooded Mae's soul. If Menno kept coming around to see Lydia, maybe by this time next year, she and Lydia would both be married.

∂⊚

During supper that evening, Lydia was pleased to see Mom chatting with Rueben. She was even more pleased when she overheard Rueben ask Mom if she'd like to go out to lunch with him soon and Mom had agreed to go.

Lydia glanced at Menno, who sat to her left. "Would you like another piece of ham?" she asked.

"Jah, sure." He took a piece and passed the platter to Ike. "How about you, son?"

Ike shook his head. "I'm full up."

"Does that mean you won't have room for dessert?" Mom asked.

Ike shrugged. "Guess that depends on what it is."

Menno nudged the boy's arm. "Don't be rude."

"What are we havin' for dessert?" Carl wanted to know.

"Lydia brought a couple of apple pies home from the restaurant," Mom said before Lydia could respond.

"I don't like apple pie," Dennis put in. "Can't we have somethin' else?"

Menno glared at the boy. "If you want dessert, then you'll eat the pie."

"Guess I won't have any then."

"I like apple pie," Kevin interjected. "Can I have Dennis's piece?"

"I think one's all you need," Menno said. "Now get busy and finish your supper."

The boys ate in silence, and after the final prayer, they scampered out the back door to play.

Menno looked over at Lydia and smiled. "That was a good meal. Now I'll help you with the dishes."

"Oh no, you don't have to do that."

"I really don't mind. I do dirty dishes at home whenever I can't get the boys to do 'em, so I've gotten pretty good at it."

"I'd appreciate your help." Lydia pushed away from the table. "Mom, why don't you and Rueben go into the living room and visit while Menno and I do the dishes?"

Mom rose from her chair. "That's a nice idea. I think we will."

Rueben looked over at Lydia and winked; then he followed Mom out of the room.

While Lydia and Menno did the dishes, Menno talked about his woodshop and how busy he'd been over the summer months. "Things have slowed down some now that fall's here," he said, "my work will no doubt pick up again when people start buying for Christmas."

A lump formed in Lydia's throat. The thought of spending Christmas without Josh made her feel like crying. It wasn't fair that she'd only had her precious boy a few short years. She was sure she'd never stop missing him.

"You okay?" Menno touched Lydia's shoulder. "Did I say something wrong?"

"I was thinking about Christmas and wondering how I'm going to get through it this year without Josh." She sniffed, struggling to hold back her tears. "The thought of going through the holidays without my son makes me wish Christmas would never come."

"But you still have your mamm."

"That's true."

"Think you'll ever get married again?" he asked suddenly.

"I . . . I don't know." She sloshed the sponge around in the soapy dishwater, sending a few bubbles floating upward. One landed on her nose, and she flicked it aside. "When Josh was alive, I was worried because he didn't have a daed."

"I think all kinner are happier when there's a mamm and a daed, but sometimes it doesn't work out that way. Even so, I've been thinking. . . ."

A horse whinnied outside, and Menno stopped talking to look out the window. "Looks like you have more company."

Lydia saw two buggies pull into the yard and stop near the barn. "It's the Stutzmans," she said as she watched Levi and his family climb out of the buggies.

She dried her hands on a towel and hurried out the back door. She smiled when she saw Levi's brothers, Peter and Andy, playing a game of tag with Menno's boys.

"You said we should stop by any time," Nona said as she approached Lydia. "So we decided to come by this evening, and we've brought some dessert." She motioned to Harold, who walked beside her carrying two jugs of apple cider. "Our girls are getting a box of doughnuts from the buggy."

Lydia's gaze went to the second buggy, where Betty and Selma stood beside Levi. Although he was average height for a man his age, he looked like a giant compared to his small sisters.

Nona looked up at Menno, who'd joined Lydia on the lawn. "We didn't realize you had other company. Is this a bad time for us to have come?"

Lydia shook her head. "Menno and his boys and Rueben Miller joined us for supper this evening. We finished eating some time ago, so I'm sure everyone's ready for some dessert by now. Let's go inside and see."

While Menno rounded up his boys, the Stutzmans followed Lydia into the house.

"If you'd like to have a seat, I'll let Mom and Rueben know you're here," Lydia said, motioning to the kitchen table.

When Lydia entered the living room, she found Mom and Rueben sitting on the sofa. Mom had a copy of *The Budget* in her lap, and was reading Reuben an article by one of the scribes.

Lydia smiled. They looked like an old

married couple, relaxed and comfortable with each other while they enjoyed the solitude of time spent alone.

"Sorry for the interruption," Lydia said, "but more company's arrived."

"Who's here?" Mom asked.

"The Stutzmans. They brought some apple cider and doughnuts for dessert."

"I didn't know you'd invited the Stutzmans to join us for dessert." Irritation tinged Mom's voice.

"I didn't." Lydia shifted uneasily, feeling the sudden tension in the room. "I saw Nona at the restaurant on Wednesday, and she said they'd come by to see us soon. I guess tonight worked out for them."

"The more the merrier." Rueben grinned at Mom. "Just think, now we get to have some fresh apple cider and doughnuts to go with our apple pie. What could be better than that?"

Mom returned his smile, although Lydia could see that it was forced. Nona was right; for whatever reason, Mom clearly did not want the Stutzmans around.

When Lydia entered the kitchen with Mom and Rueben, she was surprised to see everyone seated at the table eating doughnuts, while Nona and Betty scurried around, filling glasses with apple cider.

"I have some apple pie to serve, too." Lydia went to the pantry and took out the pies.

It didn't take long for the pies and doughnuts to disappear, and while they ate, the Stutzmans took turns sharing jokes and humorous stories. Everyone seemed to be having a good time. Everyone but Mom and Levi, that is. They both remained quiet, only speaking when someone asked them a question.

"Can we go outside now?" Dennis asked his father. "We wanna look for the *katze*."

Menno nodded. "But don't get into any trouble."

Menno's boys scrambled for the door, as did Levi's two younger brothers.

The talk at the table turned to the weather, local news, and the state of the economy. Mom still said very little to anyone but Rueben, and Levi remained silent.

Maybe if I wasn't here, Mom would be forced to talk to the Stutzmans, Lydia thought. She stood. "Think I'll go outside and see if the boys were able to find the cats. When those critters don't want to be caught, they find all kinds of places to hide in the barn." She grabbed her sweater from the wall peg in the utility room and slipped out the back door.

"We can't find any of the katze," Carl said when Lydia joined the boys on the lawn.

Peter grunted. "Who cares about the *dumm* old katze. I say we play some more tag."

Dennis, Carl, and Peter bobbed their heads, but Kevin did not. "Don't wanna play tag," he mumbled. "I wanna play with the katze."

"Me, too," Andy said.

Lydia motioned to the barn. "Let's see if they're hiding in there."

Andy shook his head. "We looked in the barn already. Didn't find any sign of the katze."

"I think I may know how to roust them out of their hiding place." Lydia headed to the barn, and Kevin and Andy followed.

Once inside, Lydia got out a bag of cat food and poured some into one of their dishes. "Usually the sound of food brings them running," she said.

The boys glanced around with expectant expressions.

"Where are they?" Kevin asked. "Sure don't see any katze yet."

Lydia nudged the dish of food with her foot, so the food would rattle. "Here kitty, kitty."

No response; not even a *meow*.

"Guess they're not hungerich," Andy said. "Maybe we outa find somethin' else to do." He looked up and pointed to the rope swing hanging from the rafters. "If we could reach it, we could swing on it."

Kevin looked up at Lydia. "You're bigger'n us. Can ya get the rope down?"

"The only way I can reach it is if I climb the ladder to the loft," Lydia said.

"Would ya do that? Would ya please get it for us, Lydia?"

Kevin's eager expression reminded Lydia of Josh. He'd often looked at her the same way when he'd wanted something really bad.

Before Lydia could respond to Kevin's request, Levi entered the barn. "It's time for us to go," he told Andy. "I've got the horses hitched, and everyone's waiting in the buggies."

Andy groaned. "Wish we didn't have to leave so soon. Me and Kevin were gonna play on the rope swing."

"You can play on it the next time you come over," Lydia said.

"Okay." Andy ambled out of the barn, and Kevin followed.

"It was nice of you and your folks to stop by," Lydia said to Levi. "Everyone enjoyed the apple cider and doughnuts, and it was fun to visit and listen to your family's jokes."

"Too bad your mamm didn't enjoy our visit. It's obvious that she doesn't like me or my family very much. It's sad to say, but some folks are prejudiced against people who are different than them." Levi frowned deeply. "My parents and siblings are little people, Lydia, not lepers."

Lydia was speechless. She'd never seen Levi get angry before. "I'm sorry for my mamm's behavior. I don't understand why she acts the way she does toward your family. She had an unhappy childhood, and—"

"That's no excuse! Nobody's life is perfect. We can rise above our circumstances and love everyone the way the Bible says we should."

Lydia nodded. "You're right, of course.

Would you like me to talk to Mom and see if I can find out why she acts so rude whenever your family's around?"

Levi shrugged and walked out of the barn.

CHAPTER 37

One week after Mae's cast came off, she decided to start quilting again. Her fingers were stiff from not using them for so long, but she'd been doing the exercises the doctor had given her and hoped it wouldn't be long before she had full use of her hand again. In the meantime, she would get her quilting blocks cut out and ready to sew.

Mae's stomach growled, and she glanced at the clock. It was half past eleven, and she felt ready for lunch. But she wanted to cut out the rest of the squares before she took the material off the kitchen table.

Half an hour later when she'd finished

cutting the last square, she heard a horse and buggy rumble up the driveway and into the yard. She glanced out the window. Rueben was climbing down from his buggy.

"I see you've got your cast off," Rueben said when he entered the house a few minutes later.

"The doctor removed it last week." She smiled and lifted her arm. "Feels a lot lighter now."

"I'm sure it does."

She motioned to the fabric on the table. "I've been cutting out material, getting ready to do some quilting as soon as my fingers start working better. Before I get too carried away with sewing, however, I need to go to Miller's Dry Goods and see if they've sold any of my quilts and might want more."

"Say, I have an idea," he said, leaning against the cupboard door.

"What's that?"

"I've got some free time right now, so why don't the two of us head over to Miller's?"

She glanced at the clock on the far wall. "Right now?"

He nodded. "Figured we could stop at

Grandma's Restaurant and get some lunch before we head over to the dry goods store. How's that sound to you?"

She smiled. "It sounds nice. It'll give us a chance to say hello to Lydia."

Lydia was surprised when she saw Mom and Rueben enter the restaurant. It was only the second time Mom had come into the restaurant since Lydia had started working there, and it was the first time Mom had come in with Rueben. This was a very good sign.

As soon as they were seated in a booth, Lydia hurried over to their table. "It's good to see you. Did you come in for lunch?"

"Sure did." Rueben smiled at Mom. "When we're done here, I'm taking your mamm over to Miller's Dry Goods Store to check on her quilts."

Lydia could see by Rueben's expression that he really enjoyed Mom's company.

"I was busy this morning cutting some quilt squares," Mom said. "So I'm hoping that Miller's will want me to bring in a few more quilts once I get them made."

"If they don't, you could take them to

one of the quilt shops in Berlin," Rueben said.

Mom looked at Rueben as though she'd never thought of that idea. Never mind that she and Lydia had discussed it and that Mom had already talked to the owner of the quilt shop in Berlin. "That's right. The last time I was there, they said they'd be interested in me bringing some of my quilts."

"When you have some quilts ready to take to Berlin, I'd be happy to drive you there." Rueben leaned a little closer to Mom.

"I'd appreciate that very much."

Lydia couldn't believe the way Mom and Rueben were acting—like a young courting couple. Mom looked happier than Lydia had seen her in a very long time.

"Guess if we're gonna eat we'd better put In our order," Rueben said.

Lydia pointed to the menu. "Would you like the special of the day, or is there something else you'd rather have?"

"What would you like?" Rueben asked, looking at Mom.

"A turkey sandwich sounds good to me."

Rueben looked at Lydia and wiggled his

thick eyebrows. "Think I'll have the same as your mamm."

"I'll put your order in right now." As Lydia turned, she spotted Menno heading her way.

"Can I talk to you for a minute?" he asked.

"Of course. Did you need a table?"

"I can't stay for lunch today. I came in because I have a favor to ask."

"What is it?"

"I was wondering if you have to work this Saturday."

She shook her head. "Saturday's my day off this week. Why do you ask?"

He shifted from one foot to the other. "The thing is . . . I have to go out of town on business on Saturday, and I can't take the boys with me. So, I was wondering . . ." He tugged his left earlobe. "Would you be willing to keep an eye on them for me?"

"I wouldn't mind at all. You can bring them over to our house before you leave town."

"I'd rather you come to my place, if you don't mind. That way, the boys'll be able to get their chores done."

"I'd be happy to come over," Lydia said.

"I'll probably be gone most of the day. Might not be home until around seven, so would you mind fixing their supper, too?"

"No. I'll look forward to spending time with the boys."

"Great. I'll come by your place and pick you up around eight on Saturday morning."

"You don't have to do that. I can ride my bike over."

"Sure you don't mind?"

"Not at all."

"I'll see you on Saturday then." Menno nodded at Lydia and headed out the door.

A short time later, Levi entered the restaurant and was shown to a table.

"It's nice to see you," Lydia said, stepping up to him. "How are things with you and your family?"

"Okay." Levi tapped his menu along the edge of the table. "Uh—this Saturday is my mamm's birthday, and I was wondering if you'd liked to join us and several others for a surprise supper we're planning for her that evening. I'm sure Mom would like having you there."

Lydia was on the verge of saying yes, when she remembered her promise to spend Saturday with Menno's boys. "I really wish I could," she said, "but I promised Menno that I'd take care of his boys on Saturday, and since he won't get home until after supper, I won't be free to attend your mamm's party."

"Oh, I see." A look of disappointment crossed Levi's face as he pushed the menu aside. "I'd better go."

"Aren't you going to order something?"

"Guess not. Thought I was hungry, but I've changed my mind."

As Levi left the restaurant, Lydia's heart clenched. She really liked the Stutzmans and would have enjoyed spending the evening with them.

I wish I could be there to see the look of surprise on Nona's face and have some small part in making her birthday special.

Chapter 38

On Saturday morning after breakfast, Menno told his boys to remain at the table so he could talk to them.

"Did we do somethin' wrong?" Dennis asked.

Menno shook his head. "I just wanted to remind you to be good for Lydia while I'm gone today." He looked over at Ike. "I'm counting on you to set a good example for your brothers." His gaze went to Carl, Dennis, and Kevin. "You need to make sure you get your chores done without Lydia having to remind you. Is that clear?"

Everyone nodded.

"Thought I might ask Lydia to go to Charm Days with us next weekend, so don't do anything to upset her, or she might say no."

Ike wrinkled his nose. "Do we hafta take Lydia with us to Charm Days?"

"Jah, Papa," Dennis put in. "We wanna do somethin' fun with just us and you for a change."

"All right," Menno said with a nod. "Just us five will go to Charm Days, but if we see Lydia there, I might ask her to join us for supper."

Before any of the boys could respond, a knock sounded on the back door. Menno pushed away from the table. "That must be Lydia now."

When Lydia entered Menno's kitchen, she found all four boys sitting at the table. From the looks of the cereal box and dirty dishes sitting out, it was obvious that they'd just finished breakfast.

"I was hoping to have the kitchen cleaned up and the dishes done before you got here," Menno said, "but the time's gotten away from me, and now I need to go."

"That's okay." Lydia smiled. "With the

boys' help, I'm sure we'll have this kitchen cleaned in no time."

Dennis groaned, and Menno glared at him. "Remember what we talked about?"

"Jah."

"Just do as you're told, and everything will be fine," Menno whispered to Ike. He looked at Lydia and shook his head. "When it comes to doing chores, they sometimes drag their feet, but once they get going they can get a lot of work done."

A horn honked, and Menno glanced out the kitchen window. "My ride's here, so I'd better get going." He pointed to a piece of paper lying on the counter. "My driver has a cell phone, so if you need to get in touch with me for anything, there's his number."

"I appreciate that, but I'm sure we'll be fine."

"All right, then. I'll see you sometime around seven." Menno gave each of his boys a pat on the head. "Be good now, you hear?"

⌀

"Thanks for helping me blow these up," Betty said as she handed Levi a package of balloons.

"Sure, no problem."

"You think Mom will be surprised?"

He shrugged. "You know Mom. She always seems to have a way of finding things out. I wouldn't be surprised if she already knows about it and has talked to everyone we've invited."

Betty's nose crinkled. "I sure hope not. Pop promised to keep her shopping in Millersburg until it's almost time for supper, and I really hope she'll be surprised." She pulled a red balloon from the package. "Is Lydia coming to the party?"

Levi shook his head. "She has other plans for this evening."

"What kind of plans?"

"She'll be at Menno's house, watching his boys all day while he's out of town on business."

"You don't like that very much, do you?"

"What makes you say that?"

"Your expression doesn't look very happy."

"I don't care what she does. It just would have been nice, for Mom's sake, if Lydia would have been free to come to the party." Levi blew up a red balloon, then a blue one, and tied them together. "Do you have a big box we can put these in?" he asked.

"Sure don't want them floating around the store all day."

"There's one in the back room that's just the right size." Betty poked Levi's arm. "Do you care for Lydia?"

"Just what are you getting at?"

"Are you thinking about courting her?"

"No. I'm not interested in courting anyone." He grabbed another balloon. "We'd better get these finished before customers start coming."

I'd never admit it to Betty, Levi thought, *but I was disappointed when Lydia said she couldn't come to Mom's party. Even though I know Lydia and I can't have a future together, I wish we could.* He clenched his teeth until his jaw ached. *Anyway, Menno seems interested in Lydia, and she'd probably be better off with him than me.*

⁂

As Lydia stepped out the back door to call the boys in for lunch, she nearly stepped on a wad of sticky chewing gum on the porch. She would have to get after the boys for that.

She moved to the end of the porch, cupped her hands around her mouth, and was about to call the boys, when a shaggy yellow dog bounded across the lawn, leaped onto the porch, and rammed into Lydia's legs. *Woof! Woof!*

She squealed and grabbed the porch railing to keep from losing her balance.

"She won't hurt ya none." Kevin hollered as he raced across the yard. He stepped onto the porch and grabbed the dog's collar. "Goldie, you'd better behave yourself. Papa said everyone's supposed to be nice to Lydia and not get into any trouble today." He shook his finger at the dog. "That means you, too."

Lydia smiled. Kevin was a good-natured boy, and the fact that he'd scolded the dog for nearly knocking her off her feet warmed her heart.

"Where are your brothers?" Lydia asked.

He pointed to the barn.

"Would you tell them that lunch is ready?"

"Sure." Pulling the dog by its collar, Kevin headed for the barn.

Lydia was amazed at the boy's strength, considering that Goldie was so big and Kevin was only one year older than Josh.

Tears pricked her eyes. Every time she

thought of Josh, she was overcome with a sense of sadness. Would the pain ever go away? Would she ever be able to look at a boy close to Josh's age and not think of him?

CHAPTER 39

By the time Lydia sat down with the boys to eat supper that evening, she was so tired she could hardly keep her eyes open. It had been a busy day. Keeping up with four energetic boys had been more draining than working a full shift at the restaurant. It wasn't that the boys were bad. They just fooled around a lot, and she had to keep reminding them to do their chores. Then there was that big shaggy dog. That afternoon, Goldie had tromped through a mud puddle and snuck into the house, leaving muddy paw prints all over the clean kitchen floor.

"I need some ketchup for my macaroni," Carl announced.

Dennis and Kevin reached for the ketchup at the same time, and the bottle tipped over, spilling Carl's glass of water all over his plate.

"Now look what you've done!" Carl glared at Kevin.

Kevin scrunched up his nose. "Didn't do it on purpose."

"You shoulda kept your hands to yourself and let me get the ketchup," Carl said. "It was settin' closer to me, ya know."

"No it wasn't."

"Jah, it was."

"Huh-uh."

Lydia was getting ready to intervene, when Ike kicked Carl under the table.

"Ouch! What'd you do that for?" Carl bumped Dennis's arm.

"Wasn't me. It was Ike."

Carl squinted at Ike. "How come ya kicked me under the table?"

"So you'd stop carryin' on about the ketchup. Remember what Papa said this morning?"

"Jah."

"Then hush."

Carl frowned and stared at his plate.

"Why don't you get another plate?" Lydia suggested. "You can save the soggy macaroni for the dog."

Carl set his plate on the counter, climbed onto a stool, and took a clean one from the cupboard.

"I'll bet Papa woulda made you eat that waterlogged mess," Ike said to Carl. "You know how he feels 'bout foolin' around at the table."

Carl shook his head. "No he wouldn't. He woulda probably put the plate on the floor and let the dog lick it clean."

Lydia gasped. "Surely your daed wouldn't do something like that!"

"Jah, he would," Dennis said. "Papa lets the dog sleep on his bed, too."

"Not *on* his bed," Ike corrected. "*In* his bed—under the covers."

Lydia cringed. She couldn't imagine sharing her bed with a big shaggy dog that had muddy paws and smelly breath. Maybe the boys were only teasing.

"Papa lets Goldie sleep on the sofa sometimes, too," Carl said.

"And when she gets thirsty, he don't care if she drinks from the toilet," Dennis added.

Lydia nearly gagged on the piece of bread she'd put in her mouth. She quickly reached for her glass of water to wash it down.

Ike took a drink of milk and swiped the back of his hand across his mouth. "Once, Papa let Goldie eat some scraps right off the table. Said it was easier than haulin' the food outside to her dish."

Lydia set her glass down and looked right at Ike. "I think you and your brothers are pulling my leg."

"Huh-uh," Kevin spoke up. "Nobody even touched your leg. We woulda had to crawl under the table to do that."

"I didn't mean that you actually pulled on my leg," Lydia said. "I meant that I think you've been teasing me about the dog."

"We mighta fibbed about a couple of things," Dennis admitted, "but Papa really does let Goldie sleep on his bed. He says it's become a habit."

Carl nodded. "Papa has other nasty habits, too. He chews his nails, picks his teeth with a—"

Lydia held up her hand. "You shouldn't be talking like that. You should be grateful that you have a daed. Now let's talk about something else, shall we?"

"Let's talk about popcorn," Kevin said.

"What about popcorn?" Lydia asked.

"I really like it!"

"So do I," Carl chimed in.

"Maybe after we get the dishes done we can make a batch of popcorn. Do you have a popcorn kettle?" Lydia questioned.

"Sure do." Dennis pointed to the cupboard next to the stove. "It's right over there."

"I'll get some started after the dishes are done." Lydia looked at Carl and then Kevin. "You two can clear the table while your older brothers wash and dry the dishes."

"What are you gonna do?" Dennis asked.

"I'll be putting the leftovers in the refrigerator and sweeping the crumbs we left off the floor."

"I'm done eating, so I'll clear my dishes now." Carl raced over to the sink with his dish and silverware."

"You get back here right now!" Ike shouted. "We didn't say our last prayer."

Carl ambled across the room and dropped into his chair with a grunt. "I forgot."

All heads bowed for the second prayer. When they were done, Lydia looked at Carl and said, "Now you and Kevin may clear the rest of the table."

By the time the dishes were done and the kitchen had been cleaned, Lydia was exhausted and had a headache. She wished she hadn't promised to make popcorn. She wished she could go lie down. Maybe the boys had forgotten about the popcorn. Maybe they would get busy doing something else and she could relax in the living room for a while.

No such luck. Dennis had already opened the cupboard door and retrieved the popcorn kettle. "Hey, Carl, get out the bag of popcorn!" he shouted.

"Why do I have to get it?"

"'Cause you're standin' right by the pantry, and that's where the popcorn's kept."

Lydia yawned, barely able to keep her eyes open. "Is the oil for the popcorn in the pantry, too?"

"Jah, I'll get it." Ike marched across the room, threw open the pantry door, and returned with a bottle of cooking oil and the bag of popcorn. "You look like you ain't feelin' so good," he said to Lydia. "Why don't you go rest in the living room while I make the popcorn?"

"I am a little tired. Have you made popcorn before?"

He puffed out his chest. "'Course I have. I ain't no boppli, ya know."

"No, you're certainly not." Lydia yawned again. "Maybe I will rest awhile. Call me if you need anything," she said as she headed for the living room.

*

"I'm glad you were free to go out to supper with me this evening," Rueben said to Mae as he helped her into his buggy.

She smiled, feeling happier than she had in some time. "It was nice of you to ask. Since Lydia's watching Menno's boys and won't be home until later this evening, I would have had to eat supper alone."

"Do you think Lydia will stay here in Charm or move back to Illinois?" Rueben asked as he guided his horse onto the road.

"Oh, I'm sure she'll stay here. She has no family in Illinois, and no job there, either. Here, she has a job and family, so it only makes sense for her to stay in Charm."

"If you moved out of your grossdaadi's house, what do you think Lydia would do?"

"Why would I move out? My daed left his place to me."

Rueben's ears turned red as he glanced over at Mae. "Well, I was thinking that if you moved to my place, then maybe Lydia could—"

"Are—are you suggesting that we get married?"

He gave a slow nod. "I've loved you ever since we were kinner, and since you and I have both been widowed for some time, I was hoping you'd be willing to become my wife."

Mae covered her hot cheeks with both hands, unable to say a word in response.

"You don't care for me? Is that it?"

"No, no, it's not that," she said, finally finding her voice. "It's just that we haven't been seeing each other very long, and . . ."

"It's not like we don't know each other, Mae." Rueben held the reins with one hand and slipped his arm around Mae's shoulder. "We're not gettin' any younger, you know. So I figure why should we waste time with a long courtship? If you're willing to be my wife, maybe we could get married before the end of this year, or early spring at the latest."

Mae drew in a deep breath and tried to think. *I know Lydia said she'd be fine with me seeing Rueben, but how would she feel if I married him? Maybe she just said those things because she didn't think Rueben would ever propose.*

"Would you mind if I take a few days to think about this before I give you my answer?" she asked.

"I . . . I guess not." The look of disappointment on Rueben's face was obvious.

"It's not that I don't care for you," Mae quickly reassured, "because I surely do. I'd just like to talk to Lydia about this first."

"I understand. But I hope it won't be too long before you give me your answer."

She leaned her head against Rueben's shoulder, relishing in the comfort of being so near to him and happy to know that he cared deeply for her. "I promise I'll talk to Lydia about it soon."

As Menno stepped out of his driver's car that evening, he was surprised to see Dennis on the back porch with a broom. "What are you doing?" he asked when he joined the boy on the porch.

"I'm sweepin' popcorn into the yard."

"I can see that, but why?"

"It's for the birds."

Menno frowned. "What's going on?"

Dennis motioned to the back door, hanging slightly open. "Go inside, and you'll see for yourself."

When Menno stepped into the kitchen, his mouth dropped open. Kernels of popcorn, some popped, some un-popped, were scattered everywhere—on the floor, all over the stove, and in Ike's, Carl's, and Kevin's hair.

"What in the world's going on in here?" Menno shouted.

Carl looked up from the pile of popcorn he was sitting in and pointed to Ike. "You'd better ask him."

The garbage can sat beside Ike, and he was frantically scooping handfuls of popcorn into it. "I was makin' popcorn, and I guess I put too much in the kettle."

"How come you were making the popcorn? Where's Lydia?" He'd seen her bicycle parked outside, so she was obviously still here. What he couldn't figure out was why she wasn't in the kitchen, supervising the boys.

"Lydia was tired. She's in the living room, sleepin' on the sofa," Carl said.

"Well, get this mess cleaned up, and then go upstairs and get ready for bed." Menno hurried from the kitchen. He found

Lydia curled up on the sofa, just like Carl had said. She looked so peaceful he hated to wake her. But it was getting late, and she'd probably like to get home. No doubt the boys had worn her out.

Menno leaned over and touched her shoulder.

She jumped and quickly sat up, straightening her head covering, which had been pushed askew. "Oh, you're home! How long have you been here?"

"Just a few minutes." He motioned to the kitchen door. "Discovered a mess in there. Apparently the boys tried to make a batch of popcorn. They ended up with it all over the floor."

"I'm so sorry. I should have been the one making the popcorn, but Ike said he could do it. He even suggested that I come in here and rest." Lydia yawned and stretched her arms over her head. "I guess I was more tired than I realized, because I fell asleep and didn't hear anything going on in the kitchen."

"It's okay. No real harm's been done, and the boys are cleaning up the mess right now."

She swung her legs over the sofa. "How

was your day? Did you get your business taken care of?"

He nodded. "Went real well. I was able to buy some new equipment I've been needing."

"That's good."

"How'd things go here? Other than the popcorn episode, did the boys behave themselves?"

"There were a few mishaps with the dog, but basically, we got along okay." She rose to her feet. "Guess I'd better get my bike and head for home."

"It's dark out and has just started to rain, so I'll put your bike in the back of my buggy and give you a ride."

"You don't have to do that. I have a light on my bike, and a little rain won't hurt me. I'm sure you'd like to spend some time with your boys this evening."

"It's no problem. I told 'em to get ready for bed as soon as they get the rest of the popcorn cleaned up. I won't be gone long, and Ike can oversee things until I get back." Menno moved toward the door. "I'll get the horse and buggy ready and pick you up close to the house so you don't get too wet."

Lydia smiled. "I'll get my shawl and outer bonnet and say good-bye to the boys."

A short time later, Menno and Lydia were heading down the road in his buggy. They rode in silence most of the way, partly because Menno was concentrating on the road, but mostly because he was trying to work up the nerve to say what was on his mind and wasn't sure of the best way to say it.

As they approached Lydia's driveway, Menno turned to her and said, "There's . . . uh . . . something I want to ask you."

"What's that?"

He stopped the horse and buggy near the barn. "I've been thinking . . . That is—" He paused and swiped his hand down the length of his face. "Would you marry me, Lydia?"

CHAPTER 40

Did you hear what I said?" Menno touched Lydia's arm. "I'd like us to get married."

Lydia was so surprised by Menno's proposal that she could hardly find her voice—could hardly even breathe. She should have expected this, because Menno had hinted it at often enough. Even so, she hadn't prepared herself for his proposal and had no idea how to answer.

"I . . . uh . . . would need some time to think about this," she finally managed to squeak.

"I understand, but I'd really like your answer by Christmas."

"Christmas?"

He nodded and smiled. "If your answer's yes, it'll make a nice Christmas present for the boys."

She breathed a sigh of relief. Christmas was still a few months away. That would give her some time to pray about things and think it all through. "I'll have an answer for you by Christmas Eve," she murmured.

"Oh, and please don't say anything about this to the boys. I don't want 'em to get all excited and then be disappointed if you say no."

"I won't say anything. It'll be your place to tell the boys." Lydia's legs shook as she stepped down from the buggy. "I appreciate the ride home," she said as Menno took her bike out of his buggy.

When he hesitated and took a step closer, she wondered if he might try to kiss her. Instead, he merely smiled and said, "I'll see you at church tomorrow morning."

Lydia pushed her bike up to the porch and nearly stumbled into the house. The fatigue and headache she'd felt earlier had gotten much worse. Her arms and legs had begun to ache, and her face felt flushed. She hoped she wasn't coming down with something. Maybe it was the stress of dealing with four lively boys all day. Or maybe it was the shock of Menno's proposal.

She was relieved to see that the house was dark, which meant Mom must not be home from her supper date with Rueben. Lydia didn't feel ready to tell Mom about Menno's proposal. She needed some time to pray and think things over first.

She stepped into the kitchen and leaned against the counter, drawing in a deep breath. It was obvious that Menno's boys needed a mother. Truth was she liked the idea of being a mother again. There was just one problem: even though Menno was a very nice man, she wasn't in love with him. When he'd asked her to marry him, he'd made no mention of loving her, either. Maybe he was looking for a marriage of convenience—a wife to help care for his children. Would it be right to marry someone she didn't love just so she could help raise his boys? Was it wrong to long for love and a bit of romance? Could marrying Menno be God's will for her? So many questions swirled around in her head, but it would take time before the right answers came. Right now, she needed to go to bed.

❧

When Lydia awoke the following morning, she could barely lift her head off the pillow. Her whole body ached, and her stomach churned. She'd obviously come down with the flu. Hopefully it was the twenty-four-hour kind. Maybe if she rested all day, she'd be well enough go to work on Monday. She really couldn't afford to miss any work.

Tap. Tap. Tap. "Lydia, are you up? If we don't eat breakfast soon, we'll be late for church," Mom called through the closed door.

"I–I'm sick," Lydia rasped.

"What was that?" Mom opened the door and stuck her head inside. "I could barely hear you, Lydia."

"Don't come in. I'm not feeling well. I think it's the flu, so I won't be going anywhere today."

"I won't go then, either," Mom said with a shake of her head. "When I got home last night, you'd already gone to bed, but I had no idea you weren't feeling well. I'll go make you a cup of herb tea and some toast."

"I might be able to keep the tea down, but you'd better forget the toast." Lydia moaned and clutched her stomach. "I feel so queasy."

"I'll fix you some peppermint tea. Hopefully that will help. Close your eyes now and rest."

When Mom shut the door, Lydia rolled onto her side and drew her knees up to her chest. She hated being sick. It made her feel useless.

When Menno entered his kitchen Sunday morning, he found Ike and Dennis sitting at the table, each with a bowl of cereal and a glass of apple juice.

Menno placed his hand on Ike's shoulder. "Where's Carl and Kevin?"

"They're still in bed. We think they've got the flu 'cause they both threw up last night. When I looked in their room this morning, they said they ached all over." Ike's brows furrowed as he frowned. "Sure hope I don't get whatever they've got."

"Oh, great," Menno said with a groan. He hoped he didn't come down with whatever his two youngest boys had, either, because work was piling up in his shop, and he couldn't expect his two employees to carry the load by themselves.

And what would he do about the boys if they were still sick tomorrow morning? He sure couldn't send them to school or leave them at home to fend for themselves if they had the flu.

"I'm going upstairs to check on your brothers. Be sure you and Dennis get the table cleared and your dishes washed," Menno told Ike before he left the room.

When Menno entered the younger boys' bedroom, he found Carl draped sideways across the bed and Kevin curled in a fetal position on the braided throw rug on the floor. The soiled sheets had been stripped off the bed and tossed in a heap in a corner, but their putrid odor permeated the room.

Menno held his breath as he picked up the sheets and tossed them into the wicker hamper the boys used for their dirty clothes. *Sure don't know how Sadie used to do it.*

He got out a clean set of sheets; then he lifted Carl from the bed and placed him on the floor beside Kevin.

"My head hurts and my belly's doin' flip-flops," Carl said with a moan.

"I know. Just rest here while I put clean sheets on your bed."

Kevin stirred slightly but didn't open his eyes. The poor little guy's hair looked like it hadn't been combed in a week, and the dark circles under his eyes were accentuated by his bright red cheeks.

Menno hurried to get the sheets put on; then he lifted one boy and then the other onto the bed.

Kevin opened his eyes just a bit and released a pathetic whimper. "I'm *grank*, Papa."

"Jah, I know you're sick." Menno placed his hand on the boy's forehead. "Close your eyes and rest. I'm going downstairs with your dirty sheets, but I'll be back soon with some tea that I hope will make you feel a bit better."

"Don't want no tea," Carl mumbled as he tossed and turned. "I want my mamm."

Menno's throat constricted. He couldn't give the boys their real mother back, but maybe in a few months they'd have a new mamm.

CHAPTER 41

When Lydia woke up on Monday morning, she felt somewhat better. Her stomach had settled down, and her body didn't ache so much, but she was still awfully tired.

I need to get dressed, she told herself. *I can't afford to stay home from work.*

She swung her legs over the bed and ambled over to the window. It had been raining since Saturday night, so whether she walked or rode her bike to work, she'd be soaking wet by the time she got there. Driving the horse and buggy was out of the question, since she wouldn't want to leave Buttercup tied to the hitching rail the whole time she'd be working. She could call one of their neighbors for a ride, but that would cost money, and she might not be able to reach anyone with this short notice.

Guess I'll walk, she finally decided. *At least it'll be easier to carry an umbrella than it would be if I rode my bike in this nasty weather.*

Lydia glanced at the clock on the nightstand. It was almost five thirty. If she didn't get a move on, she'd never make it to work by seven o'clock. She grabbed a set of clean clothes and hurried down the hall to the bathroom.

When she entered the kitchen sometime later, she was surprised to see that it was already six thirty. She'd have to leave immediately to make it on time.

"How are you feeling this morning?" Mom asked, turning from the stove.

"Better. I think it was just the twenty-four-hour flu."

"That's good to hear." Mom motioned to the kettle on the stove. "Breakfast is ready. Since it's a chilly wet day, I fixed oatmeal."

"I don't have time for breakfast. I need to leave for work right now." Lydia grabbed her jacket, outer bonnet, and an umbrella.

"You're going to work?"

"Jah. I'm scheduled to work the breakfast and lunch shifts today."

"But you were sick yesterday. Don't you think you should stay home and rest?"

"I'll be fine."

"But I'd hoped we could talk while we eat our breakfast. There's something I want to tell you."

"It'll have to wait until I get home. If I don't leave now, I'll be late."

"What about breakfast? You can't go to work on an empty stomach."

"I'll get something at the restaurant." Lydia was almost to the door when she remembered the birthday card and gift she'd gotten for Nona. She pulled out the plastic sack in from the desk drawer where she'd stored them and hurried out the back door.

❧

By noon, Lydia was so tired she could hardly stay on her feet. Mom had been right—she probably should have stayed home today. She glanced at the clock. Just one more hour, and she could take her lunch break. It would feel good to sit down and eat a healthy meal. When she'd arrived that morning, she'd barely had time to gulp down a doughnut and a cup of coffee. Mom wouldn't have liked that at all.

Lydia glanced to her right and saw Levi enter the restaurant. When he was seated in her section, she moved over to his table.

"How did your mamm's party go?" she asked. "Was she surprised?"

"It went well, and Mom was very surprised. Over thirty people showed up, so our house was pretty full." Levi smiled. "Mom deserved all the fuss that was made over her. She does a lot—not just for our family, but for many people in the community."

The tender expression on Levi's face made Lydia realize once again how much he cared for his family. He was such a kind, considerate man. She still couldn't believe he wasn't married.

"I'm glad the party went well, and I have a little gift for your mamm. I'd planned to stop by your store after work and give it to her, but I'm tired so I'll probably go right home."

"That's okay," Levi said. "Mom won't be there anyway. She has a dental appointment in Berlin this afternoon."

"I have the card and gift in the back room. Would you mind giving them to her?" Lydia asked.

"Sure, I can do that."

"Let me take your order, and then I'll get the gift."

Levi studied the menu a few seconds and then ordered a toasted cheese sandwich and a bowl of chili.

"Would you like something to drink?" she asked.

"Water will be fine."

"Okay, I'll be back soon." Lydia turned in Levi's order, then retrieved Nona's gift. When she returned, she found Levi visiting with Rueben, who'd taken a seat on the other side of him.

"I didn't realize you were meeting Levi for lunch," Lydia said to Rueben. "If I'd known, I would have waited to turn in his order."

"No problem," Rueben said. "Levi and I hadn't planned to meet, but when I came in, he asked if I'd like to join him."

Lydia handed Nona's gift to Levi. "Tell your mamm I said hello and that I'm glad she had such a nice birthday surprise." She turned to Rueben and said, "What would you like to order?"

"Don't think my nervous belly is up to much more than a bowl of chicken noodle soup and some crackers." Rueben touched his stomach and winced.

"Maybe you're coming down with the flu," Levi said. "It's been going around here lately."

"That's true," Lydia said. "I was sick with it yesterday."

Levi's forehead creased as he looked at her with obvious concern. "No wonder you look so tired. Shouldn't you be home resting today?"

"I'm feeling better than I was yesterday, and I didn't want to miss any work." Lydia looked back at Rueben. "Are you achy and weak?"

He shook his head. "My stomach's just givin' me fits. I'm sure it'll settle down once your mamm gives me her answer."

Lydia tipped her head. "What answer?"

Rueben's cheeks turned red, and little beads of sweat broke out on his forehead. "Didn't she tell you that I asked her to marry me?" he said, lowering his voice.

Lydia's eyebrows shot up. "She never said a word about it."

Rueben's face grew redder. "Guess I shouldn't have opened my big mouth. Mae said she'd need to talk to you about us gettin' married before she gave me her answer, but I figured she'd have said something to you by now."

Lydia glanced at Levi to gauge his reaction, but he just stared out the window. "I'm sure Mom will tell me as soon as I get home," she murmured. "In fact, I know she will, because that's the first thing I'm going to ask."

CHAPTER 42

By the time Lydia got home from work, she'd developed a headache and was shivering from the cold and rain.

"As soon as you get out of those wet clothes, come into the kitchen and I'll fix you a cup of tea," Mom said when she greeted Lydia at the door.

Lydia nodded and trudged up the stairs to her room. When she entered the kitchen a short time later, Mom was sitting at the table, where she'd set out two cups of tea and a plate of zucchini bread.

"There's something I need to talk to you

about," Lydia and Mom said at the same time.

Mom smiled. "You go first."

"Rueben came into the restaurant today. He said that he'd asked you to marry him and thought I already knew." Lydia frowned. "How come you didn't tell me about this, Mom?"

"I was planning to tell you right away, but when I got home Saturday night, you were sleeping." Mom paused and took a sip of tea. "On Sunday you were sick, so I didn't want to bother you then."

"You could have told me this morning."

"I was planning to during breakfast, but you insisted on leaving right away so you wouldn't be late for work."

"That's true." Lydia reached over and touched Mom's hand. "Tell me about Rueben's proposal."

"When he brought me home the other night, he said he loved me and asked if I'd marry him." Mom dropped her gaze to the table.

"What'd you tell him?"

"I said I needed to talk to you first."

"You don't need my permission to marry Reuben."

Mom lifted her gaze, tears in her eyes. "I know that, but I was concerned that you might be upset if I got married again."

"Do you love Rueben?"

"Jah."

"Then you have my blessing."

A slow smile spread across Mom's face. "Oh, Lydia, I appreciate you saying that."

"So when will you get married?"

"Probably not until sometime after the first of the year."

"That's good. It'll give me time to find a place of my own, or to—"

"Or to what? You're not thinking of going back to Illinois, I hope."

"I have thought about it, but since I have no family or job there, it wouldn't make sense." Lydia shrugged. "Besides, now that I've made a few friends here, I'm beginning to feel like Charm is my home."

"What about Menno? You've been seeing a lot of him lately. Do you consider him to be one of your friends?"

"Of course I do." Lydia's conscience pricked her. She'd expected Mom to tell her about Rueben's proposal, so it was only right that she tell Mom about Menno's.

She reached for a piece of zucchini

bread and took a bite. "There's something I need to tell you, too."

"What's that?"

"When Menno brought me home Saturday night, he asked me to marry him."

Mom's eyes widened. "Ach, Lydia, that's *wunderbaar*! Maybe we could be married the same day."

Lydia took a sip of tea and blotted her lips with a napkin. "I haven't agreed to marry him, but I said I'd give him my answer by Christmas Eve."

"If you're holding off giving him an answer because you need my blessing, you certainly have it." Mom gave Lydia's hand a gentle squeeze. "Menno's a very nice man, and I'm sure he'd make you a good husband." Her nose crinkled slightly. "Of course, his boys are quite active and might prove to be a handful for you. Is that the reason for your hesitation?"

Lydia shook her head. "The boys and I would get along fine. It's just that . . . well, I respect Menno, but I'm not in love with him. I don't think he's in love with me, either. I'm not sure it would be right to marry someone when there's no love involved."

"I understand your hesitation, but in time, love can grow out of respect."

"Maybe so. It's a big decision, and I'm glad I have a few months before I give him my answer." Lydia massaged her forehead. "My head's pounding, so if you don't mind, I think I'll go up to my room and rest awhile before it's time to start supper."

"That's a good idea. You look awfully pale this afternoon. You probably shouldn't have gone to work today."

"I have to keep working. We need the money."

"We don't need it badly enough that you should wear yourself out or end up getting sick again. Besides, the last time I stopped at Miller's Dry Goods Store, I found out that one of my quilts had sold." Mom smiled. "So the money I earned will help with our expenses, too."

"I'm glad to hear it, but how come you never mentioned it before?" Lydia asked as she continued to rub her forehead.

"Because I put the money aside so I could surprise you with a nice Christmas present this year."

Lydia grimaced. "I don't need anything

for Christmas, Mom. What we need is money to pay our bills."

"I know, and I'll use some of the money for bills, too." Mom took another sip of tea. "After Rueben and I are married, I won't have to worry about earning money, and if you marry Menno, you won't have to worry about working, either. I'm sure he makes a good living with his woodshop, and if you married him, you'd be well taken care of."

"I won't marry someone so they can support me, and neither should you." Lydia stared hard at Mom. "Is that why you agreed to marry Rueben . . . so he can provide for your financially?"

Mom shook her head so hard that the ties on her covering swished back and forth. "I love Rueben very much. I was only trying to say that once we're both married, neither of us will have to worry so much about our financial situation."

"I haven't said I'd marry Menno, and I'd rather not talk about this anymore." Lydia pushed away from the table. "I'm going to my room to lie down. Please call me when it's time to start supper."

≈◌

"Papa, Kevin threw up again!" Dennis shouted from upstairs.

Menno groaned and pulled himself off the sofa. He'd come down with the flu last night and had missed work today, leaving John in charge of the shop. Ike was the only one in the family who hadn't gotten sick, but he couldn't be expected to do everything on his own. As it was, Ike had stayed home from school today to do all the outside chores and help Menno care for the other three boys. Unless by some chance Ike was immune to the flu, he'd probably come down with it before the week was out.

"Papa, did ya hear what I said?" Dennis called again. "Kevin made a mess all over his bed."

"Jah, I heard and I'm coming right now!" Menno hollered as he trudged up the stairs. In the ten years he'd been married to Sadie, he'd never had to care for the boys when they got sick. Until Sadie got cancer, she'd always tended to them and had done a good job of it, too. It was hard enough for Menno to play nursemaid when he was well, but feeling this lousy made it ten times worse. He wished he could go over to Lydia's and talk her into marrying him right now.

≈

Things had gotten busy at the store, and it wasn't until nearly closing time that Levi remembered to give Mom the gift from Lydia.

"This is for you," he said, handing her the gift and card.

"What's this?" she asked with a look of surprise.

"I saw Lydia at the restaurant today. She asked me to give you this and said she was glad you'd had such a nice surprise party."

Mom smiled. "That was so nice of her. I didn't realize she knew I'd had a birthday."

"She knew because I invited her to your party."

"You did? Then why didn't she come?"

Levi frowned. "She spent the day watching Menno's kinner while he went away on business."

Mom tugged on Levi's shirtsleeve. "That frown you're wearing makes me think you might be jealous."

"Jealous of what?"

Mom lifted her gaze toward the ceiling. "Not what . . . who? I think you're jealous of Menno and the fact that Lydia's been seeing him."

Levi folded his arms. "Lydia can see whomever she pleases."

She gave his shirtsleeve another tug. "I think you have more than a passing interest in her. Don't deny it, either, because I've seen the sappy look on your face whenever Lydia's around."

He shrugged. "I do like Lydia, but . . ."

"Then why don't you ask her to go out with you?"

"I can't do that, Mom. You know I can't."

"Is this about you thinking that you need to be around here all the time to take care of us?" She planted her hands against her hips. "Because if it is, then I think I need to remind you that when you were in bed with tonsillitis, your daed and I got along quite well."

"That's true, but it was only for a few days."

"If we could manage for a few days without your help, then we'd manage just fine if you decided to get married and move out on your own."

Levi turned his turned his hands palm-up. "That's only part of my concern."

"What's the other part?"

"I'd rather not talk about this."

"Are you afraid of rejection?"

"What do you mean?"

"Do you think Lydia might not return your feelings?"

"I'm not sure how she feels, and that's not the real issue anyway."

"What is the real issue?"

A muscle on the side of his cheek quivered. "There are other things to consider."

Mom leaned forward and stared at him. "Does it have something to do your family being little people?"

He cringed, but slowly nodded. "I've never admitted this to you before, but I'm afraid if I married, one or more of my children might be born with dwarfism."

The slow intake of Mom's breath let Levi know that he'd shocked her. "Would that be such a bad thing? Are you ashamed of us, Levi?"

"No, of course not, but there are many challenges a child born with dwarfism must face."

"Your brothers and sisters have done quite well, don't you think?"

"Jah, but the teasing they've had to endure has been hard on them."

She shook her head. "It's not just little people who are teased. Some folks, especially children, get teased for no reason at all."

"I guess you're right, but my concerns go deeper than the possibility of teasing."

"What else are you worried about?"

"I'm worried that any woman of normal size wouldn't want the challenge of raising a child who would never grow tall and might have some physical limitations." He wiped his damp forehead with the back of his hand.

"So this is really about trust, then isn't it? You don't trust God enough to help you find a wife who would accept your family the way we are and who would love and accept a child born with dwarfism."

Levi just sat there, unable to respond.

She placed her hands over his. "Levi, you need to set your fears aside and put your trust in God, just like Jeremiah 17:7 says we should do. 'Blessed is the man that trusteth in the Lord, and whose hope the Lord is.'"

He let her words sink in.

"You know, Levi, from the time I've spent with Lydia I've gotten the impression that she accepts us just the way we are. She's a good woman. The kind the Bible talks about in Proverbs 31:10: 'Who can find a virtuous woman? for her price is far above rubies.'" Mom placed her hand on Levi's arm. "I think you need to set your fears aside and ask Lydia out before she ends up marrying someone else, and then it'll be too late."

"Maybe you're right." Levi heaved a sigh. "Maybe I should ask her out."

CHAPTER 43

Are you sure you want to go to Charm Days with me?" Lydia asked Mom as they ate breakfast together on the second Friday of October. "Now that you and Rueben are planning to be married, I figured you'd want to go with him."

"We plan to go to supper this evening, and we'll also attend some of tomorrow's events, but today, Rueben has several horses to shoe." Mom gave Lydia's arm a gentle tap. "Besides, you have to work tomorrow, and since you have today off, it'll be fun for us to spend some time together."

"You're right. It should be fun."

Mom's eyebrows furrowed suddenly. "I'm surprised Menno didn't invite you to go to Charm Days with him. I'm sure some of his boys will be involved in the wooly worm race."

"Maybe Menno wants some time alone with the boys. If that's the case, then I'm fine with it."

❧

"Where's Carl and Kevin?" Menno asked Dennis and Ike, who were doing the breakfast dishes. "I've called them several times to get dressed and brush their teeth, but neither one of them has answered me. I even went up to their room, and they weren't there."

"Did ya look in the barn?" Dennis asked. "I'll bet they went out there to fool around."

"They'd better not have." He glanced at the clock on the far wall. "If you boys don't get going soon, you'll all be late for school."

"Wouldn't wanna be late today," Dennis said. "And we don't wanna forget our wooly worm caterpillars, neither."

"That's right," Ike put in. "When it's time to go over to Kiem Lumber for the wooly worm race, we'll all be cheerin' for you and Carl."

Dennis's eyes lit up. "My worm's gonna win; I just know he is."

As the boys continued to jabber about the wooly worm race, Menno hurried from the room. Stepping outside, he cupped his hands around his mouth and hollered, "Carl! Kevin? Where are you boys?"

A few seconds later, Carl ambled out of the barn. Kevin traipsed behind him.

"We were lookin' for a better container to put my wooly worm in," Carl said. He lifted the coffee can he held in his hands.

"What was wrong with the empty sour cream container you had him in before?" Menno asked when the boys joined him on the porch.

"Thought it was too small. Wanted to give him lots of room to crawl around so he can exercise and win the race."

"Well, go inside and get your teeth brushed." Menno opened the door. "It's almost time for you to leave."

"Are you comin' to watch me and Dennis race our worms this afternoon?" Carl asked.

Menno nodded. "Said I'd be there, didn't I?"

"Jah, but you get busy in your shop sometimes. Figured if that happens, you'll probably forget about the race."

"I won't forget." Menno gave both boys a tap on the head. "Now get inside, you two."

As Levi stood among the crowd of onlookers inside Kiem Lumber, where they'd come to witness the wooly worm race, his excitement mounted. Andy would be racing his caterpillar, Speedy, and Levi, as well as the rest of his family, had come to cheer him on. Students placed each of their worms at the bottom of a string, and without touching their worm in any way, they had to coax it along, hoping it would be the first to reach the top of the string.

Andy alternated between whistling and hollering, "Go, Speedy! Go!"

The young girl next to Andy encouraged her worm to move up the string by blowing on it, while another girl clapped her hands in an effort to get her worm moving.

Levi glanced to his left. Two of Menno's boys, Dennis and Carl, were also racing wooly worms.

"Come on, Lightning!" Dennis clapped his hands and jumped up and down. "Get up that string . . . zing . . . zing . . . zing!"

More whooping and hollering went on from the children who were racing, as well as plenty of encouraging comments from the crowd.

Andy's worm, Speedy, was the first to the top, and Andy, beaming from ear to ear, was pronounced the winner in his age group.

Levi's family and several others gathered around Andy, patting him on the back and offering congratulations.

"It wasn't me." Andy grinned as he pointed to his wooly worm. "It was Speedy. He's just plain fast!"

Levi was pleased to see his little brother looking so happy. Andy had worked hard with Speedy, and Levi thought he deserved to win.

"Oh, look, there's Lydia," Mom said, nudging Levi's arm. "While Andy's putting Speedy away and visiting with his friends, I think I'll go over and talk to her. Would you like to come along?"

"I suppose so. What about the rest of the family? Aren't they coming, too?" After the discussion he'd had with Mom about Lydia the other day, the thought of seeing her again made Levi's stomach churn. He hoped Mom didn't expect him to ask Lydia out with her standing right there. He wasn't sure this was the right time for that.

Before Mom could respond to Levi's question, Pop spoke up. "Think I'll take a look around the lumber department." He winked at Levi. "Might want you to build us some new bookcases for the store." He turned to Peter and poked his arm. "Want to come with me and check out the lumber?"

Peter nodded and hurried off with Pop.

"What do you girls plan to do?" Mom asked Betty and Selma.

"We're goin' upstairs to Carpenter's Café to get something to eat," Selma said, with an eager expression.

Mom clasped Levi's hand, as though she knew he needed some support. "Let's go now, before Lydia disappears into the crowd." Her blue eyes twinkled as she smiled up at him. "Why don't you invite Lydia to join you for supper this evening? Maybe you can take her to one of the restaurants in Berlin or Walnut Creek, where it might not be as busy as the places in Charm seem to be today."

"I guess I could do that if I can work up the nerve." Levi moved toward Lydia, feeling more anxious and unsure of himself with each step.

"Hello, Lydia. Are you here by yourself today?" Mom asked, before Levi could find his voice.

"I came with my mamm," Lydia replied, "but she'll be meeting Rueben Miller for supper soon, so then I'll be on my own."

"Where's your mamm now?" Mom asked.

"She went upstairs."

Mom nudged Levi, but he wasn't about to ask Lydia anything with Mom standing right beside him.

"I'm sorry I couldn't be at your birthday party a few weeks ago," Lydia said to Mom. "I had other plans that night."

"Levi explained why you weren't there." Mom chuckled and patted her stomach. "We had a fun time, and I ate way too much because my girls made my favorite meal—Frogmore Stew."

"I'm sorry I missed out." Lydia laughed. "I love that meal. Even eating with my fingers is fun."

"I delivered your card and gift to Mom," Levi said, finally finding his voice.

Mom nodded. "I appreciated the jar of homemade apple butter. Danki, Lydia."

"You're welcome."

"I think I'll go see what Harold and Peter are up to in the lumber section, so I'll see you later." Mom gave Levi's arm a pat. Then she hurried away.

Levi drew in a couple of deep breaths, hoping to calm his nerves. "I . . . uh . . . was wondering if you'd be willing to—"

"Oh, there you are," Menno said, stepping between Lydia and Levi. "The boys and I were hoping we might find you in this crowd of people this afternoon. If you have no other plans, we'd like you to join us for supper."

Lydia glanced at Levi, then back at Menno. "No, I . . . uh . . . have no plans."

"That's good to hear." Menno leaned over and tucked the end of Kevin's shirt into his trousers. "Don't know why my boys can't keep their shirts tucked in."

"Maybe it's because they're growing so much and their shirts are getting too small," Lydia said.

"That could be. Guess I need to take

'em shopping soon, but there never seems to be enough time."

Levi shifted uneasily. He was tempted to tell Menno that he'd been talking to Lydia first and had been interrupted in the middle of inviting her to join him for supper, but he quickly dismissed that as a dumb idea. The only thing he could think to do was to say a quick good-bye and walk away.

"Don't know what made me think I had a chance with Lydia," Levi told Mom when he found her in the lumber section with Pop and Peter. "She's obviously interested in Menno, not me."

"I know what you're thinking," Mom said.

"What's that?"

"You've decided to give up on the idea of courting Lydia because you think she's already spoken for."

He nodded.

"Well, as far as I know, she's not spoken for yet. If you care for her, don't give up. I think you should look for another time when you can ask her out."

Mom was right—as far as he knew, Lydia wasn't spoken for. So the very next chance he got, he would definitely ask her out.

CHAPTER 44

What are you looking so *bedauerlich* about?" Pop asked as he and Levi sat together at Pop's desk, going over a list of things they needed to order for the store.

"I'm not sad. Just thinking is all."

"Sure look sad to me." Pop elbowed Levi's arm. "Most folks don't wear a frown as big as yours if they're not feeling down in the dumps about something."

Levi forced his face to relax and even managed a weak smile. "There, is that better?"

Mom stepped up to them and tapped

Levi's arm. "I'll bet I know why you're so bedauerlich."

"Why's that?" Pop asked before Levi could respond.

"Because he thinks Lydia's being courted by Menno." She gave Levi's arm another solid tap. "Our son still hasn't worked up the courage to ask Lydia out."

Pop's eyebrows shot up. "You're planning to ask Lydia out?"

"I am, but—"

Pop elbowed Levi again. "Better move quick, or it might be too late."

"May already be too late," Levi mumbled. He couldn't believe they were having this discussion. Many Amish young people weren't so open with their parents about who they wanted to court.

"You won't know unless you ask her to go out with you," Mom put in.

"That's right," Pop agreed. "If I was you, I'd get on it fast, because word has it that Menno's lookin' for a new wife."

"Where'd you hear that?" Mom asked.

"Heard a couple of men talkin' about it when I was browsing through the lumber section at Kiem's during Charm Days."

Levi grimaced. If Menno was looking for a new wife, he no doubt had Lydia in mind, since he'd already gone a few places with her. "She'd probably be better off with him than me," Levi muttered under his breath.

"What was that?" Pop asked.

"Nothing. I was just thinking out loud."

Mom motioned to the clock on the far wall. "It's almost noon. Why don't you go over to Grandma's Restaurant and have some lunch? If Lydia's working today, you might get the chance to ask her out."

"I don't know if that's such a good idea. I wouldn't want anyone to hear me asking."

"You don't have to shout it out so the whole restaurant can hear." Pop's elbow connected with Levi's arm. "Just do it, son."

"Okay, maybe I will. Even if Lydia says no, it'll be better than staying here and subjecting myself to your elbow jabs."

Pop chuckled.

"When you get back, be sure you let us know how it goes," Mom said.

⁂

"What are you doing back so soon?" Nona asked when Levi returned to the store a short time later.

"Lydia wasn't working today, so I decided not to bother with lunch."

"Are you sure she wasn't working?" Nona asked. "Maybe she was taking a break or something."

"No, she wasn't. When I asked Edith, she said Lydia's hours had been cut and that she wasn't working today."

Nona's forehead wrinkled. "The last thing Lydia needs is to lose hours at work. I'm sure she's still paying Josh's hospital bills, not to mention all the other expenses she and her mamm must have."

"Maybe it's just a temporary cutback," Levi said. "In a few weeks, Lydia might be working full-time again."

"I hope so, but things usually slow down around here during the winter months."

"They didn't slow down in our store last winter," Harold shouted from the back room.

Nona gritted her teeth. "I wish your daed wouldn't holler like that. What if a customer comes in and hears him bellowing like an alt *kuh*?"

Levi snickered. "They'd probably think we had an old cow in the back room."

Nona playfully swatted Levi's arm. "You're such a kidder."

Levi motioned to the stack of invoices on the desk. "Is Pop done with those, or do you need me to finish them up?"

"He's done with them and is getting some boxes out for some more things I want to donate to the Care and Share Store." Nona motioned to the back room. "Why don't you help him? When I have the boxes filled, you can take the stuff to the Care and Share and then stop by Lydia's place on your way home."

"I don't mind delivering the boxes for you," Levi said, "but why am I stopping by Lydia's place?"

Nona rolled her eyes toward the ceiling. "So you can ask her out, of course."

Levi rubbed his chin thoughtfully. "I'm not sure that's such a good idea."

"Why not?"

"Because Lydia's mamm is probably home. I'm sure she doesn't like me."

"I don't think Mae has anything against you." Nona frowned. "It's me she doesn't care for, but I still can't figure out why."

"Maybe she's got something against little people," Harold said as he joined them, carrying two cardboard boxes.

"That makes no sense," Nona said. "What could she possibly have against little people?"

Harold shrugged and set the boxes on the floor. "Who knows what reasons people have for their prejudices? You and I both know that we've been teased a lot over the years because we're so short."

"I have a feeling the reason for Mae's behavior goes much deeper than us being short," Nona said.

Levi grunted. "If she ever says anything negative about my family to me, I'll set her straight."

Harold shook his head. "You won't earn any points with Lydia if you get in an argument with her mamm."

"Didn't plan to argue with her. Just said I'd set her straight." Levi picked up one of the boxes. "Guess we'd better get busy filling these so I can head to the Care and Share."

※

"I still can't believe things are so slow at the restaurant," Mom said as she and Lydia sat at the kitchen table cutting out quilting blocks.

"Hopefully it's just a temporary slump."

Lydia stacked the pieces she'd cut into a pile beside the ones Mom had cut.

"If the other quilts I left at Miller's Dry Goods would sell, I wouldn't be quite so worried." Mom sighed. "With things slowing down, it makes me wonder why I'm bothering to quilt."

"I would think people would start buying things for Christmas pretty soon. For that matter, I'm surprised more of your quilts, or at least some of your potholders, didn't sell during Charm Days when the town was full of people."

Mom shrugged. "Guess people weren't looking for quilted items that day."

Lydia heard the *clip-clop* of horse's hooves and turned toward the window.

"Who is it?" Mom asked. "Reuben?"

Lydia shook her head. "No, it's Levi."

"I wonder what he wants."

"I'll go see." Lydia hurried out to the yard just as Levi finished tying his horse to the hitching rail.

"What brings you here this afternoon?" she called.

"I was on my way back from the Care and Share in Berlin and thought I'd stop and see how you're doing," Levi said.

"We're getting along okay."

"I was at the restaurant around noon
and was surprised that you weren't working today."

"They cut back my hours because business has been slow."

"So I heard." Levi took a step closer to
Lydia, and she sensed that he was about
to say something else, but just then another horse and buggy entered the yard. It
was Menno.

"I went by the restaurant for lunch,"
Menno said to Lydia. "When I heard you
weren't working today, I decided to stop
and see if you'd be free to go out to supper with me and the boys this evening."

"That's nice of you," Lydia said, "but
Mom's already started chicken and dumplings for our supper."

Menno licked his lips, while patting his
stomach. "Umm . . . that sounds real good.
Haven't had chicken and dumplings in a
long time."

"I'm sure there's more than enough, so
if you and the boys would like to join us
you're more than welcome," Lydia said.

"That'd be great. I'm on my way home
from running some errands, but as soon

as I get there I'll make sure the boys get their evening chores done, and then we'll be over." Menno glanced at Levi. "How are things with you and your family these days?"

"Fine. Everything's fine." Levi untied his horse. "Guess I'd better get going. If things have gotten busy at the store while I've been gone, I'm sure Mom's missing me by now."

"Danki for coming by," Lydia said as Levi climbed into his buggy.

He replied with a nod, then guided his horse down the driveway toward the road.

"I didn't interrupt anything, did I?" Menno asked, leaning closer to Lydia. "I thought Levi looked upset about something, and he was sure in a hurry to go."

"I don't think he was upset. He just stopped by to say hello and see how Mom and I are doing."

"He's not interested in you, I hope."

Lydia's cheeks warmed. "Of course not. He's never given me any reason to believe he has anything more than friendship on his mind."

Menno smiled. "That's good to hear, because I wouldn't want him influencing your decision about whether you'll marry me or not."

Lydia shook her head. "The only one who'll influence my decision is God, and I'm still praying about the matter."

CHAPTER 45

Have you tried asking Lydia out again?"
Nona asked Levi a few weeks later, as the
two of them sat behind the store counter,
sipping coffee.

Levi shook his head. "I went to the restaurant again last week, but Lydia was
waiting on Menno." He grimaced. "I heard
him ask her to go out to supper with him
yet again, so I figured there wasn't much
use in me asking. He's obviously courting
her, so I think it's best that I don't get in the
way."

"Maybe she'd rather be courted by you.
Did you ever think of that?"

"If that were the case, then she wouldn't be going out with him."

"Maybe so; maybe not. I think you're giving up too soon—before you even know whether she's serious about Menno."

The bell on the front door jingled, and Levi swallowed the rest of his coffee and stood. "Looks like you've got a customer to wait on, and I've got to get busy on those shelves I promised to make for the store."

Nona turned to the customer and smiled when she recognized Rueben Miller. "It's good to see you," she said.

"Good to see you, too." Rueben placed a horseshoe on the counter. "Found this in the parking lot. If I knew whose horse threw it I could probably drum up a little business."

"Is business slow for you right now?" Nona asked.

"Not really, but it goes in cycles." He grinned. "'Course I don't really mind those days when there's no horses to shoe. Gives my back a chance to rest."

Nona had never really thought about it before, but bending over to shoe a horse would be hard on anyone's back.

"How's business doing here?" he asked.

"Are things as slow as they are with some of the other shops in town?"

"They've slowed down some, but we're still keeping busy enough. It's probably because we carry most of the basic items that people need."

"With you and Harold having a family to support, you need your business to do well." Rueben glanced around. "Where is Harold anyway? Haven't seen him for a while."

"He had a dental appointment this morning. Seems like between the two of us, we're always getting some kind of dental work done." She frowned. "Last month it was a root canal for me. Today, Harold's getting a crown. Never seems to be an end to the bills coming in."

"Are you folks needing any help?" Rueben asked. "Because if you are . . ."

"It's nice of you to be concerned, but I think we'll be fine. The other day, Levi sold some wooden toys he'd made to an English couple looking for some simple things to give their children for Christmas. He also sold some bird feeders and a couple of small rocking chairs. The extra money he's brought in has helped a lot."

"Well, let me know if you need anything,"

Reuben said. "Since I have no kinner living at home anymore, my expenses are much less than yours, I'm sure."

"We appreciate the offer." Nona smiled. "By the way, we're having a few people over for another one of our Frogmore Stew suppers this Friday evening. Would you like to come?"

"What's in Frogmore Stew?"

She wiggled her eyebrows. "You'll have to wait and see, but I promise you won't be disappointed."

He smiled. "I'd be happy to come, but would you mind if I brought a friend?"

"Of course not. The more the merrier is what we always say."

"You can have a seat at any of the empty tables you like," Lydia said when Nona entered the restaurant. "Our hostess is taking a break right now, but I'll be with you in a minute."

"Actually, I didn't come in here to eat today. Just came by to ask you a question," Nona said.

"Oh, okay. I need to check on an order I put in first, and then we can talk."

Lydia hurried toward the kitchen. When

she returned, she found Nona standing near the front counter.

"What's up?" Lydia asked.

"The girls and I are fixing Frogmore Stew for supper this Friday night, and we're inviting a few friends over. I was wondering if you'd like to join us."

Lydia smiled. "I don't think I can pass up that tempting offer."

"We'll look forward to seeing you around six o'clock." Nona hesitated a moment, then quickly added, "Your mamm's welcome to join us, too."

Lydia figured Mom probably wouldn't want to go, but she smiled and said, "I'll let her know that she's invited."

"See you soon." Nona turned toward the door.

A few seconds later Lydia's boss stepped up to her. "Can I speak with you a minute?"

"Sure."

Edith motioned to the break room at the back of the restaurant. "Let's go in there."

Lydia followed Edith into the small room. Brenda, the hostess, was just leaving the room when they entered, and she shot Lydia an anxious look as she passed by.

"What did you want to talk to me about?"

Lydia asked after Edith told her to take a seat.

"I really hate to tell you this, because you're a good worker and I know you need this job, but business has slowed down so much that we've been forced to make further cutbacks." Edith paused and her lips compressed. "Unfortunately, because you're the most recent person we've hired, your job will have to be terminated until things pick up again, which probably won't be until spring."

Lydia sat for several seconds, letting Edith's words sink in. Then, with a whispered, "I understand," she dashed out of the room.

CHAPTER 46

Are you sure you won't reconsider and go to supper with me at the Stutzmans' to-night?" Lydia asked Mom Friday evening. "I'm sure we'll have a lot of fun."

Mom shook her head. "Rueben and I have plans for this evening. He's taking me out to supper again." Her shoulders sagged. "Besides, I don't see how you can have fun when you've just lost your job at the restaurant."

"I am upset about losing my job," Lydia admitted, "but whenever I'm with the Stutzmans, I feel so relaxed. Their cheer-ful attitudes and good humor always makes me laugh, which is something I really need right now."

Mom shrugged. "Suit yourself, but my idea of a good time isn't listening to a bunch of silly jokes or eating a meal with no plates or silverware. Apparently the Stutzmans don't know anything about proper table manners."

Lydia's back stiffened. "They're not ill-mannered, Mom. They just like to have a good time, and their positive attitude has a way of rubbing off on people. At least it does for me."

"Whatever."

Lydia touched Mom's arm. "I really wish you'd get to know them. Nona's a very nice woman, and—"

"Oh, look at the time." Mom pointed to the clock on the kitchen wall. "I'd better change my clothes before Rueben gets here."

"I'm heading out now, so I'll see you later this evening." Lydia grabbed her shawl and outer bonnet, then hurried out the back door. Even though things were better between her and Mom these days, they still didn't see eye to eye on some things, including the Stutzman family. Lydia wished she knew what Mom had against those dear little people.

⁂

When Lydia stepped into the kitchen, Levi wondered what was up. Apparently Mom had invited her to join them for supper without telling him.

"It's good to see you, Lydia," Mom said. "I'm so glad you could make it."

Lydia smiled, although her eyes held no sparkle.

"Is everything all right?" Mom asked with a look of concern. "You seem kind of sad this evening."

"I've had a trying week, but I'm sure I'll feel better after spending the evening with all of you."

"What happened?" Mom asked. "Is it something you feel free to talk about?"

"Things are slow at the restaurant, and I've been laid off. If business continues to be slow, I might be out of a job until spring."

"I'm real sorry to hear that. We'll have to pray that business picks up at the restaurant soon," Mom said.

"My mamm's been hoping that more of her quilts would sell, but things have been slow at all the quilt shops, too."

"I'm sorry your mamm didn't come with you tonight," Mom said. "I was hoping for the chance to get to know her better."

Lydia's face reddened. "She . . . uh . . . had other plans for the evening."

Mom flashed Lydia one of her optimistic smiles. "Maybe she can join us some other time."

Lydia made no comment. Levi figured she knew that, short of a miracle, her mother would never have supper with them.

Mom nudged Levi's arm. "We won't eat until the rest of our guests arrive, so why don't you and Lydia go into the living room and visit with the other guests who are already here?"

"Isn't there something I can do to help you with the meal?" Lydia asked.

Levi figured she probably didn't want to spend time with him.

Mom shook her head. "The Frogmore Stew's done cooking, and since we won't be needing silverware or plates on the table, there's really not much more to do." She shooed them toward the living room. "You and Levi go ahead. I'll call everyone when it's time for supper."

Levi followed Lydia into the living room,

where Pop sat with Bishop Yoder and his wife, Sarah.

"Where's the rest of your family?" Lydia asked Levi after she'd been greeted by the other three.

"Betty and Selma are changing clothes. After helping Mom make the 'icky stuff' for the stew, they were both a mess." Levi glanced toward the back door. "Peter and Andy are outside doing their chores. I'm sure they'll be in soon."

Lydia and Levi both sat on the sofa since the three chairs in the room were occupied.

As they visited, Levi noticed that Lydia seemed to be relaxing. Hopefully by the end of the evening he'd feel more relaxed, too.

When Mae glanced out the kitchen window and saw Rueben pull into the yard, she grabbed her bonnet and shawl and hurried out the back door. Thankfully, going to supper with him this evening had given her a good excuse not to go with Lydia to the Stutzmans'.

As Mae headed toward Rueben's buggy, the shriveled leaves strewn around the yard crinkled beneath her feet. Fall was definitely upon them.

"How was your day?" Rueben asked as he helped her into the buggy.

"It was fine. How was yours?"

"Went real well. Shoed ten horses today, so I worked up a hearty appetite."

"Where are we going?" she asked as they headed down the driveway.

He looked over at her and winked. "It's a surprise." He clucked to his horse to get him moving faster.

Mae figured they might be going to Der Dutchman in Walnut Creek, which she'd told Rueben was one of her favorite restaurants. When Rueben directed the horse to turn right instead of left, she changed her mind about Der Dutchman and decided Rueben was probably taking her to Grandma's Restaurant in Charm. That was fine with her. The restaurant needed business, and if they got real busy again, Lydia might get her job back sooner than expected.

When Rueben's horse and buggy went past Grandma's Restaurant and turned up the driveway leading to the Stutzmans', Mae became concerned. "I hope you're not planning on us eating here."

He nodded. "Nona invited me the other day, and I told her I was bringing a guest."

Mae's back went rigid, and her cheeks burned like fire. "You should have checked with first me, not just assumed I'd want to eat here."

In the pale moonlight, she could see the outline of his nose. "I thought if you spent an evening with the Stutzmans and got to know them, you'd realize what nice people they are," he said, halting the horse.

"I'm not comfortable around little people." Mae's voice came out in a strange-sounding squeak.

"How come?"

She twisted her fingers around the edge of her shawl, unsure of what to say. Should she admit her fear of little people? Would Rueben understand if she did?

Finally, she drew in a deep breath and decided to plunge ahead. "Little people aren't to be trusted."

Rueben turned to face her. "Sometimes people are afraid of what's different. Is that your problem, Mae?"

She shook her head. "I'm afraid of what I know."

"And what's that?"

"When I was a young girl, an English family moved to the farm next to ours. They were little people, and their daughter was two years older than me." She paused and drew in another quick breath. This was difficult to talk about. "Angela—the little girl—came over to my house one day, and while we were playing, she broke my doll."

Rueben's thick eyebrows squeezed together. "You mean you won't go around the Stutzmans because a little English girl broke your doll?"

"That wasn't all she did," Mae said with a shake of her head. "After she broke it, I said I was going to tell on her, and then she pushed me to the floor, sat on my chest, and wouldn't let me up. She may have been short, but she was much stronger than me, and it really hurt when she pinned me down like that."

"What'd you do?" Rueben asked.

"I struggled and finally managed to get away. Then I ran downstairs and told my daed what Angela had done." Mae put both hands against her hot cheeks. "Angela lied and said I broke my own doll and was trying to blame her for it. Then she made the lie even worse by saying that I was the one who'd sat on her. I . . . I thought I could trust Angela. I thought she was my friend."

"Did you convince your daed that the little girl was lying?"

"Huh-uh. He believed her and gave me a bletsching." Mae's fingers curled into her palms so tightly that her nails dug into her flesh. "Then when I was walking to school the next day, Angela's daed ran down his driveway and hollered at me for trying to get his daughter in trouble."

Rueben reached for Mae's hand and rubbed his knuckles gently across her fingers. "I understand why you were upset, but not all little people are like that family." He flicked the reins to get the horse moving again.

"Wh—where are you going?"

"To the Stutzmans' for supper."

"B—but I just told you . . ."

"You're being lecherich, Mae. If you'd just get to know Nona and her family, you'd soon realize that—"

Mae's heart thumped with fury. "How dare you speak to me like that! I'm not being ridiculous, and I'm not going to the Stutzmans' for supper!" Mae was shrieking and visibly shaking, but she couldn't seem to help herself.

Rueben turned the horse and buggy around. "Fine! I'll take you home, but then I'm coming back here for supper like I told Nona I would."

Mae ground her teeth together. "If that's how you feel about it, then I don't care to go anywhere with you ever again. In fact, I think it's best if we don't see each other anymore, because a marriage between us would be impossible!"

CHAPTER 47

I don't know what happened to our last supper guest," Nona said, stepping into the living room. "The food's on the table, and if we don't eat now, it will turn to mush or be too cold to eat."

Everyone rose from their seats and followed Nona into the kitchen, where Betty, Selma, Peter, and Andy were waiting. They had just finished their silent prayer, when a knock sounded on the back door.

"I'll get it!" Peter jumped up and raced for the door.

A few seconds later, he returned with Rueben at his side.

Rueben's face flamed as he looked at Nona. "Sorry I'm late."

What's going on? Lydia wondered. *I thought Rueben was taking Mom out for supper this evening.*

"That's all right," Nona said. "We haven't started eating yet." She motioned to the empty chair beside Levi. "Please, have a seat."

Rueben hung his jacket on a peg near the door and quickly sat down. "Have you prayed yet?" he asked.

Harold nodded.

Everyone remained silent while Reuben bowed his head. When he was done praying, Nona gave Rueben a serving of the good stuff.

"I'm surprised to see that you've come alone," she said to Rueben. "I thought you were bringing a guest."

The color in Rueben's face deepened. He glanced at Lydia, then back at Nona. "Well . . . uh . . . my guest wasn't able to come."

"Sorry to hear that," Nona said, "but we're glad you could make it."

Harold nodded. "We've been lookin' forward to treating you to my fraa's Frogmore Stew."

Rueben shot Lydia another strange glance, then picked up a piece of chicken, dipped it into his bowl of barbecue sauce, and popped it in his mouth.

Lydia stared at her food. Mom must have been Rueben's guest, and she'd obviously refused to come. Lydia wondered what excuse Mom had given. They'd need to have a talk when she got home.

❧

"Would you please close that door?" Menno hollered when Ike and Dennis entered the house after doing their chores. "You're letting the cold air in."

Woof! Woof! Woof!

Menno set the pot of soup he held onto the stove and whirled around.

"What's that hund doin' in here?" He asked Dennis, who looked the most guilty.

"Sorry, Papa, but Goldie was cold."

"That shaggy dog's got a nice coat of thick hair, so I doubt that she's one bit cold." Menno pointed to the door. "Put her back outside . . . now!"

Dennis yanked on Goldie's collar, but the dog didn't budge.

"Don't think she wants to go," Ike said with a chuckle.

Menno frowned. "It's not funny. Now help your bruder put the hund outside."

Ike got behind Goldie and pushed, while Dennis tugged on the dog's collar. After several minutes of scuffling and shuffling, Goldie was finally escorted out the door.

"Be sure you shut the door!" Menno called over his shoulder. "Then go get Carl and Kevin, because you all need to get washed up for supper."

Ike and Dennis scrambled out of the room. Several minutes later, they were back with Carl.

"Where's Kevin?" Menno asked.

"He's sleepin' on the floor in the living room," Carl said.

Menno grimaced. It seemed like Kevin slept a lot these days, when he should be awake and raring to go. "Please go wake him up," he told Carl. "I've already turned off the stove, and if we don't eat soon, our soup will be cold."

"Don't see why I hafta wake Kevin. He'll probably be crabby and yell at me," Carl grumbled as he shuffled from the room.

When Carl returned to the kitchen with a sleepy-eyed Kevin, Menno motioned to the table. "Let's pray so we can eat."

After the prayer, Ike, Carl, and Dennis practically inhaled their soup. Kevin, however, kept yawning and rubbing his eyes.

"How come you're so tired all the time?" Menno asked, ruffling the boy's hair.

Kevin shrugged and released another noisy yawn.

"I can tell ya the answer to that," Carl spoke up. "Kevin sleeps a lot durin' the day 'cause he don't sleep much at night."

Menno looked at Kevin. "Is that so?"

Kevin nodded slowly and hung his head.

"Sometimes he wakes me up when he's foolin' around with his toys," Carl said.

"How come you've never told me about this before?" Menno asked.

"Figured you'd get mad and say I was a *retschbeddi*."

"Sometimes it's okay to be a tattletale." Menno lifted Kevin's chin. "You know better than to stay up late playing. If you don't start going to sleep when you're supposed to, I'll take away your toys."

Kevin's chin quivered. "Please don't, Papa."

"If you don't want me to take 'em, then you'd better do as I say." Menno spooned some soup into his mouth. "Ugh! This tastes flat. I must've forgotten to put in the salt."

"Tastes fine to me." Dennis picked up his bowl and slurped his soup. "'Cept it is kinda cold."

Menno grimaced. He hoped Lydia would have an answer for him soon. He really needed help with these boys, and it would sure be nice to have a wife who could cook them a decent meal, too.

As Lydia traveled home from the Stutzmans' that evening, she thought about how being with them had made her temporarily forget her worries over losing her job. Her only concern right now was Rueben. Usually cheerful and talkative, he'd been awfully quiet during supper. Something must have happened between him and Mom, and Lydia was anxious to find out what it was. She hoped it was nothing serious, because Mom had been so cheerful since she'd agreed to marry Rueben.

Thoughts of marriage made Lydia think about Menno. She realized that spending time with him and his boys had helped her get through the pain of losing Josh. Now that she didn't have a job, it would be nice to have a husband to care for her needs. But was that a good enough reason to accept his proposal? Should she settle for a marriage of convenience instead of love?

An image of Levi came to mind. She enjoyed being with him so much. Nice as he was, Menno didn't have the humor and gentle spirit Levi had. It was wishful thinking, but Lydia wished Levi, rather than Menno, had asked her to marry him.

"Like that would ever happen," she murmured. "Levi's never shown any interest in me romantically. If it weren't for Nona, I wouldn't have been invited to have supper with them tonight."

As Lydia neared her house, Buttercup whinnied and picked up speed, obviously eager to get home. Lydia guided the horse and buggy up the driveway and parked it near the barn. Anxious to get inside and speak to Mom, she quickly unhitched the horse and took her to the barn.

When she entered the house, Lydia found Mom sitting on the sofa, staring at the glowing embers in the fireplace. Her eyes were red and puffy.

"What's wrong?" Lydia asked, taking a seat beside Mom.

"I'm upset with Rueben, and also myself."

"Why? What happened?"

Tearfully, Mom told Lydia what had transpired between her and Rueben earlier that evening, and then explained why she felt uncomfortable around little people. "Rueben tried to trick me into going to the Stutzmans' for supper, and even after I told him my reasons for not wanting to go, he didn't seem to understand." Mom sniffed and dabbed at her tears. "I told him I didn't want to see him anymore. It looks like we won't be getting married, after all."

"I know you're upset right now," Lydia said, giving Mom a hug. "I think you need a good night's rest. If you're willing, we can talk more about this at another time."

Mom shook her head. "I don't think there's much more to be said." She rose from the sofa. "I'm going to bed."

Lydia leaned against the back of the sofa and closed her eyes. *Lord, please help my mamm to realize that the Stutzmans are nothing like her little childhood friend. And if it's Your will for Mom and Rueben to get married, then help Mom understand that Rueben loves her, for I'm sure he meant no harm when he tried to take her to the Stutzmans' this evening.*

CHAPTER 48

When Lydia awoke on Thanksgiving Day, snowflakes were swirling past her frosty bedroom window, and the ground was covered with a blanket of white. It was beautiful, and if she were in a better mood she might have rushed outside and caught a few snowflakes on her tongue, the way she'd done as a child—the way Josh had done when he was alive.

What kind of Thanksgiving will this be? Lydia thought bitterly. *Is there anything I can be thankful for?* She had no husband, no son, no job, and she and Mom were almost out of food. Why hadn't anyone from the community come to help them? Surely everyone knew Lydia was out of a job.

Maybe they think we have enough money saved up, Lydia reasoned. *Or maybe they think Grandpa left us some money.*

She shivered and moved away from the window. *I wonder how life would be for me if I hadn't moved to Charm. Would I have found love again if I'd stayed in Illinois? Do I really need love to have a good marriage? Couldn't I be happy just being a good mother to Menno's boys? If I married Menno, I'm sure he'd be a good provider and would take care of Mom.*

Lydia sank to the edge of the bed and buried her face in her hands. *What should I do, Lord? Should I go to Menno today and tell him that I've decided to marry him?* She lifted her head and sprawled back on the bed. Even if she agreed, it would be several months before she and Menno got married. That wouldn't solve the problem she and Mom faced right now.

She sat up again and blotted her tears with a tissue from the nightstand. *I could go to Menno and tell him we're almost out of money and food. I'm sure he'd help us if he knew.*

Lydia thought about how the last time she'd seen Menno, he'd hinted that he and the boys would be alone for Thanksgiving. Lydia figured he was probably hoping she'd invite them over for dinner, but with no money to buy a turkey and so little food in the house, it would be impossible to fix a decent dinner, let alone a big Thanksgiving feast.

More tears sprang to Lydia's eyes. *So Mom and I will sit here alone, not knowing what to say to each other, while Menno and his boys fend for themselves on Thanksgiving Day. It just doesn't seem fair.*

"Lydia, come look at this!" Mom called from downstairs.

"What is it?" Lydia asked when she reached the kitchen.

"Look in there." Mom pointed to a large cardboard box sitting on the floor by her feet.

"Where'd that come from?"

"When I went outside to give the cats some milk I found the box on the back porch." Mom smiled. "It's full of everything we need to fix a nice Thanksgiving dinner, plus a whole lot more food to fill our pantry."

Lydia leaned over and stared into the box. Mom was right; there was a big turkey and a lot of other food. She raced to the back door and stepped outside. Just below the porch, she saw two sets of small footprints in the snow, leading into the woods behind their place.

"I know who left the food," Lydia announced when she stepped back into the kitchen.

"You do? Who was it?" Mom asked.

"It was Menno, and I think he had a couple of his boys deliver the box."

"How do you know that?"

"There were two sets of small footprints in the snow."

"And here I thought it might have been Rueben." Mom sighed as she flopped into a chair at the table. "I guess he's still upset with me because he hasn't been around since the night I refused to go to the Stutzmans' with him. If not for seeing him at church twice in the last month, I probably wouldn't have seen him at all."

"Maybe he's afraid to visit. You did tell him you didn't want to see him anymore, and he might think you're still mad at him."

Mom crossed her arms. "I am. He should

have been more understanding when I explained about the little girl and what she'd done to me."

Lydia said nothing. What was the point? She and Mom had been over this topic several times since that night, and nothing had been resolved. Mom was determined to hang on to her feelings, and she was equally determined not to make the first move where Rueben was concerned. Lydia thought Mom could be the most stubborn woman sometimes. If Lydia had someone who loved her as much as Rueben obviously loved Mom, she'd make things right with him really quick.

"I guess we'd better get this bird ready to go in the oven." Mom reached into the box and removed the turkey. "Sure wish we'd invited someone to join us for dinner because there's a lot more turkey here than the two of us will ever eat."

"I guess I could go over to Menno's place and see if he and the boys would like to join us for dinner," Lydia said.

"That's a good idea. If Menno is the one who furnished the food, he certainly ought to share our meal."

"If you boys aren't ready in the next five minutes, we'll stay home and have soup for dinner," Menno said when he stepped into the living room and found all four boys sprawled on the floor with a stack of books.

Ike was the first to jump up. "No soup for me; I'm ready to go!"

The other three boys clambered to their feet as well. "Let's go!" Carl shouted. "I'm hungry for a hot dog!"

"Today's Thanksgiving, so we'll be eating either turkey or ham," Menno said.

Carl frowned. "I'd rather have a hot dog."

"You can have a hot dog the next time we eat at Carpenter's Café. Today, we're eating at Chalet in the Valley Restaurant, and you'll have whatever the rest of us have."

Menno grabbed his hat and opened the back door. The boys followed. They were almost to the barn when a horse and buggy pulled in. Menno was surprised when Lydia stepped down.

"I hope you don't have other plans for today," she said, "because Mom and I would like to have you come to our place for dinner."

"We were going out to eat at Chalet in

the Valley, but I'm sure we'd enjoy eating at your place a lot more." Menno smiled. "It'll be more fun for the boys there, too."

"Mom already has the turkey cooking, and it should be done in a few hours," Lydia said. "So you can come over whenever you like."

"How about now?" Menno motioned to the boys. "We're all ready to go, so if you don't mind, we'll head over to your place before one of the boys finds something to do and makes a big mess."

"Now's fine." Lydia climbed into her buggy. "I'll see you at the house."

❧

"I wish we would have thought to invite Lydia and Mae to join us for dinner today," Levi's mother said as they sat around the table enjoying their Thanksgiving meal. "I hope they're not spending Thanksgiving alone."

Pop shook his head. "They're probably spending the day with Menno and his boys."

"What makes you think that?" Mom asked.

"When I was having coffee at Carpenter's Café the other day I heard Menno talking to Rueben. He said that it's not

public knowledge yet, but he's asked Lydia
to marry him."

Levi's heart felt like it had sunk all the
way to his toes. It was just as he'd feared—
Lydia was in love with Menno, and Levi's
chances were nil. He should have asked
her out when he'd had the chance. He
shouldn't have suppressed his feelings.

Mom, apparently able to read Levi's
thoughts, reached over and patted his
hand. "Lydia hasn't married Menno yet,"
she whispered.

∞

"Everything sure tastes good," Menno
said, smiling at Lydia, and then at Mae.
"We appreciate your invitation."

"We figured it was only right to invite you
and the boys since you were so kind to . . ."
Mae's face reddened as she halted her
words. "What I mean is we're glad you and
the boys could share this meal with us."

Lydia nodded. "There's way too much
food here for just Mom and me to eat."

"It is a lot of food, but my growing boys
are sure putting a dent in it." Menno
squeezed Ike's shoulder. "Especially this
one, who's going through a growing spurt
right now."

Ike grinned. "Won't be long and I'll be as tall as you, Papa."

"What about me?" Carl asked as he forked a piece of turkey off the platter and plunked it onto his plate. "I'm gettin' taller, too."

"You sure are," Menno said with a nod.

Lydia smiled. "I think all of the boys have grown since I first met them."

The boys beamed and bobbed their heads. Menno was pleased that they were on their best behavior today.

As the meal progressed, the adults visited, and the boys ate more than their share of food.

Not long after they were done eating, Carl complained of a stomachache, so Menno decided it was time for them to go home. If Carl was coming down with the flu, Menno sure didn't want the boy getting sick here.

"Danki for everything," Menno said as he and the boys started out the door.

"Don't forget this." Lydia handed Menno a whole pumpkin pie. "Since you're not staying for dessert you can eat this later." She patted Carl's shoulder. "I hope you feel better soon."

He gave a nod and scooted out the door.

Once Menno had everyone seated in the buggy, he turned to the boys and said, "I'm glad you were all so good today. I wasn't going to tell you this until Lydia gives me her answer, but I've asked her to marry me."

The boys said nothing; just sat there with their eyes wide and their mouths hanging slightly open. Apparently the news left them speechless.

CHAPTER 49

A few weeks later, Mae decided to go to Miller's Dry Goods Store to see if more of her quilts had sold. She had been traveling only a short time when she spotted Levi's youngest brother, Andy, standing in the weeds by the side of the road. A young English boy with curly black hair stood beside Andy, shaking his fists and hollering something Mae couldn't understand.

She slowed the buggy and was horrified when the chubby-looking English boy knocked Andy to the ground and straddled his chest.

"Whoa!" Mae guided her horse and

buggy to the side of the road, climbed down, and secured Buttercup to a nearby tree. Then she dashed across the road. "Let go of that little boy, right now!"

The English boy jumped up and took off down the road.

Mae dropped to her knees beside Andy. "Are you okay?"

"He . . . he said mean things to me and knocked me down," Andy said with a sob. "When he sat on my chest, I felt like I couldn't breathe."

"It's okay. He's gone now." As Mae helped Andy to his feet, an unpleasant memory came to her. She knew exactly how Andy felt. She'd felt the same when Angela sat on her chest.

"Where were you going, and how come you're alone?" she asked, gently patting Andy's back.

"W—went over to my friend Johnny's after school. Was on my way home, and then that mean kid came along." He sniffed and swiped the back of his hand across his tearstained face. "He said I was a runt and that me and my family are different and don't belong in this town."

Mae's conscience pricked her, and she

grimaced. She'd felt the same way about Angela. *It wasn't right for me to stay angry with Angela all these years—even becoming prejudiced and fearful around little people because of what she did to me. She was just a child, and I need to forgive.*

"Let's go across the road to my buggy," Mae said, taking Andy's hand. "I'll give you a ride home."

"Okay."

Mae led Andy across the street and lifted him into her buggy.

When they drove up his folks' driveway a short time later, Mae halted the horse at the hitching rail. "I'll go into the house with you and explain to your folks what happened," she told Andy.

He nodded soberly. "I . . . I hope Mom and Pop won't think I started anything with that boy."

She gave his shoulder a gentle squeeze. "It'll be fine. I'll explain what I saw."

Mae followed Andy into the house, where they found Nona standing on a wooden stool in front of the kitchen sink, peeling potatoes.

Mae cleared her throat to make her

presence known, and Nona jerked her head. "Ach! You frightened me. Didn't know anyone had come in."

"I brought Andy home." Mae could barely get the words out. Being in Nona's house—a place she'd refused to visit until now—made her feel nervous, like she didn't belong.

Nona stepped off the stool and hurried over to Andy. "Are you all right? It looks like you've been crying."

"A mean kid was pickin' on me." Andy's chin quivered, and he motioned to Mae. "Then she came along and made him go away."

"I appreciate you coming to my son's rescue and bringing him home," Nona said, smiling at Mae.

Levi stepped into the kitchen just then. "I was in the living room and overhead what you said. Do you know who the boy was who picked on my brother?" he asked Mae.

She shook her head. "I've never seen him before."

Levi looked at Andy. "Do you know the boy?"

Andy's head moved slowly up and down.

"His name's Ron, and he lives in Millersburg, but he comes to Charm to visit his cousin sometimes. He's been in our store a time or two, but he's never done nothin' mean to me before today."

"What's he look like?"

"He's got curly black hair, squinty blue eyes, and he's kinda chunky."

Levi's eyes narrowed. "Well, the next time he comes into the store, I want you to let me know right away."

"How come, Levi? What are you gonna do?" Andy asked in a quivering voice.

"I'll talk to him. Or better yet, if his folks come into the store, I'll tell them what happened today."

"I think it would be good if the boy's parents were told," Nona said, "but I believe it should be your daed who talks to them, not you, Levi."

Levi frowned. "I think it'd be better if I did the talking."

"Why's that?" Nona asked.

Mae shifted uneasily in the presence of this family disagreement.

"Since I'm bigger, the boy's parents will be more likely to listen to me. If Pop tries to talk to them, they might try to intimidate him the way their boy did Andy."

"Puh!" Nona swatted the air as if flicking away a pesky fly. "Your daed's just as capable of making someone listen to him as you are. And it shouldn't matter how tall a man is, either." She sighed. "We've been through all this before, Levi. You can't always be there to help and protect us."

Levi nodded. "You're right, but if I see this kid who picked on my brother, and you and Pop aren't around, I'm definitely going to say something." He took Andy's hand. "Let's go to the bathroom and get you cleaned up."

After Andy and Levi left the room, Nona smiled at Mae and motioned to the table. "Would you like to sit awhile and have a cup of tea?"

Mae hesitated, but finally took a seat. If she was going to get over her fear of little people, she may as well start now.

While visiting with Nona, Mae told her story about Angela and admitted that from that time on she'd been wary of little people.

Nona sat several seconds without saying a word; then a slow smile spread across her face. "So that's why you've been avoiding us?"

Mae nodded, and her face heated. "When I saw Andy being terrorized by that bully, it made me realize that little people get picked on, too."

Nona nodded soberly. "Probably more so than others, in fact."

"I'm sorry for avoiding you," Mae apologized. "I know it was foolish and childish of me to cling to my fears."

"I think we all have fears from our childhood to deal with," Nona said. "I'm glad you felt free to share yours with me today."

Mae relaxed against the chair as a new realization settled over her. She and Nona might actually become friends. Now she hoped she'd be able to make things right between her and Rueben.

Menno had just stepped into the house, and was about to head for the kitchen, when he heard voices coming from the living room.

"I still can't believe Papa plans to marry Lydia." Menno recognized Dennis's high-pitched voice. "Doesn't he know we don't want a new mamm?"

"Know what I wish?" Ike said. "I wish we could move back to Pennsylvania."

"Me, too," Carl put in. "I liked it better where Grandpa and Grandma Stutzman live."

"Our aunts, uncles, and cousins are there, too," Dennis said. "I really miss 'em."

"Maybe Lydia won't marry Papa," Ike said. "She might turn him down, ya know."

"I like Lydia," Kevin chimed in. "She cooks better'n Papa does."

"That ain't no reason for him to marry her." Ike's voice raised a notch. "Grandma cooks good, too, and if we lived near her and Grandpa, I bet she'd cook for us all the time."

Menno leaned against the wall in the utility room, shocked by what he'd just heard. All this time, he'd thought the boys needed a mother, when what they really wanted was to move back to Pennsylvania and be near his family.

He pulled his fingers through the ends of his beard as he mulled things over. *I don't know what to do. I've already asked*

Lydia to marry me. If she says yes, she'll be hurt if I say I've changed my mind. On the other hand, if I marry her, it could come between me and the boys.

The whinny of a horse drew Menno's thoughts aside. He peered out the small window in the back door. Lydia's horse and buggy had just pulled into their yard.

"Oh no," he moaned. "What if she's come here to give me her decision?"

For weeks, Lydia had been praying about Menno's proposal, and she'd finally made up her mind. She still had time before Christmas to give Menno her answer, but why wait?

She glanced at Menno's shop. It was dark. He'd probably finished working for the day and had gone home. She had just climbed down from her buggy when Menno came out of the house. He hurried toward her, his boots crunching on the firmly packed snow.

"I was hoping you'd be home from work," Lydia said. "I've come to give you my answer to your marriage proposal." She drew in a quick breath. "My answer is yes."

Menno's face turned white as the snow

beneath his feet. "You're willing to marry me?"

She nodded. Why wasn't he smiling? "Is something wrong? Have you changed your mind about marrying me?"

"Do you love me, Lydia?"

She shook her head slowly and dropped her gaze to the ground. "But I care about you and the boys."

His fingers cupped her chin, and he raised it so she was forced to look at his face. "I care about you, too, but not in the way I did my wife."

"In another words, you're not in love with me?"

"No."

"So if you don't love me, and I don't love you, are you thinking that we shouldn't get married?"

"That's exactly what I think. I also think I've been unfair making my boys stay here in Charm where they have no family but me." Menno paused and jammed his hands into his pockets. "Right before you got here, I heard the boys talking about Pennsylvania and how much they missed their grandparents and other relatives. I've realized that they—and me, too—would be happier if we moved back to Pennsylvania where we could be close to my family."

"What about your business here in Charm?"

"Guess I'll have to look for someone to buy me out. But even if I can't find a buyer, we'll leave. I want my boys to be happy and well-adjusted."

"I can't blame you for that. I wanted the same for Josh."

"When I bought the woodshop and moved to Charm, it felt like the right thing. Now that Sadie's gone, and knowing how much my boys miss their family in Pennsylvania, there's really no reason for us to stay. I should have realized that before now." He took a step toward Lydia. "I hope I haven't hurt you by saying all this. I'm sure when the time's right, we'll both find the person we're supposed to marry."

Lydia nodded, feeling a strange sense of relief. "I wish the best for you and your boys." She started to move away but turned back around. "Before I go, I wanted to thank you for all the things you've left on our porch."

Menno's eyebrows pulled together so they almost met. "What things?"

Lydia told him about everything that had been secretly left on their porch, and how they'd found money in their mailbox on two occasions. "When I noticed the small footprints in the snow on Thanksgiving morning, I was sure you'd had a couple of your boys deliver the box of food."

"I'm embarrassed to say this, but I've never left any food on your porch or put money in your mailbox." His face reddened. "I knew you were without a job and had bills to pay, but I assumed since you always seemed to have food, that either you or your mamm must have some money put away."

Lydia shook her head. "We did have some, but with all of Grandpa's and Josh's hospital bills, the money we had was spent long ago."

"I'm real sorry, Lydia. I've been selfish and inconsiderate." Menno touched her arm. "Is that the reason you would have married me . . . so you'd have a husband to provide for your needs?"

Lydia had to swallow a couple of times before she could answer. "I knew you'd be a good husband and would see that my mamm and I were taken care of, but I also wanted to help care for you and your boys."

He pulled out his wallet and handed her a hundred-dollar bill. "This probably won't help much, but I want you to have it."

"Oh no, I couldn't. I didn't tell you all that so you'd feel guilty and help us out."

"I'm sure you didn't, but it's every Christian's duty to help others in need, and under the circumstances, it's the least I can do."

Lydia hated to take the money but knew it would buy her and Mom more groceries or pay a bill. So, she swallowed her pride and said, "Danki for your kindness." Then she climbed into her buggy and headed down the driveway.

"If Menno isn't responsible for all the things that have been left on our porch, then who is?" she murmured.

A torrent of mixed emotions flooded Lydia's soul. While she felt relieved that she wouldn't be marrying a man she didn't love, she also felt deeply concerned. Now that neither she nor Mom was getting married, and neither of them was making any money, how were they going to survive? Should they move away from Charm? Would there be something better waiting for them in some other place?

CHAPTER 50

On Christmas morning as Lydia was about to heat some water for tea, she was surprised to hear a loud *thunk* on the porch. She set the teakettle on the stove and hurried to the back door. When she opened it, she spotted a pile of split wood on the porch. Not far from it sat a large basket filled with food.

Lydia looked out at the snowy yard and noticed a set of footprints, only this time they were big—the size of a man's feet.

She darted into the house, grabbed her shawl, and raced out the door. Stepping carefully across the frozen snow, she followed the footprints around the side of the house, past the barn, and out to the shed, where the firewood was kept. When she spotted a man with an axe raised over his head, she halted. "Rueben?"

Rueben lowered the axe and whirled around. "Lydia, you about scared me to death. What are you doin' out here in the cold?"

"I could ask you the same question."

He motioned to the stack of wood. "I was about to chop more firewood."

"I can see that. What I want to know is why."

"It's a cold Christmas Day, and I figured you and your mamm could probably use some wood for your fireplace." His blue eyes twinkled as he grinned at her. "I've already put some wood on your back porch, but figured you'd need a lot more. There's no point in you or Mae havin' to trudge out here in the snow to get wood."

Lydia couldn't believe Rueben's generosity. Even though he and Mom had broken up, he still cared about her enough to want to help. "I saw the wood and wondered where it had come from," she said. "It was nice of you to leave the basket of food, too."

His eyebrows shot up. "I didn't leave any food. Just the wood."

"Have you ever left food on our porch?"

He shook his head. "Just some firewood a couple of times."

She slipped her cold hands into her jacket pockets. "Now that's sure strange."

"Guess someone else must've left the food." Rueben set another piece of wood in place on the chopping block. "It's cold out here. Don't you think you ought to get back to the house where it's warm? I'll have the rest of this wood chopped in no time, and then I'll leave a good stack of it on your porch."

Lydia told him thanks and hurried back to the house, anxious to tell Mom what Rueben had done.

As she neared the house, she spotted another set of footprints near the porch. *I wonder why I didn't see those before.*

She squinted at the fresh set of footprints in the snow—these were little footprints, like she'd seen once before, and they were leading away from the house toward the driveway.

Lydia shivered. Despite the cold, she was determined to follow the prints and find out who was responsible for the basket on the porch.

As she approached the end of their driveway, she spotted two little boys trudging through the snow toward a horse and buggy parked along the shoulder of the road, partially hidden behind a clump of bushes. When the buggy door opened, she gasped. Levi sat in the driver's seat!

He must have caught sight of her, for his face turned crimson. "Lydia, wh—what are you doing out here in the cold?" he asked as she approached.

"I found a basket of food on our porch and followed two sets of small footprints that led me here."

Peter and Andy turned around. "It was us who left the basket," Andy admitted. "We were hopin' no one would see us do it."

"Well, you did a good job of keeping it a secret," Lydia said. "I had no idea who left the basket until I followed your footprints."

Levi told his brothers to get in the buggy; then he handed the reins to Peter and said,

"Hold the horse steady, because I need to speak to Lydia a minute." He stepped down from the buggy and moved closer to her.

"Have your brothers left things on our porch before?" she asked.

"They did deliver a few of the things," he said with a nod.

"What about the money we found in our mailbox? Did they put that there, too?"

"No, I'm the one who did that," he admitted.

"How come?"

The color in Levi's cheeks darkened. "For one thing, I did it because there was a need, and also because . . ." He paused, and Lydia could see his breath in the cold morning air. "Never mind," he mumbled.

"What were you going to say?"

Levi tipped his head and looked at her in such a way that her heart nearly melted. "I did it because I care for you, Lydia, and even though I know there's no chance of us ever courting because you're going to marry Menno, I wanted to help you and your mamm."

Shocked by his declaration, Lydia stood staring at him, unable to find her voice.

Levi moved toward the buggy, but she

called out to him before he got in. "I'm not going to marry Menno."

He whirled around. "You—you're not?"

"Huh-uh. Menno's planning to move with his boys back to Pennsylvania to be closer to his family."

Levi's eyes widened. "What's he going to do about his business?"

"He plans to sell it."

Levi shuffled his feet a few times, kicking up some of the powdery snow. "I was wondering, if you're not going to marry Menno, then would it be okay if I courted you?"

She smiled and nodded. "That'd be just fine with me."

He took a step closer to her, and she wondered if he might be about to kiss her. She quickly dismissed that idea when she noticed Andy and Peter peeking at them through the side opening of the buggy.

Levi's cheeks reddened further as he kicked at the powdery snow with the toe of his boot. "Say, I was wondering if you and your mamm might like to come over to our house for Christmas dinner this afternoon."

"That'd be real nice. Would you like to go inside with me and extend the invitation to Mom yourself?" Lydia asked.

"No need for that," he said with a shake of his head. "She and Mom are friends now, so unless you have other plans, I'm sure she'd be willing to come."

"We have no plans. What time should we come over?"

"Mom will serve dinner around one, but you can come over anytime before that."

"That sounds good. We'll probably see you around noon."

Smiling to herself and feeling as if she were walking on air instead of slippery snow, Lydia made her way back to the house. She could hardly believe that Levi had invited her and Mom to join his family for Christmas dinner. Even more amazing was that he'd asked if he could court her. Lydia felt like pinching herself; it all seemed too good to be true.

When she stepped into the kitchen a few minutes later, Rueben was sitting at the table, holding Mom's hand. His face flamed, and he quickly let go when he saw Lydia.

Mom, who didn't appear to be embarrassed at all, looked at Lydia and smiled. "Rueben and I have worked things out. We're planning to be married in the spring."

"I'm so happy for you." Lydia leaned over and gave Mom a hug, then took a seat at the table. "Levi's the one responsible for the gifts and money that have been secretly left for us," she said. "His little brothers made most of the deliveries for him."

Mom blinked her eyes rapidly. "I had no idea."

Lydia glanced at the clock. "He invited us to join him and his family for Christmas dinner. We're supposed to be there before one, and I said we'd probably come around noon."

"That's fine with me." Mom glanced over at Rueben, and then back at Lydia. "Do you suppose they'd mind if I brought a guest?"

"I'm sure that won't be a problem," Rueben said. "And the reason I know that is because Nona already invited me."

Lydia couldn't believe how well things had worked out. Despite her missing Josh, this would be a Christmas she'd always remember.

CHAPTER 51

Over the next few weeks, several changes occurred: Lydia had begun working at the general store a few hours each day, which helped out with their finances; Lydia and Levi started courting; Menno and his boys moved back to Pennsylvania; and Levi, who'd saved up enough money for a good down payment, bought Menno's woodshop, as well as his house.

At first, Levi balanced his time between working a few hours at his folks' store and a few hours in the woodshop each day, but he quickly realized that if he was going to make a go of the woodshop, he'd have to work there full-time.

Since Menno's house needed a lot of repairs, Levi spent some of his time working on it, as well. He wanted it to be in good shape if Lydia would be willing to marry him.

As Levi sat at the desk in his woodshop, he tried to concentrate on the stack of invoices lying before him. It was hard to think about business when his mind was consumed with Lydia. He still hadn't worked up the nerve to ask how she would feel about the possibility of having a child with dwarfism. He hoped that, after they'd courted awhile and she'd spent more time with his family, she'd be receptive to the idea and would say yes when he asked her to marry him. In the meantime, he planned to save up all the money he could and spend whatever free time he had with Lydia.

On Saturday, both the store and the woodshop would close at four o'clock, so Levi had invited Lydia to go sledding with him and his three youngest siblings. Lydia had eagerly accepted. Mom had suggested that after they were done sledding,

Levi should bring Lydia to their house for supper.

Levi smiled as he stared out the window at the blanket of white covering the ground. He could hardly wait for his workday to be over so he could be with Lydia. She was all he'd ever wanted in a woman—kind, even-tempered, hardworking, gentle, and loving—not to mention that she had a most pleasing face. When she smiled, his heart sang with joy. When she frowned, he wanted to kiss the wrinkles from her forehead and make her worries melt away.

"What's that big grin all about?"

Levi jumped at the sound of John's voice. "Ach, don't sneak up on me like that."

"Wasn't sneakin'. I've been standing here for several seconds, hoping to catch your attention." John's blue eyes twinkled as he grinned at Levi. "The way you were smiling as you stared out the window made me think your mind must not be on work today."

Levi's face heated. He wasn't about to admit to his employee that he'd been thinking of Lydia. "Guess I did let my mind wander a bit," he said with a chuckle. "Was there something you wanted?"

John stroked his full red beard as he nodded. "Mark and I were wondering if you're happy with our work."

Levi's eyebrows squeezed together. "Of course. Why wouldn't I be?"

"Well, because you're our new boss and might have a different way of doing things than Menno."

"You two are both good craftsmen, and I'm more than pleased with your work," Levi said. "You and Mark have been working with wood a lot longer than I have, so I'm hoping to learn a few things from you." He tapped the stack of invoices on his desk. "I may do things a bit differently than Menno in my business practices, but I want to continue making good quality furniture here in the shop. I'm sure I can count on you and Mark to do as good a job for me as you did for Menno."

John sighed with relief. "That's good to know. Sure glad we got that cleared up."

Levi smiled. "Me, too. Now, is there anything else on your mind?"

"Nope. Guess I'd better get myself back to work on that dresser I was sanding." John whistled as he walked away.

Levi was more certain than ever that

he'd made the right decision when he'd bought Menno's shop.

⊱

"I'm so glad you're working with us now," Nona said when Lydia joined her at the front counter.

Lydia smiled. "I appreciate your hiring me."

Nona patted Lydia's arm, like she would have one of her own girls. "You're doing us a favor by working here. With Levi running his own business, our three youngest in school, and Betty working part-time at the bed-and-breakfast, it would have been a bit of a challenge for Harold and me to run the store by ourselves. Of course, we'd never admit that to Levi. We had a hard enough time convincing him that we could manage without his help so he could run the woodshop. When you agreed to work here, he was greatly relieved."

"I can tell that Levi cares a lot about his family," Lydia said. "That's one of the things I admire the most about him."

"Sometimes he tends to care a little too much, but he's getting better about letting us do more for ourselves. I think after his bout with tonsillitis, he finally came to realize that we aren't completely helpless." Nona chuckled. "Even when Levi was a boy, he tried to do things for us. Once, when he was five years old, I caught him standing on the kitchen counter, trying to get something down from the cupboard because he thought I wouldn't be able to get it. It nearly scared the life out of me seeing him up there like that." She slowly shook her head. "That boy took more chances trying to do things he thought we couldn't. I'm sure that's why I've got so many gray hairs."

Lydia smiled. "It's not easy being a parent, is it?"

"No, it's certainly not. But I wouldn't trade parenthood for anything in the world."

"I enjoyed being a parent, too." Lydia's shoulders sagged as she dropped her gaze to the counter. "I still miss Josh so much and had even considered marrying Menno so I could be a mother to his boys."

"But you didn't love Menno, right?"

"No, and he didn't love me, either, so it was best that we didn't get married."

Nona watched the tiny dust particles float through the air from the sunny window as she contemplated whether she should say something that had been on her mind. After a few moments of reflection, she turned to Lydia and said, "I know I'm being bold by asking this question, but if Levi asked you to marry him, what would you say?"

"I . . . I'd probably say yes, but he hasn't asked."

Nona was on the verge of saying more when the bell jingled and Mae walked in.

"It's good to see you," Nona said. "Did you come to shop or to visit with me and Lydia?"

"I came to bring these." Mae held a pair of woolen mittens out to Lydia. "You left in such a hurry this morning that you forgot them. I figured since you planned to go sledding this afternoon, you'd probably want them."

"I appreciate that." Lydia glanced at the clock on the far wall. "The day's sure gone by fast. It won't be long before Levi will be here to take me sledding."

"Say, I have an idea," Nona said, smiling at Mae. "We'll be closing the store soon. Harold's in the back room right now, getting out some cleaning supplies. While he's busy cleaning here, I'll be heading up to the house to do a few chores before starting supper. Why don't you go up to the house with me, and we can visit while I work? Then you can stay and eat with us when the group gets back from sledding."

Mae's face brightened. "That sounds real nice, and I'd be more than happy to help with any of the chores you need to have done."

"That'd be much appreciated."

"What did you plan for supper?" Mae asked with a curious expression.

Nona chuckled. "Not to worry. I won't be fixing Frogmore Stew. I was planning to make a pot of chili and some toasted cheese sandwiches."

Mae smiled. "That's sound good to me."

Nona stepped down from the stool where she'd been sitting and moved around the counter to stand by Mae. "Since you're here, there's something I've been meaning to discuss with you."

"What's that?"

"I was wondering if you'd like to bring some of your quilts in here to sell. We could put them on one of the shelves in our housewares aisle, or Levi could make some quilt racks—then we could display your quilts in a separate area of the store where they're sure to get noticed."

"I appreciate the offer, but since only one of the quilts I have at Miller's Dry Goods Store has sold, I'm not sure any would sell here," Mae said.

"You never know," Lydia put in. "Some people who might not go into the dry goods store could see your quilts while they're shopping here."

"That's true," Nona agreed. "Maybe you can make some potholders, table runners, dish towels, dishcloths, and pillowcases. People are always in need of those."

Mae clasped Nona's arm. "I appreciate the chance to do this. You're really a good friend."

Just then, the front door swung open, and Rueben entered the store. "Sure glad to see you're still open," he said, smiling at Nona. "I need a few things and was afraid you might be closed already."

"We're not closed yet." Nona motioned to the shelves behind him. "So feel free to look for whatever you need."

Rueben looked over at Mae and smiled. "I didn't expect to see you here today. Figured with this cold weather, you'd be sitting at home in front of the fireplace, working on a quilt."

"I came over to bring Lydia her mittens," Mae explained. "She and Levi are taking his brothers and sister sledding soon."

"That sounds like fun." Rueben jiggled his eyebrows and winked at Mae. "Should we join 'em?"

She shook her head. "I'm getting too old to be doing something like that."

"We are never too old to have fun," he said.

"That may be so, but I'd rather be inside where it's warm than outside in the cold, snowy weather."

"Say, I've got an idea," Nona said to Rueben. "Mae and Lydia will be joining us for supper this evening. Why don't you come over, too?"

Rueben didn't have to be asked twice. "Are we havin' Frogmore Stew?"

Nona chuckled. "Not tonight. We'll plan that for some other time."

A heavy blanket of snow covered the hill behind the Stutzmans' house, and as Lydia, Levi, and his three youngest siblings trudged up the hill, pulling their sleds,

Lydia found herself panting for breath. She wasn't used to this kind of exercise—especially not in the cold.

Andy and Peter bounded through the powdery snow with ease, but Selma, like Lydia, also seemed to be out of breath.

"Take your time. There's no hurry getting to the top of the hill," Levi said, slowing his steps. He gave Lydia a crooked grin, and she could tell he was in good spirits.

"How did things go at your new shop today?" she asked. "Are you enjoying the work as much as you thought you would?"

"Even more," he said. "I've enjoyed fooling around with wood ever since I was boy. Always dreamed of owning my own woodshop someday but never thought it would happen."

"Our lives are full of unexpected changes," Lydia said as Selma hurried ahead to catch up to her brothers. "I never thought I'd be working at your folks' store or that I'd be doing things like this with you."

"You mean sledding or tromping through snow so deep it seeps into the top of your boots?"

She snickered. "Both."

Levi's face sobered. "I really do appreciate you working at the store. I never really enjoyed working there that much and only did it because I thought my help was needed. I've come to realize that my folks are pretty capable, and I figure when they need my help, they'll ask for it."

"I'm sure you're right."

"The weather's been nice today," Levi said. "Even though it's cold, seeing the sun for most of the day has made me feel like spring's not too far off."

"It's hard to believe that my mamm will be getting married in March. She sure is excited about becoming Rueben's wife."

"Will your mamm move to Rueben's house after they're married, or does Rueben plan to move to her place?"

"Since his house is a lot smaller than Mom's, they've decided it would be best if he moves in with us." Lydia stopped and brushed at a clump of snow clinging to her boot. "I feel funny about living there when Rueben moves in, but they've both insisted they want me to stay."

When Levi said nothing, Lydia started walking again. They walked in silence the rest of the way.

They'd just crested the hill when Andy came to a stop.

"What are you stopping for?" Levi asked. "I nearly ran into the back of your sled."

Andy's eyes were huge as he turned to face Levi. "That big kid who sat on my chest is here."

"Where?"

"Over there." Andy pointed to four boys several yards away, who were chasing each other through the snow as they pitched snowballs left and right.

"Just ignore him. Maybe he won't bother you none," Peter said.

"Which one is he?" Levi asked, leaning closer to Andy.

"He's the chubby one with dark curly hair." Andy took a step back. "Sure hope he don't see me."

"It doesn't matter whether he sees you or not, because I'm going to have a talk with him." Levi dropped the rope to his sled. "I'll be right back."

As Levi trudged quickly through the snow, Lydia's gaze went to the group of rowdy children and she gulped. She hoped Levi wouldn't make things worse for Andy by giving the bully a lecture. If the boy ever got Andy alone, he might do something even worse to him than he had before.

Selma drew closer to Lydia. "You think Levi will get through to that mean kid?"

"I don't know, but let's hope so."

"Should we go ahead and sled, or wait until Levi gets back?" Peter asked Lydia.

"It's up to you. If you want to sled, I'm sure it'll be fine."

"Good. Let's go sledding then." Peter flopped onto his sled and sailed down the hill, followed by Selma, and then Andy, all whooping and hollering as they went.

Lydia waited with her and Levi's sleds, hoping that whatever Levi said to the English boy would put an end to him picking on Andy.

A few minutes later, Levi returned, his forehead creased with obvious concern.

"What's wrong? You look upset," she said.

"The kid's daed is out of a job, and the day he pushed Andy to the ground he was trying to get Andy to give him some money so he could buy a toy."

"Did Andy mention that to you before?"

"Huh-uh. Just said the kid called him

names, pushed him down, and sat on his chest."

"It's too bad his daed's out of a job, but that didn't give the boy an excuse to try and get money from Andy."

"You're right, but at least I know he wasn't just picking on him because he's small."

"So what did you say to the boy?" she asked.

"At first I gave him a lecture and said he'd better never pick on my brother again. Then, after he started bawlin' and explained why he did it, I talked to him some more." Levi blew out his breath with a visible puff of air. "Then I said I was sorry about his daed losing his job and that trying to force Andy to give him money was wrong."

"What was his response to that?"

"He said he was sorry and that he wouldn't do it again."

"Do you think he meant it?"

Levi shrugged. "I believe so, but I guess we'll have to wait and see."

Lydia slowly shook her head. "There are so many hurting people in this world. Don't you wish we could help them all?"

"Jah, and I got the boy's address, so I thought I might help out with some food."

Lydia smiled. What a kindhearted man Levi was. No wonder she'd fallen in love with him.

Levi motioned to his brothers and sister, trudging red-faced back up the hill. "They make it look like so much fun, so guess I'll give it a try. Are you coming?"

"In a minute."

Lying facedown on his sled, Levi pushed off and went zooming down the hill with the speed of a racing horse.

Deciding that it was time to prove her bravery, Lydia took a seat on her sled, put her feet on the steering handles, and grasped the rope with her hands. Her mittened fingers felt frozen as she clung to the rope and skidded down the hill at lightning speed. As she neared the bottom, she noticed that Levi's sled was right in her path. She pulled on the rope and pushed the handle with her left foot, hoping to steer the sled to the right, but the handle seemed to be stuck.

"Look out, Levi, I'm right behind you!" she screamed.

He quickly veered his sled to the left, and

to her relief, she whizzed on by. Lydia's sled kept going for several more feet, finally coming to a halt when it plowed into a mound of snow. The impact knocked her off, and she gasped as cold wet snow shot up her nose.

Levi was quickly at her side. "Lydia, are you all right?"

"I think so. Just got some snow up my nose, and I'm feeling kind of shaky. Didn't expect my sled to go so fast, or that the handle would stick when I tried to turn it."

Levi pulled his glove off and reached out to swipe the snow off Lydia's face. Her chest fluttered from the sensation of his gentle touch, and she held her breath, wondering if he might finally kiss her.

As a few crystalline snowflakes fell from the trees above, Levi slowly lowered his head. His lips were almost touching hers when Selma dashed up to them and dropped down beside Lydia. "Are you okay? I was really scared when I saw you fall."

"I'm fine. Just a little shook up is all." Lydia looked over at Levi and smiled. He smiled in response and gave her a quick wink. If he ever did ask her to marry him, her answer would be yes. But would he ever ask?

CHAPTER 52

On the first day of March, Levi woke up with a sore throat. "I hope it's not tonsillitis again," he groaned. Things were just beginning to go well for him at his shop, and even though he was sure John and Mark could handle things on their own, he didn't need to miss any days of work. Besides, Rueben and Mae's wedding was just a few days away, and he didn't want to miss that.

Levi pulled himself out of bed and ambled over to his closet. He felt hot, even though his room was cold. *I'll be okay,* he told himself. *Just need to take an aspirin and suck on a throat disk, and I'll be fine.*

When Levi entered the kitchen a few minutes later, he found Mom standing on her wooden stool in front of the stove. "I'm making oatmeal this morning," she said over her shoulder. "It should warm our insides even if it's cold outside."

"I'm not really hungry. Think I'll just have some juice." Levi shuffled over to the refrigerator and took out a pitcher of apple juice; then he found some aspirin in the cupboard near the sink and swallowed a couple of them down.

"What's wrong, Levi?" Mom asked, tipping her head. "Do you have a koppweh?"

"No headache, but my throat hurts a little."

She turned down the stove, stepped off her stool, and hurried over to him. "Take a seat at the table and let me have a look."

"There's no need for that. I'll be fine, Mom."

She snapped her fingers and pointed to the chair at the head of the table. Like an obedient little boy, Levi took a seat. He knew from experience that once Mom made up her mind there was no changing it, and she was obviously determined to take a look at his throat.

Mom opened one of the cupboard doors and took out a flashlight. "Now tip your head back, open your mouth, and stick out your tongue," she instructed.

Levi did as asked and was rewarded with a frown. "It's your tonsils again. They look red and swollen."

Levi groaned. "I don't have time for this right now."

"Maybe not, but you'd better see the doctor right away so you can get going on an antibiotic. Hopefully, you'll be feeling better in a few days."

"I'll phone the doctor when I get to work this morning. Maybe they can get me in this afternoon after the shop closes for the day."

Mom placed her hand on Levi's forehead. "You're running a fever, and you can't go to work when you're sick."

He grimaced. "All right then, I'll just go into the shop and lay things out for John and Mark. Then after I call the doctor's office, I'll come home and go to bed. Will that make you happy?"

She gave his arm a gentle swat. "I'm not happy that you have tonsillitis again, but if you get in to see the doctor and come home to rest like you should, then you'll get better soon and that will make me happy."

Resigned to the fact that he might miss Rueben and Mae's wedding, Levi rose from his seat, grabbed his jacket, and headed out the door.

❧

"With your mamm's wedding just a few days away, I didn't think you'd be in town today," Nona said when Lydia entered the store.

"Several of Mom's friends have been coming to help, so I decided to slip away and run some errands." Lydia smiled. "It's been good for me to keep busy so I don't have much time to think about being my mamm's witness and how nervous I'm going to feel."

Nona smiled. "I'm sure you'll do just fine." Her forehead wrinkled as her smile faded. "It doesn't look like Levi will be at the wedding, though."

"How come?"

"He woke up this morning with a sore throat, and I'm pretty sure his tonsils are acting up again. Hopefully, he'll get in to see the doctor this afternoon, so we should know something by the end of the day."

"I'm sorry to hear about his throat," Lydia said. "If he misses the wedding, that's one thing, but I doubt he'll be too happy if he has to miss much work."

"You're absolutely right about that." Nona pursed her lips as she slowly shook her head. "That boy of mine has always worked too hard."

"I guess it's better to work too hard than not hard enough."

"Jah." Nona motioned to the back room. "Harold's getting some boxes unloaded, but it's taking him longer that it should. So if you don't mind waiting on any customers who might come in, I think I'll go check on him."

"No problem," Lydia said. "I'll do whatever you need me to do."

As Nona headed for the back room, Lydia took a seat on the stool behind the counter. A few minutes later, Sarah Yoder entered the store.

"Wie geht's?" she asked, smiling at Lydia.

"I'm doing fine. How are you?"

"Other than a bit of arthritis in my knees, I'm getting along real well." Sarah leaned on the counter. "I'll be heading over to help your mamm soon, and I'm guessing she must be getting pretty excited since her wedding's coming up on Thursday."

"You're right about that. And we've all been cleaning the house from top to bottom so that everything looks nice when Rueben moves in after the wedding."

"Guess that makes sense." Sarah rapped the edge of the counter with her knuckles. "I'm surprised to see you working here today. Figured you'd be at home helping with the cleaning and such."

"I was earlier, but I came to town to run some errands and decided to stop in here and see how things are going. Nona's gone to the back room for a minute, so I'm just filling in until she gets back." Lydia smiled. "Nona insisted that I take the rest of this week off to help Mom get ready for the wedding. She even said I should take next week off, thinking I'll need to rest up after the wedding."

"That was nice of her." Sarah leaned closer to Lydia. "I was really surprised when I heard Rueben planned to sell his house, but then with your mamm's house being bigger I guess it made sense that he'd want to move in there."

Lydia nodded. "They'll be leaving for a week-long trip to Florida a few days after the wedding, so they're looking forward to that."

"I can imagine. There's nothing quite like the warm sunny weather of Florida this time of the year. Makes me wish my husband and I could go with them." Sarah reached into her purse and removed a small notebook. "Well, I've got quite a list here, so guess I'd better get busy and start shopping." She chuckled. "Can't buy too much, though, I have some things I want to take to the Care and Share after I leave your mamm's place, so the back of my buggy's pretty full with boxes."

The mention of the Care and Share made Lydia think about the box of Josh's clothes still sitting on the floor in her closet. She'd hung onto them long enough. It was time to let someone else get some use out of the clothes. "Since you'll be stopping by to help Mom, I was wondering if you could do me a favor," she said to Sarah.

"Sure, what do you need?"

"I have a box of Josh's clothes that I'd like to donate to the Care and Share. Mom knows where they are, so if you don't mind, could you take them to the store for me?"

"I'd be happy to." Sarah smiled. "You and your mamm have been through a lot this past year. I'm pleased that she's found happiness with Rueben, and I hope you'll find the same kind of happiness with a man you love someday."

"I hope so, too." Lydia blinked against the tears that had suddenly filled her eyes. She'd already found the man she loved and was sure she wouldn't be happy with anyone but him.

CHAPTER 53

As Lydia sat beside Mom, listening as Bishop Yoder preached the main sermon during the wedding service, she couldn't help but notice how Mom kept lifting her hanky and dabbing at her eyes. Lydia looked over at Rueben, who sat directly across from them. He, too, had tears in his eyes. This was a solemn, yet joyful occasion. Lydia hoped Mom and Rueben would have many happy years together.

Lydia glanced at the men sitting on the bench behind Rueben, and her gaze came to rest on Levi, who sat beside his brother, Peter. She was glad Levi felt well enough to attend the wedding service but hoped he hadn't gotten out of bed too soon.

Lydia focused her thoughts on Mom and Rueben again. Beginning tonight, Rueben would be living in the home that Lydia had shared with Mom since she'd moved to Charm nearly a year ago.

Lydia still had some misgivings about staying there, but every time she brought it up, Mom and Rueben kept insisting that she was welcome to stay with them for as long as she wanted. Mom had even said that she was sure it was just a matter of time until Levi proposed, and then Lydia would have the chance to make a home of her own.

Lydia had her doubts about that. She was beginning to wonder if Levi would ever ask her to marry him. Maybe he just enjoyed spending time with her but had no plans for marriage. After all, he hadn't even kissed her yet.

When the bishop asked Mom and Rueben to stand before him to say their vows Lydia brought her thoughts to a halt.

Mom, wearing a navy blue dress with a white cape and apron, and Rueben, dressed in a black suit with a matching vest, took their places facing the bishop.

Mae couldn't believe how deliriously happy she was. She felt the same excitement standing beside Rueben as she had the first time she'd gotten married. Although in a different way, she loved him as much as she'd loved her first husband.

She stole a glance at Rueben, and despite the seriousness of the occasion, he gave her a quick smile. What a blessing Rueben had been to her this past year. He was helpful, kind, and full of patience. Every day, Mae thanked God for bringing such a wonderful man into her life. She appreciated the fact that Rueben loved her, even during the time when she was struggling and didn't think she deserved his love.

"'Husbands, love your wives, even as Christ also loved the church, and gave himself for it.'" Bishop Yoder quoted from Ephesians 5:25. He looked at Rueben with a steady gaze. "Can you confess, brother, that you accept this, our sister, as your wife, and that you will not leave her until death separates you?"

With no hesitation, Rueben answered affirmatively.

"'Wives, submit yourselves unto your

own husbands, as unto the Lord,'" This quotation from the bishop came from Ephesians 5:22. Following that, he looked at Mae with the same serious expression and asked if she would accept Rueben as her husband and stay with him until death. She, too, answered affirmatively.

Everyone stood while the bishop prayed out loud. Then he clasped Mae and Rueben's hands together in his, and said a few more words as they officially became husband and wife.

As Mae and Rueben returned to their seats, Mae knew with a certainty that she would be happy being married to Rueben for the rest of her life.

Levi tried to keep his focus on the ministers, as they took turns saying a few words about marriage, but he couldn't keep his thoughts, or his eyes, off Lydia. Wearing a blue dress that brought out the color in her eyes, she looked pretty sitting beside her mother with such a sweet expression. He wanted so badly to ask Lydia to marry him, but when he did, he must bring up the possibility that they could have children with dwarfism. What if she said no to his proposal? What if she felt that the responsibility of raising children who were different was too much for her?

Levi knew he should trust God with this matter, but he kept going back and forth—one minute ready to propose, the next minute afraid to ask. Then there was the problem with the house he'd bought from Menno. It needed a lot of repairs, and until he had those done, he couldn't even think of asking his wife to move there. At the rate he was going, Lydia would find someone else before he felt ready to ask.

I'll talk to her about it soon, he told himself. *Maybe while Rueben and Mae are in Florida.*

Beads of sweat broke out on Levi's face, and he fanned himself with his hand. He felt hot, like he was running a fever, and his throat felt scratchy and swollen. Maybe he'd gotten out of bed too soon. Maybe he shouldn't have come to the wedding.

Levi was relieved when a final prayer was said and the closing hymn was sung. He needed some fresh air. He needed to go home and lie down.

CHAPTER 54

Mae and Rueben left Friday on the bus for Florida. Lydia felt lonely and bored at home by herself, so on Saturday, she went to town to run a few errands.

"I'm surprised to see you here," Nona said, when Lydia entered the store that afternoon. "I figure you'd be home resting and would enjoy having the house to yourself."

Lydia smiled. "I tried sleeping in this morning but woke up as soon as the sun shone through my bedroom window. Guess it's just not in me to sit around and rest all the time. Are you sure there isn't something I can do to help out here?"

"You drive yourself too hard, just like Levi." Nona slowly shook her head. "When he came home from the wedding the other day he was running a fever and his throat was sore, yet he went to work on Friday and again today."

"That's too bad. Is that why none of you came to the meal after the wedding?"

Nona nodded. "Selma complained that her back hurt from sitting so long during the wedding service, and then when Levi admitted that he didn't feel well, we decided that we should all go home."

"How's Levi feeling today?"

Nona shrugged. "He said better, but he didn't eat much breakfast, so I suspect his throat still hurts. Sure wish he'd listen to reason and let the doctor take those tonsils out. I know he'd be miserable at first, but once he healed up, I'm sure he'd feel a lot better. "

"I wish I had some influence," Lydia said, "but I'm only a friend, so he probably wouldn't listen to me."

"I think you and Levi are more than

friends." Nona flapped her hand. "Even though you've only been courting a few months, he's known you almost a year, and if you want my opinion—"

The bell above the front door jingled, and Levi stepped in. When he saw Lydia, he smiled. "I thought you weren't working today."

"I'm not. Just came by to say hello to your mamm and pick up a few things."

Nona looked up at Levi. "Are you done working for the day?"

He nodded.

"How's your throat feel?" Lydia asked. "Your mamm said you left right after the wedding because you were hurting."

"My throat hurt then, but it's doing much better today."

"That's good to hear. Do you think you'll need to have your tonsils out?"

He shook his head. "Not if I can help it."

Nona touched Levi's arm. "I'll be in the back room, helping your daed sort through some things. Would you please wait on any customers?"

"Sure," Levi said.

When Nona walked away, Levi leaned against the counter and stared at Lydia.

Her cheeks warmed. "How come you're looking at me like that?"

"I was just thinking how tired you look. Since Mom gave you some time off, I thought you'd be home resting up this week."

"I've gotten enough rest, and I need to keep busy. Besides, in a few weeks I may be busier than ever."

"How come?"

"I stopped by Grandma's Restaurant before I came here and talked to Edith. She said things are picking up and wondered if I might consider coming back to work there."

"You're not happy working here?"

"It's not that. I enjoy working here very much."

"Then why quit and start working at the restaurant again?"

"I'm not planning to quit my job here. Edith said I could work the dinner shift, so I'll be able to do that after I leave the store each afternoon."

Levi's eyebrows furrowed as he shook his head. "That's not a good idea, Lydia. You're working hard enough now as it is."

She stiffened. "I'm not a child who needs to be told what to do." *And you're not my husband,* she mentally added.

"I'm not treating you like a child. I just think you push yourself too hard. Remember what happened after Josh died and you went back to work too soon?"

Lydia's irritation increased. "That was different. I was deeply grieving then."

"If you work two jobs, we'll never get to see each other."

"We can see each other on my days off and some evenings after I get off work."

"Why would you want to work two jobs anyway?"

"I need to make more money so I can either rent or buy a place of my own. I don't want to live with Mom and Rueben for the rest of my life."

"Why would you need a place of your own? If you get married again, you'll be moving into your husband's home."

"Well, I don't see anyone asking me to marry hlm, do you?"

Levi stood with a blank look on his face.

She cringed, thinking she'd probably said too much. She hoped he didn't think she was hinting at a marriage proposal.

"I can't talk about this right now, so please keep an eye on things until Mom gets back." Levi turned and rushed out the door.

Lydia moaned. She was sure she'd said too much. She'd probably driven him away, and now he'd never ask her to marry him.

"I couldn't help overhearing you and Levi," Nona said when she came out of the back room a few minutes later. "I understand if you're upset with Levi. I'm afraid trying to be in control and telling others what to do has become a lifelong habit for him. Even though he's doing some better, it's a habit that's been hard for him to break."

"Maybe I reacted too strongly. I just don't think he has the right to make my decisions."

"Levi tends to hover and worry too much, and you were right in what you said to him. He needs to realize that he can't control every situation." Nona stood on tiptoes and gave Lydia a hug. "If you think you need to work a few hours at the restaurant each day, then you should do it. For that matter, if you'd rather work there than here, I'm sure we can manage."

Lydia shook her head. "I enjoy working here, and since I don't have to give Edith an answer right away, I'm going to pray about the matter."

Nona nodded. "Prayer's the only way to receive the answers we seek."

As soon as Lydia got home, she put Buttercup in her stall and went to the phone shed to check their answering machine, thinking there might be a message from Mom. Instead, she found a panicked message from her friend, Marilyn Byler, who lived in Illinois. Marilyn's parents had hired a driver to take them to a friend's wedding in Indiana and on their way home had been in a terrible accident. Marilyn's father was dead, and her mother was in serious condition.

Without question, Lydia needed to be with Marilyn. She called and left a message on the Bylers' voice mail saying she'd be there as soon as she could. Then she called Mavis Jones, the English woman who sometimes drove for them, and asked if she was free to drive her to Illinois.

Once Lydia had secured a ride, she hurried to the house to pack. Since there was no phone at the house Mom and Rueben were renting in Florida, Lydia decided to leave them a note on the kitchen table, in case they returned before she did. She felt bad about the disagreement she'd had with Levi but didn't have time to deal with it now, or even tell him where she was going. She'd call Nona at the store when she arrived in Illinois and leave a message with her for Levi.

CHAPTER 55

Unable to get any work done in his shop, Levi, holding a cup of coffee in one hand, paced from his desk to the window and back again. For the last three days, he'd been kicking himself for the disagreement he'd had with Lydia. He had no right to tell her what to do, and he couldn't believe the way he'd just stood there when she'd said that no one had asked to marry her.

He gripped the handle of his mug so tightly that his knuckles turned white. *Maybe I should have spoken up—asked her to marry me right then. No, that wouldn't have been a good idea. Not with Mom and Pop in the back room, probably listening to our conversation—not to mention that a customer might have come in.*

Saturday evening, Sunday evening, and again on Monday evening, Levi had gone over to Lydia's house, but she was never home. He'd tried the front and back doors, but they'd been locked. It made no sense. He didn't think Lydia would go out after dark by herself. He'd even checked at the restaurant this morning to see if she might have started working there, but Edith said she hadn't talked to Lydia since Saturday.

He'd talked to his family, but none of them had seen or heard from Lydia, either. Mom suggested that Lydia might have joined Mae and Rueben in Florida, but Levi felt sure she would have left him a message if she'd gone out of town.

Levi finally stopped pacing and lowered himself into the chair at his desk. *Maybe Lydia was at home when I went over but didn't answer the door. Well, I'm going over there every evening until she finally answers my knock.*

When Lydia entered the hospital waiting room, she spotted Marilyn standing with her back to her, gazing out the window.

Lydia slipped her arm around Marilyn's waist. "I came as soon as I got your message."

"I'm so glad you did. I can't begin to tell you how much it means to have you here with me," Marilyn said, dabbing her eyes with her hanky. "I still can't believe my daed's gone and that my mamm's lying in a hospital bed. It seems like a horrible nightmare."

Lydia patted Marilyn's back. "We can be grateful that your mamm's injuries aren't life threatening."

Marilyn nodded slowly, as more tears flowed. "It's bad enough that we've lost my daed, but Mom's terribly upset because she won't be well enough to leave the hospital for his funeral."

"That must be difficult for her." Lydia could almost feel her friend's pain and wished there was more she could say to offer comfort.

"I don't know how you've come through the loss of Jeremiah, your grossdaadi, and then little Josh. It hurts so much when a loved one dies."

"It's been hard, but I've learned that if we feel sorry for ourselves, it will suck us under just like quicksand. What helped me get through my grief was reading my Bible and spending time in prayer."

"I'll need to do that, too, and so will Mom." Marilyn leaned her head on Lydia's shoulder and released a shuddering sigh. "Life is so short, and we often take it for granted. When Mom and Dad left for Indiana, if I'd had any idea that I'd never see Dad again, I would have said so many things to him."

Lydia swallowed hard. She'd never forget the day she'd pulled over to examine her wobbling buggy wheel, never dreaming that a tragedy was about to occur. If she'd had any idea that her precious boy would be taken from her, she would have said so many things to him. She'd give anything if she could have told Josh how much she loved him and said good-bye.

"I'll stay with you for as long as you need me," Lydia said, gently patting Marilyn's back.

"I appreciate that." Marilyn managed a weak smile. "My two married sisters who live in Montana will be here soon, and then once Mom comes home from the hospital, I think we'll be all right."

"Did the doctor say how long that would be?" Lydia asked.

"Probably a week or so, depending on how well Mom's injuries have healed." Marilyn blew her nose on her hanky. "I'd planned to come to Ohio for your mamm's wedding, but with my folks gone, someone had to be here to run our bookstore, not to mention taking care of the livestock at home." She sniffed. "Of course, since Mom was admitted to the hospital, I've been here most of the time, so I had to close the bookstore and rely on our neighbor to feed the animals."

"That's okay," Lydia said. "Mom didn't think everyone she invited would be able to attend the wedding."

"I'd like to visit Ohio sometime and see where you live. Maybe after Mom's better and things settle down I can come for a visit." Marilyn clasped Lydia's hand. "Maybe it'll be your wedding I'll come to attend."

"I don't think I'll be getting married again."

"How come? From the letters you've written, I got the impression that you were getting serious about the man who's been courting you."

"I am serious about Levi, and if he asked me to marry him, I'd say yes."

Just then, a nurse stepped into the room and told Marilyn that her mother was awake and wanted to see her.

"I'll be back soon, and we can talk some more," Marilyn said to Lydia as she turned from the window.

"I'll be here, waiting."

When Marilyn followed the nurse down the hall, Lydia found a chair across the room. Leaning her head against the wall, her thoughts went to Levi. She'd tried to leave a message for him on the Stutzmans' voice mail, but it had been full when she'd called. She wished she'd been able to make things right between them before she'd left for Illinois. She wished she could tell him how much she loved him.

She sighed deeply. *Guess I'll have to wait until I get home. In the meantime, I'm needed here.*

CHAPTER 56

As Levi guided his horse and buggy up Lydia's driveway, he spotted Rueben's horse grazing in the corral. Rueben and Mae must be home. So if Lydia had joined them in Florida, she was probably home, too.

He pulled his horse up near the barn, secured him to the hitching rail, and sprinted for the house. Mae answered the door on his second knock.

"Levi, I'm surprised to see you here in the middle of the day," she said, smiling at him. "I figured you'd be hard at work in your new shop."

"I've been coming by here every evening

for the past week, hoping to see Lydia, but she's never home. Thought if I came by during the day, I might catch her."

Mae shook her head. "Lydia's not here. When Rueben and I got home from Florida, we found a note from Lydia saying she'd gone to Illinois."

"Illinois?"

"Jah, she—"

Levi whirled around and raced across the yard to his buggy. He could hardly believe it! Could Lydia have been so upset about their little disagreement that she'd left Charm for good?

As he drove away, his heart clenched. All the plans and dreams he'd had were over. *And it's my fault,* he fumed as he snapped the reins and made his horse trot faster. *I'm the one to blame for the disagreement, and I never even got the chance to apologize to Lydia. I wonder if there's anything I can do to get her to move back, or is it too late for us now?*

He thought about turning around and asking Mae if she had a phone number where Lydia could be reached, but he'd left Mark and John alone to work on a table with a matching china hutch. He'd promised he'd be back in half an hour to help with it. He'd go back to see Mae after supper this evening.

🙠

Nona stepped onto the back porch to call Levi for supper and found him sitting in one of the chairs with his head resting in the palm of his hands. Thinking he might be praying, and not wishing to interrupt, she stood quietly, leaning against the screen door. After a few minutes, Levi lifted his head, reached into his pocket for his hanky, and blew his nose.

"Are you feeling all right?" Nona asked, taking a seat in the chair beside him. "Your throat's not hurting again, I hope."

He shook his head. "I was asking God to show me what to do about Lydia."

"What about her?"

"I went over to Mae's house this afternoon and discovered that Mae and Rueben are back from Florida, but"—Levi grimaced—"she's gone, Mom. Lydia's moved back to Illinois."

Nona blinked a couple of times. "Are you sure about that?"

"Jah. Mae said Lydia had left a note for her."

"I can't believe it. Why would Lydia move back to Illinois, and how come she never told any of us she was going?"

"I think she must have been upset about the disagreement we had." Levi swiped his hand across his forehead, where beads of sweat had formed. "Thought I'd go over and talk to Mae again this evening and see if there's a phone number where Lydia can be reached."

"That's a good idea," Nona said. "Oh, and while you're there, would you let Mae know that I'm having a group of women here tomorrow afternoon to work on a quilt we'll be donating to the next Haiti benefit auction?"

"How are you going to do that? With Lydia gone, that leaves only you and Pop at the store. If you're here with a bunch of women, Pop won't be able to handle things on his own."

"He won't be alone. Tomorrow's Betty's day off from the bed-and-breakfast, so she'll be working with him in the store."

"Oh." Levi stood. "Guess I'll head over to Mae's right now."

"Without eating supper? It's ready right now."

"I'm not really hungry. Maybe I'll fix myself a sandwich when I get back."

"Okay." Nona understood why Levi wanted to talk to Mae again. The sooner he spoke to Lydia, the better the chance of him talking her into coming back to Charm. "Oh, before you go," she quickly added, "I was wondering if you could do me a favor."

"Sure, what is it?"

"I won't have time to do any baking before tomorrow, so I was wondering if you could stop by Grandma's Restaurant and pick up three pies for me to serve to the women when they come to quilt."

"No problem. I'll do that on my way back from Mae's. Any particular kind of pies?"

She shook her head. "I'll take whatever they have."

"Okay. See you later."

"Oh, and Levi, there's one more thing I want to say."

"What's that, Mom?"

"Remember that no matter what happens between you and Lydia, you need to let God take control."

"I know." Levi hurried off toward the buggy shed.

"I can't believe that no one's at home," Levi grumbled as he left Mae and Rueben's place. At the rate things were going, he'd never get to talk to Lydia.

Maybe I'll go to Grandma's Restaurant and get the pies; then after I take them home to Mom, I'll head back to Mae's and see if she and Rueben are home yet.

When Levi entered the restaurant some time later, he told Edith that he needed three pies.

"What kind?" she asked.

He shrugged. "It doesn't matter. Mom said that she'll take whatever you have."

"If you'd like to have a seat at one of the empty tables, I'll get them boxed up for you right away."

"Sure."

Edith headed toward the back of the restaurant, and Levi moved into the dining area. He was about to take a seat at a table along the wall when he glanced to his right. Mae and Rueben were seated in a booth near the window, and across from them sat Lydia.

Levi froze, shocked at the sight of her.

She must have seen him at the same time, for she blinked several times.

"Levi, what a surprise," she said when he stepped up to their table.

He scratched his head. "I'm the one who's surprised. I thought you'd moved back to Illinois."

Lydia's nose crinkled. "Where'd you get that idea?"

"When I stopped by your place today, your mamm told me you'd gone back to Illinois."

"I did, but not to move back. I went to be with my friend Marilyn, because her folks were in a serious accident." Lydia looked at her mother. "Didn't you tell him that, Mom?"

Mae shook her head. "He never gave me the chance to explain. Just got all red in the face and rushed off as soon as I said you'd gone to Illinois."

"I guess I must have jumped to conclusions." Levi looked at Lydia. "How come you didn't call and let me know where you were?"

"I tried, but your folk's voice mail was full."

"Lydia got home late this afternoon."

Mae glanced over at Rueben and smiled. "Since we were both too tired to cook, my considerate husband suggested that we come here to eat."

Rueben bobbed his head and grinned. "Always did enjoy eating their fried chicken dinners." He motioned to the empty chair beside Lydia. "If you haven't eaten yet, Levi, why don't you join us? We've just put in our orders, and when the waitress brings our beverages, you can add yours."

Levi didn't have to be asked twice. He took the seat and picked up a menu.

For the next hour, the four of them visited as they ate, but Levi didn't know how he managed to get through the meal without blurting out to Lydia the way he felt about her.

When the bill came, Levi offered to pay, but Rueben insisted it was his treat.

As they moved toward the cash register, Levi turned to Lydia and said, "I was wondering if I could give you a ride home. It'll give us a chance to talk."

Rueben nudged Levi's arm. "Thought that's what we'd been doing for the last hour. Fact is, I think we covered just about every topic under the sun."

Levi's face heated. He could hardly tell Lydia's new stepfather that he wanted to spend time alone with her so they could talk about their future.

As though sensing his predicament, Mae smiled and said, "It's fine if you want to bring Lydia home."

Levi looked at Lydia and was relieved when she nodded.

They were almost to the door when Edith called, "Levi, don't forget the pies your mother wanted."

"Oh, right." Feeling more flustered than ever, he moved back to the counter to pay for the pies, while Lydia waited for him near the door.

Once Lydia and Levi were seated in his buggy, he turned to her and said, "I'm sorry for the disagreement we had. I understand why you were upset with me. I had no right to tell you what to do."

"I'm sorry for my part in the disagreement, too," Lydia said. "I was oversensitive."

Levi gathered up the reins and directed his horse onto the road. "I'm sure glad you're home."

She smiled. "So am I, but I know Marilyn

appreciated the time I spent there, and I was glad I could be with her in such a difficult situation."

They lapsed into a companionable silence, broken only by the sound of the horse's steady *clip-clop* as it moved slowly up the road. Levi was apparently in no hurry to get her home.

When they reached the road leading to Menno's old house, Levi turned his horse in that direction.

"Where are we going?" she asked.

"You'll see."

A few minutes later Levi pulled his rig up next to the barn, climbed down, and secured the horse. "I wanted you to see what I've done with the place," he said as he helped Lydia down from the buggy.

When they entered the house, Levi lit a gas lamp and motioned for Lydia to follow him into the kitchen, where he lit a second lamp.

"Did you make all this?" she asked, taking in the new oak cabinets lining the wall near the sink. A large table with eight matching chairs sat in the center of the room.

"I sure did, but my workers, Mark and John, helped, too." Levi motioned to the other side of the room where a new, propane-powered stove and refrigerator sat. "Also bought some new appliances."

"I knew you'd been working on the place so you could rent it out, but I had no idea you'd made it look so nice."

"I've done a few things in other parts of the house, too, but there's still a lot more I want to do before . . ." Levi's voice trailed off as he moved closer to her. So close, she could feel his warm breath blowing softly against her cheek. "I shouldn't have waited so long to say this, but the truth is, I love you, Lydia. If you'll become my wife and move into this house with me, I'll be the happiest man in Charm."

Before Lydia could form a response, he clasped her hand and said, "There's just one thing I'm concerned about."

"What's that?"

"If we have kinner, one or more of them could be born with dwarfism."

"I'm not worried about that," Lydia said with a shake of her head. "Over the last year, I've gotten to know your family quite well. Little people are no different than big people." She smiled as she gazed at his face. "I'm open to and accepting of whatever God has for us. So if we were to marry, I'd love our kinner no matter what size they might be."

"Does that mean your answer's yes?"

She nodded, barely able to contain herself. "I'd be honored to be your wife."

Levi's face relaxed, and he pulled her into his arms. "That's real good to hear."

Lydia could hear his heart beating under her ear, and her chest fluttered from the sensation of being so near to him.

They stood like that for several seconds before Levi pulled slightly away. Slowly, he lowered his head and captured her lips in a kiss so sweet it nearly took her breath away.

Never, in all the times that she'd been in this home, had she imagined herself living in it as Mrs. Levi Stutzman. She could hardly wait to see what the future held for her and her husband-to-be.

EPILOGUE

Two years later

Lydia glanced at the calendar on the kitchen wall. It didn't seem possible that today was Levi's and her second wedding anniversary, or that their precious daughter Nona Mae, who'd been named for both of her grandmothers, had just turned a year old.

She smiled as she watched her sweet little girl playing happily on the living room floor, rocking her doll in the small wooden cradle her father had made for her birthday. Even though Lydia knew that Nona Mae would grow up to be tall like her parents, she wouldn't have loved her any less if she'd been born with dwarfism.

Lydia sighed. So much had happened since she'd lost her job in Illinois and moved to Charm—some good, some not so good, but all leading her closer to God.

"What's that dreamy look about?" Levi asked, stepping into the room and placing his strong hands on Lydia's shoulders.

"I was just thinking about how much God has blessed us and remembering back to the days when I first moved to Charm and had my doubts about whether I'd ever feel as if I belonged. Now I'm happy and content to call Charm my home." Lydia tipped her head back so she could look at Levi's face. "Would you like to know what I'm happiest about?"

He nodded.

"I'm happy to spend the rest of my life with you, Nona Mae, and any future kinner we might have."

"And I'm happy that you looked past my imperfections and agreed to become my fraa." Levi leaned over and kissed the top of Lydia's head. "My mamm once reminded me of the words of Proverbs 31:10: 'Who can find a virtuous woman? for her price is far above rubies.' I thank God for giving me such a woman. Happy anniversary, Lydia, and I hope we'll have many more."

Recipe for Nona's Frogmore Stew:

Ingredients for The Yucky Stuff:
    1 cup catsup
    1 cup cooking oil
    1 cup apple cider vinegar
    1 cup salt
    1 tablespoon black pepper
    Hot water to fill a large canner cooker
        about ½ full
    1 (3 ounce) package crab boil
        seasoning mix

Ingredients for The Good Stuff:
    15 to 18 small red potatoes, left whole
    1 bag baby carrots, left whole
    2 pounds smoked sausage (or
        Little Smokies), cut into 2-inch
        lengths
    3 pounds skinless, boneless chicken
        breasts, cut into bite-size pieces
    2 (½ pound) packages of fresh
        mushrooms
    Small onions (as many as you wish)
    1 pound medium shrimp, cleaned
    2 green peppers, cut into large
        pieces

(continued next page)

Mix all the ingredients for The Yucky Stuff except for the seasoning packet in a large cooker. Once all The Yucky Stuff is mixed well and the salt is dissolved, drop the seasoning packet into the cooker. Set a wire basket into the cooker. Once the broth is at a rapid boil, begin putting The Good Stuff into the wire basket in the order and for the times listed below. Lower the basket into the boiling mixture; then stir lightly after each addition so it mixes together.

To Cook:

Bring broth to a rapid boil and make sure it keeps boiling all the time. Add potatoes and boil 5 minutes. Add carrots and sausage. Boil rapidly for 5 minutes. Add the chicken pieces and boil 5 minutes. Add mushroom and onion. Boil for 5 minutes. Add shrimp and green peppers. Turn off the stove burner, but keep kettle covered, and let it set for 5 minutes. Drain the liquid broth away from the food by lifting the basket out. Dispose of The Yucky Stuff, then dump The Good Stuff into a roaster or big mixing bowl. Take it to a table that's been covered with a clean, plastic tablecloth. (Make sure that no one is seated at the table yet.) Dump the food out on the table so there's a pile of food in front of each place where a person will sit. Pass around some barbecue sauce, shrimp cocktail sauce, sour cream, and melted butter so that everyone can put a glob of whatever they want in front of them on the table to drag their goodies through. Eat with your fingers and enjoy! Recipe feeds 8 to 10 people.

Recipe for Lydia's Maple Nut Cookies:

Ingredients:
  2 cups brown sugar
  1 cup butter
  3 eggs
  1 ¼ tablespoons maple flavoring
  ¾ cup milk
  4 cups flour
  2 teaspoons baking soda
  ¼ teaspoon salt
  ¾ cups nut, chopped

Frosting:
  ¼ cup butter
  1 egg, beaten
  1 teaspoon maple flavoring
  1 ¼ cups powdered sugar
  2 teaspoons water

To prepare frosting: Combine all frosting ingredients and mix well.

To prepare cookies: Preheat oven to 350 degrees. Cream brown sugar and butter in large bowl. Add eggs, flavoring, and milk. Beat well. Combine flour, baking soda, and salt in separate bowl. Add to creamed mixture. Fold in nuts. Drop by heaping teaspoons onto greased baking sheet and bake 8 to 10 minutes. Frost cookies when cooled.

OTHER BOOKS BY WANDA E. BRUNSTETTER:

INDIANA COUSINS SERIES
A Cousin's Promise
A Cousin's Prayer
A Cousin's Challenge

BRIDES OF LEHIGH CANAL SERIES
Kelly's Chance
Betsy's Return

DAUGHTERS OF LANCASTER COUNTY SERIES
The Storekeeper's Daughter
The Quilter's Daughter
The Bishop's Daughter

BRIDES OF LANCASTER COUNTY SERIES
A Merry Heart
Looking for a Miracle
Plain and Fancy
The Hope Chest

SISTERS OF HOLMES COUNTY SERIES
A Sister's Secret
A Sister's Test
A Sister's Hope

DISCUSSION QUESTIONS:

1. When Lydia and her son moved to Ohio, she felt lonely and missed her home and friends in Illinois. Sometimes due to unforeseen circumstances, people are forced to move from a place where they feel comfortable to a place that's strange and unknown. What specific ways might there be for someone to get used to living in a new place?

2. What are some things we can do to help others who are new to our neighborhood feel welcome and part of the community?

3. When Lydia and her mother faced financial challenges, many people helped, including someone who left anonymous gifts. Lydia and her mother, like many other people, had a hard time accepting help from others. What do you think is the reason for this? Is there ever a time when we should refuse help from others?

4. What are some ways we can help someone in need without making them feel obligated or embarrassed about their situation?

5. Some gifts are given directly to a person, while other gifts are given in secret. When is the time to give someone a gift without letting them know who it's from?

6. Some people are prejudiced against those who are different. What do you think is the reason for most prejudices? What does the Bible say about prejudice?

7. Lydia's mother was prejudiced against little people. Her prejudice came about because of a childhood trauma. Have you ever suffered a childhood trauma that affected you so much that you avoided someone you were afraid of or didn't trust? What advice would you give to someone who's dealing with a childhood fear?

8. Levi was worried that his parents couldn't run the store by themselves, and he tried to do too much for them, often sacrificing his own needs and wants. What are some ways we can help others without making them feel as if we think they're not capable?

9. Lydia's mother tried so hard to please her father that her own needs went unmet. How far should an adult child go in honoring or caring for their parents?

10. The loss of a child can be devastating. How can a parent deal with such a loss? What are some ways we can help someone who's lost a child?

11. What interesting facts about the Amish way of life did you learn by reading *Lydia's Charm*?

12. What life lessons did you learn from reading this book? Were there any specific scriptures that spoke to your heart?

ABOUT THE AUTHOR

WANDA E. BRUNSTETTER is a bestselling author who enjoys writing historical, as well as Amish-themed novels. Descended from Anabaptists herself, Wanda became fascinated with the Plain People when she married her husband, Richard, who grew up in a Mennonite church in Pennsylvania. Wanda and her husband live in Washington State, where he is a minister. They have two grown children and six grandchildren. Wanda and Richard often travel the country, visiting their many Amish friends and gathering further information about the Amish way of life. In her spare time, Wanda enjoys photography, ventriloquism, gardening, reading, stamping, and having fun with her family. Visit Wanda's Website at www.wandabrunstetter.com and feel free to e-mail her at wanda@wandab runstetter.com.